RHIANNON HARGADON

QUEENS OF MOIRAI

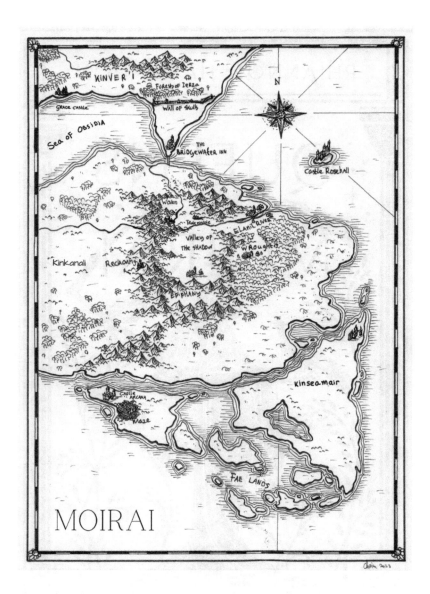

MOIRAI

CONTENTS

For my mother, who always believed that this was my path;
and for Elizabeth, who opened the gate and shoo'd me out.

PROLOGUE

*S*now fell on the graves of the children. *Here it was always winter, white and knife-cold, and the boy hated it. He hated the castle of dark-blue stone. He hated the handsome king, he hated the sounds and smells, the guards and the food.*

The boy longed for fire.

He longed for his cozy bed and the familiar view of the blue river and green, rolling hills ... but the boy knew he would die in this bleak place, far from the warmth of his people. For the Queen must stay, and his mother would never leave her.

It's not the fairytales that lie to us, but the people we love, *his mother always said, as if that would explain things.*

It was before dawn when the boy heard the insistent knocking at the door. Half asleep, dead tired, he wanted nothing more than to ignore it. "Go away," *he mumbled into his pillow.*

Around him the other servants slept hard, exhausted from long days and nights working in the castle.

The hand knocked again. Rap rap rap.

As the youngest, and the person whose cot was nearest to the door, it was his responsibility to check. Nico knew that, yet it was so tempting to ignore.

"Open the door!" *a female voice demanded.*

"Sure, sure, I'm coming!" *he grumbled, as he lurched out of the low cot and wrapped his threadbare blanket tightly around himself. The room was bitterly cold, and he rubbed his hands together as he went to open the door. He yanked hard, hard enough to make his hands ache, on the rusted knob. He was not quite big enough to work around the Castle—he could not carry the scythes, the axes, or the other weapons—but soon he would be.*

A woman in a heavy cloak stood in the snow and moonlight, her blue eyes staring at him.

"May I help you?" He didn't recognize her but the cloth of her gown and robe were quite fine, which meant she must be one of the priestesses.

Her brow knit together. "You're just a boy."

Offended, Nico puffed out his chest. "I'm eight, and the fastest in the castle with a blade."

"I'll bet you are. I wanted to see if you would help me with something, if you would do something very important for me."

"Of course." The boy couldn't believe she was asking so politely. Most of the priestesses ordered him about as if he were a field hand, or else ignored him completely. He didn't pause to wonder why she was asking in the dead of night; everyone knew the priestesses walked at midnight.

"Do you know where the children are buried?"

He shuddered. That Gods' forsaken field of snow was dotted with tiny graves. Still reeking of blood, the children had been pulled from the Queen's warm womb and tossed into holes in the snow, left to freeze to death, all because the Queen didn't want children. She said the House of Atropos was cursed, that the King and his mother shouldn't have even one descendant. The priestesses dug holes in the snow and tossed the children in, still alive, leaving them to die.

His skin crawled. "Yes," he mumbled. "I know where it is."

"One of them is still alive. I've marked the place and you will know it... Can you do that? Can you bring her here, keep her warm, and give her

milk?" She held out her hand, and it was full of goblin gold, more than Nico had ever seen.

Still, he hesitated. It was impossible to survive outside in the midst of this snowstorm—he would only last minutes. And the prospect of going out there in the dark, with them, terrified him. But it was true that a single coin would feed the entire house for a month, and there were at least twenty in her palm, enough to buy himself and his mother a house far away from here.

"Why?" he asked. "The Queen killed many babies already." He gave the woman a look of disgust.

She leaned close. "This baby is special, Nico. She's chosen. She'll rid us of the plague of undead and reunite Moirai one day ... if you and I can help her."

Fair-skinned, the woman's hair was soft brown and waved around her face. Her blue eyes were like a piece of the sky had been tugged down from Heaven. She was beautiful, he realized, in the same way that angels and princesses were. And she smelled just a little bit like flowers.

"Will you save her with me? And keep her safe? Can you be her hero?"

If he wasn't decided before, that single word did him in, just as she knew it would. Nico puffed out his chest again. "Of course I will." He fixed his chin, and gave a firm nod. "I'll go right now."

"And you'll keep her next to you? You won't let her get cold?"

"Never. I know how to take care of a baby." He didn't know how, but he didn't want the beautiful lady to doubt him. Perhaps she'd come back and bring more coins later, if he did a good job.

"Thank you," she murmured. "I can always count on you."

Later, the boy would regret his words. He couldn't know, not then, how much work it would be to raise the infant, how many years he would need *to lie and kill to keep her safe. He didn't know who the girl would become or that there would be other babies, more for him to take care of.*

So Nico strode through the killing fields with purpose, the snow spilling over the top of his boots with every step. Trembling and aching and anxious to be done with his errand, he scanned the ground. Maybe she was mistaken, he thought. Maybe the baby was already dead. Then he saw it, just as she said: two sticks, stark and black, laid in a simple cross on top of the snow.

Nico stared down at it for only a moment, just one, and began to dig.

CHAPTER 1

F ingers burning with cold, I clung to the wall of Grace Castle and took deep, steadying breaths. Thirty feet below, the icy waters of the Sea of Obsidia surged, its waves reaching upwards as if eager to gobble us up and spit out our bones.

My sister, Arabella, called back to us in the dark, "Don't look down!"

I considered a reply, but my lips were stuck together—the extreme cold had frozen them closed, and to open them at all might cause them to bleed. Plus, every noise risked drawing attention to us, the three children who hung on the side of a tower by our fingernails. It was more important to keep my grip on the frost-covered stones of the castle, to keep moving, hand over hand, silently forward, following my brother and sister.

We were survivors, the three of us. Aged fifteen, fourteen, and twelve, we'd already faced incredible odds to live this long. We were miracles—buried at birth in the snow of Kinver'i. Unlike our other seven siblings, who died from the frigid temperatures, we three still lived. It was too dark to see either of my siblings ahead, but I could feel their souls as if they were a touch upon my skin.

Tonight was our most daring attempt yet. In total darkness, shoeless, trembling, we picked our way down the rough indigo stones. The tower was only the beginning—if we reached the bottom, we'd still need to brave the sea, the forests, and an endless kingdom of snow.

We could stay and die.

Or go and die.

Arabella had a bag lashed to her back with provisions we'd hidden away these last few months. She was neither faster nor stronger, the youngest of us three, but she was braver than Taliesin or myself and could always be counted upon to be first. She climbed out the window without hesitation—we knew exactly where to place our feet. For part of the climb, we'd had years of practice. For the rest ... well, that'd be luck.

My threadbare black gown billowed in the wind, and its tattered edges slapped against my paper-white legs. My toes scratched and scraped against every rock. My hands shook as I took hold of another stone.

We're going to make it, I said to myself, for at least the twentieth time. I gulped a freezing lungful of air and pressed my forehead to the Castle wall, then said a quick prayer to Nyx, my great-great-great grandmother. *Help us,* I begged.

"Morena." My brother Taliesin was nearer than I'd thought. "It's working—the plan is working."

I glanced to my right. He was surprised, as was I. I grinned at him. "I can't believe it either."

We all hated the tower, though it was arguably safer than the monsters we'd face outside. Although we had only molded bread and water, thin soup that always left hunger gnawing at us, we wouldn't have any food outside those walls. We could easily starve while we wandered in the forests of Lerza.

"If she falls—" I said aloud to my brother.

"She won't. You won't. I won't." Taliesin was ever the optimist. "Besides, *if* any of us fell, we'd better die. Otherwise, Nico would kill us for ruining the plan."

As demi-gods, descendants of the Fates, we'd survive much. A fall of forty feet into the sea? Even a human would live through that. He was right—Nico had risked everything to help us plan this. We couldn't fail him.

Arabella called back to us again in the night. "Tally! Morena! I'm at the stairs."

"Do the words *be quiet* mean nothing to you?" Taliesin hissed, not loud enough for her to hear. She'd probably forgotten the most important part of the instructions. "We should hurry," he said to me.

"Probably." My cheek pressed against the cold blue stone. "Do you think he was able to get us the boat?"

One of the few living people left in The Grace, Nico raised the three of us, taught us to read and write, and how to throw a knife. He'd promised to tie a boat to the dock for us. Still, I couldn't help but worry—when I'd looked out from the tower window before sunset, there was no boat at the dock.

"Nico will come through," Taliesin said. "By this time tomorrow, we'll be long gone, and Arabella can celebrate her birthday outside the tower."

It was the only thing she wanted, the one item our little sister ever asked for. *Go out?* She'd pleaded, aged two, and pointed at the door. Every year since she could talk, she'd said the same thing. *Go out?*

We all wished for freedom, and we would gift it to ourselves this year. Taliesin and I started forward again, slow and steady, our blond heads close together, our elbows occasionally grazing. If we hurried, we might fall. If we *didn't* hurry, we would be killed for sure. Sunrise would come and reveal our absence to our guards, show our footprints in the snow. There was still much to do—we had to get to the dock, board the skiff, and cross the sea. We had to be out of sight before anyone knew we'd left.

Behind me, in the dark, a light flickered inside the Castle. Arabella watched us, so she noticed immediately. "Impossible," she muttered, loud enough for both of us to hear.

"What?" I hadn't seen it, not yet.

"Damn," she said in response. "Someone is awake."

The waves below lapped at the Castle. The snow fell. I shivered and clung to the stone. Perhaps it was nothing, but *I thought* I heard something, so I had to pause and listen—really listen—just to see if I'd imagined it.

Click. Click. Click Click Click.

Low and quiet, almost unnoticeable. Tally and Arabella heard it, too.

"Gods curse us." At twelve, Arabella had a mouth like a pirate—constantly swearing. "You two have to hurry up." Without waiting for a reply, she whirled. Her ivory nightgown was luminous in the black night. The stone staircase we sought was just ten paces ahead.

Click. Click. Click Click Click.

An inhuman screech tore through the air. I squeezed my eyes shut, expecting a clammy hand or yellowed teeth to seize my shoulder. "Our jailers have noticed." I continued forward across the stones. "Maybe this was a bad idea."

It was *worse* than a bad idea. It was a terrible, awful idea with severe consequences. I couldn't imagine how angry *she* would be. But what choice did we have? We'd been prisoners in this Castle tower all our lives.

I tried to climb faster, but I had to be careful. My handholds must be sturdy and sure, or I would plummet to the frozen waters and rocks below. But the Cullen were close. I could feel them. Even though I couldn't see the wild creatures behind me, I shuddered.

I reached out and grabbed the next blue-black stone covered with frost. Just a single day of sun would have made this easier. I put all my strength into my right hand, gripped the stone tight, and hunted for another foothold. *At least I'm tall*, I thought. It's easier for me to climb and jump and reach.

"There." I huffed as my toes touched upon a minuscule outcropping. I shifted as quickly as I dared, my fingernails tearing on the stone.

Click. Click. Click Click Click.

"Easy," Taliesin said, "we're almost there."

I reached forward again and grabbed another stone.

"Thank the Gods," I gritted out. "We have to—"

My words hung in the air like a man on the gallows, his stool jerked from under his feet. My thoughts were lost in a scream as I fell.

"I've got you." Taliesin's face tightened with strain as he held on, and I dangled over the churning waters of the sea. My toenails scraped against the rock ledge; my knees banged against the indigo stones as I scrambled to find a foothold.

"I won't let go." Taliesin's hand was tight around my wrist as I dangled off the side of the castle, the wind howling around us. As our eyes met, I suddenly remembered a windy night, long ago, when I'd rocked his small body in my arms until he'd fallen back asleep.

Taliesin pulled and huffed, then hauled me up onto the stone stairs. I landed hard on my knees and took several gulping breaths.

Click. Click Click.

The Cullen who crawled behind me shrieked, and a second later I heard a dull thud. It lost its grip just as I had and fell to the rocks below. I heard a low growl of delight somewhere to my left, just above us.

"I can't see how many of them there are," Taliesin said. "But I bet they're latched onto the stones like spiders."

"Good thing it's impossible for them to be quiet," I replied.

Their decaying teeth made the clicking sounds, gnawing, anticipating the chase. Cullen weren't fast, but they felt no pain nor fear, and would think nothing of crawling down the uneven stones of the Castle wall. If one fell, another would replace it. Once they caught us—if they caught us— they would drag us straight back to our tower and lock the door. *Click. Click. ClickClickClick.*

Taliesin leaned over the wall and loosed a vicious punch into the darkness. A Cullen shrieked as it plummeted to the frozen Sea of Obsidia below. "We've made it this far. Now we run to the dock."

Arabella sprinted down the stairs, far ahead of the two of us. Just barely, I could see her red hair streaming behind her like an open flame, and her gown, pale as snow, flashed white in the darkness.

She could have stumbled, rolled her ankle on the uneven stones. She could have banged her hip into the low walls, scraped her shoulder on the sudden turns as I had. But Arabella was born with an inherent grace of all the Gods—she flew down the steps in the darkness. She didn't look back. She didn't wait.

Irritated, Taliesin tugged me forward. When I tripped, he righted me. He would never leave me, so he could only move as fast as I could. Around and around we went as we sprinted down the spiral staircase.

In the east, the sky was still darkest blue. We caught up to Arabella near the base of the tower and sprinted toward the dock. I could just see the end of the dock through the fog. A boat bobbed in the water. My heart leapt with sudden joy. *We had a boat with a bag of provisions in it!* Nico had come through for us. The thought of freedom, so near, so sweet, propelled our feet faster. The three of us reached the ground, our bare feet pounding the snow as we ran.

Nico told us to run along the stone wall and follow it, turn right at a small arch, then we'd be on dock. We'd never done this, we didn't know the terrain, and Taliesin slipped. I helped him up.

Faster. We are almost there.

We rounded the final corner, we made it to the archway. But just beyond, the Queen waited. Flanked by Cullen, her red lips were frozen in a cruel smile. Even though I'd seen her less than a dozen times, each time haunted my dreams— here was the Queen of the Blood Throne, Malinda the Mad ... our mother. Her arms tucked behind her back, she waited for us as if we'd told her to meet us there.

My heart stalled and I jerked backward, frozen with fear. The three of us skidded to a halt, like a trio of cornered rabbits who've come face to face with a fox.

"Departing so soon?" our captor asked. "The sun has yet to rise." Her face was inscrutable as a group of her undead bodyguards chomped their rotted teeth and seized us.

We struggled against them, our frail bodies no match for their strength. Arabella beat at hers with pale fists, I hung my head and accepted our capture. Whatever would happen next, would happen. There was no escaping them now.

Cullen dragged us forward across the frozen boards, toward her and the edge of the water, and though I tried to keep my eyes on the sea, on the dock, anywhere else, I couldn't help but look at *her,* the Queen of the Blood Throne.

She must have just eaten a heart, I thought with a shudder. Years ago, Nico confided in us that the Queen stole hearts—stole them and *ate* them. We laughed but believed him when one of our maids came back with a hole in her chest three days later.

It was my job to take the blame, to take whatever punishment would befall us, horrific, violent, or otherwise. But it was Arabella who stepped forward, in front of her two older siblings.

A flash of rage detonated in the Queen's eyes as she scanned Arabella and me. But her voice was even, flatly calm, as she spoke: "I must say, I'm disappointed in you, Morena. You're supposed to keep these two in line." She sneered as she glanced between Taliesin and Arabella. "It is not safe for children to be out in the real world. Too many monsters. You know better."

Just the sound of her voice sent fear screaming through me.

"It's quite dangerous to crawl along the rock like that," she continued. "You might have fallen. You know what can happen if you're afraid or injured. You could have accidentally killed one of them. And what a tragedy that would have been. This is why you're supposed to stay inside."

I didn't dare answer. Instead, I put my head down and watched as chunks of ice floated past in the coal-colored sea. Sometimes I heard the screams of her victims, far off and faint through our tower window. I smelled the coppery scent of blood on the wind. I knew what sorts of deeds Malinda did, even if I'd never seen them.

As I stared down at the dock, I noticed the hem of her gown had blood along its edge, browned and old. The Queen wore pert little black boots, with silver buckles, and one of those buckles had smears of blood upon it. Taliesin shivered next to me, his underfed body wracked by the cold.

Only Arabella, the youngest, dared to look directly at our captor. She was too young, too reckless, to be afraid.

"What would you have done if you'd succeeded? Braved the ice floes of the sea, hiked through hundreds of miles of snow..." the Queen stared down at our feet... "shoeless?"

"Anything would be better than staying here." Arabella's voice trembled. "Living in your hell."

"Sure of that, are you?" The Queen smiled sweetly at us, her rebellious children.

Behind her, the Cullen guards swayed and clicked their teeth, their faces darting back and forth. The Cullen stench rolled over us, and I stared down at their bare gray feet instead of at their disfigured jowls working from side to side. Undead slaves, guards, and agents of torture—she controlled them completely and her army continued to grow. They wouldn't understand our words, they only understood her unspoken commands.

"Taliesin." The Queen focused those prehistoric eyes to my brother. Taliesin—sweet, steady, kind —lowered his gaze to the emerald pendant at her throat.

I spoke up. "Don't blame him. It was not his idea."

Tally did not crumple or cower, even though I could scent his panic. "My Queen."

He jolted at the caress of her gloved hand along his jaw. I could sense her heavy mood like a storm gathering in the distance.

"*My Queen*, he says. Not, *Mother*. Have you forgotten who I am?" She gripped his thin shoulder in her gloved hand. She leaned in and her nostrils flared delicately. "What I've done for you, when many would kill you just for the pleasure of spilling Fates' blood?" She smiled, her teeth too white and too sharp against her blood-red lips.

"You should thank me. You wouldn't last forty-eight hours in the woods past the sea." She faced away from us, clasped her hands behind her back as she walked toward the edge of the dock. "Yet here you are. You haven't appreciated my efforts." She tilted her head to look up at the sun rising over the mountains.

The Queen turned back to our group, her breath steaming in the frigid air. "I'm ready for breakfast. Shall we?" She picked up her skirts and stepped daintily over the boards back toward the Castle, brushed past us as she left.

Arabella caught my eye and shrugged her shoulders ever so slightly. *That's it?*

I couldn't believe we'd gotten off so easily. I'd expected beheading. Worse. To do nothing was out of character for the Queen of the Blood Throne.

"Arabella. Morena. You'll return to the tower." She didn't glance backward as the Cullen separated in front of her, allowing her a path through their grayed and decayed bodies.

She paused. "Taliesin, you won't be joining them." His eyebrows drew together as his head jerked up. "Perhaps without your influence, my daughters will focus on studying and staying undetected, rather than learning how to scale the Castle walls."

Arabella jerked toward her as understanding slammed down like a lightning strike.

"Malinda—wait—" I began.

The Queen addressed the Cullen soldiers, ignoring us completely. "Take him to the bottom of the sea."

They seized upon him instantly, their claws hooking his clothing, their reddish eyes rolling. The Queen turned to her only son for one last look. "Do *not* come back," she told him. "Not ever."

Arabella lurched toward Taliesin, but Cullen had already dragged him to the edge of the dock and shoved him off, into the icy waters of the sea. Before she could reach them, the Cullen vanished beneath the inky surface of the water with my brother struggling between them.

"No!" I screamed. But it was too late. My brother was gone and even I, one of the Three Fates, could not bring him back.

Chapter 2

Fated eyes cannot cry. No matter what misfortune might befall the women descended from the goddess, Nyx, we can't shed a single tear. So my wretched eyes blinked and watched in horror as the water churned. They saw my brother sink beneath the waves, the bubbles on the surface. They noted the moment that the sea swallowed him up. They saw when it settled back into quiet ripples.

Malinda's Cullen returned us to the tower, up the spiral staircase to the circular room we'd spent our entire lives in, now fewer by one. The door slammed shut, and a key turned in the lock with a resounding click.

Mute as a tree, I stood in the middle of the room.

Around me, Arabella whirled and raged. She hammered at the door with her fists. "You have insulted the Fates!" she screamed. "We'll kill you if it's the last thing we ever do!"

She took a pair of scissors and stabbed a dirt-smudged pillow. She wept and pounded her head into the stone walls, and when I pulled her away, blood dripped down her forehead and cheeks.

"Stop it," I begged as I pushed her onto our thin mattress. "Just stop!"

Arabella's despair was a bonfire that nothing could extinguish, and I could not soothe her. She carried on for hours, and as her screams echoed off the walls, I wished—oh, I wished—that she would shut up so I could think.

I'd always believed that our mother cared for us. Stupidly, despite all evidence to the contrary, I thought that our imprisonment in the tower was for our own good. When our mother said it was to protect us from enemies, I believed her. In the past, when Arabella seethed with impatience and cursed the Gods, I'd told her to wait. To *wait*. Taliesin always obeyed, his gaze ever hopeful on the door. My brother, a prince, waited all his life for us to escape. Now, he was dead. There were no more months or years left for him.

My brother Tally came to me that night in my dreams, a nightmare where he dragged me down into the sea, and the icy water filled my mouth as I screamed. His eye sockets were empty, half of his chest eaten away, and I awoke looking at the tower door, waking as its rusted bolt fell into place.

Click.

It was Arabella who first convinced us to escape; she pleaded and begged until we finally relented. I know that it wrecked her to think back and wonder, the guilt consuming her until only a shell remained.

Black and white, white and black, the sea continued to beat against the base of our tower. I watched the water closely, fearing a monster wearing my brother's skin would return to us. If that happened—if it did—I would take our one candle and burn the place down with all of us inside. Suicide by fire would save us from becoming Cullen.

"We'll keep trying," Arabella said when she'd finished crying. Her pale arms flashed in the moonlight like bleached bones as she arranged the blankets around us. "We can hide food, just like we did before." She sounded hopeful.

I ignored her words, my face toward the window and the sea. I was in no hurry to relive that terrible sequence on the dock when they'd pulled

Taliesin under the water, the terrified look he gave us when he realized he would die, his golden head disappearing under the surface.

A dull mirror hung over the desk, and I stared at my reflection in the glass. I hated my face: golden blonde, pale-skinned, a replica of Malinda. Our eyes were different—mine were worse, hell-black and empty—but anyone could see I was her daughter, and I longed to do something to make that untrue. I imagined peeling my skin down from my forehead, past my chin. Taliesin looked like Malinda, but his resemblance to her had not saved him.

"He might come back," Arabella said.

"If he came back, he'd be Cullen, which'd be worse than death." I hoped that the currents had carried him far off, far enough that he'd never return. I had no desire to see my brother return to the Queen of the Blood Throne for orders.

"Do you remember when Nico first tried to train you?" Arabella said wistfully.

"How could I forget?" Years before, Nico Ecclesiastes had brought knives instead of food. "Let us see, little spider, what you are capable of," he'd said, "or you can use this." He unstrapped a massive, speared weapon topped with a half-moon blade from his back.

You must be joking, I thought to myself.

"You're the granddaughter of Atropos. It's time you learned about your powers." Nico handed me two knives, each sheathed in brown leather, the blades engraved with runes.

"I know what my powers are," I said.

"Then show me." He stepped away, leaving me sitting on the tower floor, and leaned against one of the indigo stone walls.

"I might hurt you," I said. "I don't want to." I tossed the knives down.

"You won't even scratch me." Nico looked bored as he half-smirked. "Now, give it a try."

Arabella and Taliesin watched with interest. This was the most exciting day they'd ever had in our tower.

"You can do it, Momo," said Taliesin, then aged six.

Reluctantly, I picked up the weapons, removing their coverings. I stared at Nico until my eyes crossed, thinking murderous thoughts ... and nothing happened. This was not the first time I'd doubted the mage marks on my spine, nor the last. For though my grandmother was the controller of DeathDeath and one of the Three Fates, it appeared I'd inherited none of her abilities.

"It'll come," he assured me, handing me a ration of bread and books. "And until it does, I'll teach you how to defend yourself with a knife."

Nico taught us everything: how to dance, speak, and read. He was shockingly educated for a servant. He regaled us with tales of the Fates, the lore and fairytales of Moirai and the human lands, places with unpronounceable names, and dragons and goblins with caves so full of gold you'd drown in them.

Arabella adored him.

And Nico did teach me to use a blade, though mostly I used it to cut our hair. Long and golden, mine knotted terribly as it dragged across the uneven stone floors. Taliesin preferred his shorn completely, close to the scalp. Nico read to us while Taliesin sat in front of me, getting his hair cut:

"And so the goddess Nyx made the Three Fates: Clotho, Lachesis, and Atropos, to control Life, Time, and Death. Referred to as the Maiden, the Lady, and the Crone, Clotho was small and slight, Lachesis beautiful beyond compare, and Atropos had white-blonde hair. Together, the three ruled the kingdom between Heaven and Earth called Moirai."

"Are you a Fate?" Arabella asked Nico enviously.

"Of course not. Fates are goddesses—the only females that Zeus fears." Nico was fifteen and a full head taller than me. "Morena is a Fate." He gave me a pointed look. "And one day, she will rule Moirai."

Taliesin peered over his shoulder at me, mute with wonder, seeking confirmation.

"Sit still, or I'll cut you," I commanded my brother. "The blade is dull."

"*The Three Fates' War upended the natural order of Moirai, Olympus, and Earth itself. Animals lived for hundreds of years instead of weeks. The fates of the Gods were suddenly uncertain, and unthinkable tragedies unfolded—Icarus fell to his death, Hercules went mad, Adonis was mauled by a boar.*" Nico turned the page.

"*Life versus Death, Death versus Time: unintended consequences piled up, and things meant to operate in perfect harmony were now pitted against each other in a ceaseless battle. From that moment onward, everyone who died became Cullen, and no one—neither bird nor beast, friend nor foe—rested in peace. Instead, they came home, not alive and certainly not dead. It was during the Three Fates' War that Nyx burned the three-seated throne and cast them out of their castle.*"

One ancient text claimed that the war between the Three Fates began over a human man named Tasos, who'd seduced all three Queens of Moirai. Three deities fighting over a single lowly human seemed impossible. We'd read that years ago, and all of us children were scandalized.

As a result of that war, Atropos, my grandmother, fled North to an area called Kinver'i, which translated into 'The Truth is Told.' She built this castle, The Grace, where we were now prisoners. Where her story ended, no one knew. Atropos and the other Fates vanished, never to be seen again. She passed her bottomless black eyes to my father, Melchior, and me. I felt her creeping powers in my bones, like an ever-present tickle in the back of my throat:

To create destruction and mayhem, plagues and pain;

To see in total darkness;

To speak to the soul, rendering humans unable to lie;

The ability to kill without raising a hand, instead tugging the soul from the body like a thread from a spool;

Immortality, for the Fates could not die.

I was too afraid to try and use these powers or even test them. What if I accidentally killed one of my siblings?

"So, Atropos might be trapped in a tomb for a hundred years, and if you opened the door, there she'd be still," he told my siblings as they huddled close. "Bored stiff." Nico wiggled his eyebrows, and we laughed.

These small sips of joy sustained us through long days in the tower, long days that became long years, years where we watched the sea from our window like little birds trapped in a stone cage.

We invented intricate stories to distract us. We called the stories *The Descendants of the Fates* or *Queens of Moirai*. In them, it was not Malinda who ruled but Arabella and I, with Nico and Taliesin as our brave knights. The true Queens of Moirai arose—new Fates and new Gods—and struck down our captor. In these fantasies, we rebuilt Moirai into the magical haven it once was and envisioned our happy ending.

After Taliesin's death, Nico vanished. I paced the room like a shadow without an owner, waiting for his return.

In the days that followed, Cullen brought our food. I flinched away from them, and Arabella cowered.

"If you would only strike her dead." My sister was in a dark mood. "Then we could leave this wretched place. Free."

Strike my mother dead? Am I even capable of such a thing?

Even if I was descended from Atropos, even if Malinda did deserve a gruesome end, even if my power was more than these unreliable whispers, even if I were powerful enough to make the Gods themselves bow before me... How would I even know it?

"Malinda is nothing," Arabella insisted, "a woman who got lucky and married into our family. The blood of the Gods runs in our veins—not hers. You have the mage marks across your spine— you're a Fate, and it is you who shall sit upon the three-seated throne with me by your side." Arabella was vehement. "One day, we will stand on the Wall of Skulls, and we'll travel to the Castle Epiphany, and you will rule." She said the words like a prayer. As if she could say them loud enough and the Gods would grant her truest wish.

She wept and raged, and we remained locked in the tower.

Arabella's tears plagued me and caused an ache so deep in my bones that I feared they would be hollowed out. I didn't mind the crying—I envied her for that. Even as a babe, malnourished and cold, I'd lain silent in my crib and blinked at the stones and the snow.

So as my sister threw her pillow at the wall, eyes streaming, snot-nosed, blubbering ... I knew with certainty that she was not a Fate.

When she bathed in our copper tub, the water so cold that it raised gooseflesh on her cream and porcelain skin, I saw that she was without any of the purple-dark marks on her back. Unbranded by the God.

Unlike me.

I was mage-marked; I was chosen. Though both of us were Atropos's granddaughters, I carried the cursed honor of controlling DeathDeath. The Three Fates owned the magical abilities to control Time, Life, and Death, and *I was DeathDeath.*

I didn't dare to tell her; she would be too angry, and I was worn down by my own emotions. The two of us were only children, alone and unsure of what to do, with no one to comfort us. Tally's mattress lay on the floor, empty and cold, and I hated myself for not understanding, for not knowing *why*.

You would assume that DeathDeath would have all the answers; I assure you I do not.

Of course, Arabella carried Fated blood in her veins, so she would have some magic someday ... but not the same as mine. She was vulnerable and fragile, whereas I was allegedly immortal, destined.

I couldn't do anything except create the smallest of shadows in my hand, each no bigger than an ink drop. I couldn't kill, I couldn't maim, nor plague... I hadn't even known the day my brother was going to die. Atropos knew when people would die, up to the exact minute. I was, unquestionably, the worst representative of DeathDeath our kingdom had ever had.

I huddled close to the single candle at the desk, a low tallow stub. Outside, ice snapped against the stones—an intense winter storm had blown in while we talked, and each raindrop crystallized into star-shaped hail before striking the ground with such force that they chipped the window casements.

"One day, we won't be afraid anymore. We'll both have power, and our power will be much greater than hers—she will cower before us. She'll be the one who screams for our mercy." Arabella imagined bloody futures with epic battles full of righteous fury, and I thanked the Gods that our future was not hers to control.

I preferred a different future, where we snuck out of The Grace during the night and never looked back. We'd live in a new world of flowers and sunlight and never hear from Malinda again.

Viciously, Arabella twisted the sheet in her hands. "Don't be such a coward. Malinda deserves DeathDeath—a brutal one at that. If I'd had your power, I would have killed her years ago."

"Would you?" I responded.

Arabella scratched at the desk with her fingernails, mutinous as she waited for a reprimand. In her anger, she gouged the wood, damaging one of the few lovely things we had in the tower. My tangled hair tumbled across my face as I bowed my head and bit my tongue.

Later, I went to see what she'd written.

I am a knife without a blade.

I rubbed my fingers over the words, pondering their meaning. Beside me, the flame of our candle flickered. Would we ever escape this god-forsaken place? If Arabella ever did have magic, I prayed it would not be too strong nor come too soon. Her moods were volatile, her temper frightening.

Let her be ordinary, like any other maiden, someday married to a knight.

"Come to bed," she said, watching me stare at her words. "Don't waste the candlelight."

With a heavy sigh, I blew out the only light in the world. In the pitch-black night inside the tower, I made my way to my sister in the dark.

Click.

I jerked awake, worried that Cullen had snapped Arabella's neck right next to me. But there was no Cullen, just the two of us in the tower room. However, the door to our room hung ajar, the corridor beyond a dark and dangerous void.

Open. Unlocked. Unguarded.

This had never happened before. I put out my hand to shake Arabella, but then I paused. She was fast asleep. It could be Nico helping us to escape. Or it could be a trap intended to provoke us into another escape attempt. Terrified, I waited for Cullen to walk through the door. But nothing happened.

Almost against my will, I pushed back the blankets and swung my legs onto the floor.

I peeked out into the corridor. Typically, there would be Cullen guards, mindlessly shuffling and clicking their teeth. I'd seen their shadows under the door for years and smelled their stench long enough to recognize it, but the corridor was empty.

Though my curiosity was piqued, I hesitated in the doorway. Our three mattresses were shoved close together. Arabella's red hair was barely visible, her pale arm stretched across my pillow.

I should close the door. And just forget this whole thing.

Instead of listening to my instincts, I eased out of the room and gently closed the door behind me. Faced with three choices: an archway on my left, an archway on my right, and the spiral stairs that went up and down the tower, I didn't know what to do or where the missing Cullen might be. I chose left.

The left archway led to a corridor lined with black iron doors. Gently, I pulled at a handle. It was unlocked. The stone-floored room held a small bed with a sagging mattress and no other furniture.

I tiptoed down the corridor and peered into another room. At any moment, Cullen guards could appear out of the walls like ghosts, and I'd be thrown back into the tower.

The only sound was the whisper of cobwebs swaying. From our last escape attempt, I knew our castle, The Grace, was square-shaped with four towers. Ours was the east tower, the one closest to the sea. Each floor was identical: ten doors, five per side. With no signs of life, the thick layer of undisturbed dust suggested that these rooms hadn't been used in years. Only our corridor, our specific stairs, had the dragging footprints of the Cullen.

"There has to be a front door somewhere," I muttered.

And a throne room, a kitchen—where are they? Where does Malinda sleep?

I continued my quiet exploration, noting the unlit torches, the moth-eaten tapestries, and furniture piled in the corners of desolate rooms.

Each window I came to was bricked over. When I finally came to a small slit, too narrow for even my hand to fit through, I glanced out and immediately leaped back. Not far below me were the Cullen. Thousands upon thousands stood outside, shoulder to shoulder. They swayed in place or lay in heaps, like a great rotting army who'd won and found themselves with nothing else to do.

Armies were meant for only two things: defense or invasion. And though I'd spent my life as a prisoner if I'd had to place a wager on which one it was, I would have bet on conquest. Who would want the frozen wastelands of Kinver'i or its Cullen-infested castle? It was far more likely that Malinda planned to invade some wealthier neighbor with deep pockets, full coffers, or at least better food.

I drew a rough map in the dust at my feet. So far, I'd only traveled the corridors and floors between the east and north towers. The north held a Cullen army of tens of thousands. The Obsidian Sea lay east and south. That left west as the best way out—the absolute opposite side of the Castle. I erased the map on the floor, then wiped my filthy hand on my tattered black nightgown.

I peered back toward the corridor and was startled to find that a candle was now lit. Just before, the hall had been completely dark.

"Hello?" I whispered, in no mood to draw the Cullen to me. Silence. I should have known better.

Like a ghost, I glided through the shadowy corridor to the candle and its merry glow. It had no wax drips; it hadn't been lit for a minute. Sighing, I blew it out. "Fine, I'll go this way," I said to whatever thing lurked in the shadows.

I went west. West, *west,* my body pulled along like an unraveling thread, and I hurried as much as I dared, hoping that a Cullen wouldn't pop out from one of the doors. Once or twice, I stopped to sniff the air, but there was no smell. Typically, rotting Cullen left their stench everywhere. Still, these corridors smelled so much of nothing that they might have been described as smelling of moonlight.

The silence pressed upon my ears like a weight, and I belatedly realized that the western part of the Castle might be spelled. I squinted into the dark. Perhaps these corridors weren't just unused, but something else. They felt wrong, somehow...

Smothered, I realized. As if their life and energy were suppressed by a great force. There were no monsters. There were no mice; there was not even the slightest breeze. I expected spiders as big as a fist, but there was nothing at all. The house itself and the tiny breaths of life in it were absent.

I took the spiral staircase to the top of the west tower. It was identical to ours except for the door; instead of being dull black, it was painted rose and iris, indigo, and gold. I peered at the images, desperate to decipher them, which was very difficult since they had all been violently desecrated.

Slashes and scrapes cratered the wood like an ax had been taken. Though the paintings were horribly disfigured, I'd read enough books to recognize the Three Fates. Their imperious faces stared down at me: Clotho, the Creator, holding a spindle; Lachesis, the controller of Time, clutching an hourglass; and Atropos, the Reaper, one hand wrapped around shears, the other a scythe. Their eyes were scratched out, and their lips cut away.

The crushing feeling intensified. A small voice inside me screamed, *Run! Turn back!* But I'd come too far to be scared off now. Fully expecting the strange door not to open, I gave it a hard shove.

Like a blind bat, I tumbled into a room vastly colder than the rest of the Castle. Broken glass littered the floor, and as I picked myself up, I pulled a small piece from my hand.

A trickle of blood ran down my finger. Red. Neither black nor white nor gray. I put my finger in my mouth and sucked it away.

Careful not to step on the glass, I inched into the foreign room. Full of snow and wind, gray clouds and cold that froze my eyelashes together, I quickly noticed that the walls were ripped open, and multiple stones covered the floor. Icicles hung from the fireplace mantel. Outside, thick boughs of evergreens brushed against each other in the wind; the sound was like witches whispering curses in the dark.

I noticed *her:* a woman so gray-haired and gray-skinned that she blended into the stone. She lay in the center of the room, face up, sleeping, her hands at her sides. This was strange enough. But stranger still, no snow lingered on her clothes or face. Dressed in a fine black gown, her white hair combed carefully back, the woman seemed to be peacefully waiting.

I stretched out my hand, slowly, carefully; I wondered if I might shake her awake.

CHAPTER 3

———◆◇◆———

I watched her unmoving form, primed to run from the room.

"Hello?" I said after a long pause. "Who are you?" She did not stir. "How did you get here?"

My head whipped around to ensure no Cullen followed my voice and that I'd closed the door behind me.

The woman's lack of response unnerved me, and I drifted over to her side. My head felt like I was underwater, pressure building in my ears. Up close, I noticed the woman was covered in a thick layer of dust. She did not draw breath.

Another prisoner in The Grace, only this one is even worse off than myself.

Not asleep, but surely not dead—if she were, she'd become one of the Cullen.

I felt such intense sympathy that I put my hand on hers. A surge leaped from her skin to mine, a blinding flash that burned as if her skin was aflame. I yanked my hand from her, looking down to see the cut from the glass bleeding freely again.

Free me.

It wasn't a voice in my head, more like someone spoke words to my soul. In that instant, I knew who she was.

"Atropos?" I breathed, my face slack with shock.

A Fate so powerful that even Gods feared her ... here, in front of me. Once upon a time, even Zeus himself had trembled and begged Atropos for forgiveness.

I watched the figure warily, gathering my courage and trying to calm my racing heart. The wind whipped through the tower, covering me in chills. Though the sky was open above, it felt like something pressed down on me.

I stepped the tiniest bit closer.

Smothered. Squashed. Extinguished.

It was a deeply uncomfortable pressure, and I felt my ribcage protest. There, beneath her skin, I felt it—a *spell*. It radiated off her like poison gas. Atropos was spellbound to this stone table.

Pure, unadulterated fury rolled through me and for the first time, I forgot to be afraid. Two Fates, Atropos and me, both controllers of Death itself, were locked away in The Grace.

If Malinda had bound her here because she was a threat, then that meant Atropos could beat her. Atropos could help free us from the tower—I knew it in my bones. I had to free her.

I swiftly moved back to the door, avoiding the stones and broken glass in my path. After taking one last look at her, I pulled at the ruined door. I could still feel her binding spell, but the weight disappeared once the door was back in its place.

As I quickly walked back to the tower, I considered the situation. Things had not improved—if anything, it was worse. My bleak mood chased my steps, and all I really wanted to do was be back in my room, in the safety of my bed, and pretend none of this night had ever happened. I took the corner too quickly, just another turn in our dark, damp castle—

And smashed headlong into a Cullen.

Hot, blinding pain ripped through me. He chattered at me, his sagging jowl working, where eyes had once been now just empty holes.

"Oh," I said. I stumbled backward, and as I did so, I put my hand to my waist.

It was wet. Surprised, I glanced down at my palm and my sleeve and the indigo stone floor, and it was only then that I saw the dagger clenched in his fist. My mouth opened and closed like a fish.

He stabbed me.

Suddenly light-headed, I fell back against the wall, my head thudding into the stones. The Cullen, meanwhile, grasped my blood-covered hands and clicked his teeth at me, then stepped forward and started tugging me back down the hall, a thick smear of blood left in my wake.

I yanked my arm from his grip, crying out as the wound on my stomach twisted and gaped. He turned on me, clawed across my arms. I kicked out, snapping the bones of one of his legs. He crumpled to the ground, and I pulled myself onto my knees to get out of his reach. Teeth still snapping, he began to crawl towards me, his broken bones jutting out from behind him.

The pain in my abdomen was sharp but the fear was stronger.

Get away from me.

The Cullen reached for my ankle. As he did so, the rotting skin on his hands sloughed away, falling onto my leg like rain. I gagged hard enough to hurt. I rolled so that I was facing him and kicked out as hard as I could, directly at his disgusting face. His head popped from his shoulders with a dull crack. It plunked across the hall, rolling to a stop. I squirmed from the hand that still gripped my ankle. His body didn't follow, but over in the corner of the corridor, his teeth clacked with impotent rage.

I drew myself up into a tight ball against the stones, as far away as I could manage from his headless corpse. My gown was blood-soaked.

I am going to die. I knew it. I'm not a Fate. Not special. Not anything.

I whipped my head to the side, tried to fight the nausea that suddenly rose like a wave and the roaring in my ears. My heart was beating so fast I could feel it everywhere. It felt hot and bright, like a shooting star, and I couldn't focus. Limp, I looked down the hall toward Arabella—I lay not eventwenty steps away from the tower door. I'd almost made it back, I wanted to get to her. I wanted to tell her I was sorry that I'd made us stay so long, that we should have tried to escape sooner. That if we had tried years ago, Taliesin wouldn't have died. I wouldn't have to die now.

But I was so far away, I wasn't going to make it. Inky blackness surrounded me, narrowing my vision, and I felt a primordial pulse.

This is what it is like to die, I thought.

Honestly, it wasn't so bad.

"Thought you'd go for a stroll, I see."

The corridor was indigo, cold—crystalline. My fists beat upon the surface of a layer of ice, desperate to break through. I jerked awake, my onyx eyes burning. I was still sitting in the corridor, leaning against the wall.

I grimaced as I placed my hands to the wounds, but the pain was gone. My gown was still red, still bloody, with a long slit ... but my skin was unmarred, gleaming and pale in the darkness of the corridor. If not for the blood, I would have thought it all a dream.

I really am one of the Fates. I'm immortal. I can't die unless it's by my own hand.

"What are you doing outside your room?" Malinda asked. "And where did you get a key?"

I barely heard her question. Instead, I studied my hands, which seemed different somehow, longer, more powerful. My palms itched, and I felt like I might be able to crush the stones of the Castle with them.

Confused, I searched for the Cullen and his head, but the corridor was otherwise empty.

"What?" I asked, finally turning my gaze back to her.

"I asked where you got the key, Morena." There was anger in her voice but also genuine curiosity.

"I don't have a key." Instead of stammering, like I might have done in the past, the words were smooth. And I was curiously, strangely, unafraid.

"The door was magically unlocked?" She towered over me. Her high-collared gown was a pale amethyst color, trimmed in prim white lace. Bloodstains decorated the satin like umber roses.

"So it would seem." Slowly I stood, expecting pain, but quickly realized that I felt differently than normal—strong, young. "Where did the Cullen go? The one who stabbed me."

She inspected my face as if she could read it, as if a lie might be written there. "There was no Cullen here when I arrived." She could see the cut in my gown, the bloom of red where I'd bled out, the giant smear of blood down the hall. Understanding dawned.

"Your magic arrived. You can feel it, can't you?" she asked.

"Yes" I answered, still scanning the hallway, noticing cracks and crevices, the feeling of each breath entering my chest. A small spider in the windowsill. Despite just being stabbed, I felt like I could swim the entire length of the sea. I was no longer cold, no longer tired.

"Go to bed," Malinda told me. "Don't wander the halls of this house. It still isn't safe." Malinda grasped my shoulders, turned me toward the tower door, and gave me a small shove.

Perhaps it was habit by then, to listen to her. That despite my new-found immortality and power, I didn't have to be told twice. I returned to the room without protest, and a moment after I closed the door behind me, I heard her key in the lock.

Arabella was still asleep, her face peaceful, her brow unwrinkled—blissfully oblivious to everything that had happened. I sat down at the desk and ran my fingers over her savagely carved words.

A knife without a blade.

Now I could see the letters perfectly, even without candlelight. Now I was the blade.

As dawn broke outside the tower window, the sun rising over the edge of the sea, I knew I would not tell Arabella about the open door, nor of Atropos on the stone table and the Cullen horde standing idle; not about being stabbed in the hallway and Malinda finding out, nor the new strange feeling in my chest.

There was no reason to tell her—nothing had truly changed. Giving her hope would only make her more volatile. Despite my promise to Atropos, we were as empty-handed as ever. I did not know how to use the powers that seethed beneath my skin—I did not trust myself to wield them safely. I did not know how to get past the Cullen guard. I did not have any tools with which I might free her. All I had was myself, and I was too afraid.

I assumed that I couldn't kill Malinda with my own bare hands - I reasoned that Atropos was the key. She was a gift from the universe, a weapon to wield if I could just solve the riddle of her binding and undo it. With Atropos freed, I'd have a teacher—someone to coach me how to use my powers. Then, together, we could punish Malinda. I glanced at the pile of books on the desk. Surely, somewhere in those pages, was the solution.

The first words Arabella spoke were of our brother. "I was so sure we would escape. I felt it so strongly."

I closed the book I was reading, a thin volume entitled *The Life and Times of the Gods*. So far it had yielded no insights about The Fates, nor what I should expect as one of the them. "You have many feelings."

My dismissal settled into the long silence between us, nestled into the blank spaces of our words.

After a while, she spoke again: "If only my magic would come. I hope it's something great and terrible, so I can destroy this place." Arabella rubbed away her tears with the back of her hand. It was a gesture so childlike that for a moment it hurt, remembering the little bundle she'd once been. I'd nuzzled and cuddled her until she'd gotten too big for such things.

"Don't cry," I chided her from across the room. "You'll make yourself ill."

"I won't." Her eyes flicked past me, over my shoulder toward the tower window. Widened.

"What?" I asked. The first thought was that it would be Taliesin, reborn as Cullen, climbing back through the tower window.

"In the sky. It's a bat. A really big one." Arabella bumped against me as she came closer, forcing her way into the tight space next to the only window in the tower.

I tugged a strand of her red hair. "You stepped on my foot."

She gave me a slight shove. "I want to see."

An explosive screech tore through the air, the wind whistled past his outstretched wings, and the tower was draped in shadow as a wave of wintry air struck us both in the face. Much to our shock, it was a dragon that soared past our window, heading toward the mountains. Silver membranous wings stretched as wide as the dock, and his heart beat so firmly that both of us could hear it.

"It's a dragon! I've never seen a dragon! Nico said they don't come north. What could he be doing here...? I bet he's hungry." Arabella looked back at our table. "Let's throw an apple at him. Maybe he'll take it as a sign of aggression and burn the Castle down."

I rolled my eyes. "Always so violent," I muttered.

I'd never seen a dragon either, and my first reaction wasn't to hope it would burn down our castle. Of course it hadn't occurred to my sister that we'd still be locked in the tower, and we'd burn just as fast as Malinda.

Awed, I stared at the giant beast outside. His icy blue eyes burned in their sockets, and somehow—I do not know how—I felt as if I could speak and he would understand.

"If we throw an apple, it'll be nicely," I told her. "Politely."

Despite the smallness of our rations—we'd received just a slice of bread and an apple for our meals that day—I half-wished to throw an apple to the dragon myself. Gods knew, he was a long way from home in the bitterly cold north.

"Hello!" Arabella yelled. "You there! Are you hungry?"

"Shhhh!" I hushed her loudly. I didn't want our mother to find out, though it was probably too late for that. A dragon roaring directly outside our window was pretty hard to miss.

Arabella hurled an entire apple out the window with all her might. Of course, my sister was twelve and she'd never been outside other than our escape attempt. So, it wasn't the best throw—it was terrible, and weak, and the apple wouldn't have even made it to the edge of the sea—but the dragon snatched it within its jaws with a sharp *crack*. The stone floor of the tower vibrated under our feet.

I grabbed her arm before she could launch another toward the beast outside. "That's our last one."

"So?"

My stomach grumbled in response—that was my apple, and I'd been saving it. But I knew Arabella would never accept that answer. Our days stretched on into oblivion—no relief, no escape—and if feeding our only food for the day to a dragon would be our entertainment this month, she was willing.

"Let's cut it into pieces," I suggested. "And only give him half."

She pursued her lips, primed to pout and refuse. But it was still *my* apple, and she knew that. "Fine."

Quickly, she bit a few huge chunks out of the apple and placed them into my hand.

"We'll both throw it," she said charitably.

"Ok," I agreed.

Arabella hurled one of the larger pieces out the window. The dragon flapped its great wings and hovered in the air, then easily caught the nibble between his teeth.

"If you want to thank us, you can get us out of here!" Arabella called.

"What a good boy," I tossed some of my pieces to him, shivering when each beat of his wings sent a blast of frigid air into the room. "Would he eat us, you think?"

"If he had the chance? Maybe." Arabella seemed hopeful. "Then we'd be out of our misery."

"Taliesin would have loved this," I replied. "He always wanted to see a real-life dragon."

Instantly, our happy mood evaporated. Arabella placed her remaining sliver of apple on the windowsill with a dull thunk. I felt overcome by bitterness. He would have loved it, but he was dead. And the dark-green beast couldn't stay, for if he did, Malinda would clap him into chains. *He has to go,* I thought, miserably. *Malinda will imprison him, just like us.*The dragon, game for whatever other fruit we might toss his way, waited expectantly. We studied each other. His skin was iridescent silver, like fish scales that caught the light, some seemingly soft pink or golden. Muscular legs and wings beat at the air, yet he was sleek, and his wings spanned wide and semi-translucent, letting the light through. On his head was a crown of horns, under which a pair of arctic-blue eyes watched the tower and the two girls at its window.

Somewhere beyond the Obsidian Sea was his home—a land of verdant hills and jungles of flowers and waterfalls, where castles of ivory stone were carved into the sides of violet mountains. Kinkanali and Kinseamair still held magic —unicorns, Fae, and dragons—and this proved it. This meant that Nico's stories were real, that The Epiphany was real, that the other Fates had descendants who lived in great glass palaces and dined on hot food and spiced wine.

I had imagined it, I had dreamed it, but never had I thought it *real.*

How I wished, wished I could touch the dragon, or climb upon his back. I leaned out the window. "Malinda will never let you go if she catches you. You have to leave."

As if he understood my words, the dragon made what I swore looked like a nodding motion and flew away. As his silhouette became smaller and then disappeared, I realized that I'd forgotten to give him the last piece of apple. Crisp and juicy, it was still in my hand. I placed it in my mouth and chewed slowly, savoring the last of its sweetness.

"Maybe he'll come back and rescue us." A long, pregnant pause followed, while Arabella waited for me to join in her storytelling, but I did not.

I no longer wanted Arabella's fairytales. I wanted out—*out*—to follow the blue-eyed dragon to wherever he might lead. And to do that, I knew with sudden, cold certainty, that if we ever were going to leave this place, to see the land of our dreams ... it would require someone to kill my mother.

CHAPTER 4

———◆○◆———

P erhaps it was Taliesin's death, or the failed escape attempt, or the departure of the dragon, but the fire in Arabella rose to a fever pitch, eating at her. Perhaps she imagined Taliesin would come back; certainly she imagined a great confrontation with Malinda. But surely she did not imagine the reality, which was that life went back to exactly as it had been: long days of the two of us in silence, the walls of the tower forming a cave around us.

Some days I didn't leave the mattress. Every time I opened my eyes, I saw my sister pacing the room in the threadbare black gown that was far too short, revealing her ankles, then her calves. Whenever Cullen brought us food, she screamed and cursed, sometimes threw things at them, until even they seemed afraid. If she'd known how, she would have used my powers to wipe all of Kinver'i off the map, killing everything in reach; we would have left Grace Castle behind us, nothing but a pile of ashes. Or so she said.

But Arabella caught a cold. It became a small sniffle, which became a cough, which became a fever. At first, it seemed like nothing. Just one of her usual illnesses which left her a bit more tired and infinitely more cranky, then subsided after a few days. So I did not take it seriously. I did not give her my food rations or extra blankets at night as I should have.

One morning, I awoke and Arabella was groaning. I reached across the sheets and touched her – her skin burned against my palm. I cursed and withdrew my hand; there was nothing to do now but wait it out. We had no medicine. As the sun rose in the sky, she worsened, and I took the snow from the windowsill and packed it into a bowl, wetted one of our old socks and placed it on Arabella's forehead. It cooled her skin temporarily, and I put small mouthfuls of snow on her tongue to help her throat.

The next day was worse. Still Arabella's fever did not break, and she grew more and more distant, rambling and muttering. Despairing, I adjusted her blankets. Would the Cullen not come soon? Even when they did, how could I tell them that she was ill? Would they understand me? Would Malinda rejoice, and be happy that she could be rid of another of her children with little effort?

I could *feel* the shadow of her death date hovering, and I pushed it away like a pesky fly. I didn't want to know about that. *Not now, not soon.*

As I stroked my sister's matted scarlet hair, I talked quietly to her. "I'm going to get us out of here. We're going to have vengeance. I have a plan. I *promise* you it will be different."

I still didn't know how I'd make that true. Atropos was still cursed, stuck on the stone table. There was no one to help me, no one to talk to.

Arabella's silence was a crushing weight on my shoulders.

I can carry her, but if I am carrying her, I won't be able to move fast. I won't have Arabella to carry extra provisions, or extra things like a blanket.

Dimly, I heard a noise, but instead of the rattle in Arabella's chest, it was the sound of the rusted doorknob turning.

Malinda entered the tower room, holding a candle. Clad in a decadent wine-colored gown draped in silvery lace, the Queen's face was red-lipped perfection. Her green eyes sparkled with life, unlike Arabella's which were now glassy and unfocused.

I rose unsteadily from the bed. "What do you want?" I demanded, instantly awake. "Why are you in our room?" I inched protectively towards Arabella.

"Get dressed and come with me."

Why does she need me now? I can't leave Arabella like this.
Maybe she knows.

Maybe Malinda knew I'd found Atropos. Perhaps she'd torture me and confine me somewhere else, far from Arabella, and my baby sister would die alone. I licked my lips anxiously.

The Queen held open the tower door and gave me a stern look. "Hurry up."

I couldn't let Arabella see the Queen do that to me. I squeezed her hand as I got to my feet. Arabella struggled to breathe as she gasped at me. "Don't go ... I have a bad feeling."

"I'd be surprised if you didn't," I muttered and yanked a black gown over my head. I felt my sister's hot forehead again and pressed a kiss to it. "Remember my promise."

Of course, I didn't know how soon I'd be back. Or if I would be back at all. Malinda was unpredictable and ruthless. *All the more reason not to keep her waiting. The sooner I do whatever she wants, the sooner I return to Arabella.*

Malinda and I left the tower and she glided through the corridors. As I'd thought, the throne room and my mother's rooms were in the center of the Castle, its outer walls and towers providing vital barriers and safety.

In the throne room, her chair glistened under a cathedral ceiling. Blackened blood oozed from its arms and seat, and then pooled on the blue marble floors. I shivered slightly, but not from the cold—no, it was the prickling feeling on the back of my neck that told me we were being watched.

We walked straight through the throne room, between enormous indigo pillars carved into skulls and twisting flowers. The smell was terrible. Our home reeked of the dead: the long dead, the freshly dead, the ancient dead who were so dried out they were barely more than skeletons dressed in rags. Here, the Cullen clattered about, patrolling, sweeping floors. In the absence of war or people to murder, Malinda had her undead army doing menial chores, and the Cullen absentmindedly clicked their teeth as they worked.

I studied the planes and arches of the ceiling, up at the stained-glass windows that lined each room, where dim starlight was forced into brilliant color and pattern. They were all death scenes: morbid, macabre, and gruesome.

Casually, Malinda picked up a skull that was gathering cobwebs along a windowsill, and continued our walk through the Castle. Beneath our feet, the floors of her throne room writhed as words appeared and disappeared from them, shifting as if they breathed. I cleared my throat. "What do the floors say?"

"It depends," the Queen answered. "The prayers of our people vary depending on the situation."

I doubted if she'd ever read them, much less answered them. "What do they pray for?"

"Death."

"I don't want to be a killer," I began.

The Queen bared her teeth, each one honed like a bone knife, and completely lost her temper. "IT'S NOT ABOUT KILLING PEOPLE!" she thundered, suddenly looming over me, her eyes transformed by her wrath.

Every hair on my body stood upright as I stared down at the floor, at the writhing script that twisted and looped, the words of the dying or damned begging for mercy.

The Queen, as if able to read my thoughts, pointed at the floor. "YOU WALK ON THEIR WORDS." She stomped her foot down, hard enough to break bones. "YOU ARE A GOD. EVERY MAN, WOMAN, and CHILD WILL DIE AS *YOU* DEMAND. THAT IS YOUR DESTINY. DO YOU UNDERSTAND?"

She threw the skull she held at the wall, and it smashed into pieces, shards skittering toward the edges of the room.

"I understand," I mumbled, trying to hold back the sick feelings churning in my gut.

I followed her silently after that, until we entered a small study where a cozy fire crackled. There were half a dozen candles lit to brighten the space, and in the corner a dead cat stared at me from his pillow. One of his legs was entirely bone, its last scrap of fur hanging off the knee like a tattered flag. He was purring.

"Sit." The Queen gestured to a plush chair. "Wine?" She studied a table laden with decanters of various sizes and shapes, then poured herself a generous glass from a tall cylinder full of greasy liquid.

"No thank you," I replied, as I sank into a worn sofa.

Malinda took a seat across from me, and sipped from her goblet as she contemplated my face. I could see each soft eyelash, a small beauty mark along her eyebrow. Her ever-changing eyes which today were flecked with gold, like the forest at sunset, where the shafts of light bounce off the leaves and rich earth. She blinked, and for a moment, just a moment, I saw the flash of the Fae lineage she usually hid.

"Taliesin's death was hard on you."

My face paled. "Don't say his name." My voice was a broken vase, a sharp edge in the dark. "He was *my* brother. *My family.*"

"Is." Malinda poured herself another glass of wine. "He is your brother, although he is gone. And he is my son."

Her words held not a speck of remorse. I wished that my cursed eyes could weep, yet I was grateful that they could not. Outside, the wind wailed. The dead cat purred on its pillow. The room was curiously still as the Queen studied—no, *inspected*—me.

"Are you curious about why I came to your room?" she asked.

"No." The word popped out of my mouth before I could stop it.

The Queen smiled, revealing her small, white teeth. "Don't lie. You aren't very good at it."

I tried not to let my fear show. "I don't know why you came to my room."

"Another lie, Morena." She folded her hands across her lap. "I know much more about what goes on in my house than you think. But I'll let it pass. You are a Fate, a descendant of Atropos. You take souls. That's what you are supposed to do."

Malinda glared at me another beat, as if she would say something else. I breathed slowly, in and out, and tried to calm my racing heart. She patted a package next to her. "I've brought you a gift." From the small velvet bag, she withdrew an odd, oval shape, and placed it onto the table between us.

"A ... what?" I stared at her in shock. She could have announced she was having me murdered—that would not have been a surprise at all—but a *gift?*

I reached across the desk, half afraid whatever it was would jump at me. Flipping it over, I had to hold back a gasp. The gift was a mask, heavy and sinister, crafted with obsidian and bones and pearl. The cheekbones were savage, like white blades cleaving through night. It smelled of firerose—strong magic—probably crafted by Fae. It was the face of a ghoul.

"Put it on." The Queen leaned forward, her face giddy. "I want to see it."

I flipped over the wretched thing, slowly bringing it to my face. I wondered what kind of evil might be infused in it as I tied its ribbons around my head. With my hair and face hidden, and my black eye sockets, I was terrifying. Much more terrifying than my appearance though was the *feeling* of wearing it; my skin crawled, my hair prickled. There was *something* wrong about the mask, even though I couldn't identify exactly what it was.

"I can't see you at all," Malinda marveled. "Atropos said that with it, she could live two lives ... a Fate and its shadow. It provides safety, invisibility. Men and Fae will sense you, fear you, but not be able to grasp you—you're a dream just beyond their reach, invisible. Only those who you wish to see you will be able to, but those should be few and far between."

"How could they sense me, but not see me?" I tried to turn off the invisibility, to let Malinda see, and the focusing of her eyes let me know that she was telling the truth. I could decide if I was visible or not, and to whom.

"Can you see hate? Can you see fear? Can you see cold?" Her face grew thoughtful. "If you ever leave, take the mask with you. Remember that the original Fates turned on each other. Their descendants are your enemies."

The thought of having enemies besides Malinda sunk like a rock in my stomach. "Have they ever come beyond the Wall of Skulls?" I asked. "Are they truly a threat?"

Perhaps Malinda worried that I wouldn't agree. Perhaps she, in that moment, thought I was braver than I truly was. "I'd like you to read something," she murmured, as she handed me a stack of parchment.

The pages were tattered, as if she'd read through them over and over. My gaze flicked over the documents. "This is a declaration of war." I skimmed the words. "It says that if you wish to avoid it, you are asked to hand over your daughters..." I stopped, re-read it. "Why would they want us? Who sent this to you?

"It is one of many I have received. Pompous lords and wealthy men from all over, wanting you and your sister." The confusion must have been clear on my face because she huffed. "To breed you. To marry you off to one of their insipid sons, using you and Arabella for creating heirs. They want that so desperately, they're willing to do almost anything to have it." She was disgusted as she snatched the papers back from me. "Arabella would go to one, and you to another."

"Can't they get their bride stock elsewhere?"

She smirked. "These letters have been arriving since before you were born. What other women in Moirai have the blood of Atropos in their veins? What others can control Death and darkness and plagues? There is no better weapon than the two of you. Human kings, presidents... Even Ares himself asked for your hand."

Is this why you kept us in the tower? Why we're locked away like treasure, never to see daylight?

It explained much, but not everything.

Malinda continued. "I'm going to upgrade your rooms. The tower is abysmal." She looked directly at me. "You'll want more food. Medicine. Books."

An unsteady silence between us followed. Something had changed, something serious, for her to invite me here. The Queen pretended to study the heavy silver rings that decorated almost every finger of a rotted hand sitting on the side table next to her. I studied the room, examining all of the strange objects that littered the shelves and her desk.

"And what do you want in return?" I said. A vise of fear gripped my heart. She wouldn't offer these things if she didn't expect payment.

"Your help of course," she replied smoothly. "Cooperation for my plans."

"What plans?"

She smiled. "Keeping the tongues of their spies still. Securing our borders."

I weighed the trade in my mind. "We need thicker blankets. Firewood." I said after a beat, my voice nervous.

"I agree," she replied, with an enigmatic smile.

I was young and untried, but I understood that Malinda was *bargaining*. She wanted something from me badly enough to bring me here, to offer me these things ... but why bother bargaining, when we both knew I didn't really have a choice? Surely better blankets wouldn't make up for whatever it was that she wanted?

And yet I realized that if ever there would be a time for me to take advantage of Malinda, this was it. I thought of a dozen more requests, each bigger than the last. All in exchange for something that was only to protect myself and Arabella.

"Trips outdoors." I could tell by her expression that I'd gone too far, so I quickly amended my request. "A garden. Inside the Castle."

"A greenhouse?" Malinda tapped long tapered fingers against the arm of the chair. "For herbs and such?"

I nodded.

"Look here," she murmured, and handed me a small, wooden, scrying mirror. "See what I see."

Hesitant, I studied the face reflected back to me. I was still wearing the mask tied tightly around my head. A demon.

"The mask will allow you to be my enforcer. You will make sure that our enemies do not cross the Wall. You will punish those who defy me. You will help me protect our people from the other Fates, and their descendants. More importantly, you'll learn to protect *yourself*."

It was clear enough, yet my heart and soul recoiled and screamed in my chest. I couldn't help her. With me as her helper, Malinda would be all-powerful, and essentially unstoppable. None of our enemies would have a chance. *I wouldn't have a chance.*

"Men are full of lies, Morena. Their tongues bring pleasure some-times, but mostly pain. You'll learn that eventually. So I need you to question my prisoners, soul to soul, so that I can have my answers. Then I need you to kill them."

If I could have killed her then—right then, while we stood there—then maybe ... but I realized immediately that it was pointless. The Cullen would defend her; I couldn't get close enough to kill her, and I didn't know if I'd succeed even if I did attempt it.

I took off the mask and placed it carefully on the table. "Nothing will ever make me *want* to be a killer." My voice cracked and betrayed my nerves.

Quick as a snake, her cold hand darted forward and gripped my face. Hard enough to hurt, hard enough to make me look at her. "This is your birthright. It is what you were born to do. Pretending otherwise is a waste of our time." She let go of me as if I were disgusting to touch, and sat back in her chair, her face strangely composed.

"Besides, you can't refuse. If you do, your sister will be dead within a fortnight."

I knew she spoke the truth. Arabella would die in the tower, if not from this fever than the next. A deal with Malinda might be my only chance to save her. If Arabella had food—if she had medicine and a fire to warm her—then she could recover.

Just until her magic came.

Just until she was healthy enough.

Just until I could find a way out.

While Arabella regained her strength, I could learn to use my powers. I could find a way past the Cullen and find a way to unspell Atropos.

I surveyed the room. My eyes were immediately drawn to a painting—a small, delicate, black and white watercolor of a woman in black, arms extended in a plea. Melancholy and alone, it was meant to look like me. Taliesin had drawn it with ash from our fire.

"How did you get that?" I asked Malinda. "That's mine."

"I took it. You didn't notice." Malinda snapped. "Now give me an answer or get out."

If I embraced my powers, if I used the mask and its invisibility, I would explore the Castle further. I would look for a way to free Atropos. Some-day, Arabella, Atropos, and I would share The Grace as a real family.

I sneaked a glance at the Queen. She held a gray orb in her hands. Her golden hair, a match to mine, tumbled down over her shoulders, rich and lovely, her face as pale as my own. We were mirror images, yet her lips seemed permanently fixed into the expression of the victor who has drawn blood from a foe. Mine were always downturned, on the verge of despair.

She had won. Somehow, she always won and I always lost. If Arabella died, I would have nothing left to fight for, and no reason to refuse her anyway. If the deal I made kept Arabella alive, I would be forever enslaved to her, a prisoner forced to do her evil deeds for the rest of my immortal life. In my hands, the great obsidian mask glittered.

Malinda wanted my power; she wanted my life. But what was my life worth to me, if I spent it powerless, locked in the tower? What would it be like, if Arabella died too? A God I might be, but I was locked in a cage, with no one but corpses to rule.

"I agree," I replied, knowing the price of acceptance and knowing I had no choice.

CHAPTER 5

"**D**on't gag. It's unladylike." Malinda stepped through the pile of maggots on the dungeon floor and studied our prisoner with a practiced eye.

Blood dripped from a gaping wound across the male Fae's ribs. His blood was blue, thick, and reeking of infection. Sweat and piss, anger and fear—that's what he smelled like. Chains around his wrists attached him to the ceiling. This Fae was in bad shape—Cullen had cut out his tongue, broken his back, sliced his chest open, and cracked his ribs.

She hadn't waited long to summon me—it'd only been two days since I'd agreed to her deal. One of Malinda's faithful Cullen shook me awake by one shoulder, then escorted me down flight after flight of stairs, lifting a partially shredded tapestry to reveal a hidden door.

Ill and weakened, Arabella did not stir from her sleep as I left. As much as I worried for her, I was grateful not to have to explain Malinda's bargain, nor its terms. Which, it turned out, were terrifyingly simple.

Question the prisoners, give Malinda the answers. Cut their hearts from their chests and give those to Malinda as well. Whether they were for food, decoration, or memorabilia was none of my concern. Or so she said.

As a sign of her goodwill, Malinda held up her end of the deal. Within minutes after my return to the tower, Cullen brought medicine and hot tea, a thick wool blanket so red it matched Arabella's hair. They brought more firewood, freshly chopped, and built us a fire. They ladled out a stew, hearty and hot, into iron bowls. It was such a radical change that I immediately decided that I didn't feel like eating much. Instead, I dutifully spooned it between Arabella's dried lips and bid her drink the water, the tea, and the medicine. I watched her fall back asleep wrapped in that crimson blanket, my face sagging with relief.

But still, I asked myself if it was worth it as I stood in the corner of the dungeon awaiting orders. Now masked, wearing the heavy black robes Malinda provided, I felt sick and wrong... stained. Even as a witness, I was made unclean. The blood, the stench, the terror in the air around me —

This cannot be my path. I cannot do this.

"Speak as little as possible," she said.

This wasn't a problem. I'm not sure I could have opened my mouth without screaming.

"I grow tired of waiting for your answers," she purred to the male who dangled from the dungeon ceiling.

He was old, ancient, if one counted the number of wrinkles on his forehead. Maggots feasted on his skin and innards, and those that lost their grip due to engorgement spilled from a wide gash in his side. Like rain, they fell to the dungeon floor in a sloppy, wriggly pile. He would die by my hand or die from infection, doomed to become one of the Cullen. Clear-eyed, her hands steady, Malinda lifted his whiskered chin with a gloved hand. Then she frowned, her lovely lips forming a stark red line of displeasure.

"Tell us about the Eye," she demanded, "or yours will not be the only bloodshed tonight."

Down the hall, beyond the iron bars and the locked door, I heard a wail. One of the Cullen entered the cell, his jaw hanging off, teeth yellow, skin peeling back from his bones. His skeletal hands dragged in a girl. Dark-haired and filthy, the girl could have been anyone, the daughter of a servant, perhaps. She pushed at his rotting hands, her hair whipping around as she struggled.

How strange it was to see a girl my own age. Her hair was like a raven's wing, and I couldn't stop myself from touching it. Invisible to her, I lifted a few dark strands and let them fall. Silky. Soft. Untangled and straight as an arrow. Her eyes darted back and forth, looking for a place to escape. I knew better than anyone how she felt; I knew the futility of hope. I clenched the fabric of my robe in my fists, my hands at my sides.

"Happy to see your beloved daughter?" Malinda asked the Fae.

The girl writhed toward the door, trying to get away. The Cullen shoved her backward, toward the center of the cell.

The spectacle seemed to entertain Malinda, and she beckoned to me. "Come. Let Death pay this female a friendly visit."

The girl jerked her head up. She couldn't see me, of course, but she could feel my sinister presence, the waft of cold from my robes as I approached. Her mouth opened and shut like a fish gasping for air.

"No," she whimpered. "Please don't."

Malinda chastised the elder prisoner again. "If you will not tell us what you know, I must persuade you."

I could tell by the look on her face that she wouldn't give any respite. He should have said the Queen already if he knew anything. If he didn't tell Malinda what she wanted to know, she would make sure he begged for Death.

You are not my mother; you are too cruel and vicious to be a mother. Mothers always love their children.

After a long pregnant pause, Malinda glanced at me. "We'll practice on the girl first. Death, reveal yourself."

I made a conscious effort to let the Fae see me. The male screamed an incoherent garble. Malinda returned to the Fae, whose eyes bulged as he saw Death hovering over his daughter like a dark cloud of doom. "Oh. Are you willing to talk to us now?"

He hesitated again. Whatever he knew *must* be very important if he would sacrifice his own flesh and blood. But perhaps he did not yet know what Malinda had planned or how terrifying she might be. I didn't know either, but I surely didn't want to find out.

If the Cullen hadn't held her so tightly, the girl would have run screaming from the room. But she was caught fast, unable to flee.

Malinda leaned forward, her crimson gown pouring down on the stones. "Touch her and take her mind. You'll want to replace her thoughts with your own."

What thoughts? Thoughts of escape?

Underneath the mask, I was skeptical. I was suddenly glad Malinda couldn't see my facial expressions as they drifted from surprise to disgust.

Was it truly that simple?

Malinda could sense my hesitation, and she gripped the girl's face tightly. "We haven't got all day."

Hands shaking slightly, I reached forward and touched one tentative finger to the side of the girl's head, where her soft hair met her skin. *Madness.* I tried to think of the things I'd seen that most terrified me in this brutal place, walking through the castle rooms and re-imaging them for the girl.

The blood-soaked altar. A severed head, abandoned in a dusty corner. The floor was covered in blood, the throne drinking it. The demon of the northern tapestry, his face screaming for vengeance—I made him real.

Madness.

Delusions, deceptions, shadows, and ghosts flooded her brain. I wiped away the reality of the stinking cell and the Cullen corpses holding her and replaced her thoughts with infinitely worse visions, hallucinations meant to drive someone mad. The girl fell to the ground, writhing in agony. She screamed, long and shrill, then raked her fingernails down the soft flesh of her face, desperate to escape. I grimaced under the mask, momentarily grateful that Malinda couldn't see my expression. Torture was not required for answers. That part was purely theater or Malinda's own sick enjoyment.

It's a terrible thing to be a descendant of the Fates.

I let go of the girl, and her cries subsided into whimpers.

"Impressive," Malinda congratulated me. "That was just a taste. Are you still unwilling to tell me what I wish to know?"

The Queen circled the male Fae and dragged her nails across the open wound of his torso. "Still feeling stubborn?" He shook his head.

"Fine." Malinda addressed me again, and her smile was so evil that the marrow in my bones curdled. "Now him. Speak to his soul and ask him about the Eye."

I bowed my head and breathed deeply. Then, I reached for the vague feeling buried in my veins. I envisioned a valley surrounded by mountains, where I could stand in the moonlight among violet flowers, not a sound to be heard: *The Valley of the Shadow of Death.* I'd never been there, only read of it, but it was a calming vision.

I held my breath as I leaned closer to the Fae. Malinda said that men's tongues liked to lie, that their lips could clamp shut. Would they really answer truthfully to me? I cast my senses out into the red meat of his chest, through his lungs, bones, bones, and heart.

And much to my surprise, there it was—a soul, faint, like a shy sunrise on a December morning. A small ball of light beneath his heart.

The Fae frowned, his swollen eyes still closed. He was tired, weary, and in pain. His life was wrapped around the light like a web, a thread of delicate silver, like gossamer-spun sugar. And when I held out my hand, the thread came to me – I grasped one end between my fingers. Gently, I tugged it, unwinding and inspecting it. His life untangled as easily as a thread on a spindle. My nostrils flared as I smelled something, clover, and for an instant, I could see it: a peaceful home, a lake far from here.

Death has come for you. Are you ready?

Not yet, his soul answered. *I am not ready. Not yet.*

A wave of nausea gripped my throat, acidic and green. No matter where the feeling came from, I knew it to be true—the Fae was not ready, and I felt a deep sense of obligation to give him that time. I cursed the Gods underneath the mask and took a deep breath. As a Fate and the descendant of Atropos, I decided when lives ended—not the Fae, not Malinda, and not this one individual.

While he could ask for my time, he could not make it so. Death could take anyone, at any time, ready or no.

Tell me what she seeks. Tell me of the Eye or whatever it is she wants you for.

Keep it safe, his soul said again, beseeching. *She is clever. Too clever.*

Keep what safe? Who?

The girl was once entrusted to me. I hid her well.

The girl in the corner still sat writhing and moaning. She seemed ordinary, but if what he hid was *her...* I was certain that the humble Fae was guilty of whatever Malinda sought him for. I also didn't want to know anything else about it. If I pushed and were more precise, his soul would have no choice but to tell me the truth, and then Malinda would demand to know what he said. I was a terrible liar—so I could not conceal it. She'd see if I tried to hide anything. It was better not to know anything more.

Say nothing else, I said to his soul.

With a sinking realization, I knew there was no way he would leave this cell. I should kill him quickly before he revealed too much. I had to kill him right now, with Malinda watching. If I didn't, he would tell her whatever secrets he held—if not today, if not tomorrow, then eventually. She would wring them from his flesh and bones by force, and this poor Fae would crumble under the weight of her brutality. Killing him was the kindest thing I could do, and it would protect whatever secrets he had.

I unsheathed my dagger, grateful his daughter could not see me.

I need not ask his forgiveness. I need not assure him. But his Death felt senseless, without purpose or meaning, and it felt *wrong,* a conflicting destiny that I was setting into motion.

It felt awful.

Death, spare me, his soul entreated.

I couldn't lift the blade.

If not me, spare my daughter.

I took a deep, steadying breath. Silently, I promised him that I would. Malinda still watched; she tapped her foot behind me and observed with impatience.

I slit his throat in one smooth motion. The Fae slumped forward, dead, and the daughter screamed.

Father. Father. The cries of her soul echoed through my skull, clanging like an iron bell. I'd never met my father; I could not imagine caring for a parent as this girl did.

"You killed him," Malinda said, clearly annoyed.

"He did not have what you sought, and he did not know where it was," I lied to the Queen of the Blood Throne.

"What of his heart?" Malinda eyed me suspiciously. "Was it not worthy?"

I could not stand to have given the kind Fae's heart to such a monster. But she needn't know that either. "Infection," I said. "I do not think it would have lasted much longer."

Malinda clucked her tongue in annoyance. "Fine. Cut him up with that," she pointed toward the corner of the cell where a scythe stood waiting, propped against the wall and gleaming like a shaft of moonlight in the dark.

"As you like." I walked to the corner of the cell, streams of midnight unfolding behind me. I picked it up. It was a strange weapon, heavy, and I weighed it in my pale hands as I returned to his lifeless body.

"Do you know how to use it?" she asked.

I squirmed underneath my skin as I looked at the scythe. "No," I said tonelessly. "But I'll figure it out."

With a weak, half-hearted swipe of the scythe, I beheaded the Fae. It shouldn't have been so easy, but the blade was sharp and well-kept. His blood sprayed across the walls like a spring, which I tried and failed to dodge. Biting my lip and mostly looking away, I kept cutting. Each swing of the blade whistled through the air as I removed his arms, then feet, then legs. Bile churned in my stomach.

This is who I am now? I asked myself over and over. *This is what I do?*

I would have stayed a thousand more days in the tower if I'd known it would have avoided this moment.

He felt no pain, I reassured myself. *I promised him—we made a deal. Dismembering him now will keep him from becoming Cullen. A mercy.*

When I was done, I contemplated the girl, eyes now vacant, blood streaming down her cheeks like tears. "Who is she?" I wiped the bloody blade of the scythe with a corner of my gown.

"Nobody. A nothing." Malinda was lost in thought, staring at the blood on her hands.

If I killed her now, quickly, she would suffer less. If I killed her now, perhaps the Cullen wouldn't devour her alive, and Malinda wouldn't have an opportunity to torture her again.

But I'd made a deal with the Fae; he'd spent his last breath begging for the girl, and I'd promised to spare her.

"Let's keep her," I suggested. "In a few weeks, I can cut out her heart and bring it to you." In a few weeks, I could figure out some other excuse. At least I'd bought the girl some time.

Malinda's face might have been carved from stone. "Fine. Leave her there." Then the Queen tugged open the dungeon door and motioned me to come along. Like a dog after its master.

Underneath the mask, I smiled. I'd won my first victory against her.

And a victory, no matter how small, always tastes sweet.

CHAPTER 6

D eath leaves its mark on the living. My hands became blood-stained, just like Malinda's. My tongue grew heavy with the weight of stories and screams. My eyes hollowed, my heart numbed. As the months passed, my powers bloomed and ripened. The dates of my victim's deaths readily revealed themselves, fluttering above their heads like a moth. The date was always *today*, and their deaths became the calendar by which I measured time.

And a long time passed. Long weeks, followed by long months and even longer years.

I wore the mask infrequently at first, but then I grew so accustomed to it that I forgot to remove it. In truth, I preferred invisibility. Sometimes, I even walked as an equal among the Cullen. Whenever possible, I stole away to visit Atropos, her sleeping face my only comfort. Of the two of us, she was the lucky one. She peacefully lay there, while I was trapped in service to Malinda. I told her everything—about the Fae and their blue blood, the scythe that sometimes seemed to speak to me, and how difficult the mask became to remove. I told her of how the shadows called, that I longed to lay down in them and never get up again. I told her of my guilt and shame, of the nightmares that plagued me.

Imagining conversations between the two of us, I gave myself the advice I thought my grandmother would give. *Be philosophical about it. This is the nature of Death and suffering. All things suffer. All things die. Sometimes sooner than planned.* Her still, silent form comforted me and rationalized my actions and assured me that things would get better. That one day – one day – I would free us both from this hell. I believed her.

Whilst I labored in the dungeons, Arabella's life changed just as dramatically. Her fevers disappeared; the constant rash that covered her neck and back receded. True to her word, Malinda sent jewels and gowns, piles of games, books, and Arabella acted pleased. She draped herself in silks and cashmere, rubies as large as an egg. Her appetite for finery was ceaseless, and no matter how much the Queen sent, it was not enough. She always requested yet another item.

As I swept the dungeons clean, I often thought of Arabella upstairs, dripping in jewels and ordering around the Cullen as if they were her slaves. Down one corridor was a room with a massive hole in the center, with a sheer drop of fifty feet into the sea. Jumping would have killed anyone if I hadn't killed them already. Below, sea serpents writhed along the surface, waiting for me to provide their next gruesome meal.

"Chop up that one," Malinda ordered, pointing to a body. "Then the hole."

Bowing my head, I complied. Like the bodies that fell into the sea, I sank silently into the depths of myself, speaking less and less as time went on. Some unspoken criteria drove her selection; not every prisoner was acceptable for her Cullen horde, and I didn't care to hear her reasons. Truth be told, sweeping the dead into the sea was the best part of my day—it meant the horror was nearly over. I could return to the tower, the silence of the stone and falling snow, and my sister. It meant one less Cullen for Malinda's army, an army I was doomed to lead.

So I swept their bodies over the edge and watched the beasts of the sea devour the Cullen in giant bites. My gaze lingered on the inscription that ringed the edge, engraved on the white marble that encircled the hole: *Morior Invictus. I Die Undefeated.* It was a strange phrase, nonsensical in this place. Here in the dungeon, the enemies of the Blood Throne were always defeated.

Being Malinda's henchman had its benefits. Not long after my first visit to the dungeon, I received a key to the tower door. This was for the Queen's convenience so I could meet her at a prescribed time. After a few weeks, when I didn't vanish, Malinda entrusted me with another piece of information—how to exit the Castle through a hidden passageway through the cliffs. My mouth agape, I watched as Malinda twisted a small gargoyle head around on its shoulders, and a grate swung open.

"Go on," she instructed. She held a small bronze box for a heart in her hands, already bloody, and nodded toward the opening. "It's a long walk."

To the casual observer, Malinda walked alone. But they felt me, the shadow that walked alongside her. *Hide,* I bid them. *Run away, hide.* I pitied whomever she chose. We never spoke; we both preferred silence. I, to deal with my grief over the lives I took so cruelly; Malinda ... for whatever evil plans she was weaving. Together, we glided through winding cobblestone streets, side by side but certainly not equals.

Some nights, we walked for hours and never met a soul among the moonlit evergreens. The unlucky few we stumbled upon were questioned and killed where we met them. Quickly, efficiently, I cut out their hearts, leaving their bodies warm in the snow. I handed their hearts to Malinda, who loaded them into her bronze box.

Despite the grim purpose of our walks, I quickly became addicted to being outside, where I did not have to hear any of Arabella's complaints or endure her moods. I loved the night, with its velvety sky full of bright stars; I loved the quiet and the brittle cold; I loved the feeling of walking away and not looking back, pretending that the only thing behind me was a vast expanse of white. I marveled at the feel of new-fallen snow on my face. Before now, each day followed day... relentlessly dull. Nights were my relief: quietly perfect, the starry skies infinite, the barren trees standing witness under the moonlight. Even though Malinda walked beside me, sometimes I felt at peace, perhaps even happy.

In my eighteenth year, as my birthday present, Malinda said I could walk alone. It was the first birthday present I'd ever received from my mother. Full of absurd joy, I hummed softly as I made my way through the evergreens toward the nearest abandoned village. Nestled in the mountains, it was a town of stone with less than thirty homes.

I didn't expect to find anyone. It'd been a week since the last one, an old woman so near Death I doubted if her heart would survive a day, much less long enough to satisfy Malinda's bloody cravings. But as I went around a bend in the road, I saw a man walking in the moonlight up ahead. He had a limp, and I could smell his sweat from where I walked. Silent as the night, I glided along behind him.

He paused and scanned the empty lane, the bare trees shifting in the breeze, the snow and starlight. "Is anyone there?" he called out.

I continued toward him. He should already be running. Certainly, he could feel Death at his heels. I gripped my scythe a little tighter.

The man continued on his way, now walking faster. I drew closer and closer. When I was within reach, I extended my hand to touch his shoulder.

I will be quick. Merciful. Malinda will be glad of this young heart and reward me.

As my fingers brushed his shoulder, the man's face filled with determination and resolve. He lunged, a dagger plunging towards my neck. I leaped backward, caught off-guard, fumbling the scythe. He grabbed my cloak, despite the invisibility, and shoved me down into the snow, his hand finding my throat.

The force of it slammed a grunt out of me, and his grip flexed and closed off my air supply.

He knew I was coming.

"You think you can kill me, Reaper?" the man hissed, his spittle hitting my face. "I'll show you what I can do." He squeezed harder. My eyes bulged, and I could feel my face turning purple as I clawed uselessly at his fingers.

"What do you want from me?" he demanded.

Just die, I thought hopelessly.

He released me and toppled over, falling onto his side in the road. I lay there for a minute, gasping for air, the sky overhead full of stars. Trying to catch my breath, I glanced over at the man. Sprawled in the road, his face was pale, his eyes lifeless. Dead.

I had *wished* him dead, and now it was so. I held out my hands—they were the same. I felt no different. And yet, there he lay.

I'd learned something very valuable, which was exciting.

Glancing over at the body next to me, I wondered just what I should do now. I couldn't question him for Malinda, and his heart would stop beating long before I returned it to the Castle to hand over. This meant I'd have to find another victim before morning, which was deeply unlikely.

I groaned from the pain as I stood. I heaved a long-suffering sigh. I could either dismember him now or carry him to the Castle and drop him in the hole. Should I just leave him on the road, another member for Malinda's Cullen army?

"Next time, kill me," I muttered to his dead body. "Then at least I won't have to face her wrath."

Two of spades. I laid down the card, then raised my eyes to the window to watch the sea. Today it was raining, which was unusual in Kinver'i. It had been... I tapped a finger as I thought about it, my nails and fingertips red, on the desk. I was now twenty; five years had passed since Taliesin disappeared beneath the waves.

"I want a different crown," Arabella exclaimed, her green eyes stony and perfectly matched in her voluminous emerald gown. "A diamond crown and a ball with wine and dancing to break up the monotony of our days."

Shivering at the intense green eyes that bored directly into mine, I returned my gaze back down to the desk, to the playing cards. *Ace of Spades.* Spades always reminded me of dirt, of the killing fields of Kinver'i, where Malinda buried her children. Expressionless, I placed it on the discard pile. Solitaire was my favorite game, and it kept me from going crazy during the long days and nights in the tower.

"Your dress is abysmal. It's so worn that it's nearly faded to ash, and there are holes along the hem."

Stop, I thought. I did not care about dresses or baubles.

"Don't you want one too, sister? A crown of blades to sit upon your golden hair?" she asked me. "As our mother's most valuable possession, your appearance could use improvement."

I felt a pang in my chest as I processed what she'd said. *Her most valuable possession.* But what need did I have for a crown when so many feared me?

Arabella picked through a pile of glittering cloaks of midnight, dresses of dusty coal, onyx, and raven—all stinking of the dead. These were for me—they wouldn't show blood easily.

Buried underneath, however, was a blue dress, soft as the morning sky. Crystals crusted the bodice and formed an icy trim. Web-like gossamer flowed from it, making a cape-like train. It was as if a single snowflake had been pulled from a September day. I'd never seen anything so beautiful. Intrigued, I peered at the sparkling dress.

"This is what *I'm* wearing to our ball."

Malinda has not agreed to a ball, I almost said, but bit my tongue.

"You should wear something other than black, you know." Arabella draped a long strand of diamonds across her chest, where its tear-shaped pendant fell between her breasts. "With your height and stature, you look more like an old crow than a princess."

I drew another card. *Five of Hearts: unconditional love, self-sacrifice for another.* A card whose significance I understood all too well.

Malinda made it clear that if the nice things were to continue, I owed her my nights in the dungeon. Arabella fingered a silvery dress frothing with lace. Healthy, rosy-cheeked, my sister certainly was beautiful, though her attitude left much to be desired lately.

Quickly, I corrected myself for the unkind thought. Arabella was simply too young, too full of life, to be locked away until she withered into a crone. Of course, gowns were not enough for her, nor should they have been. No crown could substitute for her freedom.

The Cullen distributed Malinda's latest raft of presents, and then they trooped from the room, the bones of their heels clacking on the stone floor. Arabella still sat amidst all the finery, the gowns and jewels, patting them as if they were children. She didn't know or wonder about the cost to get her these things. She'd never asked what I must do to earn the prizes scattered around her. Our newfound wealth was already routine, normal for her.

So I joined Malinda that night in the dungeon per our usual schedule, and when I returned to the tower, I placed the key in the lock, but perhaps not as quietly as I could have. I eased open the door too quickly, maybe. I eyed Arabella, still asleep, and wasn't as careful as usual.

Belatedly, I noticed that one of the Cullen nursemaids was seated on the bed next to her, eyes vacant, skin decayed. This one was older, undead for several years, which I could tell by the amount of bones showing through her flesh. Her right shoulder and arm were missing, and the gray skin folded back to reveal a cracked collarbone. Next to her, Arabella was like a vampire who had left its victim drained and dead.

As if it heard my thoughts, Arabella's nursemaid clicked its yellow teeth and made a growling sound in my direction.

"I'll cut you up and throw you in the hole," I muttered to her. "Don't tempt me."

"We need to talk," Arabella said as she popped up from the covers.

"About what?"

"You haven't been hiding food under your bed. You never mention trying to escape anymore." There was a whine in her voice. "You leave at night and don't tell me where you've been. I know she takes you at night. I know the gifts she sends are in payment. Tell me what's happening. "Arabella tried to grab my arm, and I pulled away.

You don't need to know. You don't want to know.

I didn't know why I'd lied anymore, but I could not tell her now—not when it'd been so long since I'd agreed to the deal with Malinda. Each night before I crept back into my bed in the tower, I scrubbed my hands until they were raw, the dried blood cracking across my skin in large seams. I often fell into my bed well after dawn, too tired for food or water, too tired to dream.

I walked to the bedside, my black dress dragging the floor in tattered streams. My golden-blonde hair was stringy and wet, where I'd rinsed away as much of the blood as I could. I cracked my neck as I looked down at Arabella. "I don't want to talk about this right now."

"Well, I do," she said. "I also found a key. *Your key.* A key to *our* door. I can't figure it out... If you have a way out, why haven't you told me? Why let me believe we're still trapped here?"

Because you were happy. For the first time in your life, you were happy.

"I've been getting ready for our escape," I lied. "But it's taking longer than planned, and I didn't know if I'd be caught. I've been waiting for you to be well."

"I'm well enough. And even if I wasn't, I'd rather take my chances." Arabella pushed back the covers and got to her feet. "I'll put on a gown and cloak, and we will go right now."

"The food—"

"I'm sure you know where the kitchens are. We can take food on our way out, can't we?"

I stood there trying to find an excuse to stay while my sister prepared to depart. She stuffed her feet into neat brown boots, their leather not yet creased. I had to stop her; there had to be *something* I could say. We were surrounded by Cullen. Now, I knew how to kill them, but I couldn't kill all of them at once—not yet. Malinda was as ruthless as ever, and if we attempted to flee, I knew exactly what the cost would be.

And I wouldn't leave without Atropos. I'd yet to tell Arabella about finding her in the first place, and now I didn't know *how* to explain why I hadn't told her months ago.

"There's no boat at the dock," I said instead. Outside, the sea frothed and crashed at the base of our tower, the icy waves crowned with white-caps.

"We'll go another direction, away from the sea." Arabella plucked things from drawers and piled her few possessions into a bag. She'd begun to pull on her gloves.

"Arabella. Arabella, *stop,*" I commanded. "We aren't leaving."

"What? Why not?"

"Because I said so. Not tonight." I stood, easily a head taller than she, and crossed the room. "Lay back down," I ordered and tried to snatch her bag away.

Her mouth agape, Arabella stared at my hand, wrapped around hers like a shackle. "Let go of me."

"No." I'd done everything to protect her, to try and make her healthy and strong enough so that she wouldn't end up at the bottom of the sea or as another henchman for Malinda, and she was going to throw it all away.

"Malinda finally won you over."

Won me over. That was a cruel irony. If anyone was to blame, it was Arabella. She was the one who got Taliesin killed. She was the one who was always sick. She was the one without magic to protect her, so I was forced to.

"How long have you had the key?" She glared at me. "Tell me."

I didn't want to. There was no way she would ever forgive me if I told the truth. "No."

"So now you're my oppressor. Terrific." She let go of the bag, the contents spilling across the floor. "I should have known when you started acting all superior. I should have predicted it. It was always Taliesin and me making plans and constructing weapons ... while you were content to stay and wait. Now you're doing whatever Malinda says, killing whomever she wants—"

"I am not."

Her back was toward me as she paced. I was sure her face was as red as her hair. "Ever since Taliesin died, you've done nothing but stand there at the window, like a ghoul, day after day, instead of killing her like you should. It makes me sick to look at you."

I grimaced and bared my teeth at her. "I'm sick of you—you and your incessant whining. You're weak and useless. What have you done, Arabella, except get our brother killed? At least I'm working for a solution."

I shoved her away from me, away from the door, and back toward the bed.

Arabella was fast, but she hadn't expected my reaction. So when I pushed her, she tripped over the undone boot laces and fell backward onto the floor, landing with a loud thump. I expected her to jump up and slap me—with her quick temper and vicious tongue, I expected Arabella to retaliate with screams and insults— but instead, she merely glared.

What she said instead was far worse, and it struck me in the gut like a punch. "You've *become* Malinda. Doing what she would do, "she said from her seat on the floor. "You look like her. You act like her. You *treat me* like her."

"I'm doing what I have to do," I replied. "To keep you safe."

"Liar."

It felt as if there were ice in my veins. I walked to the door, took Malinda's key from my pocket, and left the tower — and I locked Arabella inside.

CHAPTER 7

———◆———

"So, of course, she stopped speaking to me," I told Atropos. I sat next to her sleeping figure in the west tower. I leaned against the stone table, my chin propped on my fists. I liked to talk with her, even if she would never respond. "I understand, though—it's a betrayal. She'll calm down in a day or two, maybe a week. Eventually, she'll see it my way."

I scratched at the mask. I would have liked to visit Atropos as my real self, but I was worried Malinda would find out. She wouldn't be happy if she knew I came here.

But with the mask, I could walk the halls of The Grace without anyone seeing me. Outside, a storm raged, and the winter wind howled across the snowy fields through the open wall. Downstairs, the sea surged, crashing into the foundations of the Castle. Each time a wave broke upon our walls, The Grace trembled.

"It's nice that I don't have to hide my comings and goings. Or strip off my bloody clothes in the hallway. And I don't have to listen to Arabella's ranting or pretend to be interested in the jewels and perfumes she obsesses over."

I felt sure that Atropos heard me. After all, she was still in there, trapped. Talking to her, at least, was better than talking to myself. "She has new rooms now, with a real bed and a rug and books, and she seems pretty pleased with herself." I scratched at the tips of my blood-stained fingers. "Malinda said I could have new rooms too if I wanted, but I said no because I like the tower. It's the only place that feels like home."

I sighed. "I wish I could figure out how to get you out of here," I muttered. "It isn't right to keep you spellbound to the table like this. It seems like Malinda has forgotten you entirely anyway."

It was a noble goal, but it seemed impossible. I lived in fear that Malinda would discover me here, and then she'd be angry and revoke my walks, take the mask, or stop providing food to Arabella. If I must stay, and Arabella must stay, so would Atropos ... right here, safe in her tower.

I changed the subject. "Malinda had two more thrones made, did I tell you? One for me and one for Arabella. So we could sit beside her. Mine is obsidian, with blades and skulls. Arabella insisted that hers should be solid gold, goblin gold. It's the most hideous thing. Nico always said goblin gold was cursed, but I suppose she forgot that."

Slowly, I got to my feet. I needed to be downstairs soon—Malinda wanted us to join her for dinner in the throne room. Hesitating a brief moment, I leaned down to touch her hair. "Soon," I told her. "Soon, I'm going to free you. I promise."

In the throne room, Arabella waited. She didn't greet me as I climbed the stairs, the mask now safely tucked in one of my wide pockets. The great clock in the hall wasn't ticking, and the room's silence was suffocating.

"Do you think Cullen have sex?" Arabella asked suddenly.

"They're dead," I said, my voice flat.

"And they do whatever the Queen says, don't they?" Arabella's face twisted into something feral and ugly.

"I don't want to die a virgin, do I? Perhaps you could find me someone younger, handsome—and make a bargain for me."

I flinched but said nothing. I wouldn't respond to her; she often said outrageous things to provoke an argument.

Malinda entered the throne room, gliding through the shadows. She smiled approvingly at Arabella, then gave me a sharper, strained frown. "We'll be having a guest tonight. You'll want to change into a different gown."

"I'm not interested in guests."

Mainly because I'd have to kill them later, and I'd rather not hear about their hobbies or watch you toy with their emotions.

"I thought you'd send me out tonight," I continued, "on a walk."

Both of their heads slowly pivoted to look at me. My sister's expression was revulsion—complete loathing. Malinda eyed me with interest.

"I can go now," I offered. *Anything not to attend a party with the two of you and my future victims.*

"Not tonight," Malinda said. "Tonight is special." She didn't say why.

As Cullen entered the room, each bearing a silver tray laden with food, I leaned longingly toward the windows. It was a beautiful night, clear and black, with stars perfectly placed in the velvet sky.

Arabella ate and drank, talking loudly to Malinda, which I tuned out entirely. When I did glance over, I cringed to see the Cullen kneeling at Arabella's feet. My sister laughed, sloppily drunk from too much wine. Her red hair was wild, and her blue gown was soiled down the front with wine. The delicate gossamer train was ripped, and the crystals dangled from one sleeve.

Later, Arabella waltzed around the room with one of the Cullen. They danced clumsily. As I watched, Arabella leaned close, her mouth hanging open.

Maybe you could make a bargain, she'd said. I scoffed and sipped my red wine. *She's never even thanked me.*

Every day, I pay in blood, and she's never thanked me.

I gripped the arms of my black throne until I feared it would crack. One of her Cullen slaves approached with a tray of meats dripping with juices, and I waved him away, uninterested. I didn't like eating meat. It reminded me too much of all the body parts I'd swept into the sea.

It was hours before Malinda allowed me to return to the tower, where I could peel away the gown and put away the mask. Bone-tired and emotionally exhausted, I closed my eyes, unable to silence the voices in my head. I realized suddenly that I didn't know what day it was. I didn't know how long I'd been a Reaper.

What day is it? I tried to do the sum in my head. I sat up and did the math again. Then again. "No," I said aloud. I sat up and yanked on my black gown, still bloody, now cold from the frigid air of the tower.

"Bells?" I said as I knocked on my sister's door a few minutes later. "Let me in."

Past midnight, she should be there. I thumped harder on the aged wood with my knuckles.

"Bells?" I called. "It's me. Wake up." She did not come.

I started to panic—what if she really had decided to bring one of the Cullen to her bed, and it murdered her?

I knocked harder. "Arabella. Stop being annoying and open the door."

The door remained steadfast between us.

"I'm sorry I forgot your birthday," I said, even though I would have preferred to speak with her face to face. Her birthday and the anniversary of Taliesin's death—I'd forgotten them both.

I put my forehead against the ancient wood with its uneven grain. "I just... I lost track of time—"

I went to rattle the doorknob. To my surprise, it turned easily, and as I stepped into the long, rectangular room, all of my apologies came to an abrupt end. An armoire was flung open, dresses strewn across the bed, and a single shoe discarded on the floor. There was no broken glass, blood, or signs of a struggle unless they'd had a clothing war.

Maybe she's upstairs. She's moved rooms again, grown bored with this one.

I hoped she wasn't down in the dungeon, doing our mother's dirty work. She could be in the crypts, she could be in the wellspring, she could be in any of the servants' rooms or the kitchen.

"Arabella?" I called out. "Bells?"

"I'm here." She sat in the dimmest corner of the room, far from the window and its moonlight, her back against the blue stone walls.

"What are you doing?" I asked. "What's wrong?"

"Do you remember Nico telling us that Fates are immortal? That being in danger makes our powers come?" Arabella fumbled at her waist, then unsheathed a silver dagger, which she pointed toward me in the moonlight.

It was my knife—I'd cut throats with it many times.

I took a step toward her. "You aren't a Fate," I said.

She sneered at me. "You know nothing. You claim to be a Fate, but you have no control of destiny. You can't even control your own, much less mine. I've had enough of playing prisoner, Morena. The goblin gold, the jewels, the Cullen—all of it. Every day, we sit and waste away." She looked at the knife and its rusted blade. "I won't wait anymore. I won't be commanded by her."

"Don't do this." I didn't really think she would do it. Even with that look in her eye, I didn't think my sister had the courage. "I know what I'm doing. The Gods will gift me, and I'll be a Fate too."

Never, never, never.

Arabella would never be a Fate. Her tears told the truth of what she was, her unblemished skin a map of her inadequacy. She never listened; she didn't know enough. It was her pride talking, her stubborn, foolish, childish pride.

"Look at you, dressed in rags, calling out every night from nightmares." Her face was flushed as she stared at me, her chin held high. "You aren't strong enough to bear the blood of Atropos—you don't deserve those marks across your back. It was me who should have held the scythe, me who should sit on the Blood Throne. I'm the future Queen of Moirai. Not you, and not her."

I could only stare at her, mute with horror. She was lost, lost to me, and there were no words I could find that would call her back to herself.

"You know," she said finally, "in my dreams, we escaped. We made it past the sea and walked in circles through the snow. You were always ahead, in the lead, and no matter what I said, you always—always—led us back. And I've always hated you for that."

She raised her head to stare at me. And there was nothing there—no trace of the love she'd once felt for me, no trace of the little girl I'd held and read to. Nothing. Malinda had taken me too far, too far away from my sister.

"May you become everything you fear," said Arabella, the youngest descendant of Atropos, as she plunged my knife into her heart. It was her twentieth birthday.

I ran toward the Queen's bedroom, Arabella in my arms and covered in blood. "Malinda!" I shouted in case she was somewhere along the corridors, the library, the kitchen, and the garden. I flew past Cullen, who shuffled through the hallways and shoved them out of our way.

This was my fault—I'd locked my sister in the tower. I'd become Malinda's pawn and betrayed her. It was my fault she didn't remember what else Nico said, that the only way a Fate could die was suicide; it was my fault she didn't recognize the signs that she wasn't a Fate.

She's dying, she's dying, she's dying... I felt her life unraveling, a glowing silver thread, and I felt powerless to stop it.

It was a surprise when I reached Malinda's door without incident. Once there, I didn't bother knocking. Instead, I slammed the red doors open, wanting to wrench them from ancient hinges. Inside, an entourage of Cullen guards clicked their teeth, agitated by the confrontation.

I slid to a halt when I saw her. Although her back was to me, Malinda stood in front of a gilded mirror, so I saw... I panicked at the sight of her; I clamped my teeth shut to hold back the scream. Malinda was covered in veins. Coal-colored, like long spider legs, they wove a map across her entire chest.

"Shouldn't you be sleeping?" she snapped, her body turning away in the mirror. Malinda was completely nude, and ribbons of black veins stretched across her tight stomach her thighs, and crept around her back. It wasn't right. It wasn't *natural.*

I'd never seen anything like it—it was almost as if she were half-Cullen. I suddenly understood why she always wore high-necked gowns and long sleeves.

Like a poisoned river through white sand, the source was a festering hole where a heart would have been. Her heart was...

Oh Gods, oh Gods...

... it was not there. It was just *not there.*

She's *heartless.* I couldn't unsee it. I couldn't understand how this might come to be; I hated myself for not realizing it sooner.

How could she be alive with that gigantic hole in her chest where a heart would be, her ribcage holding a small bronze box?

Intricately carved, its door was ajar, and in Malinda's hands was a still beating heart, the blood smishing out of it with each beat onto the blue stone floor.

I held Arabella tighter. "Save her." She was barely alive, her life thread no heavier than a snowflake.

"No." Malinda neatly put the heart into her chest, then clicked the bronze box shut. She wrapped a high-necked red robe tightly around herself. She faced me, her lush golden hair falling in soft waves.

I felt such a rush of anger I was temporarily light-headed. "Why not?"

Malinda sank into a chair by the fire, her expression pensive. "She's better off as Cullen. Happier, even."

It was at moments like these where I was at my worst. Tongue-tied and useless, I could only gape at her, speechless with shock.

Malinda chuckled. "To think I expected you to be glad."

"Why would I be glad?" Arabella was dying one breath at a time in my arms.

"Your selfish sister is the only reason you're still here." She waved a hand vaguely at Arabella. "Problem solved. If she lives, she'll be a competitor to you in every way. Just as my sister was for me."

"You're lying," I said. Malinda constantly manipulated us, both up close and from afar, as if we were paper puppets and she was the master of our strings.

"Perhaps you might have envisioned a quiet life for Arabella rather than a life of a *Queen of Moirai.*"

My next breath froze in my chest. There, in the tower, when we'd plotted and planned— somehow, she'd heard us. "I never said—"

"You did. Many times. All those stories in the tower. You're a *Fate.* You decree futures. For the rest of your days, you will need to control your mind, blade, and tongue. Everything you imagine, you might as well write in stone. Fates were created by the Goddess Nyx to declare the destiny of all creatures. Are you so stupid—"she paused on the word—"that you didn't realize your gift extends to your siblings? Did you not consider that your girlish stories would become their inescapable realities?"

"Are you talking about Taliesin?" I asked.

"You don't have to speak; you only have to think. Your will shall be done. That's why the Fates are so dangerous, why Gods and men fear you, they thirst to tame you. A Fate who is undisciplined wreaks havoc on the universe."

"If I'd known that that was all it would take, I would have decreed Arabella free."

"You might have, but instead, you named your sister as your *equal,* a *Queen of Moirai,* even though the only queens Moirai has ever had are the Three Fates, which she will never be part of. Thank Nyx that without the other Fates, all you can do is make suggestions, which the universe may yield to as it wishes."

I don't know what possessed me at that moment or from where the courage came. Perhaps it was just that I'd finally had enough of Malinda and the tower. "You're a monster," I said, voicing my thoughts. "What kind of mother doesn't love her own children?"

Malinda leaned back in the chair, the look on her face both ancient and sad. "Don't speak about things you know nothing of. I protected you; I kept you safe from the demons in this place."

She gazed at me with her vivid green eyes, like snakeskin. Above the collar of her robe, a small black tendril reached toward her jawline. "Let her die. Save yourself the pain."

I gazed down at my sister, touched her hair, and watched the blood darkening the front of her gown. "No."

Malinda laughed. "Then you'll learn your lessons the hard way, just as I did."

There was nothing but hate in my heart for this woman before me. *Die. I want you to die.*

With a furious expression, I forced my dark powers toward Malinda, fully expecting her life to unwind and her soul to come to me. I was so sure I held out my hand, palm up and open, so I could catch and crush her wretched soul into a million pieces.

But nothing happened.

"Nice try," Malinda murmured. "It won't work. I haven't a soul for you to steal. I'm surprised you didn't know that."

Heartless, soulless.

Malinda was a ghoul, so what did that make me, her daughter? My heart was breaking, breaking as my mother *laughed*. She laughed like it was a joke I'd just told instead of an attempted murder. "Let me tell you about destiny, Morena. You're Death, the third Fate. It is your destiny to kill me, just as it is your destiny to kill all the people you ever love. All of them. Including her."

"I hate you," I murmured at last. I dared to speak the words I'd always longed to say. "And one day, I will take that heart from your chest, and you will die. Permanently. Forever."

"Someday, you will. But not today, my daughter. Not today." It didn't concern her in the least. "Take her to the graveyard. She'll be Cullen before long, and you won't want to be there to see that."

Before I could say another word, one of her Cullen guards pushed me out of the room and shut the door neatly in my face.

No footprints were on the path as I made my way onto the balcony, still carrying my sister. I stepped outside and marveled as starlight, fragile as a feather, settled on her hair and shoulders. She looked as if she were sleeping. A thick blanket of snow shone white all the way to the horizon. I sighed with relief and breathed in the cold air.

"It's a beautiful night," I said to her. "Open your eyes to see it."

She was still warm, still breathing, as the winter wind blew through creaking branches. If Arabella returned as Cullen, she would belong to Malinda. If she was left to roam, I might never find her again. I could lock her in one of the crypts—imprison her so that she wouldn't hurt anyone when she became Cullen. Taliesin's tomb was empty. I could lay her inside and seal it. She'd be safe there.

Bitterly, I recalled our last argument, the one that started us on this twisted and terrible path. No, no, I could not lock Arabella in. I wouldn't do that to her again. Silence, heavy as a blanket, wrapped around us.

I stared down at her face, so much sweeter as she clung to the edge of life. "I would weep if I could," I told her. "I would drown the Cullen in my tears as they drowned our brother in the sea..." Suddenly, I knew where to go.

Trudging through the castle, I carried her down the wide staircase lit by flickering candles into the dungeons. I murmured as I pushed through the door and proceeded past the cells.

I laid Arabella on the floor, on the engraved circle of white marble, its center open like an eye. I touched her red hair gently and smoothed it away from her pale brow. "I know you hoped that you were immortal—Fate-marked in secret. Or if you just tried hard enough, your magic would save you. You were too impatient to be what I was, too blind to the will of the Gods.

"You were right about Malinda, though. The only way out of this castle is to kill her, and I can't bring myself to do it. I tried, and I failed. I failed both you and Taliesin, and I will forever be sorry about that."

Gathering a deep breath, I finished the rest in a rush. "I am weak. I don't want it badly enough. Maybe I'm only half a Fate, and Malinda's blood ruined me. Whatever the reason, I couldn't save us."

I die undefeated. Arabella's red hair fanned across the inscription, and it made a little more sense now. I prayed to Nyx, the goddess of Night. *Save her. Save her, I beg you. If you were ever going to hear any prayer and intervene for me, do it now. Bring my sister back to me.*

But the Gods were silent, and there was only the sound of the sea below.

I kissed Arabella's forehead one last time. "I know you wouldn't want to be her slave." Her breathing was dangerously shallow, and I knew my sister had but a few gasps remaining until she was lost to me forever.

"I know you wouldn't want to be Cullen. This is the only choice I have left. I hope you can find Taliesin somewhere down there..."

I gathered her up into my arms and held her tightly. She reeked of perfume and wine and Cullen, my baby sister. I had failed her, I had failed to protect her. Just as I'd failed my brother. Just as I had failed Nico. Grief ripped and tore at me worse than any beast ever could have.

My hands shook. "I'm so sorry, Bells. So terribly, terribly sorry."

Why couldn't I weep? Why couldn't I just scream and cry? And why couldn't it have been her? Why couldn't it have been *she* who was Death, and not me? Why was I, the weakest, the quietest, the most unsure...

why was it always *me?* Why had the Gods marked me as the successor to Atropos, and not my clever, quick sister who would have been so much more suited to the task?

Call it cowardice, but I couldn't watch her die. So, although I owed it to her to hold her a moment longer, I couldn't bear to do it. I couldn't stand to watch her soul as it left me bereft and alone in the dungeons of The Grace. I couldn't face the one death that I'd spent my entire life dreading.

She had few breaths left. I wouldn't watch them. With one long, last look at my sister, I rolled her body over the edge of the hole, and down it fell into the sea.

CHAPTER 8

I spent three days walking Kinver'i.

Walking while the moon shone brightly overhead, walking through the snow drifts among the evergreens, walking along the stone walls that ran along the sea. I sat in the sand in my black gown and stared at the waves, hoping the tide would take away my pain; my heart breaking like the waves along the shore.

There was no one left here. Not a soul remained. I walked with my grief among the shadows and the dead. Eyes dry, my head bowed, I wore the mask and walked among the shadows of the evergreens and hated, hated, hated my mother. Everything she had done, every choice she had made... it had ruined me. Inside I felt shattered, brittle, like whatever pieces of my heart remained had been ground down into fine powder.

At last, I returned home, home to Taliesin's empty crypt. I sat on the stairs, watching Grace Castle and the sea beyond. I pulled the mask from my face with a long, unhappy sigh.

It seemed increasingly reluctant to relinquish its hold, and truth be told, I didn't much care anymore. There was no one left to see me, no one to protect. I was utterly alone. I tucked it into my pocket.

"Sorry I'm late," said a self-assured male voice. "I'm sure you can appreciate my reasons."

I was startled at the sudden break in the silence. The man who'd wandered too close to The Grace stared down at me, his lips twisted into a wry smile. He seemed pleased with himself, like a cat toying with a bird. There was something familiar about him, like I'd gazed into those iron-gray eyes before. Flecked with black and white, like a wolf's pelt, they crinkled at the corners as he smiled. His blue tunic was decorated with silver stars around the collar. His boots, black, covered in snow, did not look as if they'd been walked in, or if they had, it was not enough to wear or mark them. Lips, lush and rounded, smirked at me; dark eyebrows slashed across his tanned skin, and his hair was the color of crow feathers. He was alive. Ridiculously, beautifully alive.

"You shouldn't be here," I informed him. I could imagine the Queen's words, telling me to take his young, strong heart. Those were nearly impossible to find anywhere near Grace Castle.

He dared a step toward me, then another. I could kill him quickly, but I'd provided Malinda with a heart last night, and I was done with bloodshed for a few days. I raised an eyebrow, wondering at his stupidity. Surely he could see my black cloak, the knives at my side, which were stained with blood?

The stranger noted my expression, my grip on the scythe. "You'll have to kill me some other time. Vitess sent me to save you, and save you I shall."

"Who?" I pursed my lips. *Who would send anyone to save me?*

"Vitess. The descendant of the second Fate, Lachesis. She's the controller of Time." A Fate like me. A Fate whom Malinda had told me repeatedly not to trust—an enemy.

His face was troubled as he took in my gaunt body, thin dress, and shadowed face. Months of sleeplessness showed in my hollow cheeks and my pale skin. He was worried not for himself but for me. This realization alone made me merciful.

"I'd rather not have your blood on my hands. So unless you'd like to lose your heart, you should go. Leave now, before Malinda knows you are here."

As if by reflex, the stranger touched the two vicious swords that hung from a belt slung across his hips. "And if I refuse?"

That made me pause. Brave or stupid, it did not particularly matter which it was. I'd never had someone willingly walk onto the Castle grounds with such determination.

"I've come," he gave me a curt nod as if to recognize his place, "to make you an invitation to The Epiphany." He offered his hand. "I'm here for you, Morena, the descendant of Atropos." I studied the design on his tunic, at the crest emblazoned with an hourglass.

He's telling the truth. The second Fate, house of Lachesis, truly had sent him to retrieve me.

I looked at his hand as if it were crawling with spiders and put my own behind my back. "The Castle Epiphany is hundreds of miles away. It would take months to travel there."

"Not if you travel by dragon." The stranger gave me an enigmatic smile.

"The Queen will never let me go. And if she knows you're here..."

He didn't seem worried. "Vitess said if you hesitated, that I should propose."

"Propose what?" I asked.

"*Propose.*" In the background was Castle Grace, dark blue and foreboding, with its crumbling towers and Cullen guards patrolling like rotting ants. "Desperate times call for desperate measures."

It was several seconds before I grasped what he meant. "Propose, as in marriage?"

Malinda's words returned to me as I gaped at him: the declarations of war, the offers of marriage. I clenched my jaw. I knew exactly for what purpose he'd come.

"My answer is no, but thank you for the offer." I stood as if to leave. "If the Cullen did not kill you, Malinda surely would, and in any case, I have no desire to spend the rest of my immortal life as a broodmare."

He interrupted me. "Begging your pardon, lady, but I assumed you'd be glad of someone—a hero come to rescue you from the tower." Again, those fascinating gray eyes met mine. There was a bite to them, a challenge, but also consideration.

A princess in a tower. Is he joking?

"I'm not the type of person anyone would want to wed."

"I doubt that's true." He stepped closer. "Don't worry. Vitess assured me that Malinda *will* let you go. With your betrothed."

I decided to question his soul directly. Wordless, he wouldn't know I was doing it.

You're here to rescue me?

Yes. His soul's response was so immediate and clear that it made me feel faint, and I put a hand on Taliesin's tomb.

The stranger stepped close to me as if to steady me. I didn't know him - not his name nor where he came from. I didn't know *anything*. He certainly knew nothing about me... He couldn't understand what he was offering or how much it meant to me. The long-dead spark of hope I'd buried deep in my chest suddenly blazed.

If the controller of Time knew our futures and I left with him ... just the possibility of leaving made my head spin. With his help, I'd have access to more books, more people, and more information. Surely someone in Moirai could tell me how to break the binding spell on

Atropos? If I just said that, I'd marry him. After we left, of course, I could do whatever I wanted.

"Vitess also said that I should bring gifts that would convince both you and Malinda that I'm serious about my offer."

I raised an eyebrow. Gifts to convince *me*? I cared nothing for finery, nor gold nor jewels. The only thing I'd ever wanted was a true family, my siblings, to be safe and far away from this wretched place.

"And?" I said at last, not the least bit curious.

There were two others who awaited in the shadows of the evergreens, and they came forward when he beckoned to them. Both wore dark blue tunics embroidered with stars; they wore rich fur cloaks clasped around their shoulders. I smelled their courage as if it were fine perfume. They were ready for a fight, shoulders squared, faces alert, and swords sharpened. I expected them to have something they carried, whatever the second Fate, Vitess, thought might sway me. But their arms were empty.

With a shock, I realized that one of them was familiar. Surely it wasn't him. It was merely someone who looked similar... some other man with rakish hair and hazel eyes, a square jaw that was just short of chiseled.

But no, I knew that face.

His eyes I would have recognized anywhere. They were the color of witches' hazel because he was *of the witches*—a glorious swirl of gold, green, and brown.

"Nico?"

I hadn't seen him since our ill-fated escape attempt three years ago. My chilly demeanor evaporated. "I thought you were dead."

"Hello, little spider," he said roughly.

With a cry, I threw myself into his arms.

"You're taller than I remember." He'd be twenty-seven now, not much older than me, but with a world more of experience. "Let me look at you."

I shook my head, afraid to let go.

He was a slab of muscle, a warrior, and I could recognize it and smell the coppery scent of blood on his skin and hair. His nose was bent like it'd been broken, and he had a new scar above his left eyebrow. But it was him, the person whom I'd always thought of as my older brother.

"I've missed you so much," I said as I buried my face in his neck. Nico knew I couldn't cry, and he knew I wanted to.

"I promised you I'd get you out of here," he murmured into my hair.

"Taliesin is dead. Arabella is dead. I couldn't save them."

"It's alright. It's not your fault." He shushed me as if I were a child and stroked my back as if I were still the little blonde girl he'd taught to read.

I was the only family he had left, and he was mine.

I will always be here for you. He'd swore loyalty to me, sworn his life and sword. And then he'd vanished.

Dead. I had thought Nico dead, even though I'd never seen any date of death hover above his head.

Nico held me, and I breathed - it felt like the first deep breath I'd taken in years.

I hadn't been touched by anyone, other than Arabella and Taliesin, in so terribly long. I held on tightly, thanking the universe, the Gods, the stranger - whatever forces conspired to bring Nico back to me.

The two men behind us cleared their throats, reminding us of their existence. Reluctantly, I released him. I stepped back, my hands cupping his face, my stained fingertips touching his soft, dark curls. I wiped away the tears on his cheeks.

Nico was unashamed. I was his only family, the last of the children he'd raised, his little sister by heart if not by blood.

The tall, redheaded Fae next to Nico bowed. "I am Lord Lorcan, overseer of Kinseamair and the lesser islands."

I knew where Kinseamair was—it was the farthest southern island of Moirai. It was rumored that it was where dragons were born and where unicorns still roamed. Lord Lorcan was, in fact, Lord of the Fae and had been so for so long that even the books I'd read had tales of him. He'd probably had shoes older than our castle. Nervous, I looked at Nico.

"He'll get you away from Malinda – we all will. I wouldn't have brought them here otherwise," he assured me.

"Are you going to come with us?" Lorcan crossed his arms across his chest as if he half-expected to drag me out of here.

"Of course, she's going to," Nico assured him. "She would never stay."

I bit my lip as possible responses ran through my mind like sand in an hourglass. Nico being here changed everything. If nothing else, I could not let Malinda kill them. I could not let them be taken captive. I could not watch another person I loved be killed.

The one who intended to propose spoke again. "Vitess *assured* me that if I brought the gifts and Nico and Lorcan, Malinda would let you go. No killing involved."

"It seems too good to be true," I replied.

"She was incredibly precise. If I don't follow her instructions to the letter ... we fail." He put his hand on my shoulder. "We'll need all our wits and a lot of luck."

His skin was strangely warm – the heat from his hand felt like it would burn through my gown. I immediately noted his smell, smoky and sweet, with a hint of apple. "Does my *betrothed* have a name? "I asked drily.

He dropped his hand from my shoulder. He seemed disappointed for the briefest of seconds, but then the look was gone so quickly I thought I'd imagined it. "Elijah."

Elijah. It was a good omen. *He who brings miracles.*

"If Malinda tries anything, we'll kill her," Lorcan assured me. "Don't worry."

"You think you can fight well enough to beat Malinda?" I raised an eyebrow at the man leaning casually against the gate, watching Lorcan, Nico, and me.

"You sound surprised." Nico grinned and leaned toward me. "If he goes head-to-head with Malinda, he'll win. And he needn't fear the Cullen either."

I must have looked skeptical because Elijah smiled and held out his hand. In his palm was a ball of fire, a real fire, an actual flame. As I watched, it leaped and grew taller until I had to step back, its heat baking against my face.

"How?" I breathed. "Malinda told me that males cannot make magic in Moirai. Only the women. Only the Fates."

Nico and Lorcan smirked, and Elijah closed his hand, the fire vanishing instantly. Gone. His skin was unburnt.

"What would you say," Nico studied me, his hazel eyes gleaming, "if I told you that you've been fed a lot of lies by Malinda and that nothing she's said—nothing—has ever been true?"

I thought of Taliesin, his golden head sinking below the waves.

Then Arabella's body falling into the sea.

I thought of Atropos, locked in the west tower, spellbound to a stone table, my father cruelly murdered by my mother.

I thought of all the men and Fae I'd killed, innocents whose hearts I'd cut from their chests so that Malinda might live.

"I'd say that sounds right," I said finally.

"Perhaps they are here to offer a truce, and they've realized their inferiority," Malinda mumbled to herself. Seated on the blood throne, she considered the stained-glass windows above us and pondered. "Or he's come to make a trade." Intrigued, but not angry - it was as positive a beginning as I'd dared hope for.

I sat straight-backed on my obsidian throne, careful not to lean against the carved brambles and rabbit skulls. "I'd like to hear what they have to say."

I feigned nonchalance, though my heart felt as heavy as a hammer on the forge. A tangle of emotions swirled through me: excitement, apprehension, curiosity, dread. I held my breath and said a small prayer to Nyx.

Please don't let Malinda kill them. Please let Vitess be correct.

The men entered. For a moment, from the corner of my eye, I thought I saw Malinda's shoulders slump, as if she'd suffered a defeat. But when I glanced over, she was watching them approach, stone-faced, her red lips glistening. Waiting.

As he drew near, I smelled him again—warm, like autumn apples and falling leaves, earth and fire. I inhaled sharply, savoring its uniqueness. Nico and Lorcan flanked him, both their faces perfect masks of civility.

After a brief hesitation, Elijah bowed deeply. "Your Majesty." His forehead almost touched the floor. Involuntarily, I gave a slight nod of encouragement. "Thank you for your kind reception. We have come a great distance to your court." His words were political theater, obviously insincere. "If it pleases you, I beg your audience."

My attention returned to Malinda. My temples pulsed with the beginnings of a headache. I dug my fingernails into my palms, taking slow, inconspicuous breaths. *I will not fidget. I will not adjust my gown. I will appear calm.*

Malinda smiled at the group. "I welcome you." This game was something she understood. The blood throne writhed beneath her. With each motion of her hand, the throne gurgled and undulated, and rivulets of blood leaked down onto the dais. I schooled my face into a frozen, polite expression as the Queen squeezed the throne's armrest, blood squelching between her fingers.

Regardless of what I'd seen in the graveyard, I still didn't feel optimistic about our chances.

"You are certainly unexpected. It has been a decade since we last had a visitor," she purred. "I'd started to forget the other kingdoms exist." She gave a tinkling, feminine laugh.

Lies.

The other kingdoms of Kinkanali and Kinseamair were all my mother thought about. Well, that and getting hearts.

"I didn't expect to see you again, Nico." She emphasized his name. Behind the prince, Nico straightened his shoulders and lifted his chin. "Your Majesty," he murmured.

Elijah regarded her without a trace of fear. "Greetings, Queen Malinda. I humbly ask that you allow Morena to leave, to accompany me to my kingdom, to the Castle Epiphany, and to take Atropos' seat on the silver throne."

The Queen inspected him as if he were a rare butterfly, one whose wings she planned to tear away and put between the pages of a book. "I note that lovely blue you're wearing. Are you Elijah, firstborn prince of House Lachesis?"

He hesitated for only a moment. "I am."

Everything in me clanged together, like scullery pots thrown together in a great jumble. He'd told me his name in the graveyard—Elijah—but not his house. He'd neglected to mention that he was a prince, a descendant of the Fate, Lachesis. Vitess was his *sister*. He hailed from a Fated family just as powerful as my own. His sister was the controller of Time, the one who had sent him to my rescue. That's why he could hold a flame in his hand.

Inside I screamed and shrieked, though externally my face remained neutral. *A prince has come to rescue me.*

It was just like the stories we'd once told, and his face matched my fantasies perfectly.

The Queen drummed her long nails along the bloody arms of her throne. "So the time *has* come."

He squared his shoulders. "We could not wait any longer."

It was as if they were talking in a secret language only the two of them could understand. "Some time ago, I was informed of a Decree. A Decree made by the House of Atropos that the kingdoms would ally." Malinda paused, reluctant to go on.

Ally? Once enemies, but now *allies?* She'd never mentioned that before.

"What did it say?" I could barely force out the words.

"That the Northern Princess—you—and the Lachesis Prince would wed," Malinda replied. "Through that union, the three kingdoms of Kinver'i and Kinkanli and Kinseamair would be reunited, and Moirai would be whole again."

Our eyes—mine and Elijah's—locked. "That Three Fates shall rule all of Moirai once more."

So it would not be a ruse, but a true marriage. A foreseen, Fate decided, arranged marriage. More than my rescuer, he would be my husband.

"Tell her the rest," Malinda prompted him.

At this, the Prince was slightly uncomfortable. "You will have a daughter. And she—she shall rule alone, not Fate-marked. There will be no more Fates."

It would be a lie to say that I wasn't comforted by his statement. If there were no more House of Atropos, the killing would end. My daughter would be normal, not onyx-eyed, not Fate-marked. She would lead Moirai not as Death, but as a queen only.

A daughter. I remembered still Arabella's scrawny little body wrapped in a blanket. I'd given her bottles and read her bedtime stories and brushed her tiny teeth. I loved watching her learn to crawl, then walk.

It was a glorious relief to know that I wouldn't spend the rest of my life here, with only Malinda and Atropos. That there was another life—a different life—waiting for me beyond these walls. And it was not my imagination, not a fantasy, but *real*. If I only dared to grasp it. If I were just brave enough to leave with him.

"For nearly a thousand years, the lineages have been estranged." The Queen said the words so softly, I almost didn't hear them.

"That is no longer true," the Prince assured her. "Not after today."

"Would you return Moirai to its former glory?" The Queen asked him. "Fix it all?"

My gaze flew to her face. Despite her brutality, she cared about this very much. And no matter what she'd said, she wasn't surprised to see these men on our doorstep. She'd *known* they would come for me, known about the Decree. I could hear it in her voice.

"I will," he answered. "*We* will." The embroidered stars across his broad chest glinted in the firelight, and his raven-colored hair shone. He leveled his gaze at me again. "*She will.*"

Married. I, someone who had never spent five minutes alone with a man, would be *married*. This handsome, tall, prince was mine.

"And if I object?" her voice questioned; not angry, just curious.

"Even you, Queen Malinda, could not alter something so set upon by the universe." Lorcan, red-haired and bearded and covered with tattoos, was formidable in the firelight.

"Where is your proof? Did you bring a document from Lachesis?"

Nico pulled a scroll from a satchel strapped to his side. "We have a betrothal agreement for the granddaughter and grandson, made between Atropos and Lachesis and Clotho. They were young when the Decree was made, but their signatures are true."

Nico did not bow and scrape. Without fear, he stepped forward to lay the scroll in the Queen's gloved hand. As he did, he stepped in the pooling gore at the base of her throne, and his boots left bloody footprints as he backed away. These, the stone slurped away silently as she read.

I wasn't sure if anyone noticed, until I saw the look of revulsion on Lorcan's face.

Elijah's tone was conciliatory. "It is what will be, Malinda. It is certain."

My mother did not seem angry. Instead, it was as if some invisible weight lifted from her shoulders. "Leave us. I will confer with my daughter."

The Queen leaned over and handed me the contract. I made a show of opening it as the men tromped from the room with their snow-covered boots. It was written in blood, so some magical being—a unicorn, a goblin—died to set these words into the foundations of the world. A magical contract, forged in blood, between three Fates, all of them younger than I was now.

Lachesis, Clotho, and Atropos agreed to my marriage, thousands of years ago.

There was no mistake; this was destiny.

Malinda assessed me in that disconcerting way of hers. "We could break the agreement," she said, her voice questioning. "And kill them now."

I raised an eyebrow. "I hold a blood contract signed between the Fates. It was foreseen."

Malinda blinked. "If I kill them—"

"No!" the word jolted out of me before I had a chance to stop it. "No... I..." I shook my head. "I do not want you to kill him." I may not have particularly wanted to marry him yet, but certainly I didn't want her to kill him.

"Then it's true. You *do* marry him." She sat back on her throne, perplexed. "If it was foreseen, it's already true that I decided not to kill him. That you are amenable, or that he would fight me for you and win."

"You sound so certain," I said after a beat. "Why would he fight?"

"For you, of course." She nodded. "And for the child to rule all of Moirai." Her lip lifted in a lopsided smile that pulled at the edges, like a sewing stitch gone wrong.

Again, the reference to a prophecy—a destiny already clear, one that others knew and I did not. In the graveyard, the Prince said that the Fate Vitess told him to propose. He'd come here not because he knew me, but because his sister ordered him to do so. I was grateful to her, and someday I hoped to thank her in person.

"Very well then," Malinda decided quickly. At her nod, the Cullen invited the trio of men back into the throne room.

The Prince cleared his throat, then gestured at the others behind him. "I've brought gifts in honor of our new friendship. And I think," he gave my mother a knowing look, "even you will be impressed."

"Very little impresses me, Prince," she responded. "But I'm willing to take a look. *After* we eat."

CHAPTER 9

The Queen stirred a bowl of soup that looked like it might have human fingers in it. Several pairs of eyes tracked her movements like a poisonous spider that could not be trusted to scurry back to its place in the shadows.

I dropped my spoon, and it bounced off the table and then onto the floor. In the silent room, the clang was deafening—Nico noticeably jumped. Beside me, the Prince carefully cut apart pieces of melon and put them on my plate. Our chairs were too close together, so our elbows occasionally brushed as the group ate silently.

I counted the seconds until Cullen attacked, and Malinda forced me to cut the heart from his chest. It all felt too good to be true, foreign, and I knew not to trust it.

"Do you have a favorite?" he asked, gesturing at the fruit on the table. I almost didn't hear him through the sounds of my blood roaring in my ears. Everyone at the table could hear his words to me.

"I like melon the most. You?"

"Winterberry."

"Ah." He took the opportunity to lean closer. "I can't wait to get out of here." I'd never seen a man—any man—close up like this before, and to be the focus of his attention thrilled me.

I swallowed my food. "I can't wait for you to *get* me out of here." Feeling ridiculous, I smiled shyly at him.

Across the table, Malinda's expression was a mixture of horror and disdain, and she slowly pulled apart a rabbit leg as she watched our interactions.

"What are those?" the Prince asked, gesturing at the flowered centerpiece in the middle of the long table.

"Amaranth. We use them for perfume."

"Do you have a favorite flower?"

"I don't know," I said, but seeing his obvious disappointment, I decided to tell a little bit of myself. "Maybe daffodils. But I've never seen one in person—only in books." Admitting my ignorance to him felt terribly awkward, and heat flared in my cheeks.

"Hmm." The Prince opened his hand, revealing his palm, and a small yellow flower bloomed.

A daffodil. It was the most cheerful thing I'd ever seen, perky and upstanding as a drop of sunshine. The flower leaned into his touch as if he were a lover.

"I've always been told that the males are born without magic," I murmured as I took the flower from his hand. "So how can you do that?"

He hesitated, then reluctantly responded. "All males with Fates' blood have powers. My powers are much less than my sister's but still considerable. Vitess and Serene are your fellow Fates. Vitess can travel through Time, to different time threads, seeing what could or will happen. She can manipulate Time by going backward and doing something different. She can also slow and speed up Time. Serene controls the elements." He pursed his lips as if knowing he'd revealed too much. Then he pondered the room full of Cullen. "Are there always so many of them?"

"Yes."

The Prince wrinkled his nose in disgust. "The sooner we leave, the sooner I can stop worrying about one of them murdering me while my back is turned."

I snorted. It was a completely inappropriate response, which I immediately tried to smother with a cough, but nevertheless, the Prince noticed.

"It's a reasonable position," I shifted toward him like a conspirator to whisper. "I also prefer we leave before she changes her mind." The sooner we left, the less likely he would be killed.

"It's hard to believe anyone would ever come here willingly," I muttered. "Especially to rescue someone like me."

"Yes. Well. I can hardly believe it myself."

"Is there a library at The Epiphany?" I asked innocently as the dishes were being cleared away by the Cullen.

"The biggest in Moirai. Some of the books are nearly a thousand years old. And not a speck of dust on them."

My body hummed with excitement, but I kept my voice conversational as I folded my napkin into precise triangles. "What sorts of books do you have?"

"Anything you could ever want. Spells, history—we even have books from the human world, some of their classics, books on vampires, werewolves, the Gods..." The Prince trailed off, distracted by the Cullen, who carted in three large treasure chests. Walnut, blackened with age and chiseled with protective symbols, each was protected by spells so that whatever contents lay inside would be safe from thieves.

"Gifts for Malinda," the Prince reminded me.

As we watched, one of the Cullen flipped open the latch and lifted the lid. Inside was a neatly laid row of wooden goblets hewn from white oak. Their golden rims glinted weakly in the firelight. Each was emblazoned with a single character. I knew what they were—*veritas chalices.* Human wars were fought over just one of the goblets—worth more than this castle and every jewel in it—and Elijah was presenting seven of them.

"One sip from those, and the drinker would have no choice but to tell all their secrets." Malinda smiled, feral and cunning. "Would you dare to drink with me?"

"I have no secrets worth keeping, Your Highness." Elijah tilted his head. "So, yes."

Several seconds passed before the Queen spoke. "Thank you."

I'd never heard her say those words in my life. I accepted it as a truce of sorts. Malinda would be cordial until she could figure out what to make of him and what to do about him. For now, he was safe. One could never expect her strange moods, which came and went like winter storms.

The Prince also had several other items with him, tightly wrapped. "For you, Morena, I bring something ... else. I wish to return something we have had for some time, something that belonged to the Fates."

Lorcan handed him something long and thin, tightly wrapped in cloth. He placed whatever it was in my hands.

"Open it."

The object he'd given me pulsed in response to his voice. Not a beat, like a heart, but a friendly chirp. I frowned down at it, and then I slowly unwound the cloth. It was a staff. Gnarled, with the top shaped like an eight-sided spider web, crusted in gray diamonds, dull with age. Runes were carved all over it, winding around it just as the cloth had done, but these were too worn to read. Squinting, I traced a finger down them, then curled my fingers around the staff to grasp it.

The fires in the room went out in a whoosh.

Power coursed through me like a brushfire, prickling every hair on the back of my neck. I inhaled sharply and found myself floating upward into the air. My constellation gown expanded and contracted around me, flowing like water and mist down from my body and onto the floor. I felt the rune tattoos across my spine begin to move.

"Holy Gods," Nico muttered, looking up as I continued to levitate.

"What's happening," I asked my mother. "What is this?"

Malinda was in awe. "Atropos' staff. It's been lost for centuries."

Not lost, hidden, the staff replied, inside my own mind. *Secret.*

"Amazing," I breathed.

Can you hear me? I replied back to the staff.

Yes. I hear only you.

The Prince looked up at me. "We've kept it safe." The look he gave me was strange. Pained, as if there were more he wanted to say but couldn't.

The power that now thrummed inside my bones was like nothing I'd ever felt. No kill—no anything—had ever felt like this. I felt utterly calm, entirely in control of it. It was indescribable, but if any word came to my mind, it was *certainty.* I was sure that this thing—the staff— was within my control.

I was confident I would never lose again, not with it in my hand, not to anyone.

Gently, I lowered myself back to the ground until my feet touched the blue stone. My gown settled back into place, still swaying slightly like cobwebs in a light breeze.

"Thank you," I said, my voice rasping. Later, I would have to consider why he gifted me this unimaginable power. At the moment, however, I decided to just be grateful and consider it a dowry.

The Queen spoke again. "Is that all?"

The Prince, straight and sturdy, considered her. "Yes, Your Majesty. That is all."

The Queen smiled. "Then I have one other demand."

For a long moment, he waited. And as he did, there was no gentleness in his gray eyes. There was nothing but naked hostility. "What is it you want? What would, as you put it, *satisfy?*" Elijah asked the Queen, his lips pursed.

"Somewhere impenetrable," Malinda replied. "A safe haven should she ever need it."

"A safe haven for ... her?" The Prince was mystified. "I am easily able to protect Morena—"

"At sea."

"At sea?" He sounded confused.

"It must be far—very far—from land. Accessible via water alone."

Several beats passed as he stumbled over what to say. "You want me to give her..." he trailed off. Elijah clenched his jaw. "You are aware, of course, that these unreachable islands belong to the Clotho family."

She knew exactly where he was thinking. "I am aware. I suspect you can agree to my ask easily with your *family lineage.*" Malinda did not back down. "And if you think that price is too much, well then..."

I tried to look relaxed, as if all this were *normal* as if I wasn't deeply worried. I had no illusions—I was gawky, tall, boney... I had no experience, a terrible family tree, a murderous mother, a dead father, and an entire kingdom of Cullen. He could easily decide that I wasn't worth the price she demanded.

"Fine. To you, Morena, I guarantee safe passage to the castle of Rosehall, which you may call your home as long as you wish. Whenever you need it. Along with any children you may bear." He looked up into my face, my black gown and crown, and my cursed throne.

Meanwhile, I stared at his boots, where tiny tendrils and baby-green vines began to pierce through the cracks between the stones. I'd never seen a man who had magic nor read of it. Yet here he was, kneeling before me. As I watched, a fern unfurled near his heel.

Seconds passed like syrup, a slow pour as he extended his closed fist and slowly opened it to reveal his palm. I watched a soft, fragrant red rose grow from his skin. Awed by his magic, every thought in my head eddied away like a stick tossed into the sea.

"If you intend to take my daughter with you, you'll need to propose," Malinda informed him.

His gray eyes met mine. *Told you so,* they seemed to say. I dipped my chin in a small acknowledgment. *And you were right.*

The shape of his mouth was like a cupid's bow, soft and pillowy, as he handed me the red rose. "Will you, Morena of House Atropos, the third Fate, reaper of men, consent to marry me-" he paused as if for dramatic effect, "Elijah, eldest of House Lachesis, and join me at The Epiphany in the kingdom of Kinkanali, and rule as one of the Queens of Moirai?"

His autumn scent assailed me like a drug. Indeed, this Prince was a gift from the Gods, a reward for my patience and suffering. He was my way out of there; he was how I would have vengeance on Malinda.

I will. A thousand times, I will.

I couldn't find the words to say yes. I couldn't form them, so instead, I nodded once. I put my hand over my heart in a fist, the universal signal of a promise made.

"May the Gods grant us favor." His voice was low, husky.

The Queen was as still as a serpent as she watched the Prince. After a beat, she stood, walked down the stairs, and extended a gloved hand toward Elijah. He considered her, then reached forward to grasp her fingers.

My mother pulled him to his feet. "Welcome to the family."

Then his eyes, steel gray, streaked with silver, once again found mine. "We leave tomorrow."

If we were to leave in the morning, I had some loose ends to tie off.

Making excuses of being tired, I slipped between the black and white banners, out a hidden door, and onto one of the many balconies of The Grace. It was a calm winter night—the moon peeked out from between the clouds, illuminating the parapets. The patrolling Cullen crawled like ants across the four towers, their broken necks oddly tilted.

From there, I took hidden stone stairs up and up, into a door on the fifth floor, down a corridor, left, and then left again, until at last I found myself at Atropos' door. I shoved it open and entered her room. I'd come to say goodbye.

Taking her hand, I told her of the Prince in the graveyard. I told her what I planned, his words, and Malinda's strange behavior. , I placed the staff next to her on the slab and tucked it against her thigh.

"This is yours," I said. "I won't keep it from you, and I have no need of it. I hope to never kill again."

Atropos continued to lay there, unmoving as the stone. I frowned as I stroked her papery skin.

I'd wondered if, by bringing her the staff, she might wake. That she would feel its magic and suddenly smile up at me. But this was apparently not the way to break the curse that bound her.

My black eyes glowed as I raised them to look at the missing wall of her room, to the gaping hole that provided a view of the west—a vast empty field, the snow pristine and undisturbed, the evergreens swaying just next to us. If I needed to, I could have leaped then and climbed down via branches.

"I will see you again," I promised her. "I will find a way to free you, and I will come back."

Then I steeled my shoulders, resolute, and made my way to the dungeons—to the female Fae prisoner. Her cell was tucked into the farthest corner, without even a single shaft of light. Most of the time, it was easy to forget that she was still here; I couldn't believe Malinda hadn't killed her already or that she hadn't starved to death.

The woman was sitting silently on the floor, tugging at her matted hair. Her dress was no more than rags, covered in her own filth. Open sores were on her hands, feet, and face. Being a Cullen would have been a blessing.

"I've good news." I slipped the keys from the pocket of my gown and unlocked the door. "In more ways than one."

Awake, I thought, as I touched her skin. *Awake and dream no more.*

She blinked in the darkness as the maddening red fog lifted, and her perpetual nightmares faded from her view. She stared at me. "Where am I?"

"You're in the dungeon. We must escape." I answered patiently. "The door is unlocked."

She wouldn't recognize me. I was blonde, a princess wearing a crown. I was no longer the Queen's enforcer, no longer the invisible Death who'd murdered her father.

"Thank you," she stammered as she began to weep. "Thank you." Her chest heaved as she realized it was no longer a dream. "I've been so afraid."

"I know," I soothed her. "That's all over now. Follow me to the boat, and the sea will take you where it wishes you to be."

"You aren't coming with me?"

"No," I said, my voice quiet with genuine sorrow. "I cannot. But it is a quiet night, and none will stop you if we leave now."

Tears running down her dirty cheeks, she stood, her legs shaky. "And my father?"

"Long dead," I answered and refused to think of the kind old Fae whom I'd beheaded. "A victim of the Queen." I felt her answering anguish and saw her wringing her hands together. "But now is no time to mourn— we must get you out of this place."

Wisely, she nodded.

I dressed the woman as if she were a child. I buttoned my cloak at the neck and smoothed back her hair. Then, I led the way out of the dungeons with long strides through the grate and the secret entrance. Finally, we came to the outermost barrier, an iron door that swung open when I slightly pushed it. Just beyond, waves lapped against the dock.

"Come now," I whispered. "It is clear."

The Fae did not ask questions. She boarded the boat I pointed to and sat down. At her feet was a bag with dried meat. It was enough for ten days, and I did not know how long it would take for the boat to drift to an island. There were oars inside the boat, a knife, a fishing net, and a cup. I'd taken as much as I dared.

"May the Gods bless your journey." I shoved the boat off into the current.

She was watchful and alert, biting her lip as she stared up at me on the dock, the golden princess clad in black. I watched her take up the oars, then continued to watch as she rowed away.

The waves of the Obsidia rolled in, steady and small, a quiet lullaby stretched as far as the eye could see. Overhead, stars shone. It was good weather for leaving, a rare night without a snowfall.

When I was sure she was far enough out at sea, I withdrew the obsidian mask from a deep, interior pocket of my cloak. I ran long fingers over its midnight surface, over the bones made of pearl. At some point, I'd become attached to the mask—it allowed me the small measure of freedom I'd had; it had hidden me in the shadows.

Goodbye, old friend. I hope to never wear your cruel face again.

I hurled it into the sea with all my strength, so far that I could not pinpoint where it sank.

This might be the last time I ever stood here, just like this. I turned in a slow circle, taking in the shapes and shadows, trying to memorize every detail of the Castle and the sea's view.

Suddenly, there was a deep, rumbling breath above me. I scanned up the stones to the roof. Perched there was one of the dragons they'd rode here on—silver, with wings large enough to wrap around an entire tower.

The dragon's unbearably blue eyes watched me warily. When I was sure it didn't intend to eat or burn me alive, I walked back inside.

CHAPTER 10

I awoke to one of the Cullen shaking me by the shoulder. Blearily, I peered around the room. It was daylight, the pale sun shining through the tower window, the ocean outside strangely calm.

I donned a midnight gown embroidered with golden thread decorated with small constellations. Modest, severe even, it was one of the only newer gowns I owned. I pinched my cheeks hard to bring a bit of color into them so I wouldn't look like a pale corpse standing next to the Prince.

I hadn't slept much—how could I, with this hope beating in my chest? For the first time, I felt like a future was within my grasp.

Just before I left the tower, I contemplated the sea one last time. I traced my fingers over the words scratched into the desk.

I pondered the three empty mattresses huddled together in the corner, one draped with the red wool blanket.

I'd throw myself off the roof of the tower to my death rather than stay imprisoned another day.

Nico, Lorcan, and Elijah met me atop the tower, dressed in blue. My entire body felt as tight as a harp string, and my skin hummed with anxiety.

I could see all around from the top of the castle—the mountains to the north and west, the empty expanse of plains to the east, and the Sea of Obsidia to the south. The village I'd walked to and been attacked in was now a barren ruin. There was no sign of the Cullen horde—a vast expanse of emptiness, snow, and rubble. Somewhere far off, on the other side of the sea, was *his* kingdom, the land of Kinkanali.

The Queen was emotional as a stone as she watched Nico load my few belongings into a pack tied to the foreleg of a silver dragon. The Cullen were mysteriously absent, busy elsewhere in the castle. I was grateful not to endure their incessant jaw-clicking and growling for my final minutes before leaving. I took a deep, bracing breath of the cold and then went to stand next to the dragon. Up, up, up... until the dragon bent down to stare at me.

I know you.

Very unexpectedly, I realized that this dragon was the *same* silver dragon that had come to Arabella and me almost four years before. I hadn't recognized him last night in the dark, but he'd come back for me after all—and now he would carry me away.

But not with my sister. Instead of Arabella, I had just one tattered satchel with two black gowns—a pitiful showing for anyone, especially a princess.

Malinda stepped forward, and I almost flinched. With long, pale hands, she tugged the edges of my cloak forward, adjusted the skull pin that caught, and held it together. I couldn't look her in the eye. I'd never had her fuss over me this way or stand this close, and I could smell her thick floral perfume, the scent of rot underneath that it hid.

Did she want to say something? I didn't hope for an apology, of course ... but some acknowledgment of what she'd done, a reason for the many years of pain. For Taliesin. For Arabella. If there was ever going to be a moment where my mother explained herself, I thought it would be right then, before she lost the last of her children forever.

"Don't come back," she said. Her voice was as cold as the northern winds that blew across the tower, and when my gaze flicked to hers, her eyes were so green that I was momentarily stunned. "Not ever."

I bit my lip and nodded, my voice failing me.

The great silver dragon blinked at me as I reached forward and grasped the rope hanging from his back, hauling myself up to the leather saddle securely fastened between his wings.

I patted him more to reassure myself than out of affection.

Please go. I want to go. Thank you.

Soon.

His soul's response was immediate and booming. I want to hug him around his neck and never let go. Later, once we were all off this roof, I would.

Lorcan settled onto the back of his own dragon, as did Nico. The Prince, meanwhile, climbed onto the back of mine. He would ride behind me and ensure I didn't fall.

Meanwhile, Malinda stared up at me, a curious expression on her face, as if she wanted to speak but could not. Around us, the sky lightened from blue to icy dawn, and the inky water below looked less menacing.

"I will keep her safe," the Prince assured Malinda as he pressed his fist to his heart in our gesture of a promise.

She stared up at him, her red lips pursed. "I know," she replied, her voice emotionless.

After a beat, my dragon leaped from the roof and into the air. I clutched the rope and bit back a shriek, and my stomach plummeted down to my boots. As his great wings flapped once, twice, three times, it created great drafts that stirred the ebony banners and churned the flags of the House of Atropos.

My heart raced as we soared away, over the sea and snow, straight toward the sunrise. The Kareen mountains stood in the distance, their crags like jagged fangs against a gray sky. Ahead, I could see nothing but the sky, and the sun rose like a lovely pink pearl. I shouldn't have wanted to look back ... but I did anyway.

Malinda stood alone on the rooftop, though we were too far away for me to see her expression. She raised one hand toward me, a final farewell gesture, but I felt a promise that this was not the end, that I would see her again. It so filled me with dread that I had to turn my head.

The dragons quickened their speed, and my thoughts and worries were wiped clean as we roared upward through the clouds. Crystallized air screamed past my ears, and my lungs burned from the frigid air. I flexed my frozen fingers on the rope tied around the dragon's neck, wishing I'd brought gloves.

As we broke through the clouds, radiant, streaming, ethereal sunlight surrounded me. The sky was endless and bright blue. My hair tore free from its braid, wild and golden in the wind. As I inhaled, I was overcome with this incredible feeling—a tingle so foreign and strange I almost didn't recognize it.

Happiness. This is how it feels to be happy.

Beneath me, the beast's enormous ribs expanded and contracted, steady and sure. I relished the life coursing through its veins, the heat against my legs. Its dragon heart pumped—*smush, smush, smush*—providing a soft drumbeat.

I am free. Free of Malinda. Free of my past.

I was traveling steadily toward a new kingdom. I was without Atropos, but I was free.

I'll come back for her, I vowed. *No matter how long it takes.*

Nico flew next to me, and I caught him grinning as his dragon, a purple-ridged beast with a savage face, plummeted through a cloud and then dived toward a mountainside. He spoke to it as they flew as if they were conversing.

Leaning as far over as I dared, I peered down. I hoped to see vibrant cities and farms where the people flourished. But the terrain of Kinver'i was barren, with empty fields and frozen lakes that resembled empty eye sockets. As far as I could see, there were no houses, villages, or towns. Much to my disappointment, the world beyond my nightly walks was remarkably the same—a vast expanse of nothing.

Here and there, the Cullen roamed. Like ants gone astray, they wandered through the vast wilderness, seeking their next meal. I shifted in my seat on the dragon and clutched the rein tighter as I saw one of them look up toward us and pause. They weren't going north toward The Grace, back to their commander. They traveled east toward the sun, just as we did.

We brought the dragons down into a quiet forest a few hours later. Prehistoric firs and evergreens with trunks nearly as large around as the dragons towered overhead. Breathless and rosy-cheeked, I slid off the back of the dragon, but the ground was so far away that I immediately stumbled and fell.

The Prince steadied me as my back slammed into his chest. "Easy there."

I whirled around, acutely aware of his nearness, and brushed the hair back from my face. It was tangled from the fierce wind, and my cheeks and nose were cherry-red. "Sorry."

His sinfully handsome face looked down at me, and his lips quirked, drawing my eyes to them. With his wild black hair, messy from flying, eyelashes and stubble dark against his cheek, he was more like a villain than a prince from a foreign land, sunkissed, like a pirate. I'd never understood the word until this moment. His lips were soft and pink. It was a good, expressive mouth, and I wondered if he'd smiled often. Maybe he'd had the kind of childhood where he had a mother and father, where he'd been encouraged and loved.

"It's fine," he said. "I wouldn't want you to fall after I promised Malinda to look after you." But this time, his voice was clipped as if there were frost along its edges.

"Where are we?" I stepped back from him, unsure I wanted to be so close.

"The Forests of Lerza," he said. "You know it?"

The Forests of Lerza were hundreds of miles from my home. "Only from books," I replied and sniffed the air.

Something strange.

There was no smell other than evergreen and oak and snow. Nor was there any hint of the many things that made the forests *alive.* So I held my breath and listened. There was no sound but the whisper of the wind in the boughs, the occasional thud of snow shaken free.

Perplexed, I cast out my magic, seeking souls to reap. Any living thing— any soul—would immediately answer my call. I received immediate flickers from Elijah, Lorcan, and Nico, which I discarded immediately. I continued to listen and wait and search.

For a long time, almost further than I could reach, there was nothing. It was as devoid of life as Grace Castle. No villagers. No deer. No horse or dog. No rabbit ducking into the underbrush, no fox lurking in the shadows of the evergreens. Not even an old crow. Nothing. Nothing other than us.

"What's wrong with this place?" I replied. "Why is it so—"

"The Cullen ate them," Nico answered.

"Ate? What do you mean?"

"The Cullen eat the animals. Or torture them until they are barely alive. Most of Kinver'i is empty; there is nothing left." Lorcan's voice was thick with venom. "Just another thing to thank the House of Atropos for."

"Why are you looking at me like that?" I asked. "I didn't make the Cullen, and I don't control them."

Lorcan quirked an eyebrow. "My mistake. I assumed that since you murdered on behalf of Malinda, you also controlled her army."

I blanched. Elijah's back was toward me, but something in his posture told me that not only was he listening but that he awaited my reply. He'd leaned against his dragon, his palm flat against its side, but the dragon watched me with a sapphire eye.

"No," I started to say. "I—"

"You don't need to lie." The Prince didn't even turn. "We all know the truth."

I stared at the slope of his broad shoulders, clad in that beautiful cobalt cloak. "I don't control them. They guarded us, kept us in the tower. I don't know how she does it."

"So you aren't the Reaper?" His back was still toward me. He already knew; the question was only meant to confirm it.

My future suddenly felt precarious as a soap bubble—it might pop with the slightest breath.

"She said that Arabella would die if I didn't help her. And she'd already killed Taliesin. I used my powers to question them, soul to soul." The words came out as a whisper.

"Every life you took made another Cullen for her army," Nico said.

"Yes." My gaze was firmly rooted on the ground; I didn't want to look up and see Nico's expression, I didn't want to see Lorcan's either. I already knew what they all would think of me.

"How many do you think there are?" Lorcan puffed on his pipe, watching the treeline.

"Thousands. Maybe ten thousand. I never counted."

"Did your victims suffer?" The Prince asked. "Were you quick?"

"I cut their throats. They felt little."

"They call you the Grim Reaper." Lorcan piled sticks onto the small campfire, and the damp wood smoked and smoldered. "And they say you're as tall as two men, made of night itself."

"I've heard," I said uncomfortably.

"Imagine how they'd feel to know that the brutal enforcer who steals their loved ones is a girl. A princess."

The Prince held up a hand. "Death decides when a life is over. It is her right."

"But was it their time? Was it *her* decision? Or was it Malinda?" Lorcan was vehement. "If it was Malinda, it was murder."

Lorcan was right. It *was* murder, though I'd never wanted any of my people to die. I wondered if they knew the full extent of my misdeeds; my reputation was not quite the same as knowing the list of all the wrongs I'd committed. "I didn't want that life. I'm happy to be free of it," I assured him.

The Prince touched my shoulder, then sat beside me on the ground. "Kinver'i was never yours to look after. It was hers. Malinda failed our people. She's the horror, the nightmare inflicted upon us all. You were just her prisoner." His eyes were clear, with not a shade of suspicion.

"You're here now..." he said pointedly... "and you're on our side."

Nico tossed small twigs into the campfire. The Prince patted the dragon and walked toward us, his face carefully blank and looking everywhere but at me.

Desperate to change the subject, I looked at Nico. "If our escape plan had succeeded, we would have been doomed. We would never have made it this far."

In the vast expanse of nothing, of snow and ice and bitter cold patrolled by Cullen, my siblings would have been killed, and I would have been returned to the tower to Malinda.

Nico bowed his head. "I tried to tell Taliesin as much. But he wanted to make Arabella happy."

"With few animals left to hunt, you would have had to make do with the rations you carried," Lorcan said, puffing on his pipe. "Assuming, of course, that you knew how to hunt in the first place." He quirked his brow at me.

The only thing I'd ever hunted was man. Those men were neither smart enough nor fast enough to avoid their Fate. I decided to keep this particular thought to myself.

With his control of the elements air and water, the Prince transformed the barren clearing into something truly magical, with castles to shelter us. Quietly, appearing from nowhere, small snow castles arranged themselves from the soft powder. Tiny turrets perched on blocks of wintry white squares, each decorated with a swirling roof. Micro-sized and stunning in detail, none would fit all of us and each was meant to be sleeping quarters for one.

I was awed and stared at him as he worked. His brow furrowed as he erected a small fence made of ice to surround the camp—a fence, I realized, to protect us from Cullen. It would keep out intruders, just in case any came near as we slept.

"You know, we thought he'd drop dead if he touched your hand," Lorcan said, by way of conversation. "Or that you'd curse us all, and we'd become Cullen at your command." He slid closer.

I furrowed my brow. "That's not how the Fated power works."

"How would anyone know that?" Lorcan snorted. "Many have gone over the wall into Kinver'i. Few return. None of them have ever seen you. Though Nico did his part, telling us how wonderful you were."

Across the clearing, Nico shifted uncomfortably.

I supposed that the Lord of the Fae was trying to make conversation. Unfortunately, I hadn't had a lot of practice in the finer details of making friends. I racked my brains trying to remember anything about Lord Lorcan or the kingdom he ruled, Kinseamair, just so that I might say *something*. I knew that it was a string of southern islands, south and east from the Lachesis kingdom. I knew that it was a land of the Fae. And I remembered that his castle was more famous than any other—and for all the wrong reasons. Surrounded by a labyrinth as far as the eye could see, any who dared attempt to explore it went mad or disappeared. Lorcan, as its ruler, was ... I wrinkled my nose, searching my memories.

Master of Mages, Keeper of Mysteries. That's what they called him.

Anything that shouldn't be placed in human hands, any object confiscated from witches gone bad, all of it was placed in *his* castle, the Arcana. Lord Lorcan alone had access to the oldest records, spellbooks, and recipes. If anyone would know how to free Atropos, it was him. I plastered a much friendlier look on my face as Lorcan patted his pocket and brought out his long pipe again, intricately carved, and then, from his other pocket, procured a small bundle that smelled remarkably like dried horse dung.

"In ten years, only one of us has ever made it inside The Grace," he said.

I didn't even have to feign interest. "Nico?"

"Correct."

Nico crossed his arms, his biceps bulging against the fabric. He'd changed so much since I'd seen him last. By the time I was fifteen, before our escape attempt and he disappeared, I assumed it was Nico who would be my first kiss. Our eyes met, and for a moment I had the strange sensation that he was thinking the same thing that I was. He broke our gaze with a subtle shake of his head.

"How is it possible that you escaped unscathed?" I asked. "Why didn't the Cullen kill you years ago like all the others?"

"My mother put a protective spell in place years ago. It's why I could walk among them without them tearing me apart." He shrugged. "She couldn't save herself, but she saved me."

Lorcan paced the snow-filled clearing as he smoked his pipe. "I first met Nico when Malinda sent him to The Epiphany on *assignment.*"

Assignment. A vague word that hid all manner of sins. Yet I knew *exactly* what he meant. There was only one kind of errand Malinda cared about; the kind that brought Death and destruction.

"A few years ago, Malinda sent me to kill Vitess," Nico confirmed. "Which I failed, of course, because Vitess undid my attempt. That was the first time she asked about you, about Arabella. Shortly afterward, she started inspecting your future... That's when she unearthed the prophecy, and found the parchment arranging your marriage."

Interesting. The Prince crafted a small, cozy campfire.

I addressed him next. "If Nico spied for you, you knew Queen Malinda kept us as prisoners."

"Everyone knew." Elijah shoved his hands into his coat pockets as the tinder caught, as the flames guttered and smoked. "Vitess checked every time thread, and she assured us that *this* was the time, and *this* was the exact route we must take. No modifications."

"This was the only way to get you out of the tower," Nico said with conviction. "Even though there were many other unsuccessful attempts."

I could only name one, the ill-fated escape when Taliesin was killed. But I had no reason nor desire to argue, and no way to know if things would have turned out differently. I flexed my fingers toward the fire and considered the future, the one in which I ruled Moirai alongside the Time controller, Vitess, my mysterious savior, and Serene, the creator and descendant of Clotho.

"Is it the same there in Kinkanali?" I asked. "The dead do not die?"

Nico nodded. "In the other kingdoms they burn the bodies, that way there is no time for the Cullen to overtake them, as they have in Kinver'i. You'll smell the smoke when we arrive."

"The pyres are always kept burning." The Prince's mood was stormy, like the seas around my tower.

Briefly, I wondered if he knew about the Cullen army hidden in the northern woods, if he knew just how many thousands of them Malinda had at her command. No simple pyre would contain so many.

"And Kinver'i?" I couldn't help but ask. "Is it truly empty? There are no people left?"

The three men shared a look, a debate as to whether or not to tell me the truth. Lorcan answered. "There are outposts. Hidden cities, beneath the snow and ice. Serene made islands of safety, surrounding them with waters too perilous for the Cullen to cross."

Serene, the controller of Life, the other Fate, spent time saving my people... while Vitess was saving me. Together, she, Vitess, and I made three. Three Fates, reunited.

The Prince gestured at one of the snow castles. "We should get some sleep."

I chewed on my lip nervously as I followed the Prince through an arched doorway. Our breath formed clouds as we stood side by side, and I wrapped my arms tightly around myself.

"I assumed you would be accustomed to the cold," he said easily, apologetically. "Otherwise I would have brought more blankets."

He unpacked one of his bags, revealing just two blankets— barely large enough for two. He began to fashion those into a bed for the two of us—one to sleep upon, one to cover us. We'd have no choice but to lay close. Meanwhile, I'd never slept next to anyone but my siblings and Nico. Would it be different? Would I be able to sleep, with his strange scent in my nose, his nearness and bare skin so near to my hands?

I undressed quickly, my face as red as Arabella's hair. I lay down next to him in my underclothes, quickly pulling the blankets up to my neck. He dutifully added another layer of blankets over us, then his blue cloak, in the hopes that it would keep me warm through the night. Meanwhile I huddled into my nightgown, convulsing, trying not to shiver uncontrollably.

However, I immediately realized this wasn't necessary. The Prince radiated warmth like a merry fire. I could feel it alongside my arm even though we weren't touching, and it banished the frost that never seemed to leave my bones. He still had that incredible smell, like cinnamon and oak, smoke and sweet apple.

"This is the farthest you've ever been from home, isn't it?" He paused. "You will be a queen without any knowledge of her people."

"There don't seem to be many citizens interested in meeting the Atropos family," I remarked. "If any still live."

The Prince pursed his lips as he stared at the ceiling. "They fear your mother. But their feelings toward her aren't how they'd feel about you."

Maybe.

"What time will we leave tomorrow?" I asked, my voice cracking awkwardly in the middle.

"Before sunrise."

"And how much longer will it be until we reach The Epiphany?"

The minute we arrived, I planned to sprint to the library, and begin my search for the spell to free Atropos. My grandmother needed me, and I wasn't going to fail her. Once I freed her, Atropos could save us from Malinda.

"A while." All his responses were terse, like the ice that frosted the stones of the tower.

"Did I do something to offend you?" I asked. "Because if I did..."

The Prince sighed, some of the tension ebbing from his body. "You didn't do anything. The Epiphany is days of flying, and rough weather most of the way." He pushed more of the blanket my way. "You'll need to lie closer, if you don't want to freeze tonight."

"I'm used to the cold." But still, I reluctantly moved nearer to him, if only slightly.

I waited for him to speak, but the Prince seemed uninterested in making conversation. The space between us suddenly felt like a yawning crevasse, with me on one side and he on the other.

"Well ... good night," I mumbled and prayed for sleep to come.

CHAPTER 11

I was caught in the dungeon again, the blue blood of dead Fae coating me. All around, corpses were sprawled, their eyes unseeing and dull.

"Another." Malinda leered as she placed an icy blade in my palm. There was always another blade, another Fae, another room to visit down the endless corridor of iron bars. I had to kill them all, everyone, if I wanted to save Arabella. I was the Grim Reaper. I decided their death.

My face was half gone, revealing the bone and obsidian mask underneath my skin. I tried to pull it off, but it was welded to my bones, screwed in too tightly for me to shift it. There was something else, something crawling under my billowing robes. I ripped them open, and my skin dissolved, revealing a crusted heart full of worms.

"Just like me." Malinda grinned.

"Stop it!" I cried and thrust the knife into her stomach. "Stop, stop, stop." When I pulled the blade free, water ran from the wound instead of blood. I looked at the Queen's face, but she was no longer there. It was the Prince. I screamed.

He shook me awake. "Morena. Morena. It's a dream."

I couldn't tell the darkness of the ice castle from the brutal rooms of the dungeon. But his firm, warm arms gripped me, and that warmth made me realize that I was somewhere else. His scent filled my nose—smoky, sweet cinnamon.

"It's alright," he said. "You're safe."

I still trembled.

He summoned a flame that hovered over us like a floating candle, and it lit the interior of the snow castle. I scanned the room as my heart rate gradually slowed.

"Most of the time, I can't tell if they're real," I whispered. "I don't know how many there were if these are memories or just nightmares."

"You mean, you don't know how many you killed?" His voice was gentle.

Of course not. "Too many. Even one was too many."

I sat up, needing to breathe, suddenly aware of his closeness. "Why do you always smell like apples?"

Caught off-guard, it took him a moment to reply. "We have an orchard at the Castle. I always have apples for breakfast. Do you want one?"

I would have said no, but as I opened my mouth to decline, I realized I was ravenous. "Yes, if you have one."

The Prince sat up, revealing his broad, bare back as he rummaged in a bag. He handed the apple to me, then recovered himself. I tried not to think about what I'd noticed: that he was wearing nearly nothing under the blankets.

"I keep wondering why Malinda kept you in the tower. Did she ever tell you?"

"She did, but I don't think it was the reason. As a child, I told myself it was to protect us, that she loved us, and it was the only place where the monsters couldn't get us." Memories flitted through my mind as I crunched through a bite of the apple.

He waited for me to continue as he lay back and crossed his arms behind his head with the ease of a man who had slept many a night on the ground. Not as a soldier, though—strangely, the Prince seemed more like someone who simply enjoyed being outside.

"Of course, later I realized the Cullen were *hers* and that she tried to bury us alive at birth, that to her we were already dead ... that we were simply a nuisance."

Throwing the empty apple core to the side, I lay on my side to face him. From this close, I could see the stubble along his jaw and the crinkles around his eyes that came whenever he smiled.

"Sometimes I thought..." I hesitated to tell him the truth, then plunged ahead..." She was always trying to make me appreciate and embrace my power. It made her angry that I hoped it would go away."

"Once you're Fate-marked, you can't be rid of it. Everyone knows that. Fates can't have normal lives—being responsible for Gods and men demands too much." He studied me. "If you can change the course of destiny, and if you can raise the dead and the demons of hell, I should think that you could achieve anything you wanted to."

"I don't think it's unreasonable to hope that I might be able to walk around my own home, have dinner at a table, sleep in bed, or have a parent who hugged me."

He was silent for a long time. As the minutes passed, I started to believe that he'd never respond. "Did you want to kill your mother? For everything she's done?" he asked finally.

"*Kill* is too kind of a word for what she deserved."

"What stopped you then?" he asked. "You could have done it—why didn't you?"

"I didn't want to risk Arabella's life once Taliesin died."

"And once Arabella was gone?"

I couldn't meet his gaze, so I stared at his mouth instead, which was also a mistake. I immediately began to think of kissing him instead of answering. My response took much longer than it should have as a result.

"I did try, once, and failed. That was just before you arrived. I tried to take her soul, but she didn't have one. There was nothing there but emptiness."

"So Malinda still lives, heartless and soulless, and here you are... Death let loose out in the world for the first time, unprepared."

I blinked my black eyes. "You think I'm a risk?"

"I think we don't have a choice."

"What does that mean?" I propped my head on my hand and studied him.

"We need Death on our side. We need the Three Fates reunited and back in charge. Without you, there are only two, and the world remains unbalanced. You could have been an ogre, and I still would have kissed your hand and loaded you up on that dragon."

I laughed. I didn't know how to handle the sudden warmth in my face or the feelings that bubbled beneath my skin—but I laughed.

And the Prince stared at me. "I know we haven't known each other very long, but I feel I am beginning to understand you. Your cloak is black, but your heart is not."

The statement shocked me. No one had ever said something so kind; in fact, I couldn't think of many times that anyone outside of my family had spoken to me. An unfamiliar feeling settled in my chest. Something warm and embracing. Thankfully, he changed the subject before I had to respond.

"I hope you'll like her, my sister. She's fearless and very intense. Honestly, she's sort of terrifying. I expected you to be just like her, only more intimidating."

Briefly, I thought of my reputation as the Reaper. I felt confident that none of the citizens would describe me as intense but *terrifying*? Definitely. I considered him with my onyx eyes. "I don't need to intimidate people when I can kill them with a thought."

"A fair point." Despite my statement, he seemed unafraid. "My gifts manifested when I was eight. At the time, I used my power to squirt water into my sister's eye, which she found incredibly annoying. She punched me, I hit her, and then our mother yanked us apart by the backs of our necks."

"It seems like you two are really close."

The Prince smiled as he drifted along the memory. "Yes. We are."

Taliesin would have liked him.

I started telling him about my childhood in the tower without really knowing why. "As you can imagine, we were crazy with boredom, and we invented games and tried to entertain ourselves. Taliesin liked to exercise, running and jumping across the beds. Arabella was more of a risk-taker. Once, she dared us to crawl out the tower window and try to hold on as long as possible."

"Sounds like a terrible idea."

"It was. We could easily fall and bash our brains out on the rocks. Arabella started to go out on the ledge. Her hands were shaking so badly I knew she couldn't hold on. So I stopped her by saying I would go first." I hesitated, remembering that night, thinking of all that had happened since and how none of it would have happened if that one moment had been different.

"I climbed out of our window and let my feet slide down the wall. All I could hear were the waves below and the roar of the wind..." I trailed off, remembering. "But I didn't fall. I found a foothold. That was when we knew it was possible that we could escape."

"Didn't Arabella care? If anyone fell, I mean?"

"Not at all. If we died, we'd be better off." A ghost of a smile flashed across my lips. "I put my forehead against the stone and prayed to Nyx." I flashed back to our escape when Taliesin died. What a fool I was to think Nyx cared what happened to us.

A lump formed in my throat, so it was hard to continue. "Arabella insisted we could climb down; Taliesin thought not. The two argued while I was still hanging off our tower like a bat."

"What would you do after you climbed down? Swim the Obsidian Sea? Hike through weeks of snow and rabid Cullen?"

I shrugged. "We stupidly didn't think that far ahead. We didn't think about how we would survive; we just ... assumed we would succeed."

"You were fools."

"We were children." The hard edge crept back between us. "Prisoners. Unloved and untended."

He sighed. "I see. We should get some sleep. Tomorrow is another long day." He rolled over, leaving the scent of his skin in his wake. It was smoky and sweet, and I wanted to bury my face against his neck and inhale deeply.

Disconcerted, I rolled over onto my back and stared at the ceiling of the snow castle he'd made. We were not far enough from The Grace; at any moment, Cullen could ransack us and ruin my chance at freedom, kill him or Nico or Lorcan, and it would all be for nothing. And then what would I do? What chance would I have if the Prince couldn't get me out of Kinver'i?

Luckily, I didn't have long to think about it before sleep claimed me. This time, there were no dreams.

We planned to leave just after sunrise, the soft fingers of dawn barely tracing the sky. Crisp and cold, the world was sleepy and hushed, and the silence was tranquil. I had just raised my boot, preparing to climb onto the back of the dragon, when my head jerked up, nostrils flared wide.

Blood. I smelled blood. A lot of it. Far off, someone began to scream. I looked at the men around me, mentally counting. They were all here: Nico burying our campfire, the Prince packing a bag, and Lorcan speaking with a dragon.

Yet these cries for help were so loud I couldn't hear anything else. I'd never heard sounds like this before. But assuredly, these woods were not empty; something was screaming for help. Making a quick decision, I whirled toward the voice and raced from the clearing.

"Where are you going?!" Behind me, Nico sounded panicked.

My feet flew over the ground, barely touching the snow, and my black gown streamed behind me.

I'm coming.

As I ran, the shadow behind me elongated and lengthened, growing wings spilling over the earth wider and wider, a yawning current of black. *The Shadow of Death.*

I pushed the thought away.

I found them in a clearing, one of the Cullen ripping and shredding a stag from behind with sharp teeth. Where his eyes once had been was a set of rotting empty holes. The stag kicked and bellowed as he rolled in fear.

"Get away from him!" I shrieked as I soared through the air. The words would be unintelligible to a human, to a Fae. It was the old language, older than time itself.

The Cullen jerked as if it'd been struck. He dropped the stag and slunk away, stopping a few yards off and clattering his teeth in impotent rage. The stag fell to the ground in a heap, and I fell with him, pulled him into my lap. He bleated in agony, blood pouring from the many open wounds across his hide.

"I am here," I said aloud.

My numbness melted away as I held the stag. I suddenly recalled a dog, distantly, dreamily, it might not have ever existed, from when I was young. Nico brought me a dog, but the dog hadn't survived even two weeks in the Castle. Cullen had torn him apart, and he'd lick at my hands with his last breaths. I might have been five years old.

"There there," I said to the stag. Bitten and mauled and bleeding, he was somehow still alive. I'd gotten here in time. Nothing was broken, he would not die.

Bitterly, I berated myself. I'd bargained for better bread while Malinda and her Cullen army annihilated every living thing in my kingdom. I'd blindly ignored the suffering of my people—in fact, I'd been her aide because I was more concerned with myself. When I'd found the Cullen army camped outside the windows of Grace Castle, I'd done nothing about it.

I'd killed many more than I could count, blocking out their screams and suffering and telling myself I had no choice.

No choices left but bad ones.

I'd failed my people and my siblings. This was the first time I'd *saved* something, and it moved me. I, *Death,* had saved one life.

It was only one.

It didn't redeem me.

But still, I felt the tiniest tingle of pride as one of the cracks in my heart sealed back together, a sliver of gilding in a sea of black. I'd lost everything else, including my soul, but just this once, I had done the right thing. For once, I was fast enough. I'd done something good.

I kissed his forehead. *I give you fifty years, decades to sire fawns.*

He'd have to find mates, which might be impossible in Kinver'I... but that was out of my hands. The stag nuzzled my hand in gratitude, and I hugged him tightly. "You will not die. Not yet. Not for a very long time."

"What the hell are you doing?" the Prince thundered. "Unhand that animal right now."

He'd come into the clearing while I held the stag, and he'd seen my face against his neck. The beast scrambled from my lap, frightened by his tone, wounds still seeping bright red. Blood smeared my face, my hands, and the ground underneath us.

"Don't you touch that animal again!" he yelled. "And you—"he flung his magic toward the Cullen I'd forgotten, and in a blink, it was encased in a cage of flames that sprang from the dirt at its skeleton feet. It screamed as it burned, shrill and incessant.

I stood up wearily. Of course, he would assume that I was there to kill the deer, to feast on its organs with the Cullen. How he saw me and why he'd been hot and cold was suddenly clear. I was a monster; I was a threat. The daughter of Malinda the Mad, Queen of the Blood Throne. I was a killer, crafted and honed.

"Were you going to eat that deer?" He glared at me. "How can you—"

The stag leaned toward my side to protect me from his anger.

Go find your mate, I told him. *Be well.*

I gave his head a light pat, and he bounded away, leaving the Prince goggling at me, his mouth hanging open. "Explain."

I shrugged. "Why bother?" I replied. "You've already decided what you thought you saw. You're willing to marry me but not get to know me." I was embarrassed and ashamed but also angry that he would make assumptions.

The Prince reached for my arm. "Morena—"

"No!" I pushed his hand away. "Why rescue me if you feel like I'm a monster among you?"

I dragged my hands down the bloody bodice of my black gown. "Do you think I *wanted* this life? Did I *ask* for these black eyes to be put in my head, a scythe in my hand? Do you think I *wanted* to look like her, be like her?"

I barreled on, not letting him have a word in edgewise. "I'm a *vegetarian*. "I wiped the blood on my face with a long black sleeve. "And actually, since you didn't ask, I don't even *like* killing things."

"What?" The Prince gaped at me like I'd lost my mind.

"You heard me."

I walked past him, back toward the camp, where undoubtedly everyone was talking about how horrible I was, a murdering ghoul, a black-footed terror... and they were right but also *wrong*. My rare temper grew, a slow boil of lava with nowhere to go, burning a hole in my throat.

I whirled back to face him. "I saved the stag. And I gave him more years to live so he might replenish this wood with Life instead of Death. I hated the tower. I hated the blood throne. But I suppose I must be just like her since she's my mother. My reputation is so firmly entrenched that no one needs to ask me how I feel. Or what I want."

I was glad to not be able to cry. If I could, I would have needed to wipe away the tears. "I guess there's good news, though. No matter what you *say*, even if your blood runs cold just looking at my cursed face... "

I pointed at myself... "you are going to marry me. You are going to love *me*."

I tried to laugh, but it felt as if I were choking on the words. "So if you don't want me, that's just too damn bad."

Much to my shock, the Prince strode across the clearing, pulled me into his arms, and kissed me, bloody face and all. I inhaled his sweet, smoky scent, and my heart fluttered. Though I was uncertain at first, he was light and fire, and I leaned into him, craving his warmth.

He ran his hands up into my hair, tugged me toward him. As we melded together, fitted like the sides of a coin, unable to tell half from the whole... I had a dark thought.

His was a soul I was going to claim forever. I for him, and he for me.

CHAPTER 12

We flew for the next six hours. And even though we didn't speak, I couldn't stop thinking about it. I touched my lips, remembered our kiss, and smiled as my dragon soared over snow-filled forests. The Prince sat ahead of me, so all I could see was the back of his neck, my arms wrapped around his waist, and it was enough.

My first kiss.

Gory, overdramatic, and at the scene of a near murder. It seemed appropriate for a Reaper from the House of Atropos. And he hadn't held back or been scared off. He'd lingered ... and his tongue touched mine, and then...

The dragon under me shifted suddenly, nearly tossing me off the saddle as the wind gusted. I scrambled, red-faced, and clutched at his waist. My hands protested and burned—I had three blisters already, and we had two more days of flying.

And two nights, my subconscious helpfully added. *Two nights of laying side by side in the dark.*

Stop that. It was just a kiss.

Yet I couldn't stop thinking about it. I remembered every flutter of my stomach, the rasp of his chin on mine, the warmth of the sun on my shoulders. The whole world felt cracked open, beautiful, and full of possibilities. I suddenly had *hope,* a precious, dangerous thing.

No girl should dare to dream like that.

We took a break in mid-afternoon, and Elijah, Nico, and Lorcan made conversation as they prepared food. I huddled close, extended my aching hands toward the flames, and listened to their easy banter.

"That smells incredible," Lorcan moaned, sniffing noisily. Thick and well-seasoned, a root stew boiled in the iron pot over our fire, and all of our mouths watered. Thanks to Elijah, the fire roared despite the dampened wood and the snow falling all around us.

"No thanks to you," Nico replied as he stirred the pot. "If you hadn't been stomping around the underbrush, I could have charmed that rabbit to hop into our pot."

"Don't complain," Elijah murmured, cutting a small, hard loaf of barmbrack into quarters. "We're lucky to eat when some citizens have so much less."

"How far are we from The Epiphany?" I couldn't help but ask again. I wanted to arrive as soon as possible so that I could begin my research on how to free Atropos.

"Another day. Two, maybe." The Prince held out a piece of the barm-brack to me. The traditional bread of the Fae was dotted with winter berries and clove; when warm, it was delicious. I steadfastly avoided looking at him.

Lorcan closed his eyes. "I can't wait to dive into a warm bed with a willing female."

Nico coughed loudly and blew into his hands to warm them. Meanwhile, I fixated on the sounds of the forest, the drip of icicles melting from branches.

Lorcan took a pipe from his pocket and a set of matches to light it. "Some said you were mute, that the Queen of the Blood Throne had cut out your tongue." He took a deep draw and then huffed out the smoke. "I can't imagine you'd be anything but ecstatic to be leaving."

The Prince sat beside me and handed me a bowl of stew without comment.

For a while, there was no talking. We only ate.

"How are you feeling," he asked quietly. "And your hands?" He glanced down at the blisters on my palms, which I immediately wished I'd hidden.

"Fine."

"We could fly another six hours and reach the inn."

The inn?

The two other men overheard and looked at each other, then at the two of us. "Why did we stop at all?" Nico asked.

"I thought Morena might want a break and a meal."

"How very chivalrous of you," Lorcan mumbled.

Nico ladled soup into a bowl, eyebrows raised as he glanced between The Prince and me.

"I'm fine to continue," I said, even though the blisters on my hands begged otherwise. "I don't mind flying longer." An inn meant a hot bath, a bed...

"And we'd stay there tonight?" Lorcan asked Nico.

"We'd be crazy not to. Although that old shack is one heavy rain from falling into the river."

No one wanted to sleep on the ground again when there was a chance of a roof over our heads, so we continued.

Just before nightfall, our dragons touched down in fields swollen with rain, and at one end of the field was a rickety bridge made of rotted wood and frayed rope. This kept it somewhat safe from Cullen, as the river around it made it an island. At the edge of the bridge was a slab of a man holding a battle axe.

Beyond the bridge, just barely visible through the fog, I spotted a decrepit building, uneven, dark brown, the entire structure drunkenly leaning toward the rushing water below it. Indeed, as Nico said, it did look as if it would topple in at any moment.

"Good to see you, Wart." Lorcan clapped the brutally scarred man on the shoulder as we passed; his face was as immovable as a headstone.

I hunched my shoulders and skulked by, though I needn't have bothered—I was as unrecognizable as I'd ever be, with leaves in my hair and dirt smudges from the campfire on my face. No one would know me as a princess, Malinda's daughter, or the Reaper ... if they knew what I looked like, which was doubtful.

The Prince gestured open-handed as the four of us tramped through the inn's mud-filled stableyard. Smells of old clothes and wet dogs immediately assaulted my nose.

"Four rooms?" the innkeeper asked, patting the pockets of an apron that barely covered his enormous round belly.

"Just two. We'll share."

In unison, Nico, Lorcan, and I all stared at him. There was no proper reason for us to do that—he was a Prince. He could surely afford more rooms.

Lorcan spoke first. "Yes. There are thieves in these parts. We wouldn't want one of them to meet Death too soon." He smirked.

I hid a responding smile, and Nico coughed out a laugh. The rationale of me, Death, being afraid of a common thief was absurd—I didn't need his protection. The Prince seemed to know that because he ducked his head immediately, avoiding our gaze.

He left me at the door to our room, mumbling something about taking care of the dragons. The room was surprisingly tidy, with a window overlooking the rapids. The bed had a red quilted blanket, handmade.

Despite Nico's criticisms, I realized it would be downright luxurious after sleeping in the snow. The small hearth with a cheerful fire added to the appeal.

"It's better than the tower," I muttered as I dropped my bag.

Outside, through a second door, I spotted a steaming pool at the edge of the river, tucked in the corner of the garden. Long branches arched over the water, partially covering it. It was quiet, away from the rapids.

"Mmm..." I sighed with pleasure—I hadn't had a bath in days. Sometimes, when I turned my head quickly, I swore I could still smell the lingering scent of the Cullen among the strands of my hair.

There was no towel, but I could use my cloak well enough, and my hair would dry by the fire. I moved quickly, eager to get myself into the warm water, but by the time I was back outside and ready, the Prince was already there.

I stopped in my tracks at the edge of the clearing. He was taking off his clothes. Slowly, he folded his tunic and laid it across a tree limb. Underneath was all muscle, corded, and soft golden skin beneath all that buttoned-up blue. Across half of his chest were tattooed leaves.

I gobbled up the view as if I were starving. As if he felt my gaze, he turned to stare back at me, and his gray eyes matched the fog. He didn't flinch. He didn't look away as he pushed down the waistband of his pants.

My heart might have stopped beating as my gaze followed the muscles of his waist, the line of his hips—

The Prince walked into the trails of mist that rose from the hot water and submerged himself up to his shoulders. It was quiet but for the sound of dripping and bubbling. The Prince sighed with contentment and tipped his head back, resting it against a rock ledge. Waiting.

Do I stand here? Do I say something? Do I just go back inside?

I licked the sweat from my upper lip. Nico snored softly in his room, audible through the thick mud walls of the inn.

"You can join me. I won't bite."

The air tasted of minerals and mud, acidic in my nose. I knew I should say or do something, but still, I hesitated, not brave enough to disrobe but not willing to walk away. The air was laced with fog, chilly and damp.

"Tomorrow, we'll be at The Epiphany. You'll meet the other Fates and embark on a brand new life. A queen of Moirai."

It should have been a celebratory moment, but for some reason, the Prince sounded worried. Maybe it was because tomorrow, I'd be meeting his family, seeing his home, meeting his friends. He didn't know if I'd have some sort of outburst and lose control, harming his innocent citizens.

"About before," I began, "at The Grace, you said the proposal was a ruse. But then you showed my mother the Decree, and it claimed that I'm betrothed to Elijah Lachesis. Was that a lie?"

"It isn't a lie. The betrothal is real."

"Why didn't you just say that in the graveyard?"

He sighed and rubbed his eyebrows. "Would you really marry me? Despite knowing nothing about who I am?"

Nothing could be as bad as what I've done.

But I wasn't quite brave enough to say this aloud—not to him, not right then.

"This is harder than I thought it would be." His voice was strained, and I could tell that he was torn.

I suddenly realized he was nervous—maybe he'd never kissed anyone either, and now he didn't know what to do next.

"I should go," he said.

"You should stay." The brazen voice that came out of my mouth was pure Malinda, and at that moment, I was actually sort of grateful to her.

"You want me to stay?" The Prince's voice was gruff.

I moved closer until I could see the rise and fall of his chest, see the water that coated his dark eyelashes, and a small white scar along his collarbone, marring his deeply tanned skin.

"Yes," I replied, my breath strangely steady. I removed my black robe.

His expression darkened. He studied my mouth, then downward to my chest. I felt a blush rise on my cheeks but didn't move. If I was to be his, *his wife,* of course, he should see me. After all, he'd let me see him, hadn't he? And he didn't flinch. I could be just as brave as he was.

Arabella once said that I was like snow—my skin was cold and beautiful, untouched. It was one of my best features: blemish-free and porcelain. And though I was always too thin, I didn't feel ashamed of my body. It served me well—it ran when I wanted it to; it was strong enough to get me through years of suffering.

I couldn't explain exactly what I hoped would happen. I'd read enough books in the tower to know a little about men and the things they expected. My eyes were glued to his chest, the thud of his heart visible beneath his tan skin. It increased speed when he looked at me.

The Prince slowly stood, the water sluicing down his abs and thighs. I could see each ridge of his body, the muscles under his taut skin. He exited the pool and came toward me. He stood so close we could have touched, his skin steaming, mine as white as moonlight.

"The bath is all yours," he murmured. Then he walked away, leaving me alone.

When I went back to my room an hour later, the Prince was asleep ... in our bed.

Now that I could stare at him unobserved, I let my eyes travel up and down his face like it was some kind of undiscovered paradise. His soft golden skin reminded me of peaches, especially where his throat met his collarbone. Malinda would have likely slit his throat just there, alongside the pulse. I grimaced and shoved that thought from my mind, then returned to discovering his body—finely honed, muscular but not overwhelming.

I lay down next to him. He didn't stir.

Gently, as if touching a snowflake, I traced the edge of his shirt. I drifted my index finger left, ever so slightly, until it grazed across his chest. Slowly, so slowly, I drew a circle there, a tiny one.

Mine.

Seven months, six days, five hours, forty minutes.

I jerked my hand away.

That was his Death date. Unbidden, it slammed into me.

What is this? It must be a mistake. How could his soul be doomed to die so soon?

Gently, I tugged at the thread of his life and it willingly unspooled into my hand. A liquid silver thread, I handled it carefully, not wanting to crush it. Soft light glowed along his collarbone, and I darted a look at his face. He was still sleeping.

There was no mistake: his soul trembled and twined around my hand like an eager vine. I could easily cut this thread, and his life would end. I could also easily tally his days, and I saw that there weren't many left.

My heart beat faster, much faster, as I narrowed my eyes on my index finger. I could see the number of years allotted to each soul as easily as if it were written on a piece of paper. He would lead a *short* life—not years, but months. Ripped from me, all potential for the life I imagined. We'd get married, have a child even, but she'd never know him.

I suddenly understood his discomfort. His sister, who could see the future, had likely warned him.

Don't get too attached. Don't fall in love. You won't live too much longer.

Of course, as one of the Three Fates, it was my duty to recognize the will of the universe. As the descendant of Atropos, controller of Death, I could add or take years away as I saw fit. As Death, it was my job to take souls on schedule. But as his future wife?

I could make some exceptions.

Gingerly, I stroked the silver thread. Thinking.

I can't make you immortal. But you'll live as long as you're with me. You may walk alongside Death... How long should it be? *Three hundred? Three hundred years. The threads of our lives shall be tied—knotted close. As long as I am with you, you will live.*

Forever? his soul asked me.

Not forever. But long enough.

The strong, sweet smell of firerose tinged the air as I envisioned us having dinner together and enjoying breakfast on a terrace overlooking the sea. We'd walk through fields of flowers, and children would play at our feet. I imagined his days, me at his side, and I pushed his appointment with Death further and further out. Days unnumbered spun out on the thread of his life, faster and faster and faster, a kaleidoscope of memories for him and me. For the Fates, there were always many versions of the truth, each equally true at the same time, and I could make this version the chosen path if I wanted.

I carefully put his soul back, the thread now much longer, by pressing my hand against his heart.

"Morena." The Prince inhaled slowly, his gray eyes still closed. "What are you doing?"

I jerked my hand away. Fear gripped my stomach and clenched my chest. I kept my voice steady, refusing to look at anything above his throat. "Nothing."

The smell of firerose hit him—magic hung upon the air. Recognition dawned, and he sat up, cold air snapping between us, his steady warmth suddenly absent. "What did you do?"

"I only wanted to help—"I stumbled over what to say. Did he understand what I was doing? Maybe I should explain or tell him how few days he had left.

He yanked on his cloak. "Do not meddle with destiny. It isn't safe." Then he walked out, leaving me alone.

I waited for hours, but my Prince did not return. I continued to lay there, curled in a ball, wondering if I'd done the wrong thing or hadn't thought things through... But I wasn't sorry for it. I'd extended his life, unfairly perhaps, but that was my right.

Was it fair that I, an immortal, should fall in love with someone who would die so soon? Of course not. Also, it was possible that in every future, I'd modified his destiny so that he would live longer. So why did he act like what I'd done was so wrong?

I decide. I'm Death. I choose the times of Death for all mankind. It is my divine right—why shouldn't I exercise it?

CHAPTER 13

C ullen piled upon each other, layer upon layer, dutifully freezing into hardened logs. Not alive but not completely dead, their stinking corpses acted as the barrier to entry. Many were staked in place, forming perfectly rectangular, squirming towers.

They clicked their teeth together as they groaned and shifted. As they decayed, their muscles leathered, maggots feasted on innards, and the slop and gore formed putrid cement. No one would approach that wall and want to touch it. None would dare to climb it. And the stench of it—dear Gods—there were tens of thousands.

Malinda's Cullen formed the southern border of Kinver'i. The Wall of Skulls. Rumored to be more than twenty feet tall, it had to be a thousand miles long. *Intimidating to our enemies*—that was how Malinda had described it. I'd never thought to ask for details. Indeed, I'd never considered what she'd done to build the wall.

Despite all I knew about the Queen of the Blood Throne, seeing her handiwork still shocked me. These were her people. Her own citizens. She'd killed my siblings and imprisoned me, but somehow, I'd still not expected such brutality from her.

Despite the dizzying height, I forced myself to watch the dark line of the wall as we sailed past it, as Cullen writhed and chattered. "I can see why everyone fears her," I told the dragon as I traced my fingers against his scales, distracting myself from the horror below.

Behind me, the Prince sighed. We'd slept in the same bed. We'd kissed. We'd seen each other naked. I felt like he was beginning to open up to me and to him. So why did he seem disappointed? Why had he snapped at me and given me the silent treatment all morning?

It began to rain. Soft and steady, without ice. We soared headlong into a glacial valley, waterfalls tumbling down the mountains on either side. Gaping holes were cut directly into the cliffs, perfectly round and flanked by pillars carved with runes. The holes formed circular doors, entries ten times as tall as any man. There were dozens of them, yawning and black, unguarded and ungated. They were The Veils—gates to other worlds.

As I watched, a flock of birds, speckled white and gray, flew into one of the portals. I couldn't shake the dread that spiked in my belly in response. Their life force—the entire flock—vanished in a blink.

"What's in there?" I asked the Prince, full of dread.

"Ouroboros ... and all manner of other monsters. Once someone goes in there, they never came back." He sighed again. Clearly, *something* was bothering him. He must be nervous, I reasoned. Now that we were drawing close to his homeland.

At my waist, I rested my hand atop his, and idly, I stroked his knuckles. It was a simple, casual touch—for anyone normal. But for me, it was a beacon, and my entire being narrowed to just the friction of my fingertips against his skin. I pushed back against his chest, burrowing into his warmth. A moment later, his nose brushed against my skin at the place where my neck met my shoulder. He pressed a brief, soft kiss there.

I lost all interest in the landscape. Though I knew he'd probably reject me, I let my head drop backward onto his shoulder and turned so my mouth was near his.

"Kiss me again," I said.

The Prince looked down into my face, and his eyes perfectly matched the storms and fog, the silver clouds, the iron mountains around us. Dimly, I heard his soul's response, even as his expression said something entirely different.

I can't.

And maybe it was my black cursed eyes or my mouth, so similar to Malinda's, but he didn't. The silver dragon beneath us suddenly bucked and banked left, and I scrambled to grab the reins, worried I might fall. The romantic moment was lost.

"Air current," he said sharply, and we continued onward.

Hours later, the Prince stood in his saddle and pointed with one hand. "Just past that ridge is Trale Nuvole, the undying city." He had no sooner spoken than the dragon veered east, toward the sea and the purple mountains in the distance.

A circular ridge of lilac mountains formed a protective ring around a green valley. Like the maps promised, each of the Fates had their own castle strategically placed. From this vantage, I could see each distinctively: The Wrought, The Woven, and The Reckoning. Together, they formed a triad, and in the center was The Epiphany. There were four castles: one for each Fate and one to rule together. Nico had told us about them, but to see them in person was overwhelming. This was where all threads and all times—future, present and past—converged.

Where the Three Fates meet is where all possibilities lie.

"That's The Woven." The Prince pointed at an earthen castle with soft orange walls and a red-tiled roof. It faced east to see the rising sun, and its western side nestled into the mountain. Clotho's castle was named *The Woven* since creation wove together strands of life. I could see that trees were embedded into its foundations. Even from far off, I smelt its courtyard full of citrus and fruit trees, sweet, ripe, and ready for tasting.

"There's The Wrought."

Lachesis, the controller of time, had named her castle *The Wrought* because Time fashioned who we became. On the other side of the valley, facing west, her palace was pearlescent, with hints of purple and pink shimmering in the rounded ivory stones. Tall and narrow, The Wrought was nestled in a profusion of white flowers, each turret topped with a cheerfully waving cobalt flag. My curiosity was piqued.

His family home.

"The Reckoning?" I asked, pointing at the third castle.

"That's the one," he said, a bit close to my ear. "Yours."

I sensed its rightness immediately. Smaller than the other two, Atropos' castle was not the iron gray of chains but soft, ethereal gray, like the mists that threaded through its courtyards. The roof and four towers were topped with slate, and moss grew along its walls and stairs. Instead of flowers or fruit, it was surrounded by evergreens that swayed and swished in the wind, murmuring their secrets. On the highest part of its roof, a statue of a Reaper with its scythe in hand acted as a small weathervane. It was mine, my birthright—its throne mine to sit upon.

I shivered with anticipation. If we weren't bound for The Epiphany and meeting his family, I would have asked to land immediately so I might walk into that sacred place. I tore myself away with regret, back toward the valley.

I noticed two columns of smoke, tall and ominous, black pillars that flanked the river. "What are those?"

"The pyres," the Prince answered. "That's the scent you smell."

There was a long pause where nothing but the wind passed our ears. "So *every time* a citizen dies, in the entire kingdom, they become Cullen? It's not just in Kinver'i?" I asked.

"All of Moirai is cursed—Kinver'i, Kinkanali, Kinseamair—all of it. We don't allow or tolerate Cullen here—they'd overrun us, just as they have Kinver'i."

I opened my mouth to ask another question, but the words were swept away as I saw the grandest castle of them all—The Epiphany. The fourth castle, the one in the center, was where the Three Fates ruled as equals, and their powers converged. Dozens of Seraphim with great glimmering wings fluttered around the castle, their sunlit wings flashing as they dove and flapped around the bridge.

As Arabella had predicted, there was not a single speck of snow. Millions of leaves, gorgeous and green, shifting in a warm breeze. Birds twittered in a sky bluer than any I'd ever seen. Sheep bleated outside cheerful homes and farms—yellow and purple, rose and teal. Real, human men stacked white stones, building a temple, *thunk, thunk.* It was a new world, rich in color and sound.

Stuck in the tower, watching one gray day after another from my window, I'd fantasized that I was the child of Silas and Alexis. Now, when I married their son, I would be.

The dragons left us halfway up the mountain on a circular platform ringed by stone figures of the Goddesses—Nyx, Gaia, Khaos, Hemera, Ananke, and others whose faces were too worn to recognize. Just ahead, hundreds of stairs were cut into the mountain.

"Now what?" I asked.

"We climb the rest of the way." Lorcan rubbed the back of his neck, looking weary. "It's the only way in."

Nico put his hand on my shoulder. "Just remember, you're cho-sen, Morena. Your future is to defeat Malinda and reunite our three kingdoms. *You* are the key. The missing piece of the Queens of Moirai. Remember that." Nico Ecclesiastes faced me proudly. "I pulled you from the dirt myself because they came to me. They told me that you were chosen. Destined to lead Moirai."

The Prince eyed the world below. "I hope you'll be happy here."

I didn't bother telling him what my years had taught me, that happi-ness was an untouchable thing, farther away than the sun for some. That it was meant for others and not me. But I felt a tiny spark of hope—not for happiness, but that I might sew up the fault lines of my heart, that I might grow into someone different than who I had been.

An extraordinarily tall Seraphim greeted us as we crossed the threshold and entered an interior courtyard full of roses and a white fountain. "We welcome you to The Epiphany, descendant of Atropos."

The Seraphim radiated light like a second sun. I'd never seen anything like it. Over its chocolate-colored chest, face, and arms were swirls and symbols in gold, burned into its very skin. A golden halo ringed around its head unlike any I'd ever seen, punctuated by razor-sharp golden knives. It had four distinct wings, wings of moving beams of light, and its eyes were closed. Not sure what the proper protocol was, I bowed. Seraphim were messengers of the Gods, and I didn't want to insult one.

The Seraphim bowed in response. "I am called Neroli. Allow us to escort you."

"Thank you," I said, reverent.

With the Seraphim as our guide, our group stepped carefully into what seemed like an infinite path upward, stair after stair of polished white marble. Gravity seemed not to apply—at times, the stairs pitched and turned so that when I looked up, there was a sense of no progress at all.

The Prince at my side said nothing, his eyes straight ahead.

"Any last words of advice?" I prompted.

"No." His lips thinned as he shrugged off my hand. He didn't even glance at me, and I felt a twinge of answering worry. He was acting so strangely. Almost as if nothing had happened, as if he were angry at someone —

We continued to climb the stairs.

I expected to be exhausted, but instead, with every step, I became stronger. My scalp tingled, and I touched my face to see if my nose was different. My face fattened, my lips reddened, and my thin frame filled out. The castle healed the slights of a lifetime, and by the time we reached the throne room, I no longer looked like the half-starved girl I had been at the bottom.

Neroli brought us to a set of tall, ivory doors wrapped in gold framing. "They are here, waiting."

I dipped my chin. "Thank you."

The doors opened unaided by any hand, revealing a room unlike any I'd ever imagined. On each side, there were seven pillars, each stone carved in exquisite relief of the Queens—as girls, as women, with clothes, nude. To my left, the west, was water, an enormous waterfall falling straight past and crashing onto the rocks below it. The floor nearest to the falls had moss sprinkled with small white flowers. To my right was the sky—no walls, no banisters, just the raw edge of the stones and a very long fall through the clouds.

One of the women stood. "You should see it on a foggy day. Or when the sun rises." Clad in Lachesis blue, her azure eyes were such a light color they mirrored the sky. She was small-boned with a delicate face, and her caramel brown hair fell gently around her shoulders. She wore no jewels, and her sapphire gown was unadorned. She was every inch an innocent maiden, the kind that heroes sacrificed themselves for. Vitess was, in fact, nothing like the all-powerful Fate I'd imagined—instead, the controller of time was short, childlike, doll-like.

The first Fate was lounging beside her, clad in a fiery red gown. Her dark hair didn't meet her jaw, it was cut short like a soldier. Thick, vicious white scars marred what would have been coppery skin of her face. From wrists to shoulder, her skin was scorched with mage marks: runes and constellations, suns and moons, and *Miserere*—psalms and prayers. The laments of mankind were the sleeves she wore. Her face was angular, her cheekbones blade sharp. She was nothing like the delicate, flowery images dedicated to the Clotho house.

I, Morena, was the third Fate, their missing piece. Two Fates were seated on the silver thrones, and there was still an empty chair—my chair—one meant for the descendant of Atropos.

"Come closer." Vitess unfolded her hand and descended down from her throne. "It's taken much too long for you to arrive." Her voice lilted like a bird melody at sunrise. The controller of time was all softness, not a single hard edge to her... like a dove settling into its nest.

Meanwhile, Serene, the controller of life, rose as if she were a cat unrolling itself from a nap. My gaze flicked to hers, and I was stunned by the challenge in them. She seemed to expect me to steal something she'd just vowed to defend.

"Welcome, Death," drawled Serene, and with sharpened crimson nails, she patted the silver pedestal next to hers, her arms dark with mage marks. "We've saved you a seat."

CHAPTER 14

---◆○◆---

As our eyes met, there was a violent boom, and a crack of lightning whipped through the sky. Like a coward, I ducked at the sound.

"See?" Serene said with a smirk. "Your presence completes the Three Fates. All our powers are amplified now."

Vitess must have sensed my discomfort because she smoothed over the moment by standing. "Please," she said warmly, "join us."

I opened my mouth, then closed it again. "They said you sent them," I said to Vitess.

"I did."

"Because I'm chosen?" I couldn't help but ask, and I wanted to hear the rationale directly from her, even if I didn't believe it.

Serene held my gaze. "Do not doubt the words of the Gods." Her voice reverberated through me, fingernails down the blackboard of my soul.

I drew a ragged breath.

"We'll take things slowly," Vitess hastily assured me. "Stay and rest, see the kingdom, get to know us. You can come and go as you please, obviously. You have a receiving chamber, a library, an office, a bedroom, and your own servants..."

It wasn't obvious. Having any freedom, even a little, was more than I was accustomed to. It didn't fit, like a shoe that was too loose.

Vitess led us out of the throne room, and the men trailed behind us, ignored and mostly forgotten. As we walked, she pointed out things that might interest me—vases, art, a gilded bowl over a thousand years old.

Life incarnate, the Fate named Serene trailed her fingers along a banister. Her movements were feline and sensual, like a woman who knows what she wants and flaunts what she has. I immediately decided that I preferred Vitess, the dove, to the tiger at my back.

The other Fates guided me into my new room through pink double doors. The rug under my feet was silver and shades of ivory, and the walls were adorned with rich brocade. Alabaster columns arched over windows facing north, toward my kingdom, and a canopy bed was draped in white fur. Fluffy white pillows and silk sheets were tucked into a pale oak frame. Tall arching windows flanked by glass doors opened onto an ivory balcony. Just beyond the ledge, a waterfall thundered down the cliff. Its lightness was the opposite of my darkness.

Nico, Elijah, and Lorcan filed in behind us and shuffled awkwardly as I stood silently, taking it all in. It was all meant for an actual princess, a golden-haired girl with gowns trimmed in pearls. As I peered around the room, I felt a nagging sense of unworthiness, as if I should ask for something lesser or smaller. Eager to look anywhere except at their faces, I craned my neck upward. Far above the rafters was ... nothing—no sky, no ceiling whatsoever. It was just the glorious vault of the universe darkening to blue, streaked with orange and lavender. A light breeze tugged through my hair, warm and fragrant with the smell of roses.

"It's the Starlight Suite. I knew you'd like it because you dance at night."

Vitess knew I liked to dance? My confusion was plain to see.

"Gods, let her breathe, Vi," Serene interrupted. "She's *never met you,* remember?"

Vitess opened her mouth to reply, then, seeing my expression, closed it. "How rude of me. I apologize."

"What do you expect in return?" I asked.

"For the room?" Vitess was confused. Guileless blue eyes met my black ones. "Nothing. It's yours. You belong here with us; this is your home."

Serene arched a brow and traced a finger down the scar on the left side of her face, watching the two of us interact.

"Well," I said stiffly, "I'm very tired."

"That's fine. You can meet with Elijah later," Vitess said.

My mind slipped back to the clearing. Yes, I could meet up with him again later once I'd gotten my bearings.

"I ask you to forgive us for the deception. Malinda would not let you go with anyone else. I checked every thread, and my other attempts failed..."

I didn't understand. *The other attempts? The deception?* What was she talking about?

"What do you mean?" I asked.

"I could only succeed if Jasper went to The Grace, though he and Elijah both said it was a terrible idea." She glanced backward at the three men, and her pink lips formed a cupid's bow so adorable I felt momentarily transfixed by it.

The new name finally registered. *He and Elijah both said it was a terrible idea. He. Jasper. Who is Jasper?*

"Strange, isn't it, that he's the only one who could persuade Malinda?" Serene leaned against a door jamb, twirling a white rose she must have plucked from somewhere.

Vitess nodded to me. "Jasper retrieved you. Only he could." Vitess glanced toward the group of men behind me. "I owe you a great debt for bringing the third Fate to us."

"Of course," the Prince replied. Flanked by Lorcan and Nico, he was inside my bedroom.

It took me a few moments to realize that the voice answering was *his*. Vitess called him Jasper, and he'd responded, which meant... What did that mean?

"I'm Jasper." He said simply, without fanfare nor apology. "Your noble rescuer."

I didn't understand. But my body must have – my stomach lurched, and my heart clenched painfully. My words stuck in my throat. "You are not Elijah?"

He'd proposed to me. Held my hand. Slept next to me and ate meals with me. I'd twined my life with his and *kissed him,* then given him hundreds of years longer to live. There must be some mistake, a joke. Something I misunderstood. Surely this man hadn't come to The Grace to deceive me.

Jasper didn't hesitate. "This scheme was the only way Malinda would let you leave." His simple honesty took my breath away.

He'd kissed me, and I'd stood with him naked, and he'd *seen me...* The fragile trust I'd been building collapsed into dust.

"You knelt before me and promised me a castle. A family." My hands trembled. Even for someone such as me, who had lived my life imprisoned, violated, and manipulated.. it was a new low. I longed to pull my cloak over my head and walk away, out into the night, where I could be numb and alone in the darkness. But no. I was done doing that.

Instantly, my hurt transformed. All of my shame and embarrassment slipped into a much more comforting emotion—wrath. Without thinking about it, as quick as a snake, I slapped Jasper across the face. Hard.

"How dare you trick me," I hissed, the spitting image of Malinda. I lifted my hand to strike him again, but Jasper caught my wrist.

"Do not do that," he said softly. "I'll let you have the once because I deserve it—but not twice." His gray eyes met mine—forceful, urgent, angry.

I wanted to shred the skin from his bones; it was an unbearable weight of hurt, and I didn't know what to do with it except bury it. I yanked myself away.

Vitess spoke up. "I've tried to get you out of The Grace for years. Unfortunately, your mother is hard to fool and keeps everything closed off—she's never trusted outsiders. Trust me when I say that sending *him* was the only way."

I understood that. But I wasn't done being angry yet—not by far.

"You lied to me too." Nico had known me since I was a child; he'd taught me to read. His deception was hurtful, more personal. "You convinced me to trust him. You said the betrothal was real."

Nico protested. "That *is* real. You *are* decreed to marry Elijah. This just isn't him."

"You might have told me that before I kissed him and slept next to him."

Now I knew precisely why Jasper objected to that so vehemently. A vivid red handprint was across his face from where I'd struck him. Even though I was still furious, I felt a pang of regret and wasn't sure why.

"He slept next to you?" Vitess asked. "He shouldn't have done that."

"He did," I said, my anger suddenly gone, leaving a sense of embarrassment and shame in its wake. *And he saw me naked and kissed me.* Of these things, I said nothing. It was too painful to admit to a room of strangers, to the other Fates who now watched me with pity.

Serene coughed, cutting the silence. "Allow me to introduce my brother—my *twin* brother. This is Jasper, Prince of the House of Clotho."

My gaze darted back to Serene, to her marred face. The same smoky eyes, the same tanned skin, the same dark hair. "So you *are* a prince, but not the one I was promised to."

Seeing my expression, Jasper's lips twisted into a sad smile. "I didn't want to lie to you." He stared at me so intently it felt like a physical touch. "She told me I had to go. What was I supposed to do—leave you in the tower to rot?"

He jerked his chin at Vitess. "Ask her."

My stomach clenched and my mouth watered, like I might throw up. But I shook my head no. "I've heard enough," I told him.

"Well then. Since my mission has been accomplished, I will take my leave, Your Majesties."

Jasper, the Clotho Prince, bowed at my back and left. As he walked away, his boots were whisper-quiet on the marble floors.

It was impossible not to get lost in The Epiphany. Every corridor was the same—endless windows, marble, and sky. I kept a hand on the wall, my hand trailing along, trying to track the twists and turns but almost immediately realizing that I was utterly lost. Meanwhile, every time I drew too close to an edge, I peered down the side of the mountain, worried that I'd stumble and fall through. The wind gusted at my face, lifting tendrils of my hair.

This particular corridor was more of a bridge than a hallway—no art decorated its walls, not so much as a stick of furniture detracted from the views of the valley. Outside the dozens of arched windows, the sky was bright blue, and beyond, I could see the lavender mountains of The Veil. To my right, a waterfall trickled down the mountainside.

Servants periodically passed me, each with a deep bow, but no one spoke to me. Ahead, I heard voices—male, arguing—and immediately identified one of them as Jasper. *The liar.*

I ran, desperate to find a place to hide. I didn't want him to see me, and I had no interest in talking to him. Thankfully, I spotted a slender indigo door tucked into a corner. I dived inside, briefly noting the thirteen-pointed bronze star emblazoned into it.

Immediately, I felt the heat—the air in this room was warm, much more than any other, and sweat beaded at my temples. It was a tight, winding passageway with stairs descending in a spiral. Every ten feet or so was a small candle tucked into an alcove. It reminded me of corridors at The Grace—crudely carved, jagged edges everywhere, with barely room enough for one person.

Gods, I hope this isn't a dungeon.

I ducked my head to keep it from slamming into the ceiling. The passageway opened into a cavern with a pool at its center, steaming and turquoise. Sitting on a stone in the center, like Venus arising from her shell, was Vitess. "You're late," she said.

We definitely had not agreed to meet there and certainly hadn't discussed a time. I sat on one of the rock outcroppings, unsure what to expect.

Vitess casually rubbed her hands across her small belly. Her nipples were pert and light pink. Completely naked, her long brown hair snaked over her breasts and pale skin, falling nearly to her waist. "Do you know why I tried so hard to rescue you?"

"No," I admitted. "I don't know why."

"I'm sure Nico's told you. He's not lying—you're the one who will reunite Moirai and the one who will usher in a new age of harmony. Without you, we will all remain false, unbalanced, broken."

I steadfastly kept my eyes on my hands, on the walls of the cave, on anywhere but her. "I just don't see how that could be true."

"I don't understand either, but we do not always have to understand to know the right course of action."

"Futures can change. You changed my future to get me here. So it might not be me."

Vitess blinked up at the ceiling. "If it makes you feel any better, you can bend futures to your will with enough time and effort."

Good, because that's what you'll need to do. I studied the stones between my feet. "I haven't felt able to change much all these years. It seems you and Serene have more luck with that."

"You can't slay a monster without becoming one," she said softly. "So it was not enough."

I had no desire to be the demigod of Death. I didn't want to be a killer. I didn't want to be anything like Malinda. I'd already spent too long as her assassin. "I would undo it if I could," I said in a small voice.

"You may find abandoning both your past and your destiny an impossible dream." She looked as if she were in pain. "It took a long time to convince Elijah—he was adamantly opposed to any interference. Yet he longed for his other half. So to hear that his soulmate was locked in The Grace... Since that day, he's thought of little else except how to get you here and begin his future with you."

I stood and paced the room, and my silver gown dragged across the stones. Vitess trod water in the dark, silent.

"Why are you telling me this?" I said finally.

"Because love makes a mockery of our principles. Every timetime. You aren't ready to face your mother, yet we have no choice. Malinda is a poison, a curse on Moirai, and must be stopped. What she did to you and your siblings was only the beginning—I have seen the future and the destruction she brings."

"Then make me ready," I insisted.

The second Fate rolled her eyes. "I can't, only you can. You still think it's *you* killing people—you don't know who or what you are, *still*, after all this time."

I leaned forward and put my elbows on my knees. "I'm Death. I know that."

"No, you don't. You think you're *Morena Atropos,* the lonely girl who grew up in a tower." Vitess stood in the water and put her hands on her hips, staring me down. "You think you have a brother and a sister. You fundamentally misunderstand *what* you are."

"Now you're starting to sound like my mother."

Vitess gritted her teeth. She resembled Venus, but the much angrier version—when she arose to discover that her dream was destroyed and her beloved gone.

"You're Death, yet you think you need a blade to kill someone. You think you need to learn to throw a punch. There's enough poison in your veins to kill every person in Moirai, every beast on Earth, and then you'd still have time before lunch to wipe out all the Gods of Olympus... Yet you let Malinda keep you like a pet."

"What was I supposed to do?"

"Kill her." The controller of time was emotionless as she said the words.

"If it was that simple, I would have."

Vitess sighed. "Soon, Cullen will be on our doorstep. And while there are many endings and chances, as far as I have seen ... we lose. If you don't change, if you don't embrace your path... we lose."

The dripping of water was uncomfortably loud.

"If I'm me, and you're you, just as we are right now, we're doomed." Vitess calmly finned through the water. "You'll have to finally admit who and what you are. And I'll have to break a few rules."

"I don't want to be a villain," I said firmly.

"Yet you are. You were born to a villainous house, with a villain for a mother and a worse father. It's bred into the marrow of your bones. And you know what I've learned, Morena? Heroes don't win. Heroes are kind, too gentle, and soft to sacrifice the people they love. Villains will sacrifice everything to win. So even if you don't want to *be* one, if you want to *beat one,* then..." she trailed off.

"If I do that, we'll win? Then life will be good, then I'll be happy?" I struggled to keep my voice even, to prevent it from faltering.

"Mmm," she said, staring up at the roof of the cave. "Fulfill the prophecy: kill Malinda. Amidst all that, I doubt you'd know what to do with such a fragile thing as happiness. Your hands were made for breaking things. We are too powerful for happiness."

When I looked back to the pool, Vitess floated face down in the water, her hair forming dark snakes around her. She reminded me of a drowned woman—of Taliesin and Arabella, and in the back of my mind, like a grey moth in a gray room, I felt a whisper of her impending death. This Fate, the controller of Time, would die. And I would be there.

It was well past time to go back to my room. I didn't want to know any more.

As I began to ascend the stairs, Vitess called after me. "All the versions of us exist on millions of paths we might have taken. We don't know what we'll choose, and we don't know what choices we have. But seeing what you could have, should have, or how it might have been—that drives a woman mad."

I gazed back at her. "I've been mad my whole life," I said softly. "And that's never made any difference."

CHAPTER 15

———◆○◆———

Moonlight quietly fell through the open window. Ivory roses swayed in the breeze.

My mood was pensive as I flexed my fingers in the water, swishing it about—my new bedroom came with its own personal bathing pool, a pale blue room with soaring ceilings and gilded detailing, including statues of cherubs with smiling faces. In the center, a fountain tinkled, each of its tiers overflowing with red rose petals, and in the corners, ivory candles burned.

It was so different from my life before, where I'd dunked myself in a banged-up tin tub scarcely big enough for a child.

I curled my knees to my chest and sighed. If Vitess was to be believed, my struggles were far from over. While I'd hoped to simply forget Malinda's existence, she would come *here*—dooming my new life. Of course, with the power of Three Fates, instead of acting alone, we could stop her. They were the key—and while working with them, we would reunite Moirai.

My thoughts drifted back to Jasper, the fraud I'd kissed and slept next to, the man I'd come to trust. I understood why he had to lie to Malinda, but why had he continued to lie even after we'd left? It was too cruel to lead me on, to make me believe he cared.

Stupid.

I stared at the water. I tilted my left hand over, filling it with inky darkness—a handful of violence, drawing all the shadows from the room into my palm.

If only I didn't feel so humiliated. If only I'd seen through the lies, if I'd remained as cold as new-fallen snow instead of throwing myself at him, desperate for attention, craving touch, wanting someone to hold. It felt natural when he kissed me. It felt like he saw me like he genuinely wanted me, and when he'd held me in the clearing—

...it felt like all the locked doors were open, and I could run through them, like sunlight, warmth, and green grass.

I knew it was only because I'd never been out of the tower. I'd never been kissed before. So, of course, I naively believed. I'd fallen for the first man to cross my path, like a fool. I squeezed my fist closed, and the blackness vanished, absorbed into my skin like the poison it was.

It was a small magic. I would need something much stronger if I was facing Malinda. Vitess was right - I needed help understanding my powers and more practice. I didn't know my limits, I didn't know how to be precise with them, I couldn't manipulate them as thoroughly as I would need to. The books could teach only so far; the rest would be simply doing.

"I'm Death, and one of the Fates, certainly *wishing people dead* should always work, "I muttered. Yet when I'd tried to kill Malinda, I'd failed.

After the bath, I donned a soft gray gown and combed every knot from my hair. The face that looked back in the mirror so closely resembled Malinda's that I stuck my tongue out at her.

My stomach rumbled loudly. If I wanted food, I'd have to go exploring. Slipping out into the corridor, I wondered just how many people lived here in The Epiphany and if there was any likelihood that I would see others now that the sun was up. As I walked, I noticed the marble floors were shiny, slick as glass, and every hall smelled like lemon and rose.

I found the kitchen between two cavernous dining rooms, its pantries, and surfaces crowded with food—table after table, lined up under the arched stone windows. I filled a plate with strawberry tarts. Chewing a hunk of bread as I browsed the dishes, I spied a large crystal carafe. I sniffed it—was this the famed summer wine of the Fae?

Whatever it was, the golden liquid smelled like honey and old trees. I poured myself a small cup and drank it down quickly. "Mmm," I moaned and poured another. A pleasantly warm sensation spread in my throat, down to my belly.

It took the edges away from my thinking, remembering the humiliation in the throne room hurt a little less with each swallow.

I continued to drink as I wandered the room, inspecting the vases and canisters, fruits that stank, and those that smelled of vanilla and exotic spices that made my tongue buzz. I ate here and there, but mostly, I drank.

I sat down at the large oak table and poured myself another. It was there that the man found me halfway through a bowl of winter berries, holding a half loaf of bread, various cups scattered around me where I'd sampled their stores.

"Morena?" he asked as he stepped through the door, the soft light of day bathing him in a halo.

"In the flesh," I laughed. "Come and eat." The whole room twinkled like stars, wild and delightful. I stood, and crumbs rained down from the folds of my bodice.

Swaying on my feet, I studied him. "Are you Elijah—the real one? You must be. You look like Vitess. Nothing like the handsome devil who came to Kinver'i."

He put out a hand to steady me. "You think Jasper is handsome?"

Yes. I leaned close. "No. He's a terrible bastard. Are you the jealous type?"

"Should I be?" he asked, giving a small lopsided smile.

I tipped my head back toward the heavens, expecting the open sky of my bedroom—I must be dreaming this. But there was only his face I saw.

Aquatic eyes, chestnut hair. His mouth was serious, and his face was a study in hard angles. He seemed as if he might chastise me, but I was strangely unafraid. Instead, I leaned into his arms, a reed in the wind. I felt full of light and beauty, warm and spinning. I squeezed my hands on his biceps, marveling at the muscles underneath.

Real. I'm not dreaming.

"Your jaw is too pointed." Brazen, I traced my finger down his nose. It was straight like a blade, hawkish. He was handsome in a ruthless way, and I sensed power under his skin that was somehow familiar.

"You're drunk," he said, peering down into my face. He smiled at me—unguarded—and his face was transformed when he smiled. It was only when he smiled that he resembled his sister.

"It *is* you, "I murmured. "The real Elijah Lachesis."

"It is," he confirmed.

Feeling a bit tipsy, I shifted on my feet to correct the sense of being off-balance. And without speaking or signaling, Elijah also moved—graceful, anticipating my movements. It was an understated, simple moment, but it felt like the first steps to a dance. Taking a deep breath, I swayed again in his arms, testing. And again, he responded with a fluid, accommodating, balancing move of his own.

We're dancing.

And I wasn't Death or a Fate. No chains, no death, no *killing,* just the two of us slow-dancing in the kitchen.

I'm hallucinating this entire thing. I'm lonely, and I've drunk too much wine. The Cullen are already here; I'm dead, and this is Heaven.

"I thought I'd find you in the rose garden," he said, continuing to sway with me in his arms. "I didn't imagine you'd be gorging yourself in the larder, drunk on Fae wine."

I chuckled drily and leaned my forehead against his chest. He rested his chin atop my head, and we stilled. I inhaled and exhaled, his scent caressing me. His was a scent I understood and knew well, the smell of water and stone and evergreen. His voice matched it—deep and calm, like a lake in the dark.

"It's quiet here," he said.

"I wouldn't like it if there was too much noise and people around." I pressed my cheek to his heart. "I worry if others are too near."

"Because you might hurt them?"

"Yes."

His hand caressed my back, along my spine, where the mage marks tattooed underneath trembled in response to his touch. "I'm sorry Jasper confused you. It was the only way. But please know I wanted to come for you myself."

"I forgive you," I mumbled, suddenly sleepy, like a kitten in the sunshine.

His voice held a smile that I could see with my eyes closed. "This is not what I thought would happen when I came to the kitchen."

I wanted to rest in the circle of his arms and sleep. I wanted to lay my face against his heart and hear its steady beating. Comforting. Constant. Even though we'd just met, the man in my arms felt familiar somehow, like a book I'd read before, its pages well-loved and worn. It disarmed me completely.

"Will you stay?" I couldn't say whether the drink or his presence made me ask.

"With you?" he asked. "In your room?"

I nodded, my face still hidden against his chest. My vision was blurry, and I felt myself starting to drift off—his warmth, his calming scent luring me into comfort. "I've been lonely," I admitted.

"Since you arrived?" He studied me, surprised.

"Since always." It was true. Even with my siblings, I'd always felt separate, apart somehow. I joined in their games and storytelling, but my heart hadn't been in it because I was different. Fate-marked, a monster underneath, whereas they were not.

"I'm going to take you to bed," he warned.

"Wonderful," I said, nuzzling my face into his shoulder as he effortlessly lifted me from under the knees.

"I'm dreaming," I mumbled as he carried me to my room. "It's not real."

"It seems real to me."

He settled me into the bed, then pulled the white silken sheets to my chin. I stared up into the blue sky beyond the white canopy, the sun blinding me—it was noon, and he was putting me to bed drunk. Our eyes met.

Carefully, as if the slightest movement might disturb me, he lay down next to me on top of the coverlet, then rolled to his side, studying my face. If he judged me, if he thought I was terrible, it didn't show. So whether it was a dream or delusion—I was grateful.

"Don't leave me," I mumbled as my eyelids slipped closed.

"I swear it." Then Elijah Aurelian, the true Prince of the House of Lachesis, watched me and waited.

"Mama, Vitess wouldn't let me wear the pink dress!"

A miniature of Elijah stomped her foot and tugged at her mother's dark blue sleeve. His family was seated around a large dining table, and we were having breakfast. I, Death incarnate and descendant of Atropos, sat mute with disbelief.

I was having breakfast with a family. *My* new family.

I glanced over at Elijah, who gave me a small conspirator's smile. I'd woken up that morning with a searing hangover and found him asleep in my bed, his arm thrown over me. I'd stayed stone-still for an hour, counting his breaths, acclimating to the strange feeling of being held. When his eyes finally opened, the first thing he'd asked was if I wanted to go to breakfast with him.

I couldn't even look at him without blushing like a fool.

"Archae, please take your seat. You know the purple is just as lovely." His mother's sweet words were met with a scowl.

Silas, his father, leaned forward to address his daughter. "Leave your mother be. Can't you see she's speaking to someone?" Elijah's father was an Ouroboros—a primordial snake and shapeshifter—beings who notoriously should not be trusted. I recognized his darkness despite the kindness of his voice, a power that felt similar to my own, yet different.

Archie's little lips curled in a pout, and she stuck out her tongue. The expression so reminded me of Arabella that my heart ached. Everyone helped themselves while their mother and father encouraged Archae to cheer up.

"What are their abilities?" I asked politely of the twin girls who now conspired, heads bent close together, at the other end of the table.

"Archae has limited, selective magic—she can touch a sapling and make a hundred years pass for just that tree. Enid is unmagical, which was lucky."

"Oh?" I smeared jam on a roll. How strange that the girl Enid had no magic, and Alexis called her *lucky*. It was the complete opposite of Malinda.

Alexis frowned. "Carin is young—too young to know what she is doing and too young to have much control. She has already accidentally killed people with her powers."

I blinked at the rebuke in her tone. "She's only a baby—"

"Just as Vitess was when her Fated powers came."

Seated across the table, Vitess leaned forward and dropped her voice to a whisper, giving the words more gravity. "Mother believes that the Fates were too powerful. That we should be mindful of the will of the gods and not use our powers too much."

She'd used her powers to rescue me. Her mother must not have known that.

"What do you think?" Alexis asked.

"Well. I don't know much about the will of the Gods. But if Nyx did not want us to have powers, she should not have granted them." I saw the distaste in her face. "Of course, I don't care much for killing, so it's easy to avoid using mine."

"But you've killed before. Many times." Alexis' smile was sharp, the finest point of an icicle.

"Mother. Leave her be," Elijah smoothly intervened. "She's Death, and Malinda raised her. Surely you don't think she spent nineteen years playing the harp and painting watercolors?" Although his words were friendly, his tone wasn't.

Silas let out a dark laugh. "My son is protective of what's his. He's waited a long time for your arrival."

Alexis added spice to her tea and stirred it with a golden spoon. "I was telling Vitess that we ought to schedule a ball, a celebration for the kingdom. It's the first time in over a thousand years that the Three Fates are together at The Epiphany."

I had no opinion about such things, so I nodded and said the correct things at the appropriate times.

"How are you feeling about your betrothal?" Vitess asked.

I stammered a reply. "We are getting to know each other." My face felt like it was on fire. Down the table, Elijah covered his mouth with a napkin, hiding his laugh. I doubted he wanted to tell her about how I'd drunkenly accosted him, then invited him into my bed last night.

Desperate to change the subject, I picked at my food. "Could you tell me about my parents? Do you know anything about them or my birth?"

"It was no accident they ended up together... the marriage of your father, Melchior, was much discussed. There were a great many who were interested in being his wife, and your mother was the daughter of a Fae farmer."

Silas was equally happy to tell me their story. "Of course, Malinda had something the others didn't—not only could she speak to the dead, she loved him. All those presented were interested in his castle and his crown." Elijah's father paused, then continued meaningfully. "But Malinda just wanted to kiss him, to sit at his feet. She hung on his every word."

They could have announced that my mother kept a stable of pet slugs, saddled and bred, and I would have been less surprised. I couldn't imagine Malinda loving anything, especially not the man she had brutally murdered.

"What happened?" I was riveted. "Why did she kill him?"

Alexis' expression darkened as she answered. "We don't know. Though I imagine marriage became much more difficult after he stole her heart."

I thought back to Malinda's rooms, to the bronze box inside her ribs. My *father* had been the one to take her heart? Perhaps this was the price of love—having your heart stolen. I dared a glance at my betrothed. "I'd always assumed my father was innocent."

"No." Silas looked at me with pity. "As bad as she seems, Malinda was the better half of your parents."

It was the first time I'd had even a speck of pity for my mother. But it was too hard to reconcile. I couldn't imagine Malinda as anything other than a tyrant. She hadn't taken my heart, but she'd definitely broken it. Everything I cared about, she ripped apart to rebuild me into the *thing* I was now.

"I only knew a monster, the Queen of the Blood Throne. She's never been anything else to me."

"There are people you could speak to, people who knew her," Alexis said.

"I'm not interested." I placed my fork down on the table, no longer hungry. "She murdered my brother. She imprisoned us for more than a decade. My sister killed herself."

Alexis frowned, a wrinkle forming between her eyebrows. Elijah, now holding a sleeping baby, Carin, rubbed his chin on her hair and said nothing. Only Vitess met my eyes, her irises so brightly blue it felt like they burned a hole into mine.

"Nevertheless," Elijah's mother finally said, "I'd like to have a wedding immediately. Within a few weeks?"

"That sounds nice," I muttered, forcing myself to look enthusiastic.

Elijah observed my expression and then stood. "That reminds me—I have one last gift for Morena. I'll just go and get it."

Another wedding gift? It took a moment for me to realize that he must have sent those gifts with Jasper—that they had come from him, even if he hadn't been delivering them.

A few minutes later, a side door in the dining room popped open, and Elijah re-entered with a blond man striding behind him. The man was solid, square-faced, and golden. He looked like he could be a farmer's son, with tawny, tanned skin and calloused hands, cuts on them visible. He might be a soldier—he had cuts on his hands and scars on his forearms, like one who practiced swordplay often, and he wore leather gauntlets to guard his wrists. But his hair was too long, jaw-length, and tucked behind his ears. His eyes were rich green, warm, and crinkled at the corners.

He studied me, a look of mild surprise crossing his face. "It's me," he said after a long hesitation.

His face wasn't familiar, and I couldn't recall ever meeting him. Had he lived in the village near The Grace? Had I killed someone he loved? I searched my memory for any clue to his identity.

But no name, no face, no memory came. He took a step closer, waiting for a hint of recognition. It was as if some of my memory had been erased, leaving only blankness.

"Don't you remember?" He gave a nervous, lopsided smile.

"I don't think so." I turned to Elijah. "Have you brought me a bodyguard?"

"Ask him," he said. "His soul."

He knows what I can do.

My gaze flicked back to the golden stranger. *Who are you?*

The answer was so clear.

My chair fell backward onto the floor.

The dark, the Cullen, the escape, every vivid memory washed over me as I lurched into the stranger's arms. "But you died. You drowned. You went under, and you never came back—"

Gone was the shy, gangly boy I'd snuggled and made up stories for. In his place was a man, a stranger, muscles bunched under his tunic, his chest a solid weight against mine. Taliesin was taller, heavier, thicker. I wouldn't have recognized him if I'd passed him in a crowd.

I touched his cheeks. "You're alive," I said, my voice full of wonder.

"I've missed you." My brother cleared his throat, his voice thick with emotion. "You have no idea how much."

I pulled him to me for another fierce hug. "Thank the Gods."

As we continued to clasp each other, Taliesin told his story to me. His escape from Malinda's Cullen, the year he'd spent with Peregrin, the leader of the Mer. "One of the Mer came to my aid when I lost consciousness and brought me south. Then, we came to meet Elijah and Vitess, Jasper and Serene. I decided to stay with them, to return to land." He shook his head. "We've been waiting for you for so long."

"I can never repay you," I said to Vitess and Elijah, both of whom watched us closely. "but damned if I won't try."

"I told them that, too." Taliesin pulled me in for another hug.

CHAPTER 16

E very citizen in the village was invited to the Welcome Ball. Alexis
sent a flowing, white, one-shouldered gown and a crown to accompany it. Vitess and Serene, as I understood it, would wear white also,
as befitted our roles as the Three Fates.

Gossamer and silk clung to my every curve, even though I had few to
speak of. The dress left my back and most of my arms bare—a goddess
gown. Maids fashioned my hair into golden waves and a swirling crown
of black sapphires for my head.

Not bad for a baby pulled from the snow, I thought as I examined
myself in the mirror. I was nearly unrecognizable.

My maid Ygrainne lined my eyes with kohl and brown, then darkened
my lashes. "Do I have to go?" I said balefully.

Ygrainne, shocked by my reluctance, clucked her tongue.

"In case you're worried – you could show up wrapped in horsehair,
and he'd still think you were beautiful." Serene spoke from the doorway.
"That being said, you don't look too bad."

She, herself, was beautiful. Her black cropped hair was slicked back,
and her white outfit was far from a traditional gown. Instead, it was a
set—a gossamer and gauze concoction that exposed her entire stomach,
the skirt billowing and flowing down to her bare feet, with a slit that
went all the way up her thigh. Her crown was emeralds and gold, fashioned to look like olive leaves. The expression on her face, her demeanor,

everything about her... Serene was a queen, body, and soul. We might be dressed alike, but that was where our similarities ended.

"Tally sent me to make sure that you actually show up. I'm your escort." Serene held my door open. "We're already fashionably late."

As we made our way down the hallway, I felt as if I had been transported to another world. The walls were covered in lush greenery, vines, and leaves winding their way up the marble pillars. A tiger strolled across our path ridden by a monkey. Overhead, a trio of colorful parrots squawked, and the air was thick with the scent of tropical flowers.

"A jungle theme?"

She smirked. "It was the least amount of effort."

We paused at the closed doors of the ballroom, where two Seraphim flanked its doors. I could hear the din from people gathered inside.

"Don't you two look stunning?" Vitess said graciously as she stepped into place, splitting Serene and me apart and taking her spot as the second Fate.

Welcome, my queens, your guests have been anxiously awaiting your arrival. The Seraphim's voice boomed in my head.

This was the first time our citizens would see us together, the Queens of Moirai, the Three Fates. One day, they would tell their grandchildren about this night. The trio of us, clad in white, were the answer to their prayers, goddesses restored.

The Seraphim moved in unison, undulated in beams of light as they opened the doors. We stepped forward as the staircase descended before us, revealing a massive crowd.

The grand ballroom of The Epiphany was a masterpiece of glass and marble, perched like a diamond in the clouds. The walls were adorned with intricate carvings and frescoes, and the arched windows glittered in the light of the chandeliers. The ceiling was a work of art, with archangels and cherubs gazing down on the guests with their wings outstretched. The air was scented with roses and jasmine, an intoxicating smell that made my head spin.

At the top of the stairs, we paused. The crowd fell silent.

"I thought it would be a *small* party, "I muttered.

In response, Vitess took my hand, holding me in place as every bone in my body begged me to flee.

"You were raised in a castle full of Cullen. "Serene whispered from the side of her mouth. "Was that so much easier to face than a room of citizens?"

Neroli announced us, using words like *The Fates. The Goddesses. Destiny. Restoration.* Much to my horror, the citizens began to kneel, then bow, pressing their foreheads to the floor. Their hopes beat at me like birds set free.

Vitess, grabbing Serene's hand as well, began to pull us down the stairs. She was seemingly unaffected by the crowd worshiping below us—a perfect queen for the citizens of Moirai.

The staircase seemed endless, and I prayed I wouldn't trip and drag us all down. The citizens remained bowed, but I saw the awe in their faces as we stepped onto the ballroom floor and made our way to the dais.

Graceful as ever, Vitess stood in front of the middle seat of the throne. I took my place on her left and Serene on her right. All eyes were on us as Vitess spoke.

"Citizens of Moirai, we have gathered today to celebrate." Her sweet voice echoed across the ballroom. "The third Fate, Morena, of the House of Atropos, has come to The Epiphany. With Life, Death, and Time once again reunited, we will restore Moirai to its former glory, bringing peace and harmony to all its people."

As if given an invisible cue, a servant rushed forward with goblets for us. Taking hers, Vitess raised it in the air. "To Moirai!" she announced as the citizens stood and raised their glasses.

"To Moirai and to the Fates!" someone shouted from the crowd.

"To the Fates!" the people echoed in unison, the ground rumbling from the noise.

Everyone tipped up their goblets, and I rushed to do the same. Something putrid touched my tongue, and I tried not to make a face as I swallowed.

The music started to play again, and the ballroom buzzed excitedly. I sat on the throne, looking at Serene still drinking from her glass.

"That was incredible," I whispered as Vitess leaned toward me.

Her bashful smile lit up her face, and she tucked a piece of hair behind her ear. "They just need hope. And to know that someone cares."

Warmth filled my chest at her words. She was the absolute opposite of Malinda. Soft, kind, gentle – noble. There was hope for Moirai. Especially with the Fates reunited and her as our leader.

"I'm starving," Serene grumbled, ruining the gravity of the moment. "Do you think there's mutton down there?"

Vitess sighed and furrowed her brow. "Of course there is. I knew you would request that." Even irritated, she was so small it was impossible to take her seriously.

Serene smiled at the crowd, her white teeth flashing. "If I must endure the boring conversations all evening, at least I can have great food and wine in my hand." Without waiting for a response, she strode off the dais.

"Do you want to go meet our people?" Vitess asked, her sweet smile beaming.

No. Definitely not. But I could not refuse the hope in her gaze, so I endured the stares, bows, and endless introductions. Everyone wanted to touch me, look at me, speak to me. Mute with anxiety, I met a cluster of Fae nobility and tried to act graciously while trying to remember their names. Vitess, unruffled, didn't even flinch when she saw me wipe my sweaty palms on my skirt.

I longed for a dark corner where I could block out the sounds of the mindless chatter. I clutched at Vitess as if she were a lifeline and plastered a polite smile on my face.

I scanned the room for Elijah. *Where are you?*

Of course, he was nowhere to be found.

I was accosted by foreign and strange sights and smells, rich and decadent and new. Around the banquet room's edges, golden goblets held wines from far-off cities, and enormous plates of meat burdened the tables. Milling about everywhere were beautiful women and handsome young men, with gowns so heavy with jeweled threads that they shone underneath the candlelight like stars.

It completely overwhelmed me, and I felt a nerve in my temple begin to throb.

For diplomacy's sake, I was encouraged to dance with citizens. So I found myself being whirled around, from arm to arm, spun and prodded until I felt so utterly overwhelmed that I thought I might fant. Just as I began to feel panicky, I found myself in a pair of familiar arms.

Jasper's smoky, sweet scent enveloped me like a balm. He looked impossibly handsome and relaxed. He was dressed in red, representing the House of Clotho.

"Enjoying the party?" Jasper asked

"No. I'm not." I looked over his shoulder. Alexis, Silas, and their children were on the stairs, but not Elijah. My betrothed was still not here, and the party was halfway over.

"I've wanted to get you alone to talk since we arrived, but it seems like I never see you," said Jasper.

I'd been avoiding him. If I heard his voice in the halls, I dove into whatever room was nearest.

"What is there possibly to say?"

"I did what I had to do to get you out of there."

"You didn't have to kiss me. You didn't have to touch me, or look at me, or anything else."

"That's true. I shouldn't have. I knew you weren't destined for me." He shrugged. "I was curious. I couldn't let it pass."

"Because it was an opportunity to kiss a Fate? To see me naked?"

"No. I kissed you because I wanted you. Because it felt right. It wasn't... I didn't think it would make a difference."

It might have felt right, but it was definitely wrong. He and I knew that, and so did everyone else involved. Lorcan, Nico, Elijah, Vitess—no one in this entire castle didn't know that Jasper Clotho was not the man for me.

"You still shouldn't have. You are interfering with destiny. You put *my* future in jeopardy, Jasper. I'm trying not to be angry about it, but whenever I think I might forgive the deception, here you are, and..."

...and I can't stop thinking about it.

"I wish you'd leave me alone," I said instead. "What's done is done."

"I believe I'll take over from here," said a smooth voice. "May I have this dance?"

Impeccably dressed in blue, Elijah Lachesis was every bit the charming prince at home in a glass castle.

Yes, please.

I took his arm and felt the silky fabric of his sleeve against my skin. He tugged me away from Jasper, between the marble columns, thick and white, past the flowers and tables of other guests, out into the center of the floor. When he turned to face me and pulled me closer, when his arm wrapped around my waist, it felt as if the entire room stilled. The only sound was the beating of my heart and the distant clink of silverware.

His hands touched my bare skin, and I shivered, quietly willing myself to smile, hold my head high, and not step on his toes.

"Don't be nervous," he murmured, tilting his head as he studied me.

"I'm not," I lied. Though I'd had years of dancing alone in the tower, being this close to him, with every eye on us, was something I was entirely unprepared for.

I needn't have worried. Elijah moved with fluid grace. Ours was a sweeping, slow dance, and even though I barely remembered any of the steps, Elijah quickly covered my hesitation. The look he gave me was intent as if he couldn't believe that I was here, in his arms, touching him. My mouth dried as I stared at him—it was he who looked the part of an immovable god, not I.

I leaned in and rested my head against his chest. "I don't deserve you," I said softly.

"I disagree." He tucked me closer, our bodies aligning, and I realized how strangely wonderful it was to feel small and protected. I'd always been the predator with the weapon in hand, like a dark tower among innocents. With his azure eyes on me, tracking every expression on my face, I felt beautiful. I felt wanted. I felt happy.

The citizens of Moirai watched. Even with music, drink, lights, flowers, and food, nothing in the room was more interesting than the two of us. It was a historic moment; the Prince of Time danced with Death.

As the music drew to a close, Elijah paused and traced his hand up my face. With every eye upon us, he took my chin lightly in his hand. Perfect, controlled, an immaculate prince.

"I'm going to kiss you," he murmured.

"I thought you'd never ask," I replied.

His lips quirked. "I was not asking," he said, lowering his head toward mine.

"It's not every day you can kiss Death and live to talk about it," a male voice quipped in my ear.

Turning, I found myself looking at Nico. A noblewoman and a long-nosed Fae with pickled skin distracted Vitess by asking about the Cullen attack, so she left his side, and we were alone.

"You hungry?" he asked.

At my nod, he tucked my hand against his arm and tugged me away from the many prying eyes and staring citizens.

I hadn't noticed, but I'd gone all day without a meal. With all the stress and work of preparing, meeting, and mingling, I'd simply forgotten to eat. Nico, ever the considerate older brother, led me to a table, encouraged me to pile my plate full to spilling, and then sat next to me as I devoured every last bite. Enormous chandeliers of gold swayed overhead, throwing sparking light onto gigantic vases full of lilies and dark purple vines.

"Lucky is me this night, with Death seated on my right!" A goblin with bare feet and black fingernails slipped into the chair beside me. Meanwhile, Lorcan also took a chair, along with Serene.

"Allow me to introduce Ranae. Ranae here is a connoisseur of rare objects. He's seen them all." Across the table, Serene gave a tight-lipped smile. *Guard yourself,* her eyes instructed me.

The goblin chuckled, and the sound was so high-pitched and sinister that I winced. He smelled like carcasses pulled from a swamp. His teeth were jagged, like broken piano keys. And his stringy black hair was wet, like rotting river weeds. Ranae's nails dragged the table as he picked up the wine goblet.

And I thought I was done with the beasts of hell once I left Kinver'i, I thought, uncharitably.

"You seem to be adjusting well," Lorcan said, considering me.

I made a sound of agreement and continued eating.

As usual, Lorcan was keen to talk, which I did not want to do. Irritatingly, he only seemed to speak in sexual innuendo. Serene didn't mind at all and gamely flattered him.

"Lorcan, as Keeper of Mysteries, guards some of the oldest spellbooks and precious artifacts in all of Moirai," Serene said as Elijah pulled out a chair across from me and gave me a pointed look. "There's no question he can't answer, no truth he cannot reveal."

"For the right price." Lorcan smirked and petted his red beard.

For a Fae lord's price. I suppressed a shudder. I couldn't imagine what sort of price Lorcan might demand, but I knew that I was in no mood to pay it.

"Tell us so we could consider it," Taliesin said as he slid into another empty chair.

"You haven't said what you want to know," Lorcan smirked.

"Malinda." I spoke up a little too loud. "How does she control the Cullen? How does she live on without a heart of her own?"

"Malinda *is* a Cullen. "Lorcan leaned back in his chair. "I'll give you that one for free. Surprised you hadn't already figured it out."

"How can that be?" Jasper asked him. "She does not look like one of the Cullen."

Lorcan responded in verse, rhyming as the Fae tended to do:

"The heart, unwillingly given.

That shall keep a dead man living. Or woman, I suppose."

"So she stays alive because she steals hearts." Taliesin gave me a look. "Because she had Morena steal hearts for her."

Lorcan was pleased that we'd figured out the answer. "Correct."

I sucked in a deep breath. When I'd carried my sister into her room, she'd known exactly how to save Arabella from becoming Cullen. It would have been so easy—I could have saved my sister right then.

All I would need was a heart, unwillingly given, and Arabella would still be alive.

"She's been Cullen since vile Melchior stole

her maiden's heart, and left that hole..."

Lord Lorcan's red hair and beard glinted in the dim light.

"So our mother can speak to Cullen because she is one of them?" Taliesin's shoulders were back, his head high. "That makes her easier to defeat, then. We can drown her or put her on a pyre."

One day, we would do just that. He and I, together. I knew it, saw it, with such sureness that it could only be destiny.

I still had one more question. "Was Malinda one of the Cullen when I was born?"

Lorcan relished the anguish on my face. He opened his mouth to answer, but Elijah touched my shoulder. "Perhaps that is enough for now. He has already given you one answer, and you don't want to owe him for too many."

The Lord of the Fae grinned. "You sure? I can tell you that too—if you have the stomach for it."

I was tempted. I did want to know desperately. "How do you know so much about Malinda," I asked, ignoring Elijah's look of warning.

Lorcan's smile might have undone a thousand women before me, brought them to their knees, and made them willing to give their youth and souls for an answer. "I have her journal."

Her journal.

"You... How...?"

"No more questions." Elijah's voice was firm, and he addressed Lorcan, not me. "And that wasn't a question either." He turned to me. "Later, I will deal with him. If you want, I'll get her journal for you, but you cannot keep owing him. You'll end up enslaved to the Fae, a queen of nothing, before he's through with you."

I licked my lips. "Alright," I said.

Taliesin and Nico looked like they might like to throttle Lorcan, but neither intervened.

As if she could tell I needed a distraction, Serene leaned across the table and spoke. "Dance with me."

I scanned the area around us, terrified to discover that she was, in fact, talking to me. Gone went the hope that she was addressing someone—Elijah, the goblin, anyone—else. "Me?" I asked dumbly. "I don't think so."

Her eyes were molten silver as she held out a hand. "You dance all the time. You can't be nervous."

"I've had my fill," I answered. "I'm tired."

"I just saw you dance with ten people in a row." She jerked her head at the dance floor. "Come on. I want to show you something."

With a sigh, I put my hand into hers. Stiff as a corpse, I let Serene tug me out into the center of the ballroom. All around us, the other guests whispered and stared. As old as they might be, they'd likely never seen one of the Fates up close, and certainly, they'd never seen Life and Death together on a dancefloor.

We both wore white, as was the custom. We both wore crowns, though Serene's was diamond and emerald, while mine was black sapphire. Side by side, of course, we could not be more different—I, tall, pale, and blonde, and Serene, with her jaw-length hair savagely chopped, her face badly scarred.

Every eye in the hall was glued to us, Life and Death, the two halves of the world. As the music began, we circled each other, our gazes locked like adversaries. I matched her steps as best I could, and the guests' long gowns fluttered and twirled around us.

Even the musicians glanced away from their instruments as we drew near, as the tempo increased into something more frantic, primal. Loosened now, we danced and danced, and I lost myself in the beat of the music. I felt full of life, and I laughed as Serene spun me and grasped my hands, both of us grinning.

I didn't want it to end.

Each step brought us closer to each other. The two Fates, Death and Life, in a joyous dance. I felt the runes tattooed along my spine moving, shifting, as we whirled faster and faster. The room felt bright and hot, a blur of color, too fast for me to grasp.

"Call the night," she whispered. "Show our people what you can do."

I did as she demanded.

Come to me... I imagined the darkness. *To us.*

There were gasps from the guests as a thunderclap of cold hit the well-lit ballroom, and tendrils of inky darkness exploded down the walls. Bent nearly backward, I opened my onyx eyes. Overhead, along the silver ceiling where there once were diamond-clad chandeliers, there was nothing but night sky and stars.

Serene and I glowed. Our skin pulsed with light from somewhere I did not understand, as if we'd eaten the sun. My white gown blended into the luminous glow that screamed from my skin.

"And that," she said, her gaze locking with mine, "is who you really are." I laughed, unable to hide my delight.

I held up a hand, shining white, as if I were made of moonbeams.

What a miracle after a lifetime in the dark. I truly am a child of Nyx.

Then day broke, a sun beaming through the darkness overhead, and fire fanned out from the center of the sun. That part—the fire, the light, the warmth—was purely Serene.

She grinned down at me. "Told you you wanted to dance."

"You were right," I acknowledged as the audience broke into applause. "Now, I won't want to dance with anyone else." It was the first time I felt a bond between the two of us, and it felt good—better than good. It felt like we might like each other.

We righted ourselves, and Serene gave the room a deep curtsy and a self-satisfied smile. I awkwardly did the same, then followed her off the dance floor and over to a corner where we could breathe and regroup.

"Must you always be such a show-off?" Vitess approached the two of us and then handed me a goblet of cold water, which I gulped gratefully.

Serene smirked, sultry. "Yes? I absolutely live for these moments."

"I don't understand how you did that," I said, turning toward Serene. "How did you make me do that?"

"Your powers are amplified when you're together."

Jasper slipped up next to me, his shoulder nearly touching mine. Nico and Taliesin followed.

Vitess hurried to fill the awkward silence. "You didn't know you could claim the night?"

"Serene didn't know either," Nico assured me. "It was a lucky guess."

"I'm never that lucky," Serene protested. "I knew we could do it."

"How would you know?" Taliesin asked while still panting from his last dance.

"Because I can summon the dawn." Serene ran her hand through her cropped hair. "And other things..." she licked her red lips. "Are you game to try again?"

"Is it dangerous?" I asked and raised an eyebrow.

"No. Well ... I don't know." Serene was unfazed. "But we're immortal."

Nico made a face. "I don't want to discover what happens when you fail."

Serene tilted her head, her dark hair falling forward along her jawline, her expression indignant. "Who said we'd fail?"

"We should try to combine our powers in other ways," Vitess said.

Jasper seemed shocked. "You aren't talking about a blood bond, are you? Because you know those are forbidden."

Serene smiled suggestively. "You *know* how I feel about things being forbidden."

"Why are they forbidden?" I asked idly, not really caring about the answer. I'd shed plenty of blood to know that it was useless stuff. The white goddess gown itched, and the combs of my crown dug into my scalp.

"It's for marriage bonds *only,* "Vitess told me. "But plenty of people…" She lowered her voice when she noticed Jasper glaring. "People do it anyway."

I supposed this meant that, eventually, I'd be blood-bound to Elijah, though no one seemed willing to say that directly. Overhead, the night sky was fading, and the lights of the diamond chandeliers were beginning to show through the darkness.

Surely, he saw me call the night. Surely, he was impressed.

My eyes scanned the crowd, seeking my betrothed, but he'd slipped away like the night Serene had banished.

CHAPTER 17

W hen I finally returned to my room, the sun was rising. I went straight to the balcony. My head was pounding, my skin was too hot, and my stomach churned from all the strange food and drink. I'd been paraded around the ballroom all night, a painted doll with a crown perched upon my unworthy head. Exhausted, I wondered how in the seven hells the other Fates managed to live a life where these events were normal.

It took me a few seconds to realize someone was knocking at my door. Depressed, and less than enthusiastic about having a visitor, I yanked it open only to find Elijah standing in the hall.

"Hello," he said gravely.

From floor-to-ceiling windows on the far side of the corridor, the sun cast a halo on his chestnut-colored hair. Behind him was a vast expanse of sky. He was breathtaking—all the hard lines of his face; the blazing blue eyes like slices of sapphire. The only soft thing about him were his lips, which were much too full for a man.

"What are you doing here?" My tone was surprised. "Doesn't anyone ever sleep in this castle?"

His face was a mix of appreciation and nervousness. "You said it was lonely."

Fully prepared to disarm me, Elijah held up an armful of books. "I thought we could read together." He noted my feet, shoeless, my tired expression. "Talk ... or sit together. Either or. Whatever you'd prefer."

Foolishly pleased that he remembered anything I'd said during my drunken ramblings, I opened the door wider. "Come in."

I watched as he spread a Lachesis blue blanket under the large cherry-blossom tree on my balcony, where the light pink flowers covered the grass and the waterfall surged down the mountainside. It was bound to be another beautiful day, and with every breath I smelled greenery and springtime.

I'd built up a list of things to talk to him about. I'd practiced asking about his hobbies, conversational tidbits, and witty banter. But when I looked at him, I found every word was wiped clean– I couldn't remember any of it. I couldn't tell if that was because he was intimidating, I was nervous, or if I was just too exhausted by the ball. So for a long time, we didn't speak; simply being next to each other was enough. Occasionally, I felt his eyes on me, but whenever I glanced over, he was reading, making me wonder if I'd imagined it. He flipped the pages with sure fingers, careful not to bend or crease the delicate paper. His gaze traveled the page, diligent, slow. The sweep of his long, dark eyelashes against his cheek reminded me of black velvet. Elegant. Clean.

Like me, Elijah was a person accustomed to long silences, a person who mistrusted words. But unlike me, he owned the space instead of retreating into it. He was not quiet because he was shy; he was quiet because he was disciplined with words. Something about Elijah reminded me of a drawing I'd seen long ago, a lake in a shadowy glade, flat and the color of ink.

I found myself waiting, watching his lips and willing him to speak. "What are you thinking?" I asked.

"I imagined you just like this when I chose this room. On the balcony, with the flowers." When he spoke, it was as if he were revealing something important, like he'd given equal thought to even the blank spaces between his words.

His gaze lingered on my body, my goddess gown. "Of course, I thought you'd wear nothing but black."

"I'm not sure I've ever worn white before," I admitted.

"You and I slept there, under the stars, in that bed." He studied the open balcony doors. "I still can't believe it."

Nor could I. But the idea of doing it again sounded wonderful. I slept well next to him, without any dreams to haunt me. And I felt so incredibly tired that I didn't know how I'd manage to make it to lunch without falling over. *Perhaps we could do that again,* I thought. *Lay down together.*

"You seem to know so much about me," I said.

"I do, yes."

"What's my favorite color? Food? Flower?" Surely he couldn't know everything.

"Daffodils, bread... black. You dance when you can't sleep. Your mother is cruel, and made you watch while your younger brother drowned. Your sister killed herself. You like melon and winter berry, but not lemon. Nico rescued you when you were a baby from the killing fields, and your back is mage-marked. No one has ever told me your favorite book. You've been kissed once in your life, by my best friend while he pretended to be me." He ticked items off as if they were a list.

It might have been the most he'd ever spoken to me. My mouth fell open. "How do you...?"

"I pay people to tell me your secrets." Elijah was unapologetic.

*Pay them? W*ho might he have paid to spy on me?

"You're not a hobby, Morena. You're my destiny, my wife. I might have paid more, if I'd known how I would feel the first time I saw you."

"Oh," I said, my head spinning. It wasn't as if I had secrets—my life was confined to one room.

He paused, weighing his words. "I, too, have woken with blood across my face like a curtain, unsure what I've done. I understand you." The quiet assurance he offered me was astounding. I'd never had that before. To know that someone knew what I'd done, and didn't judge me for it, or blame me, or hate me... not even Arabella had offered that kind of safety.

I lifted my eyes to his. "Really?"

Our eyes met and held and held and held.

"I swear." He didn't touch me, but Elijah's bright blue gaze felt warm on my skin.

Trying to lighten the moment, I forced myself to take a joking tone. "You're too handsome to marry me... too intimidating."

"You might try looking in a mirror." He reached forward, our lips just breaths apart, and twirled a strand of my blonde hair around his finger. "And I'm not marrying you because you're pretty."

Every nerve responded to the tone of his voice, my body tightening like a bowstring.

"Then why are you?" It was difficult to breathe.

"Because I want you." It was a simple statement, and the intensity of his scrutiny made me nervous.

I averted my gaze, toward the riot of white roses and the water cascading over my balcony. "What if I'm not what you imagined? What if you learn things about me you don't like?"

"Not possible."

"But if you do—"

Elijah reached out and took my hand. He trailed his fingertips between my knuckles, stroking my skin lightly. "Not possible," he repeated.

I couldn't believe he'd just done that. "Not many men would touch Death without asking," I managed to say, my heart unsteady.

"I'm an ouroboros—an immortal. Like you." His hands were cold, as cold as mine, though it was anticipation that made me shiver under his touch.

So I can't kill him, I thought. No wonder he was so fearless. The ouroboros who lived in the Veils and seas were mythical shapeshifters, snakes. I'd read about them, I'd seen pictures, so I understood what he was— at least hypothetically.

"Show me," I said.

He hesitated. For a fraction of half of a second, I saw something terrifying, like a shadow through a crack in the wall. But I didn't pull away. I didn't flinch. I knew it was a test, and I was determined to pass it, because I knew how difficult it was to show someone who you truly were. If he could be unafraid of me, then I could be unafraid of him.

Emboldened, his face rippled. Scales appeared where skin lay a moment before, and his nose flattened into two small holes, and his pupils lengthened. His features were strange, horrible even. His cheekbones were little more than silver ridges, the color of castle walls wet with rain. He had no ears. His was the face of a monster, not unlike the stone gargoyles of The Grace.

What would it be like to kiss him like this? His mouth was wide and full, luscious, but blue-black. Hesitant, I stretched my hand forward, stroked his bottom lip with my index finger. How different these two sides of my betrothed were. *Interesting*.

"You are not afraid to touch me?" he rasped, curious, surprised.

"I've seen worse." I dropped my hand, and looked out at the sky, at the place where the roses waved cheerfully in the breeze.

Elijah returned to his former shape, the Prince with cherry-blossom petals accumulating on his blue tunic. "You asked why I want to marry you—why?"

"Because I'm not the sort of person that anyone would want to wed." I licked my lips, suddenly nervous at the direction of the conversation.

"Untrue. For more years than I will admit, I have lain awake and thought of nothing else."

"But *why?*" I had to know. I had to understand it. "Is it merely because of the original Fates decree arranging our marriage? Because you have been told that I'm your soulmate? Or some other reason?"

The Lachesis prince, sun-kissed, chestnut haired, clenched his jaw as if I'd offended him somehow. Would he even tell me the truth?

"You suffered and I was unable to stop it, unable to save you. And it was... awful. To hear reports of you and your siblings, to know what would happen and be unable to tell you. It was..." Elijah sighed. "Maddening."

He rubbed his eyebrows, trying to ease the tension there. "I want to marry you because I've never considered anyone but you. It is only of you that I dream, and only our future that I planned."

I still couldn't believe he was even talking to me. He was so polished, so sure.

His voice was so soft. "Now that you are here, within reach, it is all I can do to stand in a room and not steal you away."

Elijah leaned forward to kiss me, shocking any reply from my lips. He turned my face, held my jaw gently with his fingers, and guided my mouth to his. I gave an involuntary shiver, which only encouraged him. His kiss was at first soft, then thorough, as if he knew my mouth and body already. When he finally paused, I was breathless, my thoughts thoroughly muddled.

Unbearably blue eyes met mine. "I don't want you to feel this way anymore, Morena. That you are unloved, that you are alone. I won't allow it."

He lifted my hand to his lips. Slowly, tenderly, he kissed the flesh of my palm, light as a butterfly wing. "Marry me, and I swear that the two of us will rid Moirai of Malinda, and we'll make her death as gruesome as you like. I will destroy anyone who hurts you, kill them so violently I will make you and your scythe look like a saint with a prayer book."

From his pocket, Elijah pulled out a ring forged of purest gold, with a ruby shaped like a teardrop.

He placed it into my hand, exactly where his lips had been.

"Marry me, and I will walk with you in the dark."

"Mostly, you just need lessons on how to *look* like a queen. It's all appearances." Vitess tucked a brown curl behind her ear.

I was in black today, a dour, plain gown of coarse linen with a high collar. "I like this color. What's wrong with it?" I asked the two of them as I studied the fabrics hanging from the walls at the Castle tailor.

"Nothing, if your look is, *I'm just waiting for someone to murder.*" Serene held up a sheer, filmy negligee. "But if you're going to wear all black, at least you could do it with style. For example, this is both sexy and terrifying."

Hopeless, I shot Vitess a pleading look, who shrugged in reply. ""All your gowns are threadbare. My mother insists that you have new dresses."

"I don't have money—"

Serene tugged me toward a wall of red fabric. "Trust me, you have so much money you could never possibly spend it all."

In the end, all my protests were for naught and I held up my arms to be fitted.

In the jewelry vault, Serene and Vitess selected necklaces, earrings and crowns for me. A trove of treasure and priceless jewels lay before me—rubies, hammered gold, silver spun into needle-like points. I bowed to their better judgment on every piece but one—a petite crown whose diamonds were so delicate, they might be made of stardust. That one I chose for myself.

"Are you sure you don't want this one? I've always liked it," Vitess said, holding up a lacy silver filigree crown inlaid with amethysts.

"You would," Serene replied. "It's hideous."

Vitess sighed and put the crown back into a velvet-lined drawer.

Later a pair of maids led me into the bath, roses wrapping around the pillars, shredded lavender floating on the surface. One of them lit candles, then they left, leaving me alone.

My thoughts drifted back to the ball, Elijah's proposal, what Jasper said as we danced, everything that had happened. Elijah understood me, his darkness perhaps rivaled mine, but I couldn't deny that I was drawn to Jasper's smiles, his optimism, his banter, the ease of his friendship. Maybe – maybe I had dwelled so long in darkness that I couldn't help but want the light.

In the end, it didn't really matter what I was drawn to. It was clear that my destiny was Elijah, that my *choice* would be him anyway. I ran my fingers through the silky water, and as I did, I noticed how the ring on my finger glinted, like a drop of blood shimmering in the depths. I sank a little deeper into the water, and then idly, looking up at the ceiling, summoned the night.

The room darkened immediately, onyx fluttering down the walls like raven's wings. *That's better.*

Far too soon I was back in front of a mirror, where a team of women patted me dry, filed my fingernails into rounded half-moons, plucked my unruly eyebrows. They cut and combed my golden hair, dried and fashioned into an elegant curls whilst another team lined my eyes and darkened my lashes.

"Am I supposed to put forth this much effort in every day?" I asked incredulously.

"Of course," answered Serene. "Queens must be beautiful beyond compare and inspire songs and poetry. What else are we good for?" She rubbed her fingertips lightly across the scars on her right cheekbone. Her dress, a goddess gown the color of rubies, flowed around her as she lounged on my couch.

"The first time is the worst," Vitess confided. "I was with the beauty team for six hours. You've only been here four so far."

It was three hours and forty minutes too long.

Ygrainne entered with a tray, every inch of it full of food. She settled it in front of me and handed me a fork. "Lavraki," she pointed at the plate. "Gavros."

"Are those vegetables—" I began.

Serene smirked. "The national dish of Moirai is fish, and you'll be having that at every royal occasion. Eat up."

I grimaced. "Couldn't I just..." I trailed off when I saw Vitess' frown from across the room.

"Never mind," I muttered. "I'll eat it."

I nibbled the fish hesitantly, worried I might vomit. When the plate was empty, Serene piled barley bread and olives on it, along with strange cheeses. I swallowed slowly.

Serene was firm. "You have to accustom yourself to the foods of Moirai. Eat whatever you want when you're alone, but in front of our people, you like what they like."

"How's the training going?" said Jasper, as he walked in with a bottle of wine so covered in dust that I sneezed.

Surprised to see him, I was momentarily stunned. Vitess covered my sudden silence by grabbing the bottle from him. "We're talking. Go away."

"I'm going, I just thought I'd contribute to Morena's education." He gave me a friendly smile. "This wine is called retsina. It's popular with the Gods, for reasons I've never been able to understand. They say Zeus himself will drink nothing else."

I didn't care about Zeus, or want Jasper contributing to my education. And I didn't trust his friendly smile either.

Vitess shook her head in a warning and Serene's eyes were narrowed, observing the tension between Jasper and me.

"Great," Serene said, and then put her hands on his chest and shoved him toward the door. "Now get out."

I was pathetically grateful for Serene's intervention. She and Vitess clearly knew I didn't want to talk to him, or see him.

"Is it that obvious?" I said quietly.

"No, not at all," Vitess said, at the same time as Serene said, "Yes. Completely."

I looked at the ugly bottle of wine. "Wonderful."

Serene picked it up and began to open it. "It's only obvious to us because the Fates are connected. We can read you more easily." She poured a glass of yellow liquid, which smelled awful.

I took a sip and gagged. "Disgusting." I spit the sharp, bitter liquid back into the glass. "What's it made of?"

"Pearl grapes and pine resin." Serene sniffed at the goblet. "It's very bracing."

Nectar of the Gods indeed. "It must be rancid," I said. "No God would drink such a thing."

"At dinners of state, or at festivals, you'll be expected to eat and drink as the people of Moirai do," Vitess informed me. "This is what was served at the Welcome Ball, remember?"

I scowled and picked up the goblet and took another sip. If I had to eat fish and drink retsina at every dinner, I would just stay in my room. And there was absolutely no way that we were serving this at my wedding.

"Honestly, it takes like poison," Vitess sputtered as she spit half of it back into a glass.

"Maybe we can serve it to Malinda." I smiled darkly.

Serene laughed. "I like it. And I have about eight others for you to try."

I balked. "I can't drink that much. I'll be too drunk to walk to my room."

Vitess poured herself a glass, and after she gulped it down, visibly shuddered. "That's the point, I think."

Serene grinned at the two of us and refilled both our glasses. "Yes. Vi is right. That is exactly the point. And if you're too drunk to walk, I'm sure Elijah would be happy to carry you." She grinned wickedly, then held up glass in a toast. "To Zeus, and his horrendous taste in wine and women, and to us, the Queens of Moirai. May there always be someone to carry us back to our beds."

We all drank, made terrible faces, and then we laughed, we three descendants of the Fates.

CHAPTER 18

———◆———

As wedding planning progressed, I spent my days hiding in the library. I was still searching for the way to break the spell that bound Atropos, though so far I hadn't had much success. Unlike The Grace, the bookshelves of The Epiphany were full – shelves covered each inch of the walls, all the way up to the ceiling, and there was not a glimmer of available space in the entire room.

Underfoot, the royal-blue rugs were thick and lush, and I'd already taken off my slippers to rub my toes in its silky softness. Unlike the throne room, this room had windows that did not open—the glass was wide and spanned one entire wall, but I needn't worry about falling down the side of the mountain in case I tripped on the edge of my dress.

This particularly afternoon, Serene and Vitess were with me, each curled up with a book.

"You know, I've been thinking..." Vitess closed her book carefully.

"Mmm," Serene muttered, without looking up. She was nodding off, as most books couldn't keep her attention.

"Some say that when Death comes, the thing that forces man to hold on, even in the midst of excruciating pain, is regret—thinking that if only he might have done that one thing differently. An unsaid word, a road not taken, a kiss not given—it holds them here like a hook." Vitess looked at me as if she expected me to have an opinion.

"And?" I said.

"What if what holds Cullen here is regret?"

"Their brains are just as empty as the rest of their bodies. They can't think or feel, they don't remember who they are. How could they regret anything?"

Cowed, Vitess frowned down at the aged ivory pages. "It was just a thought."

The clock ticked on the mantel, punctuating our silence. I gazed out the window, at the puffy clouds that drifted past in the sky.

I coughed. "I need to tell you all something."

The other Fates waited expectantly. "Um, well, Atropos is spellbound in The Grace. I searched for some way to free her, but never found the answer."

Serene tipped her head back and laughed. "Are you saying *Atropos* is in Grace Castle too?"

I adjusted the golden leaves on my head which had fallen askew. "Yes. She's Malinda's captive—spellbound to a stone slab. I thought Vitess must know already, since she seems to know everything else."

Vitess stared at me open-mouthed. "Did you find her when I unlocked the tower door?"

"One of your forty-seven tries was unlocking the tower door?"

Of course it was.

Vitess rolled her shoulders in a small shrug. "I hoped that you would flee with Arabella, but you did not. I assumed there must be some reason you stayed, but I never knew what it was."

My mind flashed back to the night I'd found Atropos, to the night when one of the Cullen stabbed me in the tower. When I woke up, healed, with Malinda glaring at me... I'd forgotten about the unlocked door entirely, and the question of who'd unlocked it.

I thought back to the other strange happenings in the tower—inexplicable, strange things. Could it be that Vitess had been there all along, silently helping coming to our aid, while I'd failed to take advantage?

Serene considered me. "So you discovered Atropos, but you couldn't figure out how to free her."

"That's right," I said. "She's probably still in the west tower."

Serene considered, and I prayed she'd know what to do with this information. "It doesn't change anything," she said at last. "When we go to kill Malinda, we'll free Atropos as well."

Vitess glanced up at the walls of the library, all the shelves around us stuffed with books. "And in the meantime, we're looking for a book that will tell us how to break a binding curse."

"Read anything interesting?" Jasper said, interrupting our conversation. When I glanced up, he leaned against one of the marble columns of the library.

Serene scowled at him. "Go away."

"I overheard your conversation. Perhaps I can help."

"Why would we want your help?" I said.

Irritated, I closed my book and stood. I would come back later when he'd left. I had no desire to be in the same room with him, and he had yet to understand the nature of my anger. It felt like I couldn't escape him; Jasper was always around, his scent lingering in the rooms where he'd been.

The two other Fates were distinctly uncomfortable as I walked past him.

"Hey." Jasper grabbed my elbow. "Don't leave."

I stared down at his hand on my arm. "Don't touch me."

"You've said that before," he said softly. "I didn't believe it then and I don't now."

"What is it you hope for?" I asked aloud. "Tell me that, at least. Are you planning to wrest me away from Elijah?"

I could almost feel the words he wanted to say, as if they rippled across his soul. But he kept his lips tightly shut in a thin line, telling me nothing.

"Exactly," I said, after a long silence.

His expression was troubled. "Whatever you're searching for can wait. There are more important things to worry about. Yesterday Lorcan left with the Bradach Bródúil, the sea pirates. Their leader, Keaton Blackmane, brought us bad news."

"What news?"

Jasper grimaced. "Malinda and the Cullen massacred the Mer. They've run out of food in Kinver'i, so they are now hunting in the seas. Keaton said we could see it for ourselves—it isn't pretty."

"It's nearby?"

"Within an hour by dragon. I was going to go take a look. Of course, if you wanted to go—well, I'm sure you have dinner plans."

"You should see it for yourself," Vitess said softly. "What Malinda is doing to us. Maybe you'll figure out how to stop her."

"I doubt that." I'd never had the ability to stop her before, certainly things were different now but not different enough.

That's how I ended up on the back of a dragon, Jasper gripping my waist, flying into the sunset and away from The Epiphany. We were going to the Salt Strait, a narrow strip of land that jutted into the sea, northwest of the castle.

For most of the ride, we didn't speak. But after he'd helped me down from the dragon, as we walked toward the ocean in the distance, Jasper started talking. "I hated the plan. I didn't want to go. It was Elijah who convinced me, who begged me. You were his destiny, and he'd already tried and failed. Serene had tried and failed."

"When I told the lie and you thought I was Elijah, your betrothed, you seemed so hopeful. I felt so jealous of him, of your future together."

"So you slept next to me and kissed me because you were jealous of him."

"Of course not."

"Thanks for the apology," I said, even though he hadn't exactly given one.

Suddenly I realized that I didn't know if Elijah would be angry at me about going with Jasper alone. We were betrothed, and even if he'd jokingly said he wasn't the jealous type...

I shook my head, exasperated, and walked away from Jasper. I hadn't gone very far when I tripped over a tree root. I looked down to discover I'd stepped through a Mermaid's ribcage, my boot twisted between two of her bones. I screamed in horror. As I leapt backward, I crushed a bleached skull. Scrambling as I fell, I shrieked again.

They were all Mer—Mermaids, Mer men, Mer *children*. The elaborate shark-teeth necklaces they wore indicated their class and status, their fins and tales wrapped with gilt and silver. There were hundreds of them—their smashed faces half-rotted, their fishy torsos crawling with flies. Bleached by the salt and wind and sun, their missing fins and fleshless jaws littered the sand, bones blending perfectly into the pearly grains. There were so many I'd thought they were stones, terrain... What I thought was a seashell, if I studied it closely, was more often a knuckle or a dried-out eyeball.

I knelt down to touch one of them, trying to understand. As I did, my horror mounted—I don't know for what reason the Mer had been killed, though whatever reason it was, they had died painfully. Their skeletons were skewered by arrows, rusted hooks as big as dining plates dragged the Mer from the sea. What was left of their faces screamed in agony.

This was no ordinary beach, it was a battlefield. Overwhelmed, I dropped to my knees. My heart was as still as their bodies, heavy as one of the iron hooks.

"The House of Atropos is a blight upon this land," I said. All of it came back to Malinda, torturing and maiming for years on end, her Cullen army gnawing through whatever crossed their path.

And Alexis tried to convince me she was nice.

"It's a problem, to be sure," he agreed. "Politically, too. We'll be lucky if Poseidon himself doesn't declare war on us."

"But it's Malinda who's the villain, the one who must be punished."

My hand settled on the Mer body next to me: female, with what remained of her torso tattooed with celestial maps. She was a priestess among her kind, rare, sacred. Half my size, the Mer priestess was once gold and amethyst, a pointed crown of coral nestled in her tangled red hair. Her face was frozen in a permanent scream and a spear engraved with an Atropos sigil was rammed through her small mouth.

Malinda did this to make them suffer. But why? What have they done?

Was this retaliation? I could conceive of nothing that would explain such deep hatred, such unkindness and injustice. No book, no manual, no spell had ever surfaced that would justify such action.

Jasper knelt next to me. "I was hoping the tide would come in and hide them."

"How many?" I raised my eyes to him. "Have they been counted?"

"Thousands." He couldn't look at me.

I processed the truth: if left unchecked, the Cullen would destroy the beasts of the sea, just as they'd taken the deer, eaten the unicorns, plucked the birds from their nests. With each death, their numbers swelled.

Pursing my lips, I begged the hungry, lashing thing inside of me to calm. "I will repay each death a thousandfold and rid Moirai of the Cullen."

He didn't seem to believe me. Instead, Jasper looked toward the waves. "The tide is coming in."

"Then I'd better hurry," I said. "I'm going to bury them."

He frowned. "You can't just... Wait!" He put his hand on mine and I shrugged it off. "*Wait.*"

I met his gaze. The expression on his face was appraising. "The Mer don't like the ground. They aren't like us... They wouldn't want her buried. They belong to the ocean."

Her small, sad body lay next to my feet on the sand. Nothing I could do would be enough of an apology for their people. But I could do this one thing.

Gently, slowly, I removed the Atropos spear from the mouth of the Mer priestess. Terrified at first that it wouldn't tug free, I was relieved when it came out easily. Then, knowing it didn't matter—I'd carried many dead much further than this—I gathered her tiny body into my arms and stood. This Mer priestess was no bigger than a child, lighter than I'd expected. I held the bundle in my arms and with a pang, remembered Arabella at age five—the nights she'd fallen asleep in my arms, her fingers grasping the edge of my nightgown for comfort.

Sister, I need your rage. I need your fire. I need you here, with me, to face our mother.

"I will carry her home," I said to Jasper.

To his credit, he didn't object. Instead, he asked if I needed help; as if I, the Grim Reaper, had never carried a body to its final resting place; as if my hands had ever been anything but unclean.

"No." I would do this alone. "No," I repeated, more gently. "I have her."

I walked the priestess into the waves, the warm water lapping at my black gown. Despite the nature of my errand, I felt some of the tension ease from my shoulders. This task was one I was very familiar with, and the only awkward thing about it was that, for the first time, I wasn't wearing the obsidian and pearl mask.

I carried her as far as I could, until I was shoulder-deep in the teal green water, and then let go. The tide, intense and swift, carried her under. But when I tried to return to Jasper on the beach, I found I couldn't. The current pulled and sucked at my feet, moving me further from the shore. The sand dropped from beneath me as if a great hand had dug a sudden trench, and I gulped a lungful of saltwater as I sank.

Currents like ghoulish fingers clutched at my legs, pulled at my black gown, urging me downward into the realm of the Mer. Twisted and turned by the waves, I lost the sense of up or down, shore or sea.

Nose and eyes burning, I started to scream and got another full mouth of water as a wave struck me in the face. Here there was no footing to be found, and I never had learned to swim. Flailing, I kicked for the surface of the turquoise water above. I broke the water for only a moment, but long enough to hear Jasper, still on the beach, yelling out to me.

"The tide has turned," he said. "Stop playing."

As if on cue, it began to rain—cold, nearly frozen slush pelted down. I couldn't see anything except the white foam and waves coming at me. The beach faded in the torrent, and I knew if I didn't make some fast progress, I'd be swept into the ocean just as the priestess had been.

I struggled to lift my head and push myself out of the water. My legs and arms were exhausted, weighed down by the heavy gown I wore. With each arm stroke, my muscles groaned with disuse.

I went under again. Down and down, like a great black bat weighted by a stone.

Faintly, I heard singing—soft, lyrical, warm. The ocean floor was an ivory bed underneath the tumult above. The edges of my vision darkened as they adjusted to the depths. I could stay underwater for a minute more, two at most, before I drowned.

What will happen if I drown? Will I reawaken, and drown again? Will I eventually breathe underwater, a reluctant gift from Poseidon just to get me to leave his domain?

Jasper's strong hands grasped me around the waist and hauled me up and up and up, back into the rain and wind. He yanked me through the water, up into the gray mist. He spoke in my ear. "For Gods' sake."

I didn't even turn my head. My body was pushed against Jasper as the waves crashed against us.

"Stop that," he said to the ocean, brushing back the currents around us. "She's not going with you."

He pulled my body to his chest, shielding me from the waves that now roared past with fury. Slowly, he walked toward the shore, carrying me in the same fashion that I carried the priestess. He moved clumsily through sucking wet sand beneath his feet, to a place between two boulders sheltered from the wind. I started to lose consciousness, the world fading out.

He laid me out on the sand. "Morena." He called my name repeatedly, touched my face. "Damn you, wake up."

"I'm tired..." I mumbled weakly, my entire body empty with exhaustion.

He exhaled, letting his forehead rest against mine. I breathed in his warmth, along with the salt air and sea.

"I was going to drown, just like Taliesin." I took a shaky breath of relief, eyes still shut.

"It would have been a noble ending."

I opened my eyes to stare up into his face up close. His sun-kissed skin was damp, his black hair dripped, and his lips were just breaths from mine. I didn't dare blink, for fear he'd vanish, a figment of my imagination.

His eyes were not the color of the moonlit sea. No, now that I was able to see them so clearly, they were an entirely different gray—silver, yes, but edged with iron, like a tarnished heirloom passed down through centuries, unevenly polished as though a distracted maid had never finished her chores.

"I heard you," I said, "thinking about me. You weren't telling the truth about the kiss."

His gaze didn't waver, and the heat of his body sank through my sodden clothes, through my wet skin, and down to my bones. I hadn't been this warm in my entire life. Above me, he shifted. It felt as if liquid fire were being injected into my veins. His rough breathing ripped apart the silence between us as each breath between us mingled.

My foolish monster's heart skipped a beat. I waited for him to kiss me, hoping.

Kiss me.

It was all there, plainly written on my face, desire shining out of my black eyes.

Kiss me.

Jasper traced his fingers across my eyebrows, my jaw, down my neck, and to the bodice of my gown. Before I'd been cold, teeth chattering, but his warmth cradled me. I breathed him in, along with the salt air and sea.

Kiss me.

"I'll kiss you," he said softly, "because *you* want me to." Then he lowered his mouth to mine, sliding his tongue against my lower lip, seeking entrance.

I very willingly granted it. As our tongues met, he crushed me back into the sand, his body shifting against mine. I did not fight him. Instead, I drew him closer, and wrapped one of my legs around his hip. *Yes.*

Perhaps I was using him. Or maybe I was celebrating being alive. Or I was being a fool, because I was going to marry Elijah Lachesis and reunite the three kingdoms. It could have been that I was sabotaging myself, that I didn't believe I deserved it so I was going to ruin absolutely everything. I didn't know; I didn't think about it.

Jasper shoved my shirt open, exposing my breasts, and as he lowered his mouth to them, I sucked in a vicious breath.

"Do you want me to stop?" he asked, his chin rasping against my skin.

Gods no.

I pulled him closer, urging him on, feeling delirious as I combed my fingers through his dark hair. The rain fell all around us; the waves crashed a few feet away. There was nowhere *to* look, except his mouth, at his smooth olive skin, at his gray eyes that matched the mist.

CHAPTER 19

That night, Taliesin invited everyone to The Woven for dinner. Jasper and I traveled there directly from the beach, our clothing soaked. On the back of the dragon, his arms were wrapped tightly around my waist. His fingers were tense where they rested against me. He didn't speak for a long while, and when he finally did, it was only to tell me that it was a mistake and could not happen again.

I should have had more self-control, he said.

This was something I already knew. But it didn't stop me from thinking about what had happened. I couldn't stop replaying the feeling of his lips burning a trail down my body. The way he looked at me under him, the hunger and confusion. Obviously I had to put an end to it. Yet the attraction between us was so strong that it was difficult to fight, despite the prophecy, despite the betrothal, despite Elijah, who had done nothing wrong.

"Do you think it's because I rescued you? Or was the first person to kiss you?" Jasper asked, almost as if he were talking to himself.

"I don't know," I answered. The reason, whatever it was, eluded me. I could feel it, just out of reach, slipping out of my grasp.

By the time we reached The Woven, the chorus of butterflies that flapped in my stomach made me feel as if I might throw up. Elijah would be here—he would *be here.* My hair was a mess, my gown... My emotions were even worse.

As Jasper and I walked down the entryway, three dogs came running toward us. They barked and yapped and jumped, and I had to hold them back with both hands. Undeterred, they continued to wriggle with joy—a matching trio of black and white hounds that definitely were not purebred.

"Sunny! Day! Worm! Stop that racket!" Taliesin admonished them. He gave Jasper and me an appraising look.

"Your dog is named Worm?" I asked, stumbling to fill the awkward silence.

"He's always covered in dirt and was born blind." Taliesin snapped his fingers at them, and the three dogs flocked to him for petting, their long tails wagging. "Come on. Come in."

I followed the two of them, Taliesin and Jasper, into The Woven.

Just dinner with my brother and his friends – Jasper being one of them. Stop blushing, stop acting guilty, stop looking at him.

Clotho's castle, The Woven, was entirely unlike The Grace or The Epiphany. Stuffed with art, sculptures, tapestries, and books, it felt more like an antique shop than a castle—at least, any castle I'd ever been in. The walls were a soft terracotta, and the floors underfoot were ivory stone mosaic, forming works of art under my feet. The furniture was overstuffed green velvet, threadbare in places, with cozy blankets tucked over the arms. Here and there, tufts of grass, flowers, ferns, and all manner of plants sprung from between cracks in the stone, from corners of the rooms. In some places, vines completely covered a wall, and dozens of tiny yellow birds were between the leaves. The throne room wouldn't have held even a hundred people. The smell of each room varied, but all were verdant, filled with earth and wood, flowers and fresh bread.

"You know, Serene is bitter that Jasper was the one who ended up rescuing you," Taliesin said glibly as we walked. "She tried multiple times to be the one to do it ... but she never made it past the Cullen." He held open a roughly cut oak door. "I know she is difficult. She has too much pride and attitude; she's hard to get to know."

"But you know her," I answered, desperate to hang onto any conversation that didn't include where I'd been. "Seemingly very well."

My brother stared at me and raised an eyebrow. "I know her *quite* well, yes. "He left zero room for ambiguity. And I could tell, by the look he gave me, that he knew *exactly* what was happening.

I blushed furiously.

Jasper, meanwhile, walked ahead of us, his boots leaving water marks on the floor. He led the way to the dining room. It, too, was nothing like The Grace or The Epiphany. Small and cozy, the table sat in front of a large fireplace, the room's stone walls unadorned. Fat candles guttered on iron stands in the corners, and plates were loaded with food. Several trays of vegetables, meats, fish, fresh greens from a garden, and spices were in small iron pots with tiny spoons. To my shock, there were no servants or maids to serve us.

Nico and Vitess sat side by side, and even though they weren't trying to hide it, the angle of his arm suggested that his hand rested on her thigh. A couple. While I was glad for them, I couldn't help noticing that Jasper and I might also look like a couple.

I leaned a little further away as Elijah entered the room. His eyes lit up when he saw me, and he came and kissed my forehead.

I am a terrible, terrible person.

"I received a letter from Lorcan," Jasper announced as Elijah took the seat on my left. "He and Keaton had a council meeting with Peregrin, leader of the Mer. He's agreed not to declare war on Moirai—he recognizes that we cannot be blamed for the actions of Malinda and the Cullen."

"Well, that's a relief," Serene said.

Nico poured wine into mine and Vitess' goblets, filling them nearly to the brim. "What's the bad news?"

"He also said that if we do nothing, or if this killing continues, he'll have no choice but to retaliate—his people are angry and want retribution. Otherwise, the Bradach Bróduil have already had run-ins with the Cullen beyond the wall. The pirates did not fare well in the skirmish."

The Cullen really are coming. The Wall has failed to contain them.

"In case of invasion, Lorcan offered his castle as a safe haven."

"That's kind of him, but evacuating the entirety of Kinkanali would be..." Serene swirled the wine in her glass... "problematic."

"The pirates say they'll carry the citizens south, to Kinseamair or Rosehall should it come to that."

"I'm not sure I believe that. Pirates are an unsavory lot—they like battle and bloodshed and stirring up trouble. I wouldn't trust them to get anyone to Kinseamair, especially not innocent citizens." Jasper leaned back in his chair and sat his plate on the floor for the dogs.

"Hopefully."

"What about Peregrin, the leader of the Mer?" Taliesin asked Elijah. "What does he say?"

Elijah sighed. "He won't give me a straight answer. I suspect most Mer have fled south anyway, hoping to avoid being hunted. They aren't much use to us anyway since the Cullen tend to remain on land."

Serene turned to look at me. "You have to learn to use your powers. As far as I can tell, you don't even know the full extent of what they are." Serene took a bite of an apple, likely grown in their orchard.

"Allegedly Atropos' powers were the ability to kill with only a thought, to injure, maim, or drive a man mad; to call the night, to cast a plague, to control the shadows..." Vitess tapped her fingers on the table, trying to remember others.

"Sounds cheerful," Tally joked. "On top of that, you also have to unite the kingdom. Which means getting married." Taliesin emptied the last drops of wine from the decanter into his goblet, studying Elijah and me. "Are you? Did he ask you yet? I note that ring on your hand, so I assume the answer is yes, even though there's been no announcement formally."

Elijah slipped an arm around my shoulders. Meanwhile, to my right, I could feel the tension radiating from Jasper like a bonfire.

I tucked my head in a swift nod. "That's the prophecy," I said breezily, a little unsteady as I thought of the beach.

Forks scraped against the plates in the silence, and I scratched at the neck of my gown.

"It'll be the first wedding in thirty years," Vitess said. "The whole castle is aflutter with preparations."

I refilled my glass with wine and took another gulp. "Are you going to marry Serene?" I said, desperate to get the attention off of my marriage.

"If she'll have me." Taliesin glanced over at her. "Will you?"

Serene had her boots propped on the table, her warrior's shirt unbuttoned low enough that I could see a tattoo peeking out. "Your masculinity would never recover. Also, marriage is stupid."

I snorted, and then the laugh bubbled up from deep inside me, a strange sound I choked over once it was out of my mouth.

"Are you laughing?" Serene pretended to be shocked. "I made Death laugh?"

"She's laughing *at you,* not with you, "Nico informed her.

Vitess grinned. Her chestnut hair was mussed, her cheeks pink. "I've had too much wine," she announced, patting her nonexistent belly. "And I ate too much."

The talk continued, and my tension slowly eased. Beside me, Elijah ate quietly, rarely joining in the conversation. Jasper, meanwhile, was much louder. Which made sense; this was his home, his castle. He and Serene bickered, as siblings sometimes do, and Taliesin and he joked almost constantly.

I let myself imagine nights in the future just like this one, where we all ate dinner together, laughed and joked, and drank too much wine.

"How is it that you came to be a spy in Grace Castle?" I asked Nico.

"He came here to kill Vitess, of course," said Serene. "He failed."

"Technically, I succeeded, and she reset time," Nico protested. "And then I died, but she wanted to know why I'd done it, so she saved me."

What a strange relationship these two have, I mused. "And then what?"

"My parents kept him prisoner for a while," Vitess said, her gaze far away as she remembered. "Because every time we removed his chains, he'd try to murder me again."

"You realize I was here on Malinda's orders. That I had no choice. If I was ever going to return to Morena and Arabella, I had to fulfill her demands."

"What persuaded you?" I gave him a quizzical look.

"Vitess convinced me she could find a way to save you. That she personally would ensure it."

Nico and Jasper's eyes met. "Of course, the plan seemed a little problematic. I went back to Malinda and told her it couldn't be done. But I also told her that I'd found the papers – the decree of your marriage. And that the Lachesis family talked of prophecy."

"You planted the seed." Realization dawned. "That's why she wasn't surprised to see you or a Prince."

"Correct. I'd told her before Taliesin died that you were betrothed by The Fates to Elijah Lachesis."

So she'd known. She'd known before I became the reaper that there was never any need for it, that I would leave Kinver'i and come here.

"I don't understand," I murmured. "Why—"

"It's better not to try and understand Malinda," Nico told me. "I don't bother anymore."

The rest of the group seemed interested in the conversation, but I had nothing else to add. I was too busy thinking about how my mother had feigned surprise, how wonderfully skillful she was at pretending and lying.

"So where were you two earlier that you showed up to dinner looking soaking wet?" asked Taliesin suddenly.

I cursed my brother silently for his obliviousness. Beside me, I felt Elijah sit a little straighter. Jasper froze, laughter dying on his lips.

So I answered first. "We went to see the Mer."

"The Mer?" He looked interested. "Why?"

"Jasper came to tell us that Malinda had massacred them, using them to train the Cullen or using them as food..."

I trailed off, my face red. "I didn't believe it. I wanted to see it for myself."

"And how was it?" Nico leaned forward.

"How was what?" I mumbled, wishing that the earth would open up and I could fall through it.

"The Mer. The beach." He gave me an appraising look. "That *is* where you went, right?"

"Of course, it's where we went," said Jasper, finally coming to my aid. "Bodies littered the shore. Morena decided she would return one of them to the sea."

Awkwardly, I bit my lip and avoided Nico's inquisitive gaze. The sooner this conversation ended, the better.

"I don't know why you're acting so weird about it," he said. "Did something else happen?"

I bit the insides of my cheeks and said nothing.

Jasper scowled. "Apparently, Peregrin had an ax to grind. The waves tried to drown her, and I had to pull her out of the water."

"Well, she never did learn to swim." That was Taliesin, who was buttering yet another piece of bread.

"So you went alone?" That was Elijah on my left. "Together?"

"No," I said.

At the same time, Jasper said, "Yes."

Serene's eyebrows were raised. Vitess was distressed. Taliesin was paying excruciatingly close attention to the bread roll. Nico coughed on his water.

"That was probably a bad idea, with the Cullen running around." That was Serene, who'd thankfully deduced the situation and tried to cover for me.

"Hmm." Elijah gritted his teeth. He carefully refolded his napkin with long, elegant fingers.

Sweat slid down the back of my neck, under my clothes.

Next to me, Jasper was still. Ready to defend me or ready to leave, I couldn't tell. With the wine still flowing freely, the rest of the table quickly forgot the discomfort. But I could feel Elijah beside me. Waiting. Quietly seething.

"I need some fresh air." Elijah stood smoothly. "Care to join me?" Despite the cordial look on his face, this was not a question.

I followed him out to the terrace. If his anger hadn't sobered me already, the crisp night air would have. He braced himself on the rail of the balcony, his knuckles white. I could feel the wrath rolling off him.

"So you and Jasper went to see the Mer." His eyes met mine, and guilt pooled in my stomach.

"I needed to see what she had done," I muttered. "And it was horrible, and then I almost drowned—"

"And luckily, Jasper was there to save you again. Correct?" He moved to stand right in front of me, his eyes unbearably blue.

I wrung my hands, scared to say the wrong thing. "Yes, he saved me. Nothing else happened." I could barely look into his eyes, and I was terrified he could see the blood coming to my cheeks.

"Oh?" He reached for the neckline of my dress. "Then what is this?"

Confused, I glanced down at his hand, holding back my dress. Embarrassment and shame roiled through me as I saw the mark... A bright red and purple bruise nestled at the top of my left breast.

Precisely where Jasper's mouth had been.

Guilt twisted in my guts like a blade. And it must have shown on my face because Elijah continued, "What did he do? Did he force you? Hurt you?"

"He would never..."

"So you asked him to, or at least encouraged it."

I had no excuse prepared, no lie to feed him.

My betrothed, my future husband, the father of my children, stepped back from me. With a look of wounded disbelief, he shook his head. "You're throwing away our future with both hands. I just wish I didn't have to watch you do it."

CHAPTER 20

"He's a wonderful man," my maid Ygrainne said quietly, as I stared down in horror at a pile of invitations.

"I know," I murmured, as I pressed my fingers to my pounding temples. Despite the breeze that blew through the windows, my room was a bit too stuffy, and tendrils of my hair mussed as I sweated in the center of thirty different bouquets of flowers.

"Which one is preferred?" The florist peered down his pencil-thin nose at me. "This one signifies anticipation. This one, gratitude." He held up a bouquet of white lilies wrapped in indigo ribbon. "Regal."

I gave the florist a tepid smile.

"No need to look so depressed," Taliesin drawled, as he sauntered into the room, calmly surveying. "Gods, it smells like a funeral pyre in here."

"Can I help you with something?" I brushed my thoughts away and pretended to inspect one of the clusters, a bundle of dark and light-pink lilies threaded with pearls.

He leaned over the table toward me, his green eyes narrowed. "How do you feel about target practice?"

I paused as my hand hovered over the bundles of flowers. "Very enthusiastic." At that point, I would have done anything to get out of wedding preparations. Somehow, and I was not sure how, Vitess had convinced Elijah not to cancel our wedding.

"Vitess says you have to learn to use your powers. As far as I can tell, you don't even know the full extent of what they are." He scooped up one of the bouquets and inhaled its scent, then wrinkled his nose. "We need to test you for both precision and for the ability to kill many at the same time. We need a place where you can experiment."

"Lead the way."

"I thought you'd say that." Taliesin glanced over at the florist. "I'm taking these," he announced, twirling one of the red and orange bouquets in his fingers, its flowers the color of flames.

The florist wrinkled his nose and noticeably flinched, then forced a smile. "Of course, sir."

Taliesin held open the door for me. "After you, little spider." He grinned as I sailed out. "Let's go kill something."

Taliesin brought me to The Woven, to a small, grassy sparring arena where Jasper and Serene faced each other with swords. Just the sight of him made my stomach drop.

You want him, but you cannot have him.

I shook my head to clear away those thoughts.

Encircled by stone pillars, I watched as the two siblings parried, attacked, and defended. Jasper was vicious, Serene controlled. Jasper was sweaty, determined; Serene irritatingly relaxed.

She could have beat Jasper with one hand tied behind her back.

"Point," Nico called out. His lithe form leaned against the Castle wall, studying the two, and the golden rays of sunset glinted on his dark, curling hair.

Taliesin corrected Jasper as a teacher would a pupil. "Do you know why you lost? You held your sword too high at the cross."

He nodded. "As soon as I did, I knew I was done for."

Serene considered, then chose a different weapon – a long, gold-en rapier. Jasper grinned as her sword suddenly glowed with fire. He snapped his fingers, and the entire courtyard danced with flame, sur-rounding the two.

"These two love to play with fire."

In more ways than one, I thought as I watched them.

"I like it hot." Serene ran a tongue over her top lip suggestively. Taliesin huffed out a short laugh.

Serene stabbed forward, now facing two versus one. My brother leapt out of the way, as graceful as a stag through a wood. Jasper walked through Serene's fire, unburnt. It didn't take long—seconds only—be-fore Taliesin knocked the sword from her hand, spun her around, and had a blade to her throat.

"Yield?" he asked.

"You wish," she said, and elbowed him in the ribs. Taliesin fell back; Jasper bent over laughing, both hands on his knees.

"Where did you learn to fight like that?" I asked Taliesin, when the two finally had finished, both drinking water. "You never won in the tower."

"I know all her moves." Taliesin rubbed his hand across his leather chest piece. "And, frankly, she lets me win."

I couldn't miss the warmth in his voice, or the look he gave the two of them. I also couldn't ignore the colors he wore—red and green for the house of Clotho. My brother had done more than find a home.. he'd formally renounced the house of Atropos.

"You're up next," Serene said, giving me a pointed look.

I walked into the sparring ring past Jasper, who grazed my shoulder with his own. I tried to ignore the electric feeling that shot down my arm. The look he gave me was teasing, like he knew what I was thinking. Being around him wasn't making things any easier.

I settled myself across from Taliesin, ready for anything. I took out my knives, one for each palm.

"Wait. No knives." Nico plucked them from my hands and tossed them aside.

"You want me to fight with my bare hands?" I asked incredulously.

"With your mind, fool," Serene replied. "Remember, you're *Death*, you don't need a weapon. You'll start with Nico. Most of the time, he's unbeatable."

Not against Death, he isn't.

"If you put me in the arena, I may kill him."

"Hopefully you will. And then Vitess here will bring him back to life."

I couldn't do it. Feeling physically ill, I blanched and looked over at Vitess, who sat primly on a bench. "We don't even know what will happen. What if I kill him permanently?"

Vitess crossed her legs and arranged the folds of her buttery yellow gown. "This isn't Life versus Death. This is me rewinding time, just for a few seconds, perhaps a minute. You won't feel anything, neither will he. I swear on my life that you won't kill him permanently."

Now that I had Taliesin and Nico back, I never wanted to do anything that might put either of them in jeopardy. Both were my brothers. But if Vitess could reset time... She wouldn't let Taliesin die, nor Jasper. She wouldn't let anything bad happen to Nico. She was more powerful than Serene or me, at least in this one particular case.

I released my breath in a whoosh. "Fine."

Nico moved with liquid grace, like a soldier born with a sword in hand. My technique wasn't flawless, but I was quick. He spun and slashed at me but missed. Now he gritted his teeth. He hadn't taken me seriously at first, but almost immediately it became obvious that I was a true opponent. He kicked at my head a few times and I easily dodged.

Keep trying. I remember all your moves, Nico—I sparred with you for years.

Just as I began to think that I might win, Nico landed a blow to the right side of my head, smashed his fist straight into my cheekbone. I saw stars, and the entire arena twirled in a rapid flash. I fell to the ground.

"Point!" he called out, though I quickly side-stepped, then hit him in the back as I stepped behind him.

I'm faster.

But it didn't seem to matter. He beat me again, then again. Each time, I grew angrier, but despite that, I could not bring myself to kill him. I kept my power tightly wrapped, bound in anxiety, too afraid to call upon it.

I stood up after losing for the fifth time. A few feet away, Jasper stood watching. Sun fell across his bare chest as he toweled off. He was stunning. It was nothing I hadn't seen before, of course, but still my mouth went dry as my gaze trailed down his abdomen, toward the ridge of his hip bones.

"Bed Jasper later—kill Nico now!" Serene called out. Vitess cringed, noticeably uncomfortable.

I flinched. Things were already awkward enough without Serene making it worse.

Vitess yelled to me. "Remember what I said."

Do you think you need a blade?

It didn't help. In the next round, Nico swiped my feet out from under me, then had the point of his sword against the soft skin of my neck within seconds. "Yield," he demanded, his witch-hazel eyes cheerful as he leaned over me.

"Never," I croaked as I placed my hand on his chest. As soon as I saw a tendril of silver light, I yanked with all of my power. The slender thread of his life unspooled from his heart like a ribbon, into my palm, and vanished as if it had never been.

Nico toppled over, dead, solid muscle and meat. Vitess raced over, and pulled Nico off me, rolled him over onto his back. I couldn't look, I was too worried about what I'd done.

"Vitess?" Serene said, a hint of panic in her voice.

"It's fine," she replied shakily. "He'll be alright in a second."

Click.

I blinked and Nico lay beside me; he stared up at the sky, temporarily stunned. My face felt damp, my back covered in sweat. Overhead the sky was brilliant blue, and fat fluffy clouds rolled by on the breeze. I felt exhausted; tired all the way down to the marrow of my bones.

Serene watched from afar. "Are you two just going to lay there?"

"Morena knocked the wind out of me, that's all," Nico said, breathless. He grinned as he rolled to his side and propped his curly head onto his hand. "Well done."

Vitess nervously leaned over to inspect both of us. "Morena didn't knock the wind out of you. She killed you."

I turned my face toward Nico. He was very much alive.

"Good job, little spider." Nico flexed his neck and groaned. "I guess you can kill without a weapon."

Serene leaned down, pulled me to my feet. "Well done. Jasper, you're next. Morena, you'll need to get him close to death, but not kill him. Make him feel the pain of a heart-attack, or the water in his mouth of drowning, but *don't* kill him. We're going to work your precision, because all brute force and obvious attacks is but a mere fraction of what you can do."

I grimaced. Of course the two of us would be paired against each other. I couldn't avoid him. If only he'd just put a shirt on, or stop giving me that knowing look, as if he could hear my thoughts.

"If you can make him feel pain, if you can take him to the brink of death but not kill him, that is just as useful. Perhaps more."

"So you want me to torture him?" I furrowed my brow and glanced at Jasper. His pants were fighting leathers, rich brown and edged in a green thread. He didn't look at me as he picked up a sword, swinging it in an arc.

"Yes." Serene's gray eyes, identical to Jasper's, appraised me. "Rip his arm off, cut his throat... something. And be quick about it—we haven't got all day."

Still I hesitated.

Vitess intervened again. "It's not permanent, remember? I'll undo it. Or Serene could probably heal him."

"Probably?" Jasper didn't seem nearly as worried as I felt.

"It seems you need a helping hand," Elijah said, stepping around me. He hadn't been there a moment before, but suddenly here he was, striding across the sparring ring toward Jasper. Everyone else looked as surprised as I was.

"I mean if you want to spar, you could just ask." Jasper seemed amused by Elijah's appearance, and he smirked.

Elijah walked right in front of Jasper, glanced at the knives from his waist. "You'll need more weapons than that," he growled.

Jasper studied him for a full second before picking up his sword. "Sure. Whatever you want."

The two of them took up fighting stances, and I glanced around the group with apprehension. Tension rippled through the air, and I met pity in Vitess' eyes. Everyone, especially me, knew what this match was actually about. My stomach turned as I watched the two of them circle each other.

Elijah moved first, lunging at Jasper. He dodged just in time, rolling away from Elijah's grasp. They erupted into a frenzy of movements. It was like a sick dance, my heart racing with every swing. At first the two were evenly matched, or perhaps they had done this so often that they had memorized each other's steps. My heart rate seemed to settle, if only slightly.

The fight dragged on, no one making progress, until I saw the smallest change to Elijah's face. Still controlled, of course, but I recognized the undercurrent of anger. He was turning into the Ouroboros. Before I could call out to warn Jasper, Elijah spun around and punched him so hard that Jasper's body launched across the yard.

He flew through the air in an arc, then hit the ground and rolled. After he skidded to a stop, Jasper lay stunned.

Elijah sauntered up to him. They were far enough away so that none of us could hear them. But when Elijah bent down to say something, close to Jasper's face, he muttered something. I saw Jasper's scowl and his retort. And then I watched as Elijah took Jasper's hand, as if he might shake it. Then he ripped his arm off. Paralyzed, the group of us watched as Elijah tossed Jasper's arm down into the grass, as it tumbled and rolled.

Jasper screamed in agony, his blood spraying the ground. Serene rushed to him, falling to her knees as she reached him. "What the hell, Elijah?! You're supposed to be sparring!"

Elijah ignored her completely, his face bleeding as he addressed Jasper. "Touch her again and I'll rip the other one off. Then, if for some reason you still don't understand that she isn't interested, that she isn't *yours*, I'll throw the rest of you in the sea. There won't be big enough pieces for even the fish to be interested." He swiped at his cheekbone, smearing the blood there.

I was wide-eyed as Elijah approached me, breathing heavily. "That's how you do it," he said. "My way is less polished, more painful, but you get the point. Next time it'll come easier to you, I'm sure."

I ran my fingers down the mirrored blade of one of the swords of the armory, lost in thought. After making sure Serene could handle healing Jasper, I came back to The Epiphany. I'd spent the night sleepless, half-expecting Elijah to show up at my bedroom door. When it was clear that that wasn't going to happen, I lay there hating myself, wondering what I was going to say once he finally did—if he ever did.

At sunrise, I went straight to the armory, desperate to work off some of the buzzing energy that simmered under my skin. The armory was nothing more than a long gymnasium, tall, with a dozen windows on each side of a plain, rectangular room. One entire wall was dedicated to swords, knives, axes—weapons of all kinds, all of which were sharpened to a fine edge. Though none of them were as sharp as the scythe that I'd left behind at The Grace.

"Be careful." Elijah stood in the doorway bare-chested, a towel around his neck. "You can cut your hand off with that one." On his chest was the tattoo of the ouroboros, a snake devouring its tail, the symbol of the infinite.

I jerked my hand away from the swords as if I'd been burned.

Elijah considered the wall of swords behind me and kept his distance. He gestured to the line-up. "Care to try me?"

"That depends." I selected a short sword with a jeweled handle and weighed it in my hand. "Are you going to control your temper?"

"It seems that violence is the only way I can share your hours." He rolled his broad shoulders in a small shrug. "I won't apologize for what I did, if that's what you're waiting for."

I didn't know how to feel. Angry? I deserved his wrath. Hurt? He had every right to be jealous. He wasn't wrong, he wasn't misguided, he hadn't imagined anything. It was me who was the problem. If anything, I would have preferred that he yell at me, punish me, instead of Jasper.

I raised the sword and gestured at him to approach, wary and unsure what to expect. Elijah attacked immediately—aggressive, sharp slashes intended to intimidate an opponent. Not a bad strategy.

"Sleep well last night?" he asked.

"No," I admitted, and my sword moved so quickly through the air, it nearly whistled.

The clang of the blades as they caught was a wild shriek, metal on metal. Elijah was unfazed. We drew close together, our swords crossed. So close, I could feel his breath against my skin. With a quick feint, he cut the laces on the front of my gown. I gasped and grabbed at the fabric, forgetting the fight.

"Point." His smile was calculating. "If you want to change..." He sneered at the mark on my chest.

"Cutting a lace isn't the same as winning," I said, slashing at him again. But he was there and then not there. Too fast for me to catch.

"Beat me." His laughter, low and soft, infuriated me; the way he moved, like water and smoke, unnerved me.

"I thought you'd be better than this."

"You won't say that when I carve the skin from your bones." I parried and feinted and stabbed, and still he evaded me.

His expression blazed with challenge. "That's more like it."

Blindly I whirled, and my sword clattered to the floor as our bodies collided. Our mouths were breaths apart, as if we were about to kiss. Unthinking, I grabbed at him, my hand closing around the blade of his sword.

"Ouch!" I cried out.

Like a flash, his arms wrapped around my waist. He tossed down his weapon. "Sorry. Let me see."

Gingerly, I opened my hand to reveal a pooling, bright-red river of blood and a cut across my palm.

His anger, his tension, evaporated once he saw the wound. "It's not that deep." He examined my hand, cradled it in his. "It will hurt though. We should wrap it."

"Yes." Transfixed, I stared at his face. There was nothing but tenderness, worry. My hand burned. The cut wasn't bad, just red, bright-red blood, steadily filling my palm. I wondered how long it would take to heal. Minutes? Hours?

I remembered what Serene said on the balcony. "Serene said that blood bonds are forbidden. Why?"

"Blood bonds are reserved for marriage rites. They create shared magical abilities, sometimes hybrid abilities. It's not well understood what the exact consequences are, as it depends on the couple." Elijah bowed his head ruefully.

"I should have been more careful with you."

It was nothing; I'd certainly had worse. "It's fine," I said as I watched his thumb trace the wound on my palm. Softly, as if he expected my skin to be made of velvet. His touch tingled, and I felt my heart rate increase.

I raised my head to look at him. "Elijah…"

Wrapping one hand around my waist, he tugged me closer. He waited a beat, then two—maybe thinking that I would push him away. I didn't. He hesitated another second, just one second, before he pressed his mouth to my skin.

Elijah had his lips against the wound on my hand, his tongue pushing into the gash. And I was not prepared at all. Without warning, visceral, soaring *need* surged through me.

Elijah gripped me tighter. "Morena."

It was as if he'd never said my name before. It sounded strange, foreign. Suddenly it felt as if the entire universe narrowed to a single point where only we were standing, where there was only his mouth and his voice.

He straightened when I pulled my hand away, when he saw how dark my eyes were, like storms of midnight. He started to release me, to step back, but he'd misread my expression—that wasn't what I'd wanted at all.

I grabbed the front of his tunic and pulled him in, devouring and wild, traces of blood still on his lips. Silky, cool, Elijah assaulted my senses. From the first taste, I felt it. Raw power coursed across my tongue, down my throat, twisting its way into my stomach. It was his blood, *his,* from where he'd bitten his lip. Mingled. Blurred. Blended with mine. His power prowled under my skin, sank deep into my bones, and rejoiced.

Elijah sucked in a breath, his body tense, as I stroked my hands up his bare chest, delighting in the feel of his muscles, his shoulders. "We should stop."

"Should we?" The roughness of my voice was unfamiliar and strange, someone else.

"If we don't, you'll start taking your clothes off, and that would be difficult to explain," he said huskily. Unbidden, he trailed his mouth from my lips to my shoulder.

I couldn't catch my breath; I couldn't think. It felt like my insides were burning for his touch. Not for the fires of hell would I have stopped right then. And it occurred to me, back in the deepest recesses of my mind, that I'd never understood the term *bloodlust* until that very moment.

"Tell me what's happening," I panted into his mouth.

As our tongues touched, I doubted if I'd be capable of understanding anything he said. My hands wandered down to the waistband of his pants, seemingly of their own volition, and I began to tug at the button there. He cursed, low and soft, as I arched into him.

"I don't want to talk about it," he growled, and then covered my lips with his own again.

But I had a spike of sudden, irrational, all-consuming anger. Jealousy. It was a feeling I'd never felt before. "Do you do this with other women?" I shoved at his shoulders, forced him to back off.

His blue eyes were clouded with lust, confused. "What? No. Never." He drew me to him again. "No. There is only you."

Only you.

"On the beach..." I said, my head falling back as Elijah kissed up my throat. "About..." I couldn't even remember his name. Not right now.

"I came to you, before. When you were in the tower." He was still kissing me, my back now against the wall of the training room, his hands pushing aside the ruined laces and loosening my dress. "As a dragon. But you sent me away. Told me to leave."

I could feel it—feel his dark power coursing in my veins—so similar to my own yet different. A shapeshifter. I couldn't hold onto that power, it slipped through my fingers like smoke, but I could feel it, waiting to be mastered. "You were the silver dragon," I managed.

"You have no idea how hard it was not to transform right then and carry you out over my shoulder. I wanted to rip Malinda's spine out through her mouth for what she did to you."

He never stopped kissing me through all of this. "Gods, Morena," he growled, and grasped my breasts, pinching their tips. "You make me feel so..."

I tugged at his hair in response, hard, and Elijah didn't even wince. He was immortal, like me. I wouldn't kill him by accident, I wouldn't hurt him. He and I would set Atropos free. He and I would kill Malinda. I felt drunk on the raw power surging between us.

I felt my center begin to change. My *skin* began to molt away—I was transforming into an ouroboros, right in front of him. The air was thick with the smell of firerose.

His lip curled in a soft smile as he saw me changing, as he saw his power in me. He pulled me closer, closer, until we were nose to nose, until it felt that if we wanted, our forms would merge, and we would be the same person, of one body and one mind. He wouldn't just love me, he could *be* me.

You'll never be alone again, he assured me. *I'll worship you day and night.* He pressed against me, and I could feel his hardness against me, and I shivered with anticipation.

If I'd known what this would feel like, I realized, I would have never wasted my time with Jasper. This primordial need, the desire, the furious roar of this thing between us that made my darkness raise from the depths with a heaving gasp, like the first breath I'd ever *truly* taken...

I wasn't going to let him go.

"I want you in my bed, Morena. With that ring on your hand." He raised his head to look at me.

Slowly, I reached down and drew the **dagger** he kept strapped to his side from its sheath. It was purely ceremonial, with a silver hilt that was encrusted with sapphire stones. He'd likely never used it.

I gripped the blade harder in my bloody fist, scraped the blade against his chest where a tattoo of an ouroboros encircled his heart. "Then let's get married."

CHAPTER 21

F lawless beauty greeted my eyes through the tall windows, and a crisp breeze blew the white curtains aside. Heavy rains the night before left the entire world fresh and green, and each breath I took felt like being reborn. The flowers along my terrace swayed gently as soft sunlight illuminated the long, white wedding dress draped over a chair.

Today was the day I'd agreed to marry Elijah, and we'd done all the preparation. There were flowers and a cake, musicians, and ribbons. It would be small to be held here in the grandest ballroom of The Epiphany at sunset.

We shared blood daily, and the euphoria and lust was all-consuming. If Elijah entered the room, I suddenly couldn't think or breathe. Forever could not come soon enough, and I fantasized about our wedding night so thoroughly and so often that Serene asked me if I'd gone deaf.

I lay in bed and spun the engagement ring on my finger. It was a bit loose, and I worried I'd lose it. An enormous ruby flanked by diamonds, the goblin gold that formed the band was twisted, vine-like. Our ring was forged in fire, a blood-red stone held in place by golden thorns. It suited me, suited him. In fact, it might be the only thing about this wedding that did—the rest was elegant Lachesis blue, crisp white, and silver.

It felt as if I moved through honey as I got out of bed, bathed, and sat on the balcony. I listened to the sound of the waterfalls and then watched the clouds roll by one by one. There were no maids, no servants—no one to sit with me. They'd come along in the afternoon, but this morning was mine.

The sudden crack of my door slamming against the wall startled me. Serene ran into the room, her eyes wild. "Someone put out the pyres."

"What?" I shot to my feet.

"The pyres. We don't know who it was, but there was a body—a body to be burned. It became a Cullen. Now, there are more. They are all over Trale Nuvole."

I scanned the horizon toward the village peacefully nestled next to the river. From up here, it looked the same. If there were screams, we wouldn't hear them. If they were dead, we wouldn't see them. Yet I knew her words were true. I could feel the creep of death among its streets, even from far away. Within hours after someone was killed by the Cullen, they would arise—undead and ready to follow Malinda's orders. If there was one, there would be two, then more. It would not be long before Cullen overran the village.

"We need you, Morena. We need you to get rid of them. There are too many."

I grabbed my cloak. "I'm coming now."

"We have to keep this quiet. I don't want the people to panic—the servants here all have family in the village."

I tied my boots quickly. "Cullen will attack anything in their path—cats, dogs, goats, people. We'll have a crisis on our hands by noon."

I hurried through, getting dressed and ready. I pulled open the closet door out of habit and belatedly realized that I didn't have a weapon with me.

"I'll need a scythe."

Serene was annoyed. "Surely you realize I don't have a *scythe* in a closet somewhere. Maybe there would be one in the village. But you have a knife, don't you?"

"It's best to behead them. They don't die, but it slows them down dramatically. Then we can dump them in the river and let the Mer devour them." I held my door open for Serene. "Let's go."

Just before I closed the door, I paused, my eyes drawn back to the chair by the balcony. My wedding dress was still hanging there, beaded and beautiful, as white as snow.

I'll be back in plenty of time. The wedding is at six.

As I followed Serene out of The Epiphany, I believed it.

The town of Trale Nuvole was eerily quiet. Jasper was already there, face taut with determination as he scanned the cobblestone streets and quiet storefronts. "Where are they?" he asked.

Serene tilted her head, the jagged edges of her black hair clinging along her jaw. "Morena?"

Both of them looked at me. The Cullen were here—the tang of copper was in the air. I scented death as well as a hound. "I can feel them," I said. "Don't let down your guard."

The three of us strode down a narrow avenue, our feet growing wet from puddles of rainwater. I hadn't realized from up in the Castle how twisted the streets were or how the buildings leaned over them, casting deep shadows. It was like a scene from a fairytale, except for the fact that there were no people to be seen. It should have been a busy market day, but everything appeared deserted.

Then we heard muffled screams. Somewhere ahead, people were fleeing, shrieking... *inside a building. There.*

"Go!" Jasper yelled.

I jolted forward, knowing they'd become Cullen within minutes if we didn't get to them. Off to our right, three men spilled out of a doorway into the road, clawing at the ground, and one of the Cullen lurched after them, ripping at their clothes.

One of their men's legs was torn open, and Serene shoved past me, her hands up and palms forward, fire shooting from her fingers, engulfing the Cullen in flames.

Another Cullen followed close behind—I pulled my knives out from the strap on my back and swung them in a furious arc, beheading the Cullen in one swoop. It would still live, but without its head, it'd be less able to navigate the streets and attack the citizens.

Again, Serene blasted one Cullen with a dose of fire that felt like it would bake the skin from my bones from across the street.

Screaming was everywhere, above the sound of their clicking teeth, alongside the sweet, sickening stench of dead flesh and blood. Ahead, one of the Cullen knelt over a Fae, his body bent, his back arched as if he were in a lover's embrace. Half of the Fae's face was gone, and his flesh dangled from the mouth of the Cullen.

I ran, and I leaped upon the Cullen, chopping and stabbing. It was slow and clumsy, but there were now so many of them ... too many. Fear threatened to overwhelm me, but I shoved it down—I couldn't afford to be afraid. I had to be ruthless, to do whatever it took to save my people. I moved like a dancer, my movements fluid and graceful even as I killed.

Beheading Cullen one after another, I left them in a bloody, writhing wake. Behind me, Serene and Jasper burned them. But no matter how many they burned, more seemed to appear. I could feel their cold breath on my skin and hear their jaws clicking as they closed in. I went faster, my movements becoming more frenzied as the fear threatened to consume me. But I couldn't give up. I couldn't let the monsters win.

My vision blurred with blood as I watched the citizens fight back. Some of them had soup spoons and arrows, others had sharpened broomsticks. They defended each other as best they could, and as if in answer, my shadow lengthened and grew wings. Desperate, I welcomed the power that screamed through my bones to the drumbeat inside my chest. An ancient power, deep and inky black, arose. Waves of darkness ebbed from my skin, each one formed into winged beasts that seized upon the Cullen. I lifted my hands, yielding to the shadows as they roared toward the Cullen, then grasped and drowned them in darkness, shoving down their throats and leaking through their ears.

Ahead of me was a little girl running, and a Cullen chased after her. I darted after them, heart pounding, blades in both my hands. She wasn't fast enough. I was too far—I saw the Cullen leap through the air and seize her, so I threw my knives as hard as possible. They both hit the Cullen in the head, sinking deep into its brain.

Chest heaving, I reached them a moment later. The Cullen had already snapped the girl's neck. She, too, would awake as Cullen. I cursed, then lugged them into the blood-soaked street's center.

"These two," I called to Serene and pointed. She blasted them both with fire. There was no time to mourn or wonder whose child she was.

We couldn't move quickly enough to contain them. The entire village would be massacred at this rate before we got through one quarter. Standing there in the street, I realized that Malinda wasn't coming for us—not really. She didn't have to leave The Grace to torment Moirai—the dead could spring up from their resting places and lay siege to cities. Her Cullen army could manifest anywhere and everywhere was at risk. *I was still at risk.* My throne, my people, and my future were in jeopardy.

Jasper brought water from the cracks in the street, filling it, sweeping Cullen off their feet. *Slow, too slow. At this rate, the town will be overrun.*

I looked back toward Serene—Vitess was there. She hovered a few feet above the cobblestones, her feet not touching the ground, her ice-blue gown shimmering and moving like water. Her hands were extended, and a soft and comforting light radiated from her.

Worried for her, I ran to her side. "Vitess! What are you doing?"

"We need time," she said, her eyes closed as she floated above me.

Turning in place, I noticed that everyone else—everything—was still. Paused. Momentarily suspended, Vitess held them firmly in place. The air itself around her rippled, undulated.

Her lips didn't move, but the air around me did. "You have to find a way to kill them without the scythe, without knives."

"The Cullen?" I asked, incredulous. "That's impossible." I shook my head. "They're already dead. They have no soul for me to take."

"Try." Her words were only in my own head. Vitess continued to float above my head like a frozen angel.

I reached out to tap a suspended Cullen in the face. He didn't blink, didn't flinch. The female he chased had frozen into a running position, looking over her shoulder, her mouth hanging open in an agonized scream. "How long will everyone be like this?" I said.

"As long as it takes."

"Have you ever frozen *me* before? "I couldn't help but ask.

Vitess did not respond.

I held up a hand. "Never mind, I don't want to know."

It was an effort to cast my power toward the Cullen, to look for anything that remotely resembled life or a soul among their broken bodies. At first, I found nothing. But after a few seconds, much to my surprise,

I found something. Wrapped around the base of their brains was the tiniest whiff of red mist, no bigger than an apple seed.

"It's not life," I told Vitess. "But maybe you're right, when you said before that maybe... maybe it is *regret*. What should I do?"

"Take it," she said.

"Why are your eyes closed? What should I do with it?"

Vitess slowly opened her eyes. "It's easier to concentrate, and holding all these lives in place is difficult. Especially with you chatting."

"Oh. Sorry." I bit my lip. I hadn't thought of that, but I supposed it was very distracting to try and hold hundreds of people frozen in place... I couldn't understand the mechanics of what she did, how she could stop time from continuing forward yet still allow her and I to be outside of time. "What do I do with the regret after I've taken it?"

"How would I know? It seems like you... ate it?" She wrinkled her nose as if she'd tasted something distasteful.

Eat their regret. Incredulous, I eyed one of the Cullen. Dull brown ringlets framed her gray face, almost hiding the gashes in her throat and across her cheek. I called to her regret silently, just as I would take a soul and snuff out a life, asking it to come to me.

It did not come. Nothing happened. I tried again, forcefully, demanding—nothing. I huffed with frustration. I didn't know what to ask—what to do—because I didn't know how to make someone give me their regret.

"Come on," I said aloud to the Cullen. "Let go."

Nothing. It remained frozen in place.

"If this is regret, and I'm not sure it is, I don't know how to make them give it to me," I told Vitess over my shoulder. "The Cullen don't listen to me."

"They will," she replied. "One day."

"It'd be nice if that day was today," I muttered, still studying the Cullen's face. I'd honestly never seen one this close up before. Of course, it hadn't been dead very long, so it still resembled a person, not an animated corpse.

"Tell me why you're still here," I told the Cullen. "What makes you stay here among the living when you could just die peacefully?"

I should have said goodbye to my son before I went out. Now he'll wake up alone, and I won't return to him. The response was so immediate I nearly jumped.

"SHE SAID SOMETHING!" I shouted to Vitess. Belatedly, I realized that I'd probably distracted her again.

To the Cullen, I said, "You must have been killed after leaving the house. You have a family." And I felt suddenly sorry for her, this mother who had left her child safe and warm, who now had no idea if he lived. It didn't seem fair to think of her only as Cullen, not when she'd been dead for less than an hour.

"It's alright," I assured her. "You did tell him. I heard you. And he's still alive. He's fine."

I didn't think she'd believe the lie. The Cullen, still frozen, had a blank expression. Just as I was about to tell Vitess the experiment failed, the red mist that curled in the woman raced toward me. It slammed into my chest, and my heart stung as if it'd been pricked with a needle. The Cullen dropped like a stone, fully dead.

"It worked!" I shouted to Vitess. I rubbed at my chest—though there was no need, the pain had already vanished.

Vitess gave a knowing smile. "Of course it did."

"Wait. Did you skip ahead to the future to see how to do this?" I gazed up at her, still hovering just above me.

"What if I did?"

"Good idea." I didn't care if Vitess pilfered through all of my future, even intimate moments if she could figure out how to kill Malinda and free Atropos. "It was almost too easy," I told her. "If only I'd known how to do this sooner."

I quickly finished off all the Cullen around us, though I flinched each time their bitter doses of red mist hit my heart. Taking souls was much easier than taking on their regret, but being rid of Cullen was worth the discomfort.

"Now what?" I asked Vitess when I'd dispatched the fifth one without any difficulty.

"Well," she replied, looking pensive. "Do you think you could handle an entire town?"

When Vitess unpaused time, villagers raced past us as they sprinted for shelter. Using his powers with air, Jasper dried the wood of the pyres, then relit them with elemental fire.

I tossed the knives down. More Cullen were in the village church—I could hear their clicking. I walked toward the double doors, their shadows following me. Not even one could escape; if they did, they would kill relentlessly, and more Cullen would be born. None of them must be left standing, and none could be left for dead.

"What are you doing?!" Serene shrieked. Her voice was frantic. "Kill them how we've practiced!"

You're leaving now, I called to them. *Tell me your secrets. Your regrets.*

As I sought the Cullen, I flung out my power over the village, coating it like a blanket. There would be a price—pain and perhaps other things—but our people would be safe.

One by one, the Cullen paused in their chase. Some turned, and some ran toward me. The red mists of regrets revealed themselves, wrapped around the spine or nestled in their breasts.

I inhaled them.

The beast inside me reared its ravenous head and gorged itself on their pain. It wasn't me—I wasn't myself—as it seized control of my body. My hands vanished into black, swirling vortexes.

Cullen fell as their regrets were plucked like petals, and I devoured their red mist as if it were a fine meal.

It took little time. Minutes.

All too soon, it was done—every drop of malevolence cleansed, the clicking and screaming finished. With a final, sweeping motion, I dispatched the last of them. They lay in a heap at my feet, their bodies still. I did not need to drown or burn them—these people were well and truly dead, at peace as they should have been from their last breath. I fell to my knees, my thoughts muddled with other people's memories, words, and ideas.

For a moment, I'd been a God.

I'd been a soul-devouring beast, capable of stripping the world of every life.

But now I was just me again, and my stomach lurched. Crawling to a gutter, I vomited repeatedly, the bile burning my throat. *Get out, get out, get out,* I begged this terrible feeling. I didn't want to be this version of me, not for even a second longer.

Gradually, the chaotic feeling faded until there was only the sound of my breathing and the thumping of my heart. Slowly, I heard other sounds—people emerging from hiding places, their weapons still ready, just in case. I put my head against one of the cobblestones, letting its cold soothe me.

It was Jasper who came, who reached me first. Covered in sweat, his skin glowed like a hot coal, like the last ember of a dying fire. He stared at me intently, his chest rising and falling. "Are you alright?"

I gazed up at him with those horrifying black eyes, my face pale. "What do you think?"

"Who taught you how to do that? How to kill the Cullen?"

"Vitess." I offered no other explanation.

Behind Jasper, towers of thick smoke billowed upward into the sky. The pyres raged, an inferno of the dead, and the small town was now a hellscape of bodies and blood. I have often wondered if the emotion he felt when looking down at me was gratitude or blame – it was impossible for me to tell.

Jasper extended his hand with a grim smile and helped me to my feet. "Let's get all these bodies onto the pyre."

CHAPTER 22

*H*e'll forgive me. I'll explain it all, *and he'll understand.*

I hurried into the Castle ballroom—still in black, still carrying the scythe, two hours late. My feet left bloody bootprints as I strode down the aisle. In the front of the room, under stained-glass windows, urns overflowed with winter roses and lilies. Candles burned brightly in their holders, festooned with cheerful blue and silver ribbons. Forty tables were set up, their china gleaming and unused. All the chairs were empty.

My shoulders slumped. I cursed under my breath harsh in the utter silence of the room. I hung my head, utterly broken. I might have looked like someone who had come to pay penance to the Gods, instead of one of their grandchildren. I'd missed my own wedding; I'd spent too long in the village, piling body after body onto the pyres with Jasper and Serene.

I could clearly imagine it. Elijah would be self-deprecating and apologetic. His handsome face would be stoic, and his eyes would crinkle as he smiled at each guest. He would have waited, of course ... but I suppose not for too long. He'd be cool, calm, and amiable, the Prince of the House of Lachesis, as he thanked them for coming, as his eyes scanned the room and stayed on the door.

He wouldn't have heard about what happened in the village—if he had, I felt sure he would have come down to help. So he'd been here, *right here,* waiting for me. He wouldn't know that chaos was already on our doorstep. I tried to wipe the blood from my face with a sleeve and immediately realized how fruitless that was.

"You're late," he said hoarsely.

I whirled toward the rear of the room. Elijah was there, seated in the shadows next to the entrance.

I froze. Slowly, slowly, I studied his azure eyes, chestnut hair, and the set of his jaw.

"I wondered if you'd show up or if you were holed up at The Woven with the Clotho prince, celebrating your victory." He stood, and the sight of him made my breath catch. He was stunning, clad in a suit that was so clean, so white, that it was like looking at the sun.

The Clotho Prince? Surely, he didn't think I'd missed our wedding for Jasper. I hurried toward him. "I'm sorry," I said.

He didn't want to hear it; his laugh was bitter. "I don't really expect an explanation. I shouldn't have rushed you, I suppose."

"I wanted to be here..." I closed the distance between us and tried to take his hand.

He jerked away. "Don't touch me. My temper is hanging by a thread."

Through our blood bond, I felt his emotions for me. I knew what this day meant to him and how much he was hurting. I felt his jealousy of Jasper and Serene, even of Taliesin. *His, destined to be his.* That's what he'd always been told.

"So," he said, reading my expression. "I'm now a man left at the altar on his wedding day. I couldn't believe you'd not show up. Then, I couldn't panic, couldn't be angry, couldn't show anything of how I felt. I had to stand there, completely humiliated by you, in front of family and friends."

"There were extenuating circumstances. They needed me in the village, there were Cullen—"

"I'm aware of the circumstances." He frowned. "The least you could have done—the *very least you could have done*—was tell me. Just so that I wouldn't have stood here, smiling and waiting on you."

"There wasn't time..."

"You could have made time. We have a *controller of time* living inside these walls."

There was nothing I could say to that; he was right.

"I was made a complete fool, Morena, a besotted imbecile who simply couldn't see that his betrothed was *just not interested.*"

"That isn't true. I want to marry you."

"Do you?" His blue eyes burned as they searched mine. "I've been trying to figure that out. But it's..." he couldn't seem to find the words. "I'm not sure. The ride to the coast, the kiss on the beach, how you look at him... it's all too much." The expression on his face was one I knew well – anguish, betrayal, exhaustion.

"I'm sorry," I said again. "I wanted —"

"It doesn't matter what you wanted. What matters is what happened. The wedding is canceled. At least until we figure things out. Until you are sure."

"I am sure," I insisted. "There's a decree. We're meant to be."

"Not right now. Not like this." Though his words were firm, I knew with absolute certainty that he didn't mean them. Elijah Lachesis loved me. I knew it; I felt it every time he spoke to me.

"What about the betrothal, the wishes of the original Fates?" I pleaded with him. Maybe it was true that I wasn't ready, but when would I ever be ready? And it wasn't his fault that I'd lived alone, unloved in the tower. I was the broken one, not him.

"If anyone wants to contradict me, let them try. The prophecy doesn't say when. It could be years before we get married. I was stupid and rushed things, rushed you because I was so..." he looked away.

My heart splintered and cracked. "Elijah—"I reached forward to touch and console him, and he jerked backward out of my reach.

"You were supposed to be *my* mate, my only love, and not want anyone else. I would save you, cure your loneliness, and fix everything. And still you're drawn to *him*."

"Please don't walk away." I pulled at the front of his jacket and clenched the white fabric, leaving bloody fingerprints on it. I felt like I might shatter like my entire body was made of ice.

He stared down at my hands, my red hands on his white tunic. "Let me go."

"Can we just talk first? I know you're jealous, but I swear it'll be different—"

"You're right, I *am* jealous. You're *my* future wife. You're going to have *my child.* "His words were deadly quiet. "Whatever happened on that beach—and I do not want to know what exactly happened—but I know it should have been me. And I know you know that. The blood bond was just me fooling myself."

He ran a hand through his hair. "I don't want to feel this way for the next five hundred years, Morena."

"No, of course not, if you'd just—"

"I'm being patient. I'm trying to be what you need. And I don't know what you want, but apparently it isn't me. Jasper doesn't *know you,* Morena. He would never understand you. He's not even meant for you. If those things aren't enough, I don't know what it would take to get him out of your head. "

He brushed my hands off as if they were a fleck of dust. "I'm leaving."

It would have been better to let him calm down. It would have been better to let go of him and let him cool off. But these are the things you learn later—how to fight and make up—and so I proceeded to say the absolute wrong thing.

"Jasper wouldn't walk out."

This froze Elijah in place.

"You wear a mask, and you let it down just long enough for me to get a glimpse of who you are, but not the real version, not the full picture. You'd let me believe I'm marrying the handsome, perfect prince, keeping your true self hidden away. How could I fall in love with you when I don't know who you are?"

He blinked. And for a moment—dear Gods—his facial expression was so furious I was frightened. He transformed into the silver snake with electric-blue eyes, and the anger radiated from him was of such intensity I wanted to kneel at his feet and cower.

"I'm done with this conversation." His face shifted, composed again, the beast inside him securely chained under the skin of the charming prince. "Do not follow me."

I fell straight into bed, bloody dress and all. I didn't care if the sheets were ruined or the maids came upon me and thought I was murdered. I let my knives fall to the floor, laid my head on the white silk pillows, and fell into a deep, dreamless sleep. The first time I woke, it was dark outside, and Ygrainne was removing my boots. I said nothing and rolled over.

At noon, Serene arrived. "Get up and stop feeling sorry for yourself," she demanded as she tugged on one of my feet. "If you mourn that immortal loser, so help the Gods, I will flay you alive."

"Go away," I grumbled, curling into a ball.

"Not happening. Your wedding is indefinitely postponed—the polite, royal term for *canceled,* by the way—because you saved *his people* from becoming Cullen. Don't you think that's ridiculous?"

It was, but that made little difference. My heart felt like it'd been crushed under the hooves of a thousand horses. The confrontation with Elijah played through my mind on a constant loop, and each time I relived it, I felt worse. Truth be told, I could have gone to him. I could have run to him before I'd gone to the village.

"Now get up."

"Ugh," I groaned. "Get out. Haven't you done enough?"

"You're a hero, our people thank you, and that cad has the nerve to make you feel bad about it."

The clock on the mantel chimed loudly, ticking away the seconds. Finally, I opened one eye and peered at the first Fate. "If you're trying to cheer me up, it isn't working."

"I'm trying to *wake you up.* I don't particularly care if you're cheerful."

With a noisy sigh, I shoved back the covers. "Why am I getting up? I have nothing to do."

"Did you know Elijah appointed thirty-seven servants to oversee your wedding? Stylist, two florists, four maids, butlers, a ring bearer, a harpist, a flutist, three people to dress you... I could go on—"

"Why does it matter?" I interrupted.

"Right now, all those people are busy scrubbing blood off their floors. Their wives, children, husbands, friends, parents ... many are dead, taken by the Cullen. *They* don't give a damn about your failed wedding."

Immediately sober, I swallowed hard. I hadn't thought of the survivors or the servants who were safe in The Epiphany as their loved ones were massacred in the village. I hadn't thought of them; I'd been too busy thinking of myself.

"What do you need me to do?" I said.

"Get up, like I said. We're going down there to help."

Help them? The villagers? I dressed in a clean gown. As I did, I thought about the complexity of my fellow Fates—how Serene seemed so tough on the outside and yet was the Fate with the softest heart; how Vitess seemed so delicate, but underneath, she was steel and fiercely loyal to a fault. *Where do I fit? Do I fit?*

I followed Serene down to the cobblestone streets where, just hours before, we'd killed, burned, and purged, mindless and ruthless, protecting our people.

"Take this." Serene shoved a mop and bucket with red water into my hands. "There." She pointed at a small building with bright white walls and orange shutters, with happy purple flowers carefully planted outside. It was a school.

I turned back to her, wide-eyed.

"Go on," she nudged me. "There's more to do after that one."

Inside, blood and gore decorated the floor. Toys and books were strewn everywhere as if someone had thrown them at the Cullen to slow them. I chewed my lip as I mopped and swept, righted the desks, and put pencils back in place. Touching their belongings was almost unbearable, and I wondered how many of the children who'd sat in this room still lived. I could easily imagine laughter and running.

It took hours, but I cleaned until all traces of the horror were gone, and the floors and my heart were dry.

"Are you done in here?" Serene said from the doorway, ankles crossed and arms folded, her expression as welcoming as a locked door.

"Yes. Where's Vitess?" I asked as I followed her back onto the street.

"Don't know, don't care." Serene incinerated a broken table and then used the power of wind to blow away the ashes.

"That's harsh." I hadn't had time to tell Serene about Vitess stopping time, about how I'd practiced killing Cullen for an hour while everyone in the village was paused, including herself.

"I mean to say," Serene exhaled loudly, "she's only good at *Time*-related things. She doesn't fight. She doesn't have any other useful magic."

I lifted my gaze. "She's there." I nodded my chin at a long, low wooden table down the lane. There sat Vitess, doling out steaming bowls of soup and freshly baked bread, thanking each citizen for their courage. We walked down the center of the street toward her, and when we finally reached her side, Serene put her hand on Vitess' shoulder.

Vitess avoided my eyes. "I thought you might need my help. Or, they might." She smiled sweetly at the elderly Fae behind us and welcomed him. "Take this, sir. Thank you."

Over the next few hours, Vitess hugged strangers, shook hands, and wrapped them in rich blue blankets. She never ate breakfast, lunch, or dinner. Her smiles were genuine and kind, and she ensured no one felt abandoned or ignored. As a princess and future queen, I'd never seen anyone who took the role more seriously, not then or since.

"Vitess should be Queen of Moirai," I said to Serene, "and leave us out of it."

"She believes in the Fates. And the Fates are *us*. Flawed as we are, Vitess wants the dream—the Three Fates ruling the world, counseling the Gods. She has no interest in being there alone."

"We don't deserve her," I muttered.

"I certainly don't," Serene admitted. "I'm not sure anyone does."

At sunset, the three of us sat together on the banks of the river, The Epiphany looming behind us. It was clear and warm; the hillside was dotted with tiny purple flowers. My heart felt like a towel, wrung out and twisted. Vitess blew the feathered seeds of a dandelion into the wind.

If anyone watched us, they probably thought we looked like three farm girls instead of deities. Certainly, we didn't look like the controllers of Life, Death, and Time. We were worn and tired, covered in blood and dirt.

"It doesn't seem right when people die on a beautiful day." I leaned back on my hands, picking apart the braids in my hair.

"Death can't wait for rainy days," Serene said. "Even though, I admit, when it rains, it feels like the whole world weeps with you ... and the earth is soft and wet and good for digging."

"You're so practical," Vitess said. "Also, creepy and morbid."

Serene laughed. "Maybe I should have been the controller of Death instead of Life."

"So what are you going to do now?" Vitess asked me. "About Elijah, I mean."

"I don't know," I admitted. I had no desire to stay at The Epiphany, where everything was glass, marble, and gilt. It all felt so terribly breakable, like a delicate box that I no longer fit inside. "He's your brother. Any advice?"

"Hmm." Her gaze was far away as she watched the bubbling waters of the river stream past. "Give him some space. Let him come to you."

"What if he doesn't?" I couldn't help but voice my worries. "What if he decides I'm not worth it?"

"Then you can marry me instead because he's a fool." Serene lounged back on the grass, red wildflowers sprouting around her.

"You're his true love. He's been dreaming of you since he was twelve years old. He'll come." Vitess assured me, her voice confident.

"I missed our wedding. He's pretty upset about it."

"No matter what he thought *then,* he knows the truth now. You weren't there, but for good reason. If he can't forgive you for that... "Serene shrugged. "He's wrong. And if Elijah truly loves you, if he's the man he claims to be, he will understand."

"I feel like crying," I admitted to them. "I wish I could."

"Yes. I've felt that way too. Often." Vitess spoke up.

"I never do." Serene toyed with one of her knives. "I just make some mountains fall into the sea, create a canyon, or burn down things. Then I feel better."

"Probably you shouldn't use your powers for that —"Vitess began, while at the same time I frowned. It wasn't as if I could kill people whenever I felt upset.

"If you don't marry him, Moirai will never be reunited." That was Serene again, speaking my thoughts aloud.

"The Decree means that Moirai will be reunited, no matter what else happens," Vitess answered. "It is impossible that she and Elijah *won't* end up together."

"We're already reunited, aren't we?" Serene ran her fingers through the grass. "Therefore, the prophecy is already partially fulfilled?"

I didn't know. Vitess didn't either.

"If nothing else, this whole episode with the Cullen proves that we're not ready," Vitess said, changing the subject. "Our people weren't ready, Morena wasn't ready, I wasn't ready..." she trailed off, her face thoughtful. "Despite the training."

Serene swished the knife, decapitating the flowers. They, in turn, dutifully grew back, this time with purple petals instead of red. "Maybe I could make Kinver'I an island. I'll flood the whole damn thing, then the Cullen can't possibly escape."

Beside us, the river rushed, swelling larger. It was a good idea for later.

"We have to face Malinda," I said quietly. "I have to. If we don't, the Cullen will come, island or not. She'll keep ruining my life and Moirai until we deal with her."

Serene turned her gray eyes to me. "If they cross that wall, I say we burn all of them."

Vitess licked her lips. "Morena can kill them by the hundreds."

I studied them both, the other Fates. We weren't ready, but Vitess was right. This was all a cruel reminder of what could happen, at how quickly our kingdom could be taken from us. "We rid ourselves of the Cullen. And after that, we kill Malinda. Together."

"Together," they each agreed.

Then, we each placed our hands over our hearts, a closed fist. A promise made between the Fates was ironclad; the universe had no choice but to bow to our will. Thus, we made our first decree.

CHAPTER 23

E lijah's mother was the last person I expected to appear at my door. In truth, I'd been waiting, hoping that he would come, so when I heard the knock, I nearly tripped over my white goddess dress to get to it quickly.

"Alexis!" I said sheepishly, suddenly embarrassed. "What are you doing here?"

Her eyes skimmed my pale face, the circles under my eyes. "I believe I'm here to apologize for my son. He hasn't been here yet, has he?"

Biting my lip, I held the door open and gestured for her to come in. "No, he hasn't."

She swept into the room, a cloud of soft scent and sky blue, her long brown hair threaded with pearls. "Elijah is a complicated man. But be sure, he's warring with himself, up in that tower, wanting you."

Alexis walked out onto the balcony, clearly expecting me to follow. She lingered by the edge, watching the waterfall, standing among the roses. They suited her—complimented her softness, her silver gown, and blue eyes—far more than they did me. I sat in the castle's shadows on one of the small stone benches.

Beyond the castle, I watched as a Seraphim flashed upward into the sky, its wings spread triumphantly, the sun bathing its celestial body in radiance. How strange, I mused, that angels guarded this castle while the dead guarded my own.

Malinda had not told me that. Instead, she'd fed me lie after lie: lies about Alexis, the Cullen, Arabella, and the other Fates. All she'd ever done was manipulate the truth and control *me*. And I'd let her do that, allowed it to happen, because I'd been so small and sad, with only that tiny window on the world.

I hadn't known that I could have freed myself, I hadn't trusted in my abilities, and I hadn't believed it was even possible, so I hadn't tried. I'd just accepted things and told myself I was making the best of the situation. When in reality... I'd just let it all happen to me. And maybe that was true about Elijah, too. Perhaps things would have been different if I felt like I'd made more of the choices instead of having them forced upon me.

I searched for what to say to Alexis and came up empty-handed.

Sensing my discomfort, Alexis spoke first. "I want to apologize for my son. He should not have walked out. He knows that you were doing your duty to the people of Moirai. I have told him as much."

Biting my lip, I considered this. So his mother had gone to lecture him after he'd left me in the ballroom. *Good.*

"He has the right to be hurt, "I said slowly.

"Indeed. When things do not go as you've planned, how you've anticipated, of course, you have a right to feel upset. But a prince does not have the luxury of reacting poorly."

I didn't say anything.

Nothing had ever gone as I'd planned.

"You control your destiny, Morena. Yours, his... everyone's. You're one of the Fates."

"Maybe I'm weaker than I should have been," I said ruefully. "I wanted to escape and was unable until Jasper showed up. I found Atropos and never figured out how to free her. I made deals, lied, and killed, but the person I most want to suffer still lives unmarked. I begged the Gods for Arabella to survive, and she did not."

I scanned the horizon again, out toward the town of Trale Nuvole. Their town I'd saved from the Cullen. For a moment, I feared I might see Malinda rise from the river like a leviathan, come to destroy us all. "I have never controlled my path, not even for a day. I have been manipulated at every turn, and nothing has ever turned out how I felt it would."

I gave her a considering look. "So you can see why I'm skeptical."

"You decide deaths. Not much else." Alexis stared at me hard. "And only through partnership, through working together, that The Fates can rule."

It made sense, but I certainly did not feel that way. Something terrible happened whenever I thought I found balance with the other Fates. Almost as if the Gods were testing us, looking for weaknesses, hoping we'd fail.

"Tell me the truth. Did you want to marry my son?"

"Yes. I did. I *do.* "And I meant it. I meant it with all my wretched heart. I'd thought of nothing else these last two days.

"Then I'd like us to reschedule the wedding. It was a mistake; there were extenuating circumstances. I'm sure you would have been there without the Cullen incident at Trale Nuvole."

I understood her feelings, but it wasn't up to her. Or me, for that matter. "He said I am not ready."

Elijah's mother waved away my concerns. "What do men know of women's hearts, full of twists and unexpected hallways? To be sure, the two of you will carve your own path. You will make your own choices. And if you choose differently than Elijah would want, well ... if you are not ready to embrace who you are, not ready to stare into the mirror, then I doubt my son is ready either."

When I spoke, I was hesitant. I didn't know how much to confess to her, what Elijah might have said. "We do, somehow, seem to match. It feels like we sometimes share the same thoughts and feelings. And I wasn't... I wasn't *trying* to ruin that. I didn't expect him to react so poorly; I thought he would have more faith in me."

"We are not equally light and dark." Alexis sighed. "Elijah, unfortunately, is more dark like you. He tortures himself and holds himself to impossible standards. I do not pretend to know his thoughts or feelings; I know him well, but a mother's insight only extends so far."

She gripped the railings of my balcony, and her knuckles were nearly as white as the stone. "Know this, Morena. The only thing more terrifying than *never* is the idea of *forever*. The two of you are destined... you will wed Elijah. So I do not worry about the ending as much as I worry about all the damage you'll inflict on each other along the way."

I almost spoke aloud, almost confided to her: Jasper's deception, my feelings, my confusion. She spoke so openly that it only seemed fair to do the same in return. But I didn't know yet if I could trust her, didn't know if I could treat her as a mother figure. Didn't know if Elijah would want me to. And I knew it was better to guard my heart and tongue when I felt unsure. So I asked her something I'd been wondering about since we first met. "Do you fear our futures? Do you worry about Malinda?"

"No," she said firmly. "I've always seen her as a tragic figure, tricked into life with Melchior, bitter and paranoid. And despite what Vitess has seen, I feel certain that your mother will not win. What woman—even one with an undead army—could stand against the Three Fates? Against the Queens of Moirai?"

Alexis was so different than Malinda. She was graceful, elegant, and kind; her skin rosy, her hands unstained... the mother I'd always wanted. She might have been my mother in another time and place.

"You write our story. You decide our end. That is your role if you only dare to do it."

"I'm not sure I know how," I confessed. "I've never liked my role or who I am."

"I know." Her smile was wistful, equal parts sadness and hope. "Such is Death. Desired and dreaded, ignored until it is nearly too late. The ultimate fear that must be faced by every one of us."

Indeed. I'd never heard it described better than that.

Alexis came to my side and placed her hand on my shoulder. "For what it is worth, I don't think you are ready. But one day, you will be."

I bit the inside of my lip until it bled, my head bowed until she finally left. I couldn't risk the words escaping my mouth. Alexis wanted me to be ready, to embrace my destiny. Meanwhile, I hoped I never would be. For where could Death lead, except to a tragedy?

Not long after, I was summoned to the throne room. Lorcan had returned, and his network of spies brought reports from the north. I debated not going but knew that Serene would likely drag me from my bed if I didn't show up. I donned one of the gowns she'd chosen for me, a one-shouldered dress the color of midnight that skimmed every curve. Its skirts flowed down my legs and swished when I moved. The breeze floated through the open balcony doors and windows, scented with jasmine and rose.

"This can't be good news," Nico said as he walked beside me. His every step was assured, steady. Occasionally, I remembered that the man who'd tickled me and taught me to read was an assassin, a witch. Like me, he didn't need weapons; he could kill with anything, including his bare hands.

I was pleasantly surprised to see Elijah waiting by the door to the throne room. His shirt—white, crisp—was unbuttoned at the top.

"Morena." His voice was raw. His hair was rumpled as if he hadn't showered, and his eyes were bloodshot as if he hadn't slept.

Good, I thought savagely. I hadn't slept much either. I felt like ripping everything to shreds, including his face. If the room hadn't been full, I would have demanded that he hear me out, and stop being ridiculous. Since we had an audience, I tilted my head toward him in calm acknowledgment. If he wanted me to speak to me, he knew where my rooms were.

"Well?" Serene demanded as The Three Fates took our seats on the three-seated silver throne. "What news?"

"Hello to you too, Serene," Lorcan smirked at the three of us. His baritone voice boomed, and with his height, he seemed to take up the entire chamber. Once again, I marveled at the tattoos that covered Lorcan—from wrists to his neck, so thick that I could barely see the skin underneath. There were vines and leaves and strange symbols I couldn't read, animals I didn't recognize, flowers I'd never seen.

"Malinda the Mad—"Lorcan broke off, seeing my face tense—" The Queen of the Blood Throne has moved the wall. South, toward us."

Disbelief clanged through me. The Wall of Skulls stood hundreds of miles from The Grace—there was no way they could hear Queen Malinda from that far away. "Impossible," I muttered.

"We can see the Wall shifting, encroaching onto Lachesis lands." Lorcan grimly stared at us. "At first, it was slow, like an accident. Now it's faster and faster. The wall moves almost daily, whether you believe me or not."

"Are you certain?" Vitess said, glancing at me. "There is no reason to move the wall—"

Serene spoke over her. "How do you know it moves?"

"We send a scout to draw a line where they are with a yellow flag. Often, those scouts don't make it back to us, but the flag remains."

Jasper grimaced from the back of the room. "It's a sure sign her invasion is imminent."

"Or that there is no food left, and they are becoming desperate. The last encampments have closed now that Morena is at The Epiphany with the other Fates. Without food, they have no choice but to expand their territory..." Nico trailed off.

Lorcan interrupted our chatter. "I have more bad news. The Cullen are building boats, amassing weapons."

No. I clenched the arm of my throne, my knuckles turning white.

"It can't be true," Vitess murmured.

"Malinda is probably already marching our way." Lorcan's spies had spent at least a few days traveling to us. "Who knows where the Wall is now, or if the Wall even still exists."

If we waited too long, the Cullen horde would be upon us. And along the way, they'd ruin all of Moirai. They'd leave nothing but dead bodies, making Kinkanali a barren wasteland as forlorn as Kinver'i.

"We can't let that happen," I stated. "She's been amassing an army of Cullen for decades. She has an army of thousands. She will come." I was sure of it.

Everyone began trying to talk at once.

"It shows clear intent to invade. We have to act." Serene pressed her fist upon the table. "We can't tolerate the encroachment."

"The Cullen will kill everyone in their path."

"No one knows if we'll *win*—"

"We can't just sit here and wait..."

"All we need is for Death to show up **and kill** all the Cullen." Serene pointed at me. "Surely you can do that?"

If we did nothing, time would run out. Malinda would invade and destroy all our lives. I couldn't afford to do nothing—not this time. "We could go *there*... "I began.

"You have to not hesitate." Vitess encouraged me. "You have to face them and not be afraid."

"Only a fool wouldn't be afraid of Malinda," Elijah defended me. He'd still defend me, even angry as he had been. "Morena knows—she's seen how Malinda works." Accidentally, our eyes met.

"We can't just let them just run rampant through Moirai." Jasper stared out the great windows toward the river and Trale Nuvole, the mountain towns whose soft lights twinkled in the dark.

"It'd be nice if we knew what to expect when we got there," Nico said.

"Yes ... that would be nice. It would be ideal if we knew exactly what would happen..." Vitess grabbed Nico's arm. "Of course!" She actually laughed as she spoke, her face giddy. "If we want to know what happens, I could go forward in time to the battle with Malinda and Cullen and find out." Her eyes were alight with anticipation. "I can travel forward a month, a year, two hours—"

"You could..." Serene interjected... "But you can't tell us all the future—that's forbidden." Time manipulation was tricky, and those who could control it weren't supposed to talk to the future versions of others or interfere with their lives.

"There are too many unintended consequences that could arise," Taliesin said. "You'd alter dozens of Time threads and futures with just a hint to one of us."

Vitess stared down at her hands, her expression pensive. "I know the risks," she said quietly. "But we have to do something. We must take action, even if it's dangerous."

We sat in silence. If Vitess traveled forward in time and watched Malinda invade, she'd know why. If she watched our battle, she'd know what we chose to do and whether our plans would succeed or fail. It seemed foolish not to take advantage of our greatest asset, her ability to view the future.

"Even if you do see what happens, how do you know that it will help to tell us?" Nico asked, voicing my doubts. "Once you tell us the future, that doesn't guarantee we'd understand or know how to prevent what happens. If we did prevent war, it would change everything after that, and who knows what would happen later. We might avoid one peril just to cause something worse."

I spoke up. "You'd have to tell us our future, and then we'd have to agree to let it happen anyway."

Serene was not unenthusiastic. "I hate that idea. If Vitess finds out that we lose to Malinda and why we lose, we should make changes so that we don't."

We sat quietly, each lost in our own thoughts. The weight of the task ahead of us was heavy, and the stakes were high.

Vitess stared through the arches, her thoughts as far away as the clouds. "I've seen many paths, but so far, we always face the Cullen here. And when the Wall moves, that means the war is *soon*."

"How soon?" that was Elijah, still steadfastly refusing to look in my direction.

"Now. Immediately. We have days. A week at most."

"How could we change things so that we don't lose?" Serene asked.

Vitess threw up her hands. "I don't know yet. I'll have to... explore a bit."

"Can we focus on the plan?" Jasper asked. "Please."

Everyone waited for me to speak, the one person who knew Malinda and The Grace best. I clenched my hands together, hoping that the feeling of my nails against my palm would keep me focused. "If you take the secret access tunnel into the dungeons, no one will know you're coming. There's a passage door to the left, hidden in shadow, next to a stone wolf. That leads to servants' corridors, and you should be able to spy on Malinda and the Cullen without being observed." I licked my lips nervously. "I can draw you a map. If someone catches you, freeze time and get out of there."

"Thank you," said Vitess.

Taliesin was thinking. "What if we face the Cullen somewhere else? Before they've had a chance to ravage our lands and add to their ranks?"

Elijah rubbed his jaw. "If we killed Malinda first, she can't possibly lead the Cullen across Moirai." The four men looked to Serene and me for our opinion.

"I agree," I said finally. "Vitess should travel to the future and see what happens. Then, if it's something bad, she returns to tell us. We can decide what to do about it once we have more details—whether to change our course or just let it happen. But facing Malinda and the Cullen at Grace Castle seems like a better plan than waiting for them to march here."

"If anything bad happens, just do what you did with Nico and Jasper in the sparring ring or in town with the Cullen," I told Vitess. "Edit Time again and make it so that it never happened, and they never saw you—including any of us."

Serene leaned toward the two of us, her elbows on her knees. "You do it immediately, so we have no time to act on the knowledge. Therefore, we can't possibly change anything about our future." She cracked her knuckles. "Good idea. You're smarter than you look."

"Please," I replied wryly, with a smirk.

"Simple enough," said Elijah, with a voice of velvety steel, his fingers playing with the hilt of the knife strapped to his thigh. I couldn't stop watching him.

Jasper nodded slowly. "Once Vitess has some answers, we'll go. We end this, once and for all."

"How, though?" asked Serene in the silence. "How will we end it?"

Vitess pondered. "If Death doesn't prevail, who will?"

It was a good point. My mother wasn't an immortal, and we were. The Three Fates would outlast her, no matter what happened.

Uncharacteristically quiet, Taliesin finally spoke: "If the Three Fates can rid Moirai of the Cullen, that would be most appreciated... since all of us mortals are likely to be maimed and tortured by them."

Serene nudged his arm. "You know I will undo it if they kill you. I'd bend the arc of Heaven itself if I must."

He caught her hand in his own. "You have no idea how much better that makes me feel."

Vitess said nothing, but she looked at Nico. The wordless look of reassurance that passed between them said volumes about their relationship.

"I'll be back soon," Vitess rose from her chair. "Try not to do anything stupid while I'm gone." Then the controller of time vanished, leaving the scent of firerose in her place.

Lorcan moved, startling me. He'd been so still, so silent, I'd forgotten he was still in the throne room with us. "You said Atropos is spellbound?"

"Yes. At least, I think so."

"That's an easy problem to solve."

"Is it?" I'd wasted almost four years trying to figure out how to free my grandmother. I'd skimmed book after book, seeking the one answer I could not find anywhere.

"Fate's blood—yours, Serene's, Vitess's. That's all it takes." The red-bearded Lord of the Fae looked at me with pity. "Only the blood of the Fates can break a curse like that. Luckily, you have plenty of it."

There was a beat of heavy silence among our group. A shiver of excitement went through my bones. What would happen once we woke Atropos? Surely, she'd want vengeance on Malinda—that much was obvious. But what would the Cullen do without Malinda and with Atropos returned? Could Atropos banish them? Crumble them into dust?

"What do I owe you for this knowledge?" I said suspiciously. "What payment?"

Lorcan studied me, up and down, in a way that made my flesh crawl. He was ruthless, completely immoral, and now I owed him at least three favors. He glanced at Elijah, whose jaw was clenched so hard his teeth might crack. "I'm not interested in you owing me," he said at last. "But Vitess, on the other hand..."

Nico leaped to his feet. "I'll slit your throat in your sleep if you even joke about touching her."

Lorcan held up both hands, his tattoos vibrant in the firelight. "Who said anything about touching her?"

Jasper stood with his jaw set. "As fun as this drama is, we should all get some sleep. It's been a long day and a long night." He inclined his head in a slight bow, then strode out of the room without waiting for goodbyes.

"We should get some sleep," Taliesin murmured. Nico nodded.

After Tally, Nico, and Serene left, Nico, Elijah, and I remained.

"The staff," Lorcan said in the silence. "That's my first payment."

"Atropos' staff? I don't have it. It's still at The Grace." I gazed at him, puzzled. "You knew that I didn't take it with me."

He bowed his head in acknowledgment. "It'll come back to you once you've conquered Malinda. And when it does, it becomes mine."

"What will you do with it?"

"Return it to the caves of Gilroon from whence it came, to the goblin slaves who were forced to craft it for her. It holds a stone that is not a stone, but the eye of one of their ancestors, and they grieve its loss."

"If you wanted it so badly, why did you let Jasper give it to me? Why not keep it for yourself instead of bringing it to The Grace as part of my dowry?"

"Because Vitess said I must. If I wished to cure Moirai of the plague of Malinda, if we were to free you, I had to provide the staff."

I blinked. How many deals, mazes, and threads had Vitess gone through to figure out precisely what was required to free me from that tower?

Lorcan made to leave, his broad back toward us. "Don't misjudge me, Morena. I'm not a bad person. Like you, I've done terrible things. Mine were in service to my people and country, whereas yours were to a tyrant. I don't think we're much different, in the end, if the outcomes were the same."

Now, it was only Elijah and me. The clock on the mantel *ticked, ticked, ticked*. I raised my eyes to him. He was seated on the couch across from me, a low table between us.

"Come here," he murmured at last.

"Why?"

"You know why."

Relieved that our argument seemed to have passed, I didn't even consider refusing—my blood was calling for him like a siren.

I rose and walked over to his couch, aware of every step. With a gentle tug, Elijah pulled me down into his lap. We didn't speak as he took my hand and then kissed it. I tried to ignore the answering pulse of lust and failed as our lips met, gently at first and then with increased urgency.

"I've missed you," he said. *Desperately.* I knew exactly how he felt.

I was entirely on his lap now, nestled against his chest. I wanted to swim in the cool lake of his arms, to slip beneath the facade and into the darkness that lurked beneath.

"We need to talk first," I said.

"Do we?" He kissed my neck, his breath cold against my heated skin. Slowly, he took his finger and drew a circle on my chest. He leaned forward and ran his lips down it, along the sensitive skin at the top of my gown. My back arched, and I tilted my head up, giving him more access, hoping he'd go further. I threaded my fingers through his hair. I didn't care if he took this dress off and we—

Someone coughed at the door.

I jerked to look, and Elijah, damn him, wound his arms around me. I couldn't move; he held on so tight. I couldn't leap away and look innocent, with his face against my breasts, me straddling in his lap.

It was Vitess. "Jasper is waiting in your room," she said quietly. "He wants to talk to you."

Much to my horror, I didn't know which one of us she was talking to. And I couldn't move or cover up what we'd been doing. Not that Elijah seemed interested in that. My face was as red as a flame.

"How long has he been there?" Elijah asked calmly.

She's his sister, for God's sake.

"About thirty seconds." My gaze darted to her, but Vitess' was impassive, her blue eyes carefully blank.

I glanced down at Elijah, who raised his head to look at me. Despite the audience, I'd never wanted to kiss anyone so badly in my life.

Don't go. Don't talk to him. Were those my thoughts or his? At that moment, I didn't know. Still do not know.

"I won't," he assured me aloud. I couldn't ignore the immediate pang of relief I felt. He glanced over at his sister.

"Tell him we're busy."

CHAPTER 24

———◀◆▶———

E lijah led me up a set of spiral stairs, through room after room of
marble, glass, and moonlight. He guided me round and round
through a maze of halls until we were in the highest tower of The
Epiphany, standing at a red door. He held it open silently, and I entered
the room.

His room, I quickly realized. A wide bed dominated one corner, with
a royal blue coverlet that was rumpled and unmade. Soaring windows
watched over all of Moirai; they circled the entire room. I was immediately drawn to the open balcony doors, where sheer silver curtains blew
toward me with each gust of wind. There wasn't a single lamp or candle
in the entire place. Elijah, like me, could see in the dark.

I turned back to him. "The past two days..." I'd barely slept, scared
he'd never speak to me again. I'd stared at the night sky and wondered if
I'd made a mistake if the *Gods* had made a mistake. I needed to tell him.

But Elijah wasn't interested in talking. Instead, he lifted me up, off my
feet, and pressed me against the stone. He covered my mouth with his
own, a sizzling, smoldering kiss that halted every thought.

Perhaps I should have been submissive, sweet, naive. Maybe he expected me to protest. But I'd been deprived of touch for too long, had
withered and suffered loneliness for years. So, instead, I held him like a
vise, determined to never let go. I wrapped my legs around his waist and
plunged my hands into his hair as he laid siege to my throat.

The total darkness made us both bold. He growled, his chest rumbling, and braced one of his hands against the wall. But it didn't feel close enough—I wanted to be enveloped. Our mouths fused together, and still, it wasn't enough.

Elijah spoke, his voice twisted with emotion: "You deprived me of a wedding. But I will have a wedding night."

"Wonderful," I said.

That one word peeled away the last vestiges of his restraint. It was also my final coherent thought before I was tugging at the buttons of his shirt, revealing his broad chest and the mage-mark of an ouroboros eating its own tail. He captured my mouth with his again, his tongue tangled with mine. He acted as if he were possessed, as if he were damned to the gallows at sunrise. There were no gentle caresses or slow words. Our kisses were greedy and mindless, both lost in a lust-fueled spiral.

In one swift motion, my back was on the bed.

"This is in my way—"He ripped my gown open, straight down the front, as if it were made of tissue. The slide of his skin as his body covered mine was both Heaven and Hell, hot and cold, and every rasp and groan undid me. I touched the ouroboros tattoo on his chest and felt it move. Moved as if it might wrap around my fingers.

He trailed kisses down my body from my neck to the line of my underwear. These, too, he removed. The cold air of his room slid over my bare skin.

He sat back on his heels to look at me. He didn't miss an inch as his gaze traveled up my long, pale legs. Elijah studied my skin as if it contained the pages of an ancient manuscript. Gooseflesh broke out, but I refused to fidget. He bent his head and kissed my knee, then trailed his fingers upward, pausing.

Once he could see me—really see all of me—I suddenly remembered that I'd never done any of this before, not any of it. And now he was staring, his eyes traveling down my body, breasts, abdomen, legs... I turned my face toward the pillow and blushed.

"You weren't so shy a moment ago." He paused. "Hmm."

Then he leaned forward and kissed me again, lightly, as he settled next to me, where he could stroke his hands along my body. "You're a virgin."

"Yes." *Obviously.*

I looked over at him, my golden hair spread out on his royal blue sheets. He kissed me softly, gently at first. He traced my ears, my nipples, my nose. As I squirmed, he kissed each of my fingers, then flipped me over to trace his tongue along the marks that ran blue-black along my spine. It seemed like an hour had passed before his hand finally slipped between my legs, and I arched against his fingers, beckoning.

Still, he only teased me.

"What are you waiting for?" I asked, breathless.

"You haven't said yes." His voice was solemn.

To marriage, to sex, to blood-sharing.

I didn't see any point in delaying. Our marriage was already written in the stars, destined. Decreed by the Fates. What right did I have to say no, even if I'd wanted to?

For once, I was not only darkness. I was the moonlight and stars; I felt beautiful and safe. He wanted me and I wanted him.

"I'm yours," I murmured, "and you are mine."

Elijah breathed against my skin as he grasped my hips in his hands and then slowly, carefully sheathed himself in me. I cried out; I whimpered as our gazes locked. He waited for the sharp edge of pain to subside, for me to relax, kissing me until my head spun.

I didn't speak; I couldn't. My fingers clenched into his sheets, his hair, his back.

"Gods, Morena," he murmured as he slowly sank into me.

He drew back, those gorgeous eyes memorizing my face. He smelled like evergreens, like winter mornings.

"Are you alright," he asked, worried.

"Yes." It seemed I was incapable of more than that. Now I was his, officially. There would be no more holding back—no secrets, no reservations, no lies. I promised myself right then that I would be the person he deserved, the person he'd wished for. I touched his face. "Yes," I said again.

Elijah pushed into me again. Once, twice. Always watching my expression, learning how he affected me. Unable to help myself, I moaned. It wasn't painful, it was something in between. A sharp edge that didn't cut me.

With slow, maddening thrusts, he set a deliciously steady pace. Leaning down, Elijah's mouth was affixed to my own so that every inhale of his was mine. I grabbed the blankets on either side of myself and drew them up, pulling them toward me and roping them across his back.

One of his hands gripped my hair, twisted in it, while his other curved around my back, held my shoulder. Despite his cool skin, he was a dragon. Power lived in his veins, and there was fire in his heart.

Repeatedly, our eyes met as he moved inside me. The intensity was searing; I felt my dark powers surge with delight as I read his expression—

He was mine. I owned him; I possessed him. The realization swept me away; it vanquished the worst parts of my insecurity and doubt. It was a feeling of triumph that I'd never known before.

Then his pace changed. Deeper. More intimate. He touched my face and kissed me again, soul-tingling kisses that greedily accepted. It dragged away all sense of control, and inside I felt like a clock, twisted tighter and tighter, desperate to find something...

"Let go, darling," he said, his breath ragged. "Let go. You won't break me."

He heard me gasp his name, helpless, lost in him.

And what was incredible was that he was as lost as I was. As I watched him lose control, it felt as if I was breaking, being remade into something new. Pleasure cracked like a spiderweb through my body. And when the finely honed edge of pleasure was so intense that I could no longer stand it, I came with a blast of midnight that toppled his lamp, shoved open the balcony doors, and howled out into the world like a banshee.

Afterward, we lay there, wrapped in his soft blankets, our chests heaving. Elijah gazed down at me, the lust-fueled haze leaving his eyes replaced by something much more tender: questioning.

"I didn't hurt you, did I?" he said as he brushed my hair back from my face.

"Of course not." I traced my fingers down the hard lines of his jaw.

"Good," he murmured.

Still underneath him, he was still inside me as I peered around the room. "So this is where you hide from everyone," I said at last.

He chuckled, low and soft. "I chose this room when I was twelve. You lived in a tower; I wanted to live in a tower. I'd look north and hope you were alright and know deep down that you weren't, know that I couldn't do anything about it."

"Why did it matter?" I asked, failing to understand. "You didn't even know me."

"Because you were my one true love. The forgotten princess locked away by an evil queen. And I was the prince who was going to rescue you."

I knew a little of what he must have felt—that feeling of being powerless to save the people you loved, the torment of not knowing what was happening. The regret and despair when you failed. I'd felt the same or nearly the same for Taliesin and Arabella. So I pulled his face down toward mine and kissed him again.

Thank you, I said to his soul. *Thank you for loving me.*

I couldn't explain how much it meant to know that someone, *someone*, had worried about me and cared. As I studied Elijah, I felt the mage-marks on my spine move and watched as the ouroboros on his chest slowly shifted. "Why do they move? And why only when we touch?"

"Recognition. Our powers live there, in them. And we are so rare—imagine how they must feel, that sort of magic, to be trapped in us, to find and touch its mate after all this time."

Elijah pulled back a few breaths, and I made a slight gasping sound. He gave a knowing smile.

"Is this a dream?" I said, wonderingly. Here was a man looking at me, not with fear or revulsion, but as if I was meaningful. Like nothing else could ever matter to him as much as I did.

"Does it feel like a dream?" he asked.

"Absolutely." I cupped his face in my hands and relished his answering smile.

This time, he did not tease. He did not delay but immediately devoured, and within seconds, I was panting, one hand pressing against the ouroboros tattooed on his chest, the other firmly wrapped around one of the posts of his headboard.

Caught between his bed and the hard lines of his body, I had no choice but to accept his teeth and lips and bruising hands. There was such permanence in his kiss, in his expression. It reassured me that this was someone I could throw my entire self at, even the jagged, angry parts, red and raw, and he wouldn't flinch.

I loved his roughness, but I loved how he yielded to me even more. How each time I touched him, he growled or groaned, no longer stoic. Every stroke, every kiss provoked him and unraveled his armor. And although he was often silent in the light of day, under the cover of darkness, Elijah sighed and murmured and praised me. His guard was down completely.

And I knew that if I wanted to—if I wanted—I could break him. That part of me might even enjoy it.

Just as I felt myself drifting off to sleep, his arm slung over me as he nestled against me, I had a terrible thought. "My mother told me once that I will kill every person I'll ever love," I said. "Do you think that's true?"

Elijah kissed me gently, his lips an immortal whisper against mine. "Not anymore."

Much later, I opened my eyes to silence and an empty bed. Elijah was gone. Rolling my neck, I examined the nightstand and noticed his pile of books. I skimmed the titles in the dim morning light: *Mysteries of the Cullen, Cullen History, Pathology, and Progression.*

Frowning, I opened one of them and skimmed the pages, only to find that he'd taken copious notes in the margins.

I'd never considered what Elijah did in his spare time, not really. I hadn't thought of the long hours we were apart, not of what he did or whom he spoke to. I'd gone to dinner and drank and danced, but he'd been here, reading, trying to find a way for us to win against Malinda.

For our future. For Moirai.

Out of the corner of my eye, I noticed a movement out on the balcony. His white shirt was on the floor, and I shrugged it on, delighting in the smell of him within its fabric. Elijah sat on the edge of the Castle, his feet hanging into space, the wind tousling his chestnut hair. I dragged my gaze away from his bare skin as he surveyed Moirai.

I paused behind him, then put my hands on his shoulders. "Aren't you afraid to fall?" I looked down and down through the clouds. I felt a little nauseated by the extreme drop.

"We all fall ... eventually." He dragged a hand through his hair, making it stand on end.

The sun had risen in the east, casting its rays over the violet mountains. The village was just waking up. Fat white clouds drifted across the sky, and Lachesis-blue flags waved in the breeze.

"It's an incredible view," I said.

He glanced back at me, still smelling of him, my hair tangled, wearing his shirt. "It is now."

I almost laughed. Elijah's body was as if it'd been sculpted from marble: his mouth, eyes, even his earlobes. I was tall and bony, all awkward angles, with very little womanly softness.

He slipped his arm around my shoulders as I settled beside him, brave enough to sit on that stone ledge because I knew he would never let me fall.

"About the wedding," I said at last. Even if he'd brushed it aside earlier, I knew we *had* to resolve it.

"I'd rather not talk about it. The past is past."

"Can you at least admit that you were wrong? That I did the right thing by saving people in the village, and you had no real reason to be so angry?"

Elijah exhaled, deep and steady. "Yes. I can at least admit that." He drew me toward his body, and I nestled close, inhaling his cool, evergreen scent. "I was selfish and wanted to hurt you as much as you hurt me."

I nuzzled his neck. "You succeeded."

"So you missed me too?" He responded by kissing my forehead. "Hm. Good."

We lingered there in the sun, talking. It was easy between us, and though we were new at being lovers, I could easily imagine our future. Mornings like this one, discussing our realm, friends, and family. We watched the sun rise over the wide world of Moirai, and we did what all couples did – we made plans. We laughed. And slowly, surely, I felt the constant tension easing from my shoulders.

Later, out on his balcony, he kissed his way up my inner thigh until he was at the crease of my leg and hip bone. He lazily traced his tongue closer and closer until he bit me lightly. He had not even an instant of hesitation or insecurity.

"Tell me a secret," Elijah murmured.

"I dream about you."

He smiled against the skin of my thighs, pleased.

"I don't suppose I kissed you like this?" He pressed his lips to my mound. "Or like this? The prince of your girlhood fantasies?" He slipped his tongue down, down ... it was soft, tender.

No, not at all like that.

I breathed heavily and writhed under his touch. Nervous self-conscious, but still wanting him to continue. Too shy to ask him.

He paused. "Actually ... I think not." He slid up my body to kiss me again on the mouth, rough and hard.

"Should we go inside?" he asked, his hand wrapped around my throat. "Where it's more private?"

We could hide, go where no one would see, and return to the shadows where monsters belonged. Or we could stay and make love in the light. I knew he'd do whatever I wanted. My eyes answered him, even if my words couldn't.

CHAPTER 25

—◆◆◆—

We told our stories and revealed ourselves one dangerous confession at a time. Because of the bond, which Elijah made sure never weakened, I felt all his emotions: the rage, the need to take and plunder, his desperate desire to possess me. I was grateful he let me in; let me see all of the vulnerable parts of him. He wasn't nearly as clean or elegant as I'd once believed him to be, and I reveled in his darkness that so closely matched my own.

We made love in the soft pink dawn, at the darkest hours of the night. With Vitess still investigating our futures, there was nothing to do but wait. Elijah and I took full advantage of the time. My heart felt impossibly heavy, filled to overflowing. It felt like a dream, silver-edged, and the taste and weight of him seeped into me. Sometimes, our greedy, red-hazed fury was absent, replaced by a stunning tenderness. I could neither resist him nor refuse him.

"This book is in elvish," I said, holding up one of the many tomes on the nightstand. "You read Elvish and Goblin?"

"Mmm." His brow was knit as he skimmed another. The light in the tower played over us as we lounged in his bed.

I assumed the language was helpful for diplomatic purposes, for the many visits from our mystical neighbors. "Say something to me in Elvish."

Elijah put the book aside and whispered against my ear: "*Pan fyddaf yn edrych arnoch chi, gwn fy mod yn caru chi. Er mai dyna'r cyfan a wyddwn o'r blaen.*"

He met my eyes. "When I look at you, I know that I love you. Even though it is all that I've ever known." Elijah kissed my shoulder affectionately.

I admired how open he was, unguarded and honest. My walls, so carefully built and tended, crumbled. I told him everything about Arabella, about my mother, about walking the lonely roads of Kinver'i with the mask on my face.

"It's a duty I never wanted," I told him. "A burden."

"Some burdens no one else can carry. You'll save Moirai, one way or another," he assured me.

"All I can do is kill; all I can grant is a quiet death. What sort of solution is that?"

"In some cases, Death is the best medicine," he murmured.

"Then we're in luck because they'll all be dead when Malinda arrives."

Elijah considered me. "No. They won't be dead. Your people will be prisoners, forced into doing vile and terrible things for the rest of their days. Can you imagine what it would be like if you could still see and be inside that terrible body, trapped into doing Malinda's bidding?"

I had no problem imagining it. It was my life in the tower before Jasper had come to rescue me.

"I hope to all the Gods that you will end our people's lives before Malinda makes them into Cullen monsters. Anyone would. You may not love being the controller of Death or the Reaper, but you're the lesser of two evils, Morena. The better option. Personally, if I could die, I would rather die by your hand than be Malinda's servant."

"I suppose." Begrudgingly, I admitted that he was likely correct. If I could not be good, if I could not be normal, at least I could fulfill my destiny.

"You're a strange creature," he mused as I drifted to sleep. "Death, but you do not like killing; a Fate who believes man should make their own destiny."

"Sorry to disappoint you," I mumbled, burrowing my face in his neck and sighing happily. Sometimes, after he fell asleep, I watched him. I traced the lines of his nose and drew circles on his chest. So gently it might have been a whisper, I touched his brown hair, then studied his eyelashes and cheekbones. Memorizing.

"Now I understand why some artists paint the same person over and over," I replied when he asked what I was doing.

For the first time in my life, I felt safe. Loved. Adored.

I wanted to learn his body and mind like it was a map – a map to my salvation.

"About Jasper..." My voice was hoarse. By bringing it up, I knew I might ruin the moment, yet I didn't think we could move forward without clearing the air and finally talking through our feelings.

He paused, then resumed drawing circles with his fingers across my bare stomach. "Before you go further, just know I've seen you with him. In the woods, at the inn. I was there."

That was different from where I thought this conversation was going. "If you've seen everything, why ask me questions? Why play games?"

"I wanted to know if you'd lie to me." He wasn't angry or tense. "I shifted into the dragon or a snake, or ... whatever was needed. I followed you."

"You sent him to my door. You told him to convince me to leave."

"I did. But I didn't think that Jasper would *convince* you... how he did. I didn't think he'd take advantage of you or the situation like he did. We've been friends as long as he's been alive. I foolishly thought him loyal."

"At first, he was just a way to escape Malinda. But then, during the journey, I felt drawn to him. He reminded me of Taliesin, with his jokes and his optimism." I spoke haltingly, unsure if Elijah's jealousy would get the better of him and spoil my sense of closeness.

He paused in his petting. "Go on."

"I think... I'd been so lonely, so lost, for so long. Without Arabella or Taliesin, I just ... and then he brought Nico back to me, and he smiled at me and made me laugh—"

"It doesn't hurt that he's handsome and tall and a prince who can grow flowers in his hands," Elijah finished for me.

"Right. But when I examined his life and saw that he would die, I felt I could never have anything. Everything good is taken from me. And so I gave him extra years. I pushed his time of Death out by hundreds of years so I wouldn't have to be alone again."

"I didn't realize you'd done that." His azure eyes were pensive.

"Yes. It was the first time I'd ever used one of my powers to save someone."

"And what about me?" he asked, his fingers still stroking me as lightly as snowfall.

I took a deep breath, trying to find my courage. "All I can think about is you. You're like a well, and I've fallen in, and I can't find a way out."

"Do you want out?" His tone was even, but I could sense his worry. He didn't want to keep me captive. He didn't want to make me unhappy.

"No." It was true. I didn't. I wanted to stay with him until even the stars burned out. Familiar, understood, and safe.

"But sometimes..." I took a deep breath. "Sometimes you leave without explanation. You vanish. I have no idea where you are; I'm alone."

"I leave when I'm angry," he said quietly. "I want to punish you but not hurt you."

I understood that feeling all too well. And yet... "I have wondered if you can be relied on to stay."

Elijah raised his gaze to mine. The dark blue flecks in his eyes could be counted, I realized, if I just looked closely enough. "Do you really think I would ever leave you?"

No. Yes. I don't know.

"We both have our demons—"I began.

"Not like that. There is nothing and no one that would ever make me give you up," Elijah vowed.

Maybe I was a fool to believe him. Perhaps it was the expression on his face, so impassioned, so sure. But I did believe; more than that, it was more than I'd ever believed in anyone else. While Jasper had had my attention, Elijah had my soul. I should have told him. It might have mattered; it might have made a difference.

"Kiss me again," I said instead, my voice raw.

So he did. He kissed me until all I felt was him. Firmly in control at first, then urgent, rough... As he did so, Elijah ran his fingers over the mage-marks on my back, and the tattoos trembled, alive at his touch.

When Vitess appeared a few days later, our entire group was waiting as if we'd known she might drop from the sky directly into the chair. We were both impatient to hear how her travels across time had gone.

She looked more tired than I'd ever seen her, her soft caramel hair frazzled and dirty. Vitess slumped, her small shoulders hunched. "I traveled forward, again and again, thinking there would be some clue, some variation. But I found nothing new."

I wiped the sweat from my brow. Serene's study was always too warm, and thick, plush, blood-red carpet covered the stone floor. The fireplace was massive, packed tightly with burning logs. She was accustomed to the heat, just as I was at home in the cold.

"Tell us everything," Elijah demanded.

"The first wave of her armies arrive here in fourteen days. When they do, Morena vanquishes them, but she goes missing. She's locked somewhere." Vitess avoided my eyes. "So the town is overrun, then the Castle. Elijah and the other dragons kill many, but we lose. We go to Kinseamair to regroup, and Serene asks me to travel back in time to see the original Three Fates to get their opinions on what to do."

"Surely not—"Serene begins to say, but Vitess cuts her off.

"You do because Taliesin is missing too, and you're... you don't know what to do."

Uncharacteristically silent, Serene looked at her feet, her black fighting leathers, and her boots. "Go on."

"So, as a result, I went backward in time to see the Three Fates. They were..." Vitess rubbed her eyebrows, a habit she tended to do only when she wasn't sure of something. "When I arrived, Lachesis had just visited Kinver'i. She'd come to see Atropos, bringing her daughter. They argued. Lachesis returned to The Epiphany. There was no war between them then, though clearly they were angry at each other. So, I went forward to a different time before Morena was born. I discovered that Melchior declared war on Lachesis and Clotho."

"Did you speak to anyone?" I said.

" I *had to*, or else Clotho would have never let me leave ... but Lachesis said not to worry about her, that she's harmless."

Lachesis. Another controller of time. She could interfere in the past or the future, the same as Vitess could. If she changed events, even subtly, that might mean we were never born. One wrong word and Lachesis could erase us all.

"You spoke to Clotho *too?* Did you tell them who you were? "Serene demanded as she pointed her dagger at Vitess. "Did they realize?"

Vitess crossed her arms in a defensive stance. "I know it's forbidden, but I still think I did the right thing."

"No, you've put all of us in jeopardy. You're not supposed to be seen, much less speak to them."

"Let's not blame each other—"I began.

Life and Death, with time caught in the middle. It was just too appropriate. I desperately did not want to have them argue because we all knew where arguments between the Fates would lead.

"I'd rather argue," Serene said. "What else did you tell her? Don't spare any details."

"I told Lachesis that the Three Fates become enemies. I told them Moirai was split apart between them and that we, the Three Fates' descendants, want to unite it."

Oh Hell. She told Lachesis everything.

"You couldn't have managed one tiny lie?" Serene was outraged.

"Well, no... What would be the point? She still has her abilities, so she could have just traveled to her own future and fact-checked me, couldn't she?"

Vitess had a point. I put my head in my hands. *Thank Nyx that I'm not the controller of time—I could never keep it all straight.*

"I don't know how you can be so untroubled," Serene said. "From this moment onward, our lives will be different."

"Unlikely. Lachesis seems to be a—what do you sometimes call me?" She glared at Serene. "A boring rule-follower?"

"In this case, I would have *preferred* you followed the basic principles of Time control, "Elijah said, "because those rules exist for a reason. You're not supposed to intervene or speak to people. We can't predict or keep track of all the outcomes. Especially not with the original Fates."

I bit my tongue. We'd been having Vitess intervene for weeks in various situations, and no one ever complained until today.

Vitess apparently had the same thought and narrowed her eyes. "Wasn't it you who told me to go in the first place?"

It wasn't. "Whoever's idea it was, I'm glad," I pleaded with them both. "Even if—"

"Now, unlike before, we have an ally, and I think she will provide an answer." Vitess exhaled a long, drawn-out sigh. Her doll-like face was pale and pinched, and she'd lost weight. "I need sleep. And it's time to think. It was a long couple of weeks."

"Weeks?" I replied. "You've been gone for four days."

"No, Morena. It's been much longer than that." Vitess left the room with a yawn, leaving the rest of us to ponder our newfound situation.

A few seconds passed before Jasper said anything. "She didn't reset Time soon enough—Lachesis had time enough to wreak havoc."

"Obviously," Nico said, his tone sharp.

Serene folded her arms. "Just knowing your future is enough to make you behave differently. Small changes have consequences."

"Keeping track of outcomes or others' actions is too complicated." Just *knowing* that I was destined to wed Elijah changed everything for me. He had me second-guessing all my interactions with him. "Even if she remembered exactly everything she said or did..."

"Even if we left right now, it would take a week to get there." Jasper stood by the fireplace, drinking Fae wine.

Elijah, across from me, steepled his fingers and considered. He was so thoughtful, so controlled, my steadfast prince clad in blue — outside the bedroom. Inside, well... I bit my lip.

"I don't want you back there," Serene told Taliesin. "Malinda told you not to come back."

"That's too damn bad." Taliesin ran a hand through his golden hair. "Morena can't face our mother with a horde of Cullen slaves without me."

"I absolutely can." I didn't want my brother there either.

"No offense, Morena, but my life is mine to risk, not yours."

Serene huffed and folded her arms.

"To recap, the plan is... kill Malinda, free Atropos?" Jasper asked the group.

"Tomorrow," Vitess announced suddenly, appearing seemingly out of nowhere.

Startled, Jasper dropped his glass onto the floor, where it shattered. "Can you *not* do that?"

"We are meant to leave tomorrow," she said flatly, handing it back to him in one piece.

I made eye contact with Serene. Vitess must have seen something strange—her expression was off, a tightness that hadn't been there before. After initial confusion, the men hurried from the room, discussing plans, gear, and weaponry.

Elijah stood slowly, appraising us. "I'll go inform the dragons. And my parents." *And meet you in the tower later.*

I nodded, still inspecting Vitess. She'd seen *something* she didn't like and must not want anyone else to be in the room when she told us about it.

Soon after, Jasper followed, leaving the Three Fates alone.

Vitess began calmly drinking a glass of retsina. Serene watched and ran a finger down the white line of her scar. "Well." Her storm-gray eyes shifted from doubt to speculation to resolve. "Was there anything else you wanted to tell us?"

Vitess sat the glass down with a click. "We take the dragons and we go."

Once again, Serene looked to me suspiciously. "More detail than that would certainly be useful."

I wrung my hands. "I wish we had more time. Are we ready for this? It feels like a bad idea."

Vitess scowled, an expression utterly out of place on her soft face. "No more delays. We must leave tomorrow."

"Of course," I assured her. "We'll do exactly as you say. If that is what it takes to win, we will do it."

"It is. You'll just have to trust me," Vitess said.

The clock on the mantel ticked away the seconds. *Click. Click. Click.* It brought back memories of the Cullen, and I shuddered. I started to ask a question, but when my eyes returned to the settee where Vitess was seated, she was gone. Vanished without comment, without a goodbye.

Serene was pensive. "She's acting very strange. I don't like it."

I didn't either, but Vitess was the one with the answers. And we had agreed – she would look into our futures and guide us. And we would, no matter what, follow her lead. We would try not to ask too many questions. "I didn't expect it to be quite so difficult," I mumbled. "And what choice do we have?"

"Well. None, really." Serene put her hands behind her head and stretched. She toyed with the gold necklace at her throat, which looked like an open eye with a fiery red stone. "Life and Death say nay, but it seems Time has decided for us."

CHAPTER 26

Three dragons, six of us. Three Fates versus the Queen of the Blood Throne.

In front of me, Jasper stared forward, his hands clasping the dragon's reins. The dragon, of course, was Elijah, who insisted on carrying me so he'd be touching me at all times. Serene and Taliesin were paired on a second dragon, Nico, and Vitess on the third.

As we crossed the Bridgewater Inn, it began to rain, and before long, we were all soaked to the skin, shivering in our clothes. The warmth Jasper put off made his clothes steam, and I huddled closer, my chest against his back. My hands, he covered with one of his own to warm them.

Elijah banked hard to the left. I clutched Jasper's waist even tighter.

Can you hear what I'm thinking?

No, thank God.

A long pause, so long that I thought Elijah wouldn't say anything else. *Not loving him being so close to you, though.*

I could feel the strain of his emotions. So I carefully rubbed the part of his scaled back, the part I could reach from my seat. *Don't worry. I'll make it up to you later.*

The dragon beneath me gave a growl of approval.

Previously, we traveled five days to reach The Epiphany. This time, we'd fly the entire route in two, stopping just once.

As if by agreement, Jasper and I didn't speak. We flew for the next twelve hours until my back ached, and my hands were stiff from the cold; snowflakes started gathering on my eyelashes and hair. Finally, I began to recognize the signs of home. Below the dragon, trees withered into leafless bones. We'd reached the Wall. The silence lengthened, stretched, and expanded until there was again nothing but a profound quiet that pressed upon my heart like a fist.

"We're here," I murmured into Jasper's shoulder.

"I know." His voice was clipped. "Are you alright?"

No, "I replied, "I am not alright."

He surveyed the land below—a vast canvas, white and empty. "Do you think she'll have Cullen acting as guards to keep us out of the Castle?"

"She wanted a confrontation—perhaps the doors will be wide open."

Elijah decided where we should rest, leading the dragons down into an open meadow just beyond the forests of Lerza. The beasts touched down softly. For such gigantic animals, you'd assume they'd make a tremendous noise, but no, dragons were more like cats—their feet light and padded underneath, the thud of their landings no louder than the snowfall itself.

But almost as soon as we landed, I heard a sound. Faint, far off, but I'd know that sound anywhere.

Click Click. Click Click.

Cullen teeth chattered—and it sounded like hundreds of them. They were heading directly toward us, able to sense hearts pounding and rapid breathing of living beings.

Taliesin tried not to look panicky and failed. He'd never gotten past his total fear of the Cullen. "They're close. Too close."

"Don't worry," Serene assured him. Then Serene bid the earth to rise, and it did. Right under our feet, the ground began to lift itself, creating a miniature mountain under our feet. The sides were so steep they were like walls, a pedestal upon which the group could sleep. Jasper again crafted small snow castles, a miniature village atop our mountain. Elijah took my hand and tugged me into ours.

"What about the Cullen?" I asked Elijah.

"They'll look, see a mountain, and wander off. They won't see us. And with these walls—"

He tapped the smooth snow that ensconced us. "They won't hear us either."

Elijah laid out our cloaks and beckoned. "We should get some sleep."

I tried, but I'd become accustomed to a warm bed, to blankets. I shivered, tucking myself into a tight ball against him.

An hour or so later, Elijah murmured into my hair. "Why are you still awake?"

"Nervousness."

Outside, the snowing stopped, and the sky was pure onyx, threaded with bright white stars. Superficially, the night was quiet ... peaceful. But the Cullen were near. Their rotting bodies, their souls like battered butterflies, their clicking teeth—I could feel them out there. Waiting.

"I have a gift for you. Something to make you feel more confident." He rummaged through his pack, then handed me a wrapped parcel.

A gift for me?

A pulse came in response. Deep, sinister, resounding in the marrow of my bones. Like a heartbeat, like a *greeting*. I couldn't bring myself to unwrap it. It was still pulsing. I could *hear* whatever was inside. It felt familiar. It felt wrong, and in a flash, I knew what my lover had brought me... I couldn't just sit here, like a fool, staring at it all night.

My hands shaking, I slowly untied the ribbon and lifted the lid. I sucked in a breath, the night air cooling my throat. It was the mask. *My mask,* the one I'd thrown in the sea—black, glittering obsidian, with bones of pearl. The skull face I'd shed when I came to The Epiphany. He'd had gone through the trouble of finding it. He'd brought it here.

"You do not like it?" he asked, perplexed.

I stared down at its terrible face, not sure how to feel. "I threw it into the sea."

"And I retrieved it. I want every piece of you, Morena, even the broken ones, even the ones you throw away and try to hide. There's nothing I wouldn't do, no price I wouldn't pay. After all..." He ran his fingers through my hair, tugged it to pull my head backward, revealing my throat, where he leaned to place a kiss... "I have plenty of gold, and only one of you."

Still, he felt my unease. "Do you want me to get rid of it?" he asked later, in the middle of the night, knowing I was awake and thinking.

"No," I sighed. "We may need it."

The rest of the night was uneventful, and shockingly—despite the sinister mask that now lay to my left—I slept as soundly as I usually did, wrapped tightly in the circle of his arms. We packed up our things and mounted the dragons, and then we were off, flying into a brilliant blue day.

Night had fallen when we crossed the Sea of Obsidia with its black waters, white-capped waves, and ink-colored sand beaches. The Castle was barely visible due to a low-lying fog and heavy, relentless snow. I could scarcely see Elijah's head, much less the Castle, the towers, or the black flags that flew from its corners.

Elijah flew straight down, plummeting toward the earth through the clouds, and my stomach felt like it was inside my mouth. Then his dragon's wings beat the air, and we settled softly into the white drifts. He'd landed on the west side of the Castle, just beyond a grove of trees.

"Now what?" Serene demanded as she slid down from the back of her dragon. Her short dark hair stood on end, spiky with rain and snow, and her skin was paler than usual, making the scars across her face nearly match her rich, vibrant, red wool cloak. Her *very red* cloak.

For God's sake. Has she never heard of the concept of stealth? I yanked Serene backward, away from the tree line, back to the shadows underneath Elijah's massive legs. "In that color, you stand out like blood on parchment. You can probably be seen for miles—couldn't you wear anything else?"

She pulled her arm away. "I like this color."

Jasper approached us. "We can't fly any closer—the odds are too high that Malinda would see us coming."

"So we hike in?" Nico asked, as his knives put themselves back into their holsters along his thigh.

"Not exactly…" Jasper gave Serene a look. "Will you please ask them?" He glanced toward the forest.

"Who?" Taliesin asked. "The Cullen?"

"The trees," he replied.

"You know they hate that." Serene frowned, furrows forming between her eyebrows.

"I know, and I wouldn't ask unless it wasn't the best way to get us all there in one piece."

"Ugh. Fine." She walked away, but not before unpinning her red cloak.

Without warning, there was a whisper of shadow and a whirl of snow, and then a raven perched on my shoulder. I stood stock still, paralyzed. It nuzzled my cheek. "Elijah?"

In the flesh … feathers.

"They'll do it," Serene confirmed as she strode back to us, knee-deep in wet snow. "They seem annoyed but willing."

"Good. Elijah, can you fly ahead and ready things at the crypts? Hopefully, these trees know where they are." Vitess spoke to the crow. She, unlike me, was well-accustomed to his shapeshifting.

The raven blinked and took off with a caw, flapping his wings.

Seconds later, Jasper was next to me. I gasped when his arm slid around my waist and jerked me against his hard chest. "What are you doing—?" I whispered furiously as he pulled me toward him. Of all the opportunistic, ridiculous things to do—

"Stay absolutely still," he commanded, "and don't scream."

Which did not stop me at all from looking up, and up, and up as a gigantic evergreen leaned over us. Like writhing tentacles, its roots formed feet that carried it over the snow.

"Jasper. Do not—"

He grinned. "Fear is a good look on you," he laughed and fell backward, his arms wrapped tight around me, into the dark, into the tree. Once we were both *inside* its wooden heart, the tree mended and folded itself shut.

Jasper's body curved around mine as tight as a vise. "Shhh," he murmured. One breath at a time, he loosened his grip.

I took a shallow sip of air. The space we were trapped in was like a coffin—no room to breathe, no room to shift, and we were completely encased in wood. My breasts slammed against Jasper's chest, his hips crushed against mine.

Outside, I could hear very faint sounds of inhuman shrieks, and the tree around us trembled, then walked us through the forest toward Grace Castle.

"We're *in* a tree, "I marveled.

"Indeed."

Inside our tiny space was complete and utter darkness, and it took my eyes a moment to adjust. It reminded me of the dungeons or nights in our tower when clouds blotted out the stars. It smelled beautiful, like aged paper, pine, smoky apple, and cinnamon. That part was Jasper, of course. His scent assaulted my senses, filling my entire nose and mouth. His body, firmly against mine, left no room for a breath between us.

"It's just until we reach the crypts. Everyone else is fine. Elijah will fly through the forest, transform, and kill any Cullen who waits there for us. If Malinda should peer out the window, she'll see a forest, trees swaying."

I would have nodded, but there wasn't enough space for the movement. "That was smart," I said as I tried to shift and move further away from him.

"Yes." His voice sent shivers down my neck and shoulders. "Trees were our favorite hiding place as children."

He moved just a little, giving me the barest amount of room. Dimly, outside the tree, I heard clicking, followed by silence.

We listened from the darkness. There was not even a hair's width of space around us. My hands splayed against Jasper's chest, where I'd tried to push him away. I could feel every inch of my skin he touched. I could only shift slowly as if moving through jelly.

I heard whispering.

"They said they'll protect us." Jasper paused and listened again.

"The trees said that?"

"Mmm. Yes. It's very kind of them, especially since all they'll get from us in return is one day being chopped up for firewood or cut into logs for a house."

"Noted," I muttered. "Thank the trees."

A few minutes later, the evergreen stopped, its giant lumbering foot-steps fading. Then, it unfolded, and the dusky gray light of a snowy evening temporarily blinded me.

Next to us, Serene and Taliesin emerged from a stately evergreen, and Nico and Vitess from another nearby.

Elijah waited for us, holding the gates to the graveyard open. Like the rest of our group, he wore black: black tunic, black pants, black fighting leathers. It was the first time I'd ever seen him in anything but blue, and he looked so dangerous that I felt my heart rate increase.

Attuned to me, he glanced over. "What?" he asked.

"Nothing." I gave him a small, secret smile. "You look good in black." He knew *immediately* what it was I was thinking of. Elijah shook his head with a small laugh.

As I entered the graveyard, I glanced up at the two sinister statues that guarded the interior. They were easily double my height, and their carved faces stared down at all of us ominously. Each was armed with a scythe, the blade honed so sharp it could have halved a snowflake. The snow here was deep, mid-thigh in places, so everyone tried to step lightly.

"We'll regroup in the crypts," I told the group as I ducked under low-hanging branches. "They are safe, and the doors are iron with locks."

Taliesin forged through the snow drifts behind me, his boots sinking in the snow. His golden hair was tied back. "Won't someone see our footprints?"

"They'll be covered within the hour." That was Jasper from the rear.
Exactly.

As for Vitess, she looked green. She hated flying and hated enclosed
spaces even more. I didn't imagine she'd had a pleasant journey.

The seven of us trudged through the burial plots, threading our way
between stones and mausoleums. When we reached his burial place, Taliesin eyed the phoenixes and skeletons with horror. "Incredible. Malinda
wouldn't lower herself to provide us with unmolded bread or firewood,
but my crypt looks like I was King of Moirai."

Serene, meanwhile, stared at the skeletal marble hands that clutched
the tailfeathers and made a noise of appreciation. "Do you mind if we
use your tomb as our base of operations," she asked Taliesin.

"No, and thanks for asking," he joked.

I tugged at the shiny marble handles and wrenched the heavy iron
doors open. The interior of Taliesin's tomb was a long rectangle, with
circular windows cut like moons along the top to allow in the light—all
too small for a person to fit through. There was only one door. It was
one of the safest places to be, shielded from the wind and snow.

But much to my surprise, a pallet was laid on the floor. There was also
a small amount of winter berries. It seemed abandoned, but someone
had clearly been staying here. *It's probably a villager hiding from Cullen.
I suppose I'm not the only one who found the graveyard a welcome refuge.*

"It'd be easier to face Malinda if we had at least a little daylight," Nico
griped. "Not all of us can see in the dark."

I froze. That was true—while Elijah and I could see perfectly well in
total darkness, none of them could.

"It can't be helped," Serene said. "And what are you, afraid of the
dark?"

"We'll rest until dawn," I assured them as they stomped the snow from their boots, and I shut the door behind us. "Elijah and I can see in the dark, so we'll keep watch."

Serene and Taliesin immediately went to one corner, and he spread out his cloak for the two of them to lay on, then used hers as a blanket. Nico and Vitess, meanwhile, seemed committed to sharing warmth but not speaking, and they slept awkwardly, back-to-back. Elijah made our bed closest to the door and beckoned me to it, leaving Jasper alone.

Everyone talked in hushed tones for a while, but their voices subsided. Elijah, his chest against my back, lazily stroked my stomach, and the area just under my breasts.

I rolled over to face him. My gaze fused with his; our blood and magic surged in my veins.

Slowly, silently, I traced the line of his cheekbone and nose with my fingertips. I touched his soft chestnut hair, the small scar on his chin that I knew came from shaving too closely. He pulled me a bit closer, and our lips met.

"Are you worried about tomorrow?" he whispered against my mouth.

Yes.

When his tongue brushed against mine, I smothered a groan. Even though everyone was around us... I felt his immediate reaction against my thigh. His hands slid down my body, first my breasts, then my waist. His hands roved further, streaked down, and massaged me through my pants. I gasped as one of his incisors pierced my tongue, and he sucked the drop of blood from it. I returned the favor, doing the same.

The rush of sharing power with Elijah was like nothing else. Every fiber of my being wanted him closer.

"I won't let anything bad happen to you," he promised.

I grabbed a fistful of his shirt and tugged at him until he was between my legs. I moaned into his mouth as I felt him grind against me.

Elijah put his lips to the shell of my ear, his breath tickling it. "No one can see us, but you'll have to be much quieter than that."

Then he pulled back, and the devious look in his eyes made my heart race. I could be quieter; I'd spent my life living as a shadow. So I wrapped my hand around his neck, pulled his face toward mine, then stifled a sigh as his hand drifted between us and crept under my waistband.

I writhed under him. *More.*

As if they had a mind of their own, my legs opened wider, yearning for him.

He smiled against my mouth as his fingers slipped inside me.

"Don't stop," I whispered. "I'll kill you if you do."

"Then tell me what I want to hear," he murmured.

I knew he wanted me to say it. He'd said it so many times and ways, and I still hadn't been able to. Now we were here, on Malinda's doorstep, and who knew what tomorrow would bring. Before midday, all my friends might die; I could be a prisoner again, locked in the tower.

I could trust him. I knew that he would raise hell to get me back to our home safely. *Our home. Mine and his.*

"I love you," I whispered. "You know I do."

For a moment, it was as if he hadn't heard. He so disbelieved that I would ever say those words that he could not process them.

"Say it again," he murmured.

"I love you," I breathed. *I love you.* Feeling as if I'd bared my soul to him, I doubted he knew how much I meant those words, how rarely I'd said them, how terrified I was that the mere act of admitting it meant that I would lose him.

Furtive, secret, he pulled down my pants with one hand. Not another word or sound passed between us as he plunged into me. Deep.

Silent tension spiraled through me like a wild, dark thing as I met him thrust for thrust, as we found our rhythm. I fought to keep my breathing steady and slow. Finally, we both came, Elijah with a low moan of surrender, I biting his shoulder.

In my own mind, I cried out his name. And whether it was a plea or a prayer, I couldn't even tell... but the smell of him, the taste of him, carved straight into my heart.

I held onto him tightly, hidden by the night. But instead of the peace I usually had after lovemaking, I felt an overwhelming surge of fear. Swift and brutal terror held me so tightly that, for a moment, I couldn't breathe. It was a bad omen, and I fought to push it aside, to ignore it. He was immortal. There was no cause for fear; it wasn't rational. But I couldn't ignore that force in my chest, a nagging uneasiness.

Don't take him from me, I silently begged the Gods. *Please don't.*

Though why I prayed to them, I couldn't say. They'd never done me any favors. Happiness had never been a thing I could hold; it was as fleeting as fog, at best, a ghost that I could sense but not touch.

But if my words carried any weight with the Gods, I would use them. Because I loved him. I loved him wholly and viscerally, even if I'd only said it aloud just this one time. I knew I could never feel the same about anyone else, not even for a day.

I rolled over, back to him, as I put my clothes back into place, stunned by the heaviness in my heart. Unaware, Elijah tucked me against him again, adjusting his cloak over us. His hand returned to its previous place, comfortably against my hip. He kissed the back of my neck sleepily.

In the total darkness of the crypt, I looked across the marble floor at my friends. Taliesin and Serene, Nico and Vitess still slept soundly, apparently unworried about what tomorrow might bring. As I scanned the room one last time before I drifted off, I met a pair of unforgiving gray eyes.

He couldn't see us - it was too dark - but Jasper had heard everything. And behind me, Elijah smiled.

CHAPTER 27

———◦◦◦———

J ust before dawn, I rose and crept outside. I settled myself on the stairs to the crypt, bone-chillingly cold, and waited. My power felt strained, tethered, ready to burst from my skin. I willed blackness into my palm, a pool of silky midnight. It cascaded through my fingers, like ink waterfalls, down onto the marble.

In the light of the Moon, snow drifts piled against gravestones, statues kept watch. The stars above speckled the heavens like tiny diamonds, ripped from the tiara of a goddess, flung to the sky.

Nyx. If you're listening, help me.

Atropos was Nyx's creation, and Nyx seemed to care as little for her as Malinda did for me. Perhaps it was genetic, I mused, that none of the women in my lineage seemed to care for their offspring. At least, they didn't care enough to intervene.

"What's wrong?" Nico sat down on the stairs next to me.

"Nothing. Go back to sleep."

"I'm good. I don't need much." Nico rolled his neck, cracking it, and then stretched his shoulders. "Besides, I'm too keyed up to sleep. I've been waiting to get back at your mother for years." He stared across the graveyard, his breath lingering in the frigid air. "So we just ... walk in?"

"Essentially," I replied. "If Malinda were in the process of murdering someone, she likely wouldn't notice. If we're lucky, that is."

"If we're unlucky, three of us will be dead."

Taliesin, Jasper, and Nico. If that happened—*if* it happened—Vitess would intervene. I had faith in the controller of Time, even when I lacked confidence in myself.

Nico extended his legs and crossed them at the ankles. Dressed all in black, vicious knives tucked into straps along his ribs and thighs, like the assassin I knew him to be. "Before we go in there, I must ask you a favor."

"What's that?" I was barely listening, too busy worrying about what we'd face the instant we stepped into The Grace.

If what Lorcan said was true, I only had to remove her heart, and she'd become a Cullen again—though who knew how long that would take.

"I want you to make a decree."

That broke my concentration. "A ... what?"

"I'm asking you, Death, for a decree. I want you to decree that I will never become Cullen, that my death will be final. I grew up with you at The Grace. I know what they're like. I know what awaits. I don't want to be one of them ... no matter what."

I stared at Nico. He had spent most of his life watching Cullen destroy our kingdom. He had seen them torment children, then witnessed fellow servants and friends be reborn as bloodthirsty corpses.

"I want to die instantly, Morena. I don't want to feel a lot of pain. So, if you please ... make it instant. And not from them."

It was the least I could do for the boy who'd pulled me from the cursed ground. He'd taught me to read. He'd taught me to dance. He'd been my parent and only friend for many years.

I could ensure that Nico would not become what he so profoundly despised.

I closed my eyes, searching for his soul. I found it easily. I mentally grasped the silver thread, gently unraveling it in my hand. I had to be deliberate and specific when decreeing his destiny.

Your death will be instant. You will never become Cullen. In a rare moment of inspiration, I added a few more things.

You will know warmth again. You will die in the arms of someone who loves you. And you will know that things will be alright. When Death takes you, it will be on swift wings.

I spun the silvery thread back up, weaving it carefully. Nico's life was so small in my hands, a fragile, perishable thing. Life—so quickly taken, yet so valuable. I knew the difference one life could make. The difference his life had made for me.

When I opened my eyes, Nico stared at me. "All done," I assured him. "Wish granted."

He smiled weakly. "I don't fear Death if you're the one who will be there at the end."

"Thanks," I said under my breath and ran my fingers over the skull. The mask sat next to me on the stairs where I could have it within sight. I could quickly put it on if needed.

Grace Castle loomed in the distance, half hidden by fog, its black flags flapping in the winter wind. We both watched it, expecting the worst.

After a second of hesitation, Nico spoke, his hazel eyes troubled. "I'm sorry that I let Jasper lie to you—I should have told you sooner. As soon as we landed that first night."

"It doesn't matter now," I assured him.

"It does, though. I decided to save you. When you were a baby, it was so hard. I didn't know what I was doing at all. I held you and rocked you and played with you. You're my family."

"If I'm your family, your true sister, then tell me about you and Vitess." I gave him a small smile.

Anything to distract me from what we'll face in a few short hours.

Nico cleared his throat. "We're together, and it's good. She's sweet and wonderful, and I don't think I deserve her. It's... easy. Sometimes it's a bit... I don't know how to give her what she wants, so that's complicated."

Complicated was precisely the word I'd use to describe my relationship with Elijah.

As if reading my mind, Nico continued. "You don't belong to him, you know," Nico said. "You are a Fate—you control your destiny, no one else. You should do what you want. When you want. Define death as you see fit. That is who you are. That's your sacred responsibility."

"Ironically, that's the same thing his mother says."

Nico watched the sunrise, which was beyond The Grace. "I know about the blood bond. I know when it started and why you're doing it. I just wish you wouldn't."

I couldn't hide my annoyance. "It's for married people, and we will be married. Why bother waiting?"

Nico frowned. "It's not *just* a marriage rite, Morena. It's old, dangerous magic. Most of the witch covens have banned it. Sharing blood allows the other person to control you, to use your magic whenever they wish—hear your thoughts, see what you see. They even feel how you feel. They can influence your feelings or trick you. Fae men use it to enslave human women all the time. Does that sound like the kind of marriage you want?"

My breath caught in my throat. *Influence you. Use you. See what you see. Enslave you.*

I felt like I might be sick. If Elijah could see what I saw and feel how I felt... he could *control* me. My head pounded and roared in my ears.

Nico trailed off, seeing my expression. "I thought you knew."

"And it's dangerous?" I already knew the answer—I'd felt it every time we'd shared blood.

"Besides the fact that you can control the other person?" Pity was all over his face. "Your mind becomes so muddled with them—their thoughts, their feelings—that you can't tell which are your own. The blood becomes an addiction. It can be hard to think rationally when your body craves nothing but them."

Memories swirled as I tried to think back to when we'd first shared blood. Elijah had cut my hand. Was that an accident?

He'd told me about the blood bond. He'd taken blood from me first without asking.

He had kissed me while his lip was bleeding. Coincidence?

All that was after he knew about Jasper and me on the beach with the Mer. And every time after that... We had bloodbonded *after* I was with Jasper. Like a sick reaction to his jealousy, he'd sought me out. And I'd wanted the bond, wanted him so desperately that I couldn't even think straight.

He never let the bond fade. He always ensured that if I stopped craving him so intensely, he was there to give me more. He kept a blade on his table and wore a knife on his belt.

Betrayal washed over me. When I swallowed, it felt like sandpaper. I hadn't suspected. If I had, I'd thoroughly ignored my intuitions because I liked how Elijah made me feel. I'd wanted to please him. Some twisted part of me reveled in the idea that he thought I was *worth* manipulating and cared enough to put thought into it. He wanted me so desperately that he'd do anything to ensure I was his.

Or his blood has warped my mind.

"It wears off," Nico said, trying to reassure me as he watched me process my anger and hurt. "If you aren't around them for a while."

"I see," I said, my voice an agonized whisper.

"I can't kill him since he's an immortal, but if you wanted to lock him in one of these tombs until you aren't mad at him, I'd help carry him in."

"I know you would." I laughed a little, even though my heart cracked into jagged pieces. To know that Elijah had manipulated me so thoroughly that he'd tricked me and lied to me—I told him I loved him. Just last night, I said those words and meant them. I'd never said them to anyone before, never made love to anyone before, and now...

The hurt in my heart was not unlike being stabbed by the Cullen.

"Do you wish I hadn't told you?" Nico asked nervously. "I thought maybe..." he ran his fingers through his hair. "I'm sorry," he said finally.

"No, I... I'm glad you did." But I wasn't glad, not even the slightest bit.

It was the absolute worst time to tell me. I was about to go into a battle against tens of thousands of Cullen and face my heartless mother. The last thing I needed was to feel this smothering despair, this bottomless sense of loss and pain. For a moment, I imagined just standing up and drifting away, leaving the entire lot of them to a gruesome destiny. The Cullen would tear them apart. I could simply walk away into the evergreens, slip into the shadows, and never speak to any of them again.

Maybe later, I told myself. But for now, I wouldn't take the coward's way out. Later, I would give Elijah hell. I would rage and vent my wrath. Behind me, I could hear the others stirring inside, getting ready, including him. I felt his presence, his gaze on my back.

Later, I would punish him and make him hurt as badly as I did. I would damage and destroy him; when he healed, I'd repeat the process until I wasn't angry anymore.

With a heavy sigh, I picked up the mask.

Hello, old friend, it purred.

Gritting my teeth, I put it on, immediately noting how it adhered to my skin, how its edges wrapped around the back of my head, and covered my hair in inky, glittering streams. It wrapped all the way around, hiding my golden hair, making it appear like a black, glittering skull sat atop my neck.

The outfit I wore molted, falling in strips, replaced by liquid night that pooled over my curves like a toxic cloak. I made sure everyone could see me. They might as well know who I was underneath and who they'd be fighting for.

I stood and turned to face them. "The Queen of the Blood Throne wants Death. Today, I'm here to oblige her."

I strode down the stone-walled tunnel. Despite the dim, almost non-existent light, I would have recognized where we were just by the sounds and smell of it. I knew where the ceilings sloped and dropped, anticipating exactly where not to step. The group behind me, meanwhile, bumbled and faltered.

Nico brushed away a thick layer of cobwebs. "Are you sure this is the right way? I feel like we're going in circles."

"Even the halls of Hell make sense when you live there," I said somberly.

The dungeon grate was just ahead, and I kept my eyes forward, fastidiously ignoring the walls crawling with spiders. Soon, we'd reach a broad, man-sized hole at the end of one dungeon corridor. It opened in front of the prisoners' cells, and I hoped those would be empty or at least unguarded. Then, we could easily walk through the dungeon, up the stairs, and into the Castle. If the plan worked, it would be the most straightforward, risk-free path. I'd taken this same route many times as I skulked out of the Castle on a mission for Malinda.

Of course, if Cullen were there, I could kill them. The concern was that one Cullen would alert all the others, ruining our sense of surprise and giving Malinda time to prepare. I'd need to kill them quietly if we were to breach the Castle undetected.

It was likely that the dungeon would be empty, the Cullen busy guarding the exterior of the Castle or the corridors near Malinda's room. They wouldn't be in the dungeon—or at least, I hoped they wouldn't.

Serene walked next to me, both of us at the front. "In case I forgot to say it, I hate that mask you're wearing. You look like a walking nightmare."

"Good. Maybe it will strike fear in the face of our enemies."

"I don't know why all of us have to be part of this," Nico muttered from the back of the group.

Jasper was directly behind us, his long strides matching my own. "If you're scared, you could always wait outside."

"It's not that I'm afraid. It's that we have no backup plan. Sure, we are all-powerful, and we'll all kill her. But there's a non-zero chance that she'll kill all of us," Nico retorted.

"Both of you need to shut up." Taliesin elbowed his way between the two. "Unless you want the Cullen to hear you, in which case, carry on."

"One, we have a backup plan. Her name is Vitess. Two, you're such a pessimist."

"I know." Nico cocked his head. "It's one of my best qualities."

Serene smothered a laugh with a slight cough.

Vitess hovered close to me, nervous, her hands fluttering like birds. "I'll go and find Malinda, then search the Time threads." I could tell she was just as worried as I was about failing everyone. After all, the only person who could possibly save us was her.

"See if you can find anything that might improve our odds of winning," Jasper said.

"Thus cheating our destinies again," Elijah grumbled unhelpfully.

"Perfectly acceptable," I said. I'd given him absolute silence since my conversation with Nico, and he was in the back of the group, nowhere near me. I didn't want him near me.

"In this specific circumstance, I think an exception is warranted."

Vitess was worried. Serene put an arm around her shoulders. "Don't let anyone know who you are or suspect who you are. If you get stabbed, grabbed, or otherwise in danger, reset time. If she kills one of us or all of us, reset time."

"Of course," Vitess assured her. "I'll reset time as long as *I'm* not dead."

"Luckily, Malinda *can't* kill us. "Serene clicked her tongue with annoyance. "We're descendants of the Fates."

Nico cracked his knuckles. "I, for one, appreciate the sentiment."

Vitess swallowed hard. "Got it."

A moment later, I turned to look back at her, to tell her not to worry, but she'd gone without a goodbye.

As for the rest of us, Serene would free Atropos, and I would face Malinda. It was too risky for all of the Three Fates to be together, so we'd split up, and hopefully, within the hour, we'd be out of the Castle. I'd been tempted to argue—but as Serene pointed out, we couldn't expect three men with functioning hearts to face off against the Queen of the Blood Throne. Not if we wanted them to walk out of there alive.

Nico mumbled to himself as he slammed his fist against the wall, crushing a gigantic orange spider. "Cullen won't hurt me. My magic protected me all those years. It won't be any different now."

"Leave the bugs alone," Serene said in exasperation. "*You* go with Morena and Elijah to face Malinda. I'll head for the west tower with Taliesin."

"Which way is the west tower?" Taliesin also was noticeably nervous.

"West. I can't believe you lived here your whole life and don't know anything," Nico said under his breath. "We'd be lost down here all night."

Taliesin glared at him. "I didn't exactly roam the halls freely."

"Shhh," Jasper ordered. "Unless your plan is to get us all killed."

I glanced back, wishing they'd all stop antagonizing each other. Even though I knew it was their way of working off anxiety, every sound might draw the Cullen to us, no matter how small.

I reached the grate and peered out from the iron bars, silent as a shadow. The dungeon was empty. From my vantage point, I could see the four closest cells down the corridor. There was no one and no sound. I sent out my magic, its inky tendrils creeping along the floors, to see if any living souls or life sparks were in the dungeon.

The answer didn't take long—*no*—and so I gently pushed on the grate. It inched open.

Nothing. So far, so good.

Vitess appeared next to me. "Malinda is in the throne room. She looks perfectly healthy."

"Not great news, but we can work with that," Nico said just before he pulled her in for a soft kiss. "Don't let me die in this hellhole."

Vitess blushed and wavered, clearly embarrassed by his public display of affection.

I pushed open the grate with my shoulder, just wide enough for each of us to scrape through. One by one, the group of us slipped into the dungeons of Grace Castle.

Jasper peered into one of the cells. "I believe I speak for everyone when I say this looks like a terrible place to die."

"Then try not to," I said dryly.

Nico unstrapped a wicked-looking knife from his thigh and handed it to Jasper. "If they catch you, use that to slit your own throat. You'll be better off."

Looking at the knife as if it were made of poisonous spiders, Jasper shook his head. "I'm going to use fire."

"Fates and their descendants..." Nico rolled his eyes. "Always relying on magic."

Vitess made a face. Meanwhile, I kept my eyes on the stairs, anywhere but back to the left corner, back to the hole where I'd swept the bodies—including Arabella's.

"Good luck." Vitess lunged forward, hugging both Serene and me tightly. "I'll see you on the other side of this. I won't let it be otherwise."

Serene looked at the two of us. "Just in case we get murdered and become soulless ghouls ... burn me on the pyre."

I nodded at the two of them. Then, our controller of time vanished again, off to check various futures. Nico and Jasper walked just ahead of us.

"Go ahead. We're right behind you," Elijah said, pulling me into one of the dungeon cells. He could feel the tension radiating from me and read my facial expression easily.

"You're angry with me," he said. "That much is clear."

"As I should be," I said through gritted teeth. "You've used our blood bond to spy on me and manipulate me."

He didn't deny it. Instead, he crossed his arms over his chest. "What would you have me do? Just watch my *wife* simper, faint, and throw herself at another man?"

"I'm not your wife."

"Whose fault is that?" He stepped closer. "Though maybe we're both better off if you aren't. I don't like to share."

Gods damn him. I shoved him against the wall with all of my strength.

"What now?" he growled. "You can't hurt me. You can't kill me. What are you going to do?"

Black exploded in my vision, and something vicious filled me. I couldn't think, I couldn't breathe...

Night radiated from me in a wave, my black cloak transforming into dark, roiling clouds.

"You dare to challenge me?" I grabbed his throat with a pale, skeletal hand. I watched the pulse in his neck. I wanted to draw my tongue down it, I wanted to hear his harsh breath, I wanted to cut him open, I wanted him under me, right here in the dungeon—

"You dare to *blame me* for the lies you told? "With all my strength, I slammed my other fist into the rock beside his face. The mask glittered, longing for his destruction.

Elijah blinked as he took in my expression, the Death head I now wore. The fact that my hands now had no skin but were only bones.

"Morena." His voice was low. His blood and magic surged in my veins, and my entire body tightened in response.

"No." I would not listen. I would not bow. The deep voice from my mouth was not mine—it was ancient, terrifying, the voice of an immortal goddess. My onyx eyes burned with hostility and all-consuming lust.

"I will kill you, snake," I said. "For your treachery."

"You won't." Elijah was still, somehow, unafraid. "Because I know what you need. And by the Gods, I want to give it to you. I want to pull you down on this stone floor, bury myself in you, and never come up again. But right now..." Elijah's voice was ragged...

"You're distracted. Right now, damn you, we must kill your mother, rescue Atropos, and get everyone out of here. We can fight and make up later."

You're distracted. He was right.

Fight and make up later. I was out of control. I was not calm.

I blinked away the red haze, the rage and bloodlust that clouded my thoughts.

I released his throat, one finger at a time. Slowly, slowly. I pulled my hand away. I started to step back.

"Don't do that." Elijah wound his arms around my waist. "Stay. Just ... calm down."

He leaned in and rested his lips against the mask, the skeletal forehead, and black obsidian. After a brief hesitation, he kissed it, softly exhaling. His hands stroked my back, comforting me.

Gradually, I returned to myself. Being unable to control my temper was new – it had never happened before. I was suddenly afraid, unsure. Whether it was the mask or being back at The Grace, my growing powers and proximity to the Fates, I didn't know... but I didn't like it.

"You can't just manipulate me like this and expect me to trust you," I said in a small voice.

"I know," he said. "And I'm sorry. I'll explain it all to you, I swear. Later, when this is over."

Later, not when we were in Malinda's dungeon where Cullen could interrupt us, not when our friends were already upstairs, all of them in danger of being killed. Later, we could fight and make up, like he said. Not right now.

Foolishly, I agreed because I thought that *later* would be possible.

CHAPTER 28

———◆———

We made our way up the spiraling blue stone stairs—unlit, every corridor dark—and through the Castle. Dust covered every surface, and the wooden floors scratched and scraped. The air was thick with the musty scent of decay and Death.

I peered into each room, expecting the worst. As we moved deeper into the Castle, the atmosphere grew increasingly ominous. Shadows moved of their own accord, and my footsteps echoed eerily through the halls. I tried to shake off my growing unease and focus on the mission. Every creak and groan of the old stone walls made my heart race.

It was no different than it was before, I told myself. I'd walked these same halls in the blue-dark cold and been numb to the horrors that might have lurked around every corner. I was stronger and faster now, more ready than ever. I was wearing the mask, invisible to my enemies. I should have felt more confident.

Elijah and I walked side by side, yet we avoided looking at each other as if afraid it would stoke the desire between us. I *wanted* his blood. *Craved* it, even. With the mask on, all I wanted to do was to wash myself in it. I quickened my pace, afraid that I would change my mind and drag Elijah into one of the empty bedrooms. Not to fight, but to...

Nico was right. My mind was consumed. Controlled. I needed to focus.

Come and get me, Malinda.

I traced my fingers along the mask. I could feel its impatience, its longing for bloodshed. My hand itched for a weapon.

I didn't know where my mother might be, but I'd take the Castle apart stone by stone until I found her. I'd make her regret the days that she'd kept me under her thumb.

Far off, out in the darkness of one of the rooms ahead, came a low growl and clicking teeth.

We continued our sweep of Grace Castle. Up ahead was the throne room.

"Where *is* she? "I muttered.

One singular scream rang out as if in response, reverberating down the corridor. It was followed by a deep, menacing laugh. I paused in the hallway; I waited for a beat, expecting more. *Serene. Vitess.*

We hurried forward, Elijah and I, running as quietly as we could until we reached the entry to the throne room. I could feel him beside me, studying the enormous indigo pillars that flanked the doorway—carved into skulls and twisting flowers, everything brutally beautiful and cold.

Like me.

I peeked around the corner into the throne room and was shocked to see Malinda kneeling next to the Blood Throne. She looked like she might be crying, and stupidly, I thought everything was going as planned.

Until I noticed Nico halfway hidden behind her. Writhing and struggling on the floor, he had onyx-colored shackles thick and heavy around his neck, wrists, and ankles.

When my mother spoke, it was accompanied by an inhuman cackle. "I will accept your heart as payment for your treachery."

I bit back a scream as I watched her drive a blade into Nico's thigh, grimacing as it sank to its silver hilt. The Blood Throne greedily absorbed the blood that poured from his wound. Nico continued trying to free his hands, and as he looked up to scan the room, he spotted Elijah and me at the doorway. *Go,* he mouthed. *Don't.*

Taliesin screamed in impotent rage and struggled to free himself from a trio of Cullen in the corner.

"I'll help them," Elijah said to me. "You kill Malinda."

I grabbed his arm. "No. Vitess will save them—"

"I won't die. I can't die. Don't worry."

I didn't believe him.

But even as I tried to drag him back, Elijah pulled away. I couldn't keep my grip against his strength. He was barreling toward Taliesin, toward certain doom, but even he was not fast enough to save my brother.

The Cullen yanked Taliesin's eyes from their sockets. He screamed, and to shut him up, one of the Cullen took a blunted hammer and slammed it into the side of his head. Taliesin fell to his knees, but the Cullen kept hitting him.

"What part of *don't come back* didn't you understand? "Malinda shrieked at Taliesin. "I told you to never return!"

He cried out just as Elijah reached him. I couldn't help responding with my own answering cry, raw with rage and grief. All the windows blew in, shattering the beautiful stained glass above us.

Malinda stopped slicing up Nico and glared back at me. She couldn't *see* me, but she knew I was there. She'd walked often enough through dark woods beside Death; she knew my scent and the sound of my footsteps.

"Why are you here?" Full of rage, Malinda yelled as she searched for me among the Cullen. "What is it that you want?"

"We've come to free Atropos!" Jasper cried and lunged toward her with hands full of fire.

She scoffed. "Fools."

While she was temporarily distracted, Nico cut himself out of the bonds she'd put on him and pulled himself back up to standing despite all his injuries. He picked up his sword.

Elijah and Jasper circled Malinda, the two princes descended from the Fates, and Malinda laughed. She *laughed.*

Jasper charged first, the fireballs in his palms filling the room with heat. But with one snap of her fingers, the Cullen swarmed us: twenty, thirty, fifty, and Jasper was buried under their rotting bodies and snapping jowls.

I was separated from them immediately, lost in the chaos of fighting.

"Morena!" Jasper yelled. "Kill them!"

I tried to focus, to seek the red mist that tethered them to themselves … but I couldn't concentrate. Cullen kept slamming into me every time I closed my eyes, unable to see me because I was invisible. Each time one fell against me, my mind went blank, and I couldn't grasp the red mist long enough to consume or absorb it.

Why, why did I think this would work? Why were we so stupid?

I gave up quickly and used blades instead. Viciously, I beheaded Cullen, one after another, again and again, and still they kept coming. Their numbers were endless.

Suddenly, there was a break in the furor, and I spotted Nico. He was striking, as well as he could, at Malinda. His sword was high, his face like a God. He was within moments of a killing blow when Malinda somehow twisted her crimson gown around the blade and snatched it away.

She shoved him backward with her hands into the bluestone wall of the throne room. His back hit with a resounding crack, and his mouth gaped. I thought it was amazement, surprise, that Malinda could be so strong that she could easily disarm him. He'd always had so much confidence that it seemed impossible that he could lose.

Malinda grabbed Nico by the hair. Her fingernails, razor-sharp and much too long, gleamed red. Then she leaned toward him and licked the column of his neck, tasting the sweat of his skin, deeply inhaling his scent. Then she smiled, satisfied, and stepped back.

That's when I saw it. My mother had impaled Nico with his own sword. His witch-hazel eyes were glassy, bulging. My stomach lurched, and I had to look away.

Vitess, where are you? I waited for the reset that would surely come, but nothing happened. Cullen surged around me, and there was no time to mourn him.

She will reset time soon.

I continued to cut a path toward Malinda in the center of the room. I realized that I couldn't see Jasper or Elijah anymore. I called out for them.

"I'm here!" Elijah called.

Through the flash of Cullen bodies, I spotted him. He was half-phased, with the head of a snake and the clawed arms of a dragon. As I watched, he blasted a group of them with fire straight from his mouth.

Jasper didn't reply, but I quickly deduced that he was in the furthest corner of the room because a collection of Cullen was suddenly lifted into the air by climbing vines that bore purple flowers so dark they were like slices of midnight. The vines choked and gagged the Cullen, repeatedly slamming them into the walls.

Still, more Cullen came. There must have been more than a hundred in the Castle, and they'd all come running at her command. I continued to fight—strike, slash, behead, strike, slash, behead—but even I was growing tired.

At one point, I dropped one of my knives, and as I bent to retrieve it, I saw Jasper. He was fighting valiantly still, but he was severely injured, one arm dangling at his side.

Vitess! Vitess! Where are you, damn you?

Malinda had done this. All of this—and for what? So that the Cullen could cover all of Moirai?

The throne room was bathed in blood, and a thundering boom rocked the Castle as one of the walls toppled forward, crushing another dozen Cullen, pushed inward by tree roots and earth.

I felt, rather than saw, Malinda coming toward me.

Can she see me?

Elijah saw my expression, how I became paralyzed as my mother approached—and made a decision. I will never forget that moment, as it was when I best understood his character.

He ran toward the two of us, then placed himself before me, colliding with Malinda. She sank her teeth into his throat and tore it open, then threw him to the floor, his bright red blood across her lips. She could now sample his power.

"Fool," she hissed down at him. "You were a fool to bring her here. I told you."

Before he could rise, Cullen piled on him, gripping each of his arms, gripping his head, and they began to pull, ripping him apart.

I screamed, but I couldn't stop them. There were too many, and I was too far away, drowning in the sea of their rotting bodies.

"Jasper, help!" I cried out. "They have him!"

Jasper blasted the Cullen out of the way with fire, torching them until only ash remained. I grabbed his arm as he sprinted by, tugging him in the right direction.

We made it to Elijah, and I dropped to my knees. They'd strewn pieces of him everywhere. Though he was still alive, knitting back together slowly, it was clear that he would provide no more help. I didn't even see his other hand—I hoped one of the Cullen hadn't tossed it off the balcony or eaten it.

"Don't worry about me," his head said, flickering, half-scaled with snakeskin and the other half more like a man. "I just need some time."

"Alright," Jasper said, briefly touching his shoulder. I could see a glimmer of their friendship, what it had been before me.

I heard her footsteps behind me. I felt, rather than saw, the Cullen parting to let her through.

Hoping for the element of surprise, I turned and charged at Malinda, my blade held high. I leaped through the air toward my mother like an avenging angel, my Death mask grinning like a demon.

She couldn't see me coming, but she *felt* or smelled me—or she knew me too well. She batted me away as easily as if I were a fly, and as I picked myself up off the stones, I saw two of the Cullen launch themselves onto Jasper's back.

He roared with rage and yanked one of them off him, threw it to the floor, and stomped on its face so hard that its skull shattered in an explosion of gore. In seconds, another Cullen took its place.

I came running with the knives, determined to step in, but one of the Cullen was in the way, wrapped around my ankles like a coil of rope. I tripped, and my forehead plowed into the floor.

Dazed, I fought through feet and legs, and Cullen, my vision blurred along the edges where blood trickled down. I saw the Cullen grab Jasper, twisting his head until they snapped his neck, and I watched as a third tore into his stomach with wild abandon.

Elijah was still in pieces.

Still, Vitess had yet to reset everything.

Something must have gone wrong.

Wiping the blood from my face, I picked up my knife again from the praying floors and moved toward her. Knowing she'd won, Malinda was returning to her throne, gasping, worn out, but victorious.

I'd be damned if I would let her sit there and celebrate.

I wove through the Cullen, side-stepping them, invisible.

"I will rip your heart out, Malinda."

I moved toward her, slow. Deliberate.

"I will carve my name on your bones."

The Queen of the Blood Throne settled onto her seat. "You owe everything to me. I'm the reason you're strong. I'm the reason you know how to kill at all. One day, you'll thank me for all this. You'll realize how much I did for you."

"You're mad," I told her. "You made my life a hell. Made me this—*thing* I am."

Now, I was only a few steps away.

Five. The knives felt heavy in my hands, and blood dripped from their blades.

Four. It sank through the stones of this cursed house, *my house.*

"Strong. I made you strong."

Three.

I narrowed my eyes at her delusion. "It could have been different. You could have loved us. You could have been a real mother."

Malinda leaned back against the throne, her face graying. The heart she used this time hadn't held up well in all the fighting, and each breath took effort. "One day, you'll understand. Your grandmother is the one to blame. Not me."

Two. I drew myself up to full height, the mask on my face glittering like midnight. The Queen of the Blood Throne smiled as if she relished the feeling of Death looming over her head.

One.

"Pray to Nyx to pardon you." I drew my dagger. "Because I never will."

The Queen of the Blood Throne closed her eyes as I swung the knife and cut off her head.

I paused, surveying the room. Dead Cullen littered the floor. Taliesin, Nico, and Jasper were dead. Elijah was in pieces. Through one of the arched windows, I could see that outside it had begun to snow.

I went to him. "Are you alright?" I asked.

Elijah forced a pained smile. "Fine. Better than ever."

Torn, I knelt at his side. I didn't want to leave him, but the task still wasn't done. Perhaps I should have called for Vitess right then, but Elijah wouldn't hear of it.

"Go find them," he insisted. "Serene and Vitess are somewhere up-stairs. By the time you get back, I'll be just as I was."

He was right, of course. With a resolved sigh, and a brief kiss to his forehead.

I was tired down to my bones as I mounted the stairs to the west tower. "Serene?" I called out. "Vitess?"

I put my hands on the banister—long, skeletal hands, the hands of the Reaper, of Death. I just stared at them, stared long and hard, because I couldn't believe they were mine, that the mask was once more on my face and I was once more in this Castle, as if I had never left. But I'd only gone three steps when I felt something shift. A tremor, like somewhere in a distant room of the Castle, a stone God had rolled over in his sleep, shifting the foundations ever so slightly.

I touched the mask, just to make sure it was still secured to my face. It was. My black robes flowed around me. I stopped, listened. The throne room was silent, but for the sound of blood dripping. The quiet, I was used to. The Grace had always been *quiet*.

But still, something was different. I swallowed, and continued forward. Up the stairs until I reached the top floor, then I made my way down the empty corridor. West. I paused at a corner. Was this the place where I'd drawn that map in the dust, so long ago? Had I always known it would end like this, Malinda headless on her bloody throne, and me alone in The Grace again?

As unerring as an arrow, I made my way to the west tower. Thankfully, it seemed every Cullen in the Castle had gone to Malinda's aid. There were none here – not so much as a finger bone. Just ahead, I saw the painted door, still closed, the same it had been every other time I'd come to visit my grandmother.

"Serene? Vitess?" I called out to the other Fates again. *Where are they?*

High-pitched screams erupted in the silence, followed by a thud and sickening wet sounds—sounds I knew too well. The sound of an animal or...

I put my shoulder to the wood and gave it a strong shove, once again falling into the room as I had so many times before. I had to adjust to the brightness, to the open wall, to the light reflected by the snow and ice.

A woman was on the slab, ripped open. There was a gaping wound from her neck to her hips, and standing above her was Atropos. *Atropos,* with her silver hair and dark eyes, a blade that glowed blue in her hand, her nails dripping blood. She was wearing a scarf, a scarf for the cold.

A scarf for the cold. And it dripped, dripped, dripped, red jewels onto the stone floor.

"Grandmother?" I said, questioning as I stepped closer, speaking as I realized that it was not a scarf at all, that it was Serene laid open. It wasn't a scarf because that didn't make sense, it was red and bloody and —

Her entrails, her bowels, were wound around Atropos' neck. Atropos was singing, humming happily as she looked toward the door.

I began to scream.

It's not real, can't be real, I am in the dungeons and Malinda must have me, it must be a nightmare. I need to wake up, I need to wake up.

"Vitess! Lachesis!"

I didn't know if either would come. I didn't know if she would hear. Inside my own skull I begged Vitess to help; I begged Lachesis to help. I begged anyone across space and time who could, to come now, and intervene.

Save us.

CHAPTER 29

Everything vanished, wiped away into the whiteness of snow and parchment, of clouds. It was a place without sky nor wall, nor bird nor beast. Nothing.

"Hello?" I called out. As far as the eye could see, it was pearl-colored, and I felt as if I were inside a substance, though it was neither earth nor water. My voice was swallowed up by the expanse, by the vast silence.

Hello?

"I'm here."

I whirled to find Vitess standing a few paces behind me, her flowing indigo gown pristine. No blood. No death. Her dress wasn't even wrinkled.

"What is this place?"

"*Nowhere*," Vitess said, casting her eyes around. "The middle and in between, the place amidst the threads of Time."

Nowhere. The middle of Nowhere. It had never occurred to me that this might be the name of an actual destination.

"They're dead," I told her. "All of them."

Vitess gazed past my shoulder, out into the void. "I know." The words felt like a slap.

"We knew that could happen." I forced myself to sound upbeat. "You'll change it."

Vitess folded her hands across her stomach protectively. "So far, I have not succeeded in altering our destinies in any meaningful way. Even if I change this one event, it does not change the next. We are casualties without meaning."

"I don't understand. You said I would reunite Moirai."

Vitess squared her small shoulders. "Serene fought *for you*, defended your brother. The Prince of Clotho and the Prince of Lachesis both sacrificed themselves to protect you." Her voice was so soft I almost couldn't hear the words. "Are we not united?"

"I thought you meant we would *win*."

"We have never won. Not that I have seen." Vitess smiled, and she looked so unbearably sad that I could stand to look at her face. "But there are many futures—as many as the stars in the sky, as varied as the leaves of all the trees in a forest. I haven't seen all of them, surely."

"I want a future where we all survive. Where we—you and I and Serene—are Queens of Moirai. Together."

Vitess was somber. "I want that too. But it doesn't seem like it's meant to be that way..."

"Change it." I blinked my tearless black eyes. "Help us win. Tell me what to do."

"I've already done that. I've cleaned up this mess before."

If that were true, I didn't remember it. "Please," I begged her. "Elijah is dead. Jasper is dead. Taliesin is dead. Nico is dead."

She flinched when I said his name, the only ruffle so far in her demeanor.

"Save them. You have to save them. Not me. Only you can."

"Even if I knew the answer, Morena—even if I told you, you wouldn't remember. It's impossible."

I digested her words. For every reset, I wouldn't remember anything afterward because I had never lived it. Each time was a completely new scenario. I wouldn't know how to win. Once Vitess reset time to a point in the past, events would unfold differently—the advice she gave, even if I could remember it, might not be relevant. It was a *new* Time thread, a new chance to live or die.

I had an idea. It was likely one of the worst ideas I'd ever had, but there was no other option at that moment. "Could you reset time repeatedly? Reset us *until* we win?"

Vitess frowned, her blue eyes peering past my shoulder into the void. "That might take a hundred trials. Thousands. We would be breaking the rules of controlling time—all of them—and not for one person, but everyone."

"I know," I took her hands in mine. She was so small, so fragile and bird-like. "But eventually, we will get it right. Eventually, Serene and I will figure it out and know how to beat Atropos and Malinda. In some future, sometime, we'd all walk away unscathed ... wouldn't we?" I was terrified that she would say no.

The second Fate regarded me with sadness. "It isn't likely."

"But it *could* happen. Over a hundred years, with so many attempts ... it is possible."

Vitess licked her lips. "If, for each attempt, I nudged you in the right direction, you would still choose. You would choose differently in a dozen moments. Maybe if all of those were aligned—maybe it's possible we'd beat Atropos." Vitess considered me. "But the magnitude of changes, keeping track of all our futures... You're asking me to alter thousands of timelines, all of our Fates. To remember every detail, every iteration, for as long as it takes. For all of you... no one could do that."

"Except you. You can." I kissed her hands, not caring if I had to beg and plead on my knees. "You're the strongest of the Fates—you are fair and wise and good, and you love us all. You're the best of us, Vi."

Her eyes were bluer than the sky. "I do, but..." she began to shake her head... "I can't—"

"You can. You'll save us, Vitess. Not me, not Serene. Only you can save Moirai. And Nico. And your brothers and sisters and parents ... it all disappears without you. Serene can create, and I can kill, but only you can decide which paths we choose. Only you can change our destinies and correct what we all make wrong."

Vitess was quiet for a long time, my words a weight upon her. What I was asking was no small thing—she would have to remember every step and path for each of us. Nico. Taliesin. Serene. Jasper. Elijah. Me. Herself. Lorcan. Even Malinda. She would have to know every choice we made, know every intimate detail, and understand us. She'd have to ensure we made the right decisions and did not deviate.

But the alternative was that we were all doomed.

"It is more effort than you can possibly imagine," she said at last. She pulled me close and hugged me tightly.

"I love you, Morena. You're my best friend." Vitess sighed. "So I have to believe in you, in us. I will do my best. Go try again."

She stepped back and pushed me.

I fell into the luminescent clouds, into the nothing, and forgot.

CHAPTER 30

I had no way of knowing what happened after that; I didn't remember the Nowhere nor realize how much time had passed. It's
impossible for me to guess how many attempts were made as Vitess tried
to guide our group to victory. Eventually, Vitess deposited me into a
different time, another thread where I was paired with Jasper in Grace
Castle.

Click. Pressing my fist to my eyes, I blinked into the bright, wintry
sunlight. Had I been talking to myself? Sleepwalking? My brain had to
search for words like I'd woken up from a long slumber.

Nico shoved against my shoulder. "I'm sorry I told you. You've been
in a daze ever since."

"Told me what?" I said, my voice hollow.

"About the blood bond." He peered into my face. "Are you sure you're
alright?"

*The blood bond. Elijah. He tricked me. Manipulated me. Controlled
me.*

It felt like I was moving through razor blades, everything sharp-angled
and silver. "I'm fine."

Faint, coming from far below the ledge, was a steady clicking, the
strange shuffling sound of thousands of bodies moving without speaking. We were high up on a mountain ledge, the wind blowing fiercely.
Down below was the Obsidian Sea and a vast army of Cullen, west and

east of the castle, north of the castle. Their numbers stretched far into the distance, across the snowy plain, across the killing fields, all the way to the forest and the base of the mountain. An uncountable number of dead, some lying in heaps, some swaying back and forth, awaited Malinda's orders.

The only place not swarming with Cullen was the water's dark surface. And there I saw, much to my dismay, a pack of Cullen putting a boat in the water. Lorcan's spies had been right about that, too.

"All of you need to listen," Vitess spoke in a low voice, entirely unlike her typical self. "Jasper will go with Morena and me. Serene, Taliesin, and Nico will go to free Atropos. Elijah?" She studied her brother. "We'll need you as a dragon on the roof."

"I can't go with Morena?" he asked, his blue eyes on mine.

"No." Gone was the delicate girl—she'd become confident, more of a leader.

"I've had to watch you die repeatedly," Vitess said, "So you'll do exactly as I say and nothing else."

She turned to Nico and pulled him forward by the knife straps on the front of his tunic. To our surprise, Vitess kissed him in front of the entire group. "Do. Not. Die."

Nico studied her for a few heartbeats. And finally, he gave a lopsided half-smile. "I'll try not to this time?"

"Once we're inside, Serene will take Taliesin and Nico with her to the west tower to free Atropos. Drip your blood on her, then run like hell for the roof. Do not stay a moment longer," Vitess said to Serene. "Not even one."

Serene gave her a strange look. Vitess had never spoken to us like this before, and neither of us knew what to make of it.

"Ok," she said slowly.

"What about before we get to the Castle?" Taliesin asked. "How are we supposed to kill Malinda when there are ten thousand Cullen between us and the front door?"

I scratched at my palms, my mouth bone-dry. I'd never managed to kill more than ten at a time, even in Trale Nuvole.

"Don't be nervous," Vitess chided me, her soft brown hair haloed by pale sunlight. "You are ready."

Then she smiled, slow and cunning, a look I'd never seen before on her face. "We'll draw them out and kill them all."

The dragons' wings shimmered in the sunlight as they deposited us on the flat plains west of the castle. We slid down to dismount, and when Elijah transformed, he hugged me tightly. I shoved him away, refusing to look him in the eye.

No. I was still angry, still so angry, about the blood bond and the spying. I shared his blood and his bed; we were destined, and still he lied to me. *Still.*

"Don't touch me," I said coldly.

"What's wrong—?"

"You know exactly what's wrong. Everyone—*everyone*—uses me and manipulates me. All for this power I never wanted, and now I learn that you've done the same."

Everyone stilled, including Elijah.

I barreled on, not caring who heard. "I wanted you to be different than who you are, but I should have known I'd be disappointed. They say it's not the fairytales that lie to us but the people we love. I should have known better. My fault."

He took a deep breath. "Morena."

"We are on a *battlefield*. We are about to face an army of undead led by my *mother*, and I find out that the one person I thought would never lie to me has been doing just that *the entire time.*"

Jasper cleared his throat. Started to say something. I cut him off. "Don't you defend him. He wouldn't do the same for you."

I breathed in great gulps, wanting to weep and bury myself in the hole I'd been pulled from.

"All I've ever wanted—everything I've ever wanted—was to be free. To have friends. To love and be loved. And you ... you took that and exploited it and twisted it and *ruined it,* just the same way Malinda did. Just the same." Suddenly, I wished I'd never been born, never experienced any of it.

"Please understand."

"No. I won't. I would *never* do this to you. "I choked on the words. "The only way you'll get me to marry you now is to lock me back in a tower."

I knew he was in pain, knew my words cut him to the core. I knew and said it anyway because my heart felt like it'd been cleaved in two. It hurt—it hurt so terribly that I didn't know what to do to ease its brutal aching.

So I strapped on the mask. Immediately, I felt its power course through me, the magic midnight wrapping around my head, my clothes melting into inky folds, dark clouds, bones, and the smell of Death. Its silky coolness rinsed over me, the hurt in my heart subsiding.

"Let's go to war," I told Serene and Jasper.

My anger channeled into courage, but still, my breath caught as I studied the vast expanse of the western plain. It was full of Cullen. Grace Castle was looming over it all; from here, I could see the west tower, the wall blown out.

Atropos. She was still there, still spellbound.

Waiting for me.

I clenched my teeth. *I am coming for you, grandmother.*

We didn't need to do much to draw their attention. As if they smelled us, Cullen began to turn toward the seven living beings facing them across the field. Those in the front began to run toward us.

Click. Click. Click. Click. They came at us howling, growling, and falling all over each other.

Serene yelled to Jasper above the approaching horde. "Drown them, crush them with earth, burn them! As many as you can, as quickly as you can. Once you start, they'll be screaming for Malinda, and she will defend them. So do it quickly before she discovers what we're up to."

Vitess made sure we were all on the same page. "No matter what, everyone has to keep the Cullen from reaching Morena. She has to be able to concentrate so she can take their regrets. And you," she said calmly to me, "do nothing. Do not draw attention to yourself. Stay silent and raise no blade until I tell you."

Jasper cast out his elemental magic, and the air crackled; the sea on our right frothed in response. His gaze locked on the enemy before us, the Cullen spread all the way to the castle, their teeth gnashing with rage and animosity.

Jasper sank the earth beneath them with a flick of his wrist, then called a massive wave. It rushed inland, knocked the Cullen off their feet, and sent them scrambling. Without missing a beat, he brought his right hand closer, closed it into a fist, and the northern mountains crashed forward to form a rock wall, a pen to hold them in. Water ran from his skin, his eyes filled with storms and rain. Fish froze in the frigid air, small mouths gasping, as Jasper pulled the water from the sea.

His expression was ruthless as he filled the western plain, and the water rose waist-deep. Growls of frustration echoed across the expanse as Jasper brought the sea inland and washed the Cullen away. They screamed in impotent rage as they were dragged into the churning waters. I was sure that the monsters of the deep and the Mer would make quick work of them.

In the north, near the mountains, the wind howled its fury, and the trees shook and rearranged themselves as the Cullen tried to cling to them. Undaunted, Serene swiped one hand, and the evergreens bowed, submerging themselves, pinning the Cullen under the water until they could rise again, free and clear of the rotting bodies.

"Amazing," I breathed as I watched them. They were a force to be reckoned with, unleashing all the primordial power of Earth and Wind, Fire and Water on the Cullen.

Nico ran past me, sword high, then cut down one of the surviving Cullen by cleaving its skull in half. Then he beheaded three more. Chopped five through the stomach, severing their spines. Hacking and swinging, he killed repeatedly while Serene protected his sides via fire. Cullen became ash—a hundred, a thousand, more.

Vitess, too, played her part—she flung out her own powers, pausing sections of the Cullen as Serene burned them alive, as Jasper drowned them. Taliesin swung his sword and beheaded them, fighting alongside Nico.

Suddenly, a river of fire fell from the clouds, blazing a path toward The Grace through the horde. Dozens caught fire, shrieking as they burned. I looked up, mouth hanging open, as our three dragons soared past, fire streaming from their mouths to bathe the ground in light and flames. Elijah led them, his silver wings wide as he circled the battlefield.

With another blast of fire, Elijah baked the remaining groups of Cullen, which still numbered more than a thousand, and we watched as their bodies burst into flames. Screaming at a fever pitch, Cullen launched themselves forward, catching everything near them on fire.

I moved between them, the heat of the battlefield nearly unbearable. Between the dragon's fire, Serene and Jasper's elemental magicks, it felt like we were in the center of an inferno, and the snow of the field evaporated around us. It was as if I walked through a nightmare.

"Morena! Now!" Vitess yelled to me. "Do it now!"

I looked at the field of them—there were still too many. There was no way I could extinguish them all. "I can't—"

"You *can*. You were born a weapon. You let other people use you, not realizing that they had nothing but empty hands without you."

Vitess cupped my face, her nose nearly touching mine. "Ashes to ashes."

"Dust to dust," I replied, not knowing where the words came from.

I cast my gaze toward the sky and called for night. The effect was immediate this time—it was just like it had been when Serene and I danced. My eyes rolled back into my head, and the clouds rolled away. The sun vanished over the edge of the mountains, chased away by the coal-black sky that reached down from the heavens. Then there was a pause, the universe holding its breath.

My power ripped through the world, cracking my chest like a knuckle as Cullen's soul roared forward into me.

Debellus an deire. All souls belong to me.

I didn't know where the words came from or what they meant. It was as if a deep well-spring within me opened, and I knew the words of the

House of Atropos as if the very marrow of my bones were engraved with the silver words of destiny. It wasn't me. I transformed into something horrible and ancient, a monster cultivated inside my throat from the dark words.

I sent the message in waves, stealing away the regret that burned in them. Like a fleeing horde, thousands of Cullen leaped away toward the trees. The Cullen fell, and as they collapsed, their abandoned bodies made greasy marks on the snow, and the red mist barreled toward me.

There was pain—pain unlike any I'd ever experienced—as their regrets poured in. Small tears formed between my fingers, and my skin broke open as my fingers stretched apart. I screamed as blood spurted from the corners of my eyes.

"I won't let go," Taliesin shouted, gripping my hand as my body lifted from the earth. "Keep going."

It hurt. *It hurt.* Blood covered Taliesin's hands as my mouth yawned wider, so wide I swore my jaw would break. He became my tether as the Cullen's fine red mist flooded my mouth.

Inside me, a war began—my heart versus the reality of who and what I was. Eating their regrets was despair and power and release and wretched terror. I devoured it all. Cullen fell, and the monster in me roared and hungered for more.

My fingernails turned purple and fell out. My spine arched, my body lifted higher by the force of it. The world I know died and was born again, in black and white, Death and Life, where I was the key and the controller of all that was and all that would ever be. Held fast in the grip of the power that I unleashed, the girl I was once dying like the tiniest speck of a forgotten star.

Inky liquid streamed from my eyes like toxic tears, and it rained down over Taliesin's golden hair, pooling on the melting snow beneath our feet. But my brother held tight and ensured I did not back down or stop as row after row collapsed into dust.

Finally, the last Cullen fell, the field littered with smears of their bodies and blood. Our battlefield cleared; the beast inside my soul was sated. I drifted slowly back to earth, my black robe streaming around me.

CHAPTER 31

W e made our way up the spiraling blue stones, the stairs unlit, of course, and through the corridors of Grace Castle. Dust covered every surface, and the wooden floors scratched and scraped. The air was thick with the musty scent of decay and death.

Vitess and Jasper followed my lead, and I did exactly as Vitess asked, leading us to the tower room where I'd spent my entire life imprisoned. At the top of one of the blue-black staircases, she leaned over to whisper something to Jasper, and then they walked swiftly away from me without a word.

Like all our worst fears, I must face mine alone.

There was no one and no sound. I sent out my magic, its inky tendrils creeping along the floors, to see if any living souls or life sparks were near. The answer didn't take long:

No.

Nothing. So far, so good. It seemed most of the Cullen had met us and died on the battlefield.

I didn't allow myself to think about what might happen if I lost, if Malinda was still stronger and wiser than me. Or what would happen if she manipulated me once more into doing her bidding.

I approached the castle's interior with a keen sense of dread; each step bringing me closer to the darker rooms where the Queen of the Blood Throne preferred to dwell.

Nearer and nearer, I narrowed the distance between me and my vengeance. I passed one of the few windows and looked out. Snow fell softly, and for a moment, it was as if no time had passed, as if I'd never left. I still felt fear, and it flailed inside me like a wounded bird. Inside I was still me, the quiet girl that she'd locked in a tower — I was no shadow. I was no nightmare.

And still... I was her Death, inescapable and final. Afraid or no, I would not turn back.

The blood throne was the same as it was when I'd left it. There it sat, oozing and red, blood bubbling up from its seat like a morbid fountain. Skeletons hung like wretched chandeliers from the arched ceilings and eaves. The stained-glass scenes of war and that circled the room watched me cross the room; I leaned against one column of indigo stone for a moment, drawing a deep breath. Beneath my boots, prayers writhed on hammered silver floors.

I forced my gaze up to Malinda, the Queen of the Blood Throne. She stilled.

Mother.

Her red robe hung open, revealing the black pulsing veins that wrapped across her breasts and belly like serpents. No doubt, some unwilling heart was locked inside the bronze box beneath her ribs. She needed a new one, though — her face was paler than usual, her lips pink instead of ruby.

"Mother," I greeted her and took off the mask as I knelt at her feet, shaking my blonde hair free.

I wanted her to see my face when I carved her to pieces.

Her brows narrowed. "I told you never to come back."

"Yet here I am." I stood. I refused to cower before her.

"For what purpose?" I could see her eyes calculating, like a rat looking for its way out of a trap.

"To free Atropos. To circumvent your foul plans."

"Plans? What plans do I, an abandoned Fae in a frozen land of the dead, have?"

I didn't expect her to lie. Even though I hadn't known what she'd say, but I hadn't expected her to feign ignorance. I was no longer a child, no longer her captive, and I didn't have to believe any word that crossed her lips. I could not be forced to follow and do exactly as she bid me. Not anymore.

"I know the Wall moves, Malinda." I rose to my feet.

The flash of surprise across her features was well-orchestrated and completely fake. "Atropos the Unyielding cannot leave her cage—unless your goal is annihilation. And even still, I would not allow you to free her." Malinda clenched the arms of her throne and leaned toward me.

"What right do you have to keep Atropos prisoner? What right did you have to keep me?"

"The same right as every parent: protection."

"Protection?" I growled. "You would seek to protect Moirai from me? You made me this way. You broke me. You twisted me and ruined me. You made me who I am."

Murderer. Butcher. Assassin. Grim Reaper.

"And you grew strong. Wary. Capable. Thanks to me."

I looked at her, at the crimson robe that pooled on the floor under her knees. I studied the emerald green of her eyes, green as the hills of Kinkanali, an exact match in color to Arabella's. I examined every feature of her face for perhaps the first time, horrified to see pieces of my siblings and myself there. She truly was our mother; I'd hoped all these years that somehow it was all some grand lie.

"I'll enjoy tearing you apart," I said finally.

Malinda didn't move, didn't stir from her throne. Her lips twisted into a sinister smile. "What have I told you about lying?"

Don't lie to me. You aren't very good at it. Her words echoed down the halls of my memories.

Malinda's flawless face, so similar to my own, was impassive and cruel. I stood there, stood there, and *hated her*. It thrummed and ached in the marrow of my bones, rising to rear its ugly head, to lash its black tongue. I was Divine Might, the sword of the Gods, come to bring her to justice.

"Did you ever wonder why the Cullen are here in Moirai, daughter? Have you ever thought about Death, the mechanics of it?"

"They're your army. An army you built to destroy Moirai." I drew my knife and palmed its handle, accustomed to its lines and weight.

"Did I?" Malinda waved a hand in dismissal. "Then why a wall? If I'm so terribly keen to lay waste to our southern neighbors, it seems like a wall would be counterproductive." She tapped her fingers on the throne's armrest. "And it does seem if I wanted an *army*, the Cullen wouldn't loaf about this castle sweeping floors."

"They're your army," I insisted through gritted teeth, "for your campaign to reclaim the south."

"*You* made them." The Queen of the Blood Throne was smug. "Cullen are, after all, *Death's* creations, are they not?"

"You're lying. That's not possible." I gripped the knife.

"Without Death, the living are doomed. Death—*that's you*—must take souls so the dead rest in peace. If, however, Death is busy or has moral qualms about doing her job... our people have no choice but to linger. Trapped."

Lying, terrible monster. I knew Malinda was playing with me, more of her trickery to confuse me. "I don't know what you're talking about," I said simply.

"They are your army, Morena. Yours until you dismiss them or use them. I just contain them."

If only I could cut her throat and be done with it all. "I don't believe you," I said.

At that exact moment, the throne room darkened as if storm clouds blotted out the sun. There was a rumble of thunder, and it echoed throughout the castle. I tilted my head and met Malinda's gaze. I tried not to smile.

Atropos was free; Serene had completed her task.

Malinda sat straighter on her throne, senses tuned, perhaps listening to whatever Cullen remained in the castle. "What have you done?" She leaped to her feet and grabbed my arm, her eyes full of ire.

"You brought the other Fates to unbind Atropos?" She seemed shocked.

I jerked my chin at her. "I did."

"You have doomed us, girl! Did you not read the books Nico brought? Everything I have done—spellbinding Atropos, keeping you in the tower, giving you that mask— it was to keep you safe from *Atropos, our enemy.*"

The words clanged through me. *Our enemy.*

She isn't lying. My smile died on my face. "What?"

Malinda glared at me as she shook her head and scanned the room for routes of escape. "You, my daughter, are a *fool.* You have befriended your enemies and set free the monster who will devour the world."

She cursed as she dragged me outside to the balcony. "She was fashioned from the brimstone of Hades. She danced among the demons of Tartarus ... and you *freed* her."

"You might have warned me," I protested.

"How was I to know that you're so stupid that you'd release her?" she replied, her tone acidic. "Now you'll give her what she wants most, a daughter. Another Fate from her bloodline to rule Moirai. She'll never rest until Moirai burns to ash, and she sits on a throne of bones with the other Fates dead under her feet."

Even as my lips formed the words, I hated myself for asking. "I thought the only way for a Fate to die was suicide."

My mother spit on the ground in disgust. "Who told you that lie? Any Fate can kill another. That's why you must never trust Clotho or Lachesis, or any of their descendants ... and why Atropos is who you must fear most of all."

Taliesin and Jasper found us on the balcony a moment later, my mouth still working, trying to formulate a response.

Malinda surveyed the field of dead Cullen. "There are no others?" she asked, shocked.

"No. None." Jasper answered her, stepping to her side. I didn't understand it, but he'd never seemed to fear her.

"Good. Maybe you have a chance of survival."

With a crack that sounded like an oak splitting, the sky above us turned dark, filling with smoky storm clouds. Beneath my feet, I felt the Earth tremble.

She walks. Atropos was coming for us.

Where Serene and Nico might be, I did not know. Or Vitess, where had she gone? I glanced back, into the castle through the stone-arched doorways, and saw Atropos emerge from the shadows. Impossibly tall, clad all in black, her platinum white hair was tied back into a braid.

Even though Malinda had just warned me, I almost called to her. *Grandmother.* I'd spent too many years hoping for her to be the mother I'd never had. In my imagination, I hurled myself into her arms, and Atropos swept me up and hugged me tightly. Relieved to be reunited, she'd say how she'd done her best to protect me. Maybe she would apologize for failing me.

Those were the silly visions of a sad, lonely girl. The moment I saw Atropos, living, breathing... I knew they'd never come true. Instead, I recalled some of the books Nico brought to the tower.

Atropos, the Inflexible. The Unyielding. Devourer of souls. The damned.

I'd never taken any of those seriously – some books would say the same about me. Future histories might say we were equals. We both represented Death; we both took Life. But the difference between the two of us was stark. Her presence was ominous; mine was mere silence.

Despite being alive and awake, her face looked as if it were carved from marble, and her eyes were lit with unholy sickness. Her lips twisted and curled in a sinister grin, like a demon who'd spent a hundred years plotting man's downfall.

"Listen to me, daughter, and listen well." Malinda jerked my arm and pulled me to face her. "That demon is not an ally. A god is not an ally. The Fates are not your allies. Your lover is not an ally. Trust no one, Morena, not even your own family. There is no such thing in this place as loyalty, only lies. I know. I have soaked this cursed ground in the blood of the innocent to pay my debts, and there is no honor here."

Malinda shook me. "These things will break you if you let them. Do not love them. Do not."

Wide-eyed, I stared at my mother. They were the ramblings of a mad woman, a broken woman, one I'd never seen before. She'd worn her own mask all these years. I'd never gotten so much of a glimpse of this woman, and I didn't know her.

Atropos held out her hand as inky ropes came from her palms. I watched in horror as the shadows twisted through the air and reached for us.

"No!" Malinda shouted and shoved Taliesin and me behind her. "You will not have them."

The shadows seized us all—I couldn't move or kick as they closed around me like a vise. Their black hands held Malinda's throat and pulled her upward until her feet barely touched the ground. They parted Malinda's robe, revealing her pale skin underneath like clouds unveiling the moon. Malinda fought, kicking and hissing, but the shadows held her tightly. They unlocked the bronze door. Then those shadows plucked Malinda's borrowed heart like a dripping jewel from her chest.

We were all wide-eyed as Malinda slumped in the arms of the shadows, her skin immediately fading to sickly yellow-gray, her face withering like old flowers tied to a beam. Her beautiful golden hair began to fall out in long strands in two seconds. The flesh of her neck peeled away to reveal her spine and jaw. She'd aged quickly, a hundred years in a few moments.

Atropos reached us. "Which hero should I thank for setting me free?"

I didn't dare speak, but Atropos immediately noticed my black eyes and golden hair. Her answering smile was like nails raked down a knife edge. "A daughter at last," she breathed, face going slack with ecstasy. "A Fated descendant of Atropos."

Her black gaze settled on Taliesin and Jasper. "And I see you've brought toys to play with."

They winced as the shadows tightened their grip.

"Stop it," I begged Atropos, knowing my words were futile.

It was Jasper who saved us, summoning wind and fire that burned and blew the shadows away. The four of us fell to the ground, gasping for air, bruising our knees on the stones. We scrambled to our feet, Jasper's magic still holding the shadows at bay.

Atropos cackled. "A Clotho, a son with Fated magic! A twin!" She rubbed her hands together with gleeful malevolence. "Oh, this is wonderful."

Malinda looked over at Taliesin and me; it was the only time I'd ever seen her face soften.

A hairless skull leered at us; her beautiful green eyes burned bright in their sockets. She addressed the three of us, the prince she'd been told to trust, and her two remaining children.

"Run," she said. "And when you can, burn this place to the ground."

Then my mother, Queen of the Blood Throne, the last of the Cullen horde, threw herself at Atropos with a cry of pure fury.

CHAPTER 32

———◆◇◆———

We didn't have time to watch their confrontation. Behind us were shrill screams, sounds of bones snapping followed by an ominous silence. We did as my mother ordered, sprinting back through the throne room toward the halls that would lead us out of the castle.

I looked back and saw roping shadows twisting after us, and I pushed myself to run harder, faster. I threw walls of night, obsidian and solid, at Atropos. These temporarily delayed the shadows but didn't stop them—they crept under and over, peeking through cracks in the walls.

Jasper whirled toward the Cullen, his hands full of flames. As I ran past him, he threw fireballs forward, igniting and charring the black vines to a crisp. "Leave it! Keep running!" I shouted back over my shoulder.

We hurtled through a set of doors, out onto a different balcony, the one with the stone stairs. The very same stairs we had fled down so long ago as children, when we had attempted to escape the tower. Taliesin and I sprinted down with Jasper close behind, somehow keeping our footing on the icy stones.

Just ahead, I could see that a skiff was tethered to the dock, bobbing in the black water.

Nico comes through again.

"Hurry!" Taliesin yelled back to Jasper as he untied the rope and shoved the boat off.

I jumped from the edge of the dock, then Jasper followed. Immediately, water began to drip off Jasper, to seep from his skin. Transfixed, I panted from exertion as he touched the tips of his fingers together, as the sea responded to his magic and pulled the small boat away into the sea.

Briefly, I felt guilty for leaving Serene—she must have been somewhere back there, trapped in Grace Castle. She might be dead. But I couldn't do anything about it now; with a strong wind at our back and the currents underneath the boat yanking us forward, Jasper was quickly putting distance between us and the dock. We went north, straight into the Sea of Obsidia.

Overhead, a loud shriek rang out, and I threw myself into the bottom of the boat.

"It's them!" Taliesin said, grabbing at my arm. "The dragons!"

Three dragons, their outlines visible through the clouds, flew overhead. One swooped lower, and I could barely make out a small face peering over the side. "Elijah!" I screamed out with a surge of joy. "Serene!"

She peered over the edge down at us and waved. Then Elijah fired a stream of fire back at the castle, dousing it in orange and red. Serene held up both arms and called to Earth; I heard the roar of stone and grumble of dirt and trees as the world shifted, as the ground itself rolled and rose up. Before my eyes, a deep moat all the way around the castle formed, and the Sea of Obsidia rushed to fill it.

"She certainly looks alright," I said to Jasper. "They made it out. But where's Nico?" I asked. "I don't see him or Vitess."

"I'm much less worried about those two," he answered. "They're probably above the clouds, riding one of the other dragons."

The smell of firerose was thick around us as Jasper put all his power into getting us away from the castle – wind to blow us, water to push us.

"They'll be fine," Taliesin assured me. "Vitess knows what she's doing."

I turned back toward The Grace. One last look. Our castle burned, smoke billowed into the winter sky. It was now a singular island in the midst of the Obsidian Sea. I couldn't even see the black flags and banners. Pieces of the dock floated along the waves.

My teeth chattered. Between the cold, the wet, and the snow, I was frozen to the bone, and I shivered convulsively as I pulled my black cloak tighter around me. Taliesin was stoic, but he'd shoved his hands deep into his pockets and hid his face from the wind.

"Where are we going?" I asked Jasper, and wiped my running nose with my sleeve. "There's nowhere safe, nowhere where Atropos can't reach us."

A strange expression came over his face. "There is one place," he muttered. "Remember? I promised Malinda."

Rosehall. It was almost as if she'd known this moment would come; somehow my mother had known that I would need a safe haven.

The boat began to slow, Jasper growing tired. We were far from Grace Castle now, and I began to breathe easier. Still, I watched the dark smoke around my tower with disbelief, and a strange feeling of incredible sadness. It was my prison, but it had also been my home. And I thought... I thought perhaps I saw someone along the shore, an oily smear outlined by flames, a flickering shadow looking toward us.

My brother, meanwhile, stared at the shore. "It can't be."

Atropos. I rubbed my eyes. It was her. My mother hadn't killed her.

The boat stopped moving, paused as if suspended... And then it began to go backward.

"Jasper?" I grasped at his sleeve. "Jasper." The boat picked up speed. "What's happening?"

"I'm not sure," he muttered.

Above us, the sky darkened, and the night came falling like a boot upon our necks as if a sudden winter storm had come from the castle itself.

"It seems like her shadows are bringing the boat back to her, counteracting the water." He lifted his arms again, demanding that the water and wind yield to him.

I peered down at the sea. As I watched the coal-colored waves, they became an undulating mass of crimson and skulls of hands that grabbed at the boat.

You cannot escape me, Morena. Atropos hissed inside my skull so loudly that I had to put my head in my hands. Not real. It wasn't real. Atropos made us see things, just as I had when I'd driven the Fae mad in the dungeons.

"Don't look at the water," I said to Jasper. "Close your eyes, keep going!"

I worried about Serene and Elijah overhead. I worried about us in this boat with nothing around us but the open ocean. Her magic was so strong – much more powerful than my own. The boat was truly going backwards now, pulled by the shadows that stretched across the sea.

"We have to do something," Taliesin said, his eyes screwed tightly closed. "We can't just let her reel us in like fish on a hook."

But what could we do? What could the three of us do against Atropos, the original Fate, Death Incarnate?

Help us, I begged the Gods. *Help us get out of here. I'll do anything.*

A roar filled my ears as I scanned the water behind us, and I saw a crack beginning—*a crack in the middle of the ocean, between us and Atropos*—and as I watched, it widened like a yawning mouth. Seawater rushed and whooshed as it fell into the hole, cascading down into the depths.

"What in the seven hells is that?" I shouted, and Jasper turned to look.

"A Veil—that's our way out of here!" There was no fear in his voice as he bid the water carry us toward the ever-growing hole in the sea.

Behind us, Atropos stood on the dock and raised her hands toward the sky, and I watched as more inky black spirals formed from her palms, stretched up and up like twin columns of smoldering doom. We neared the edge of the sea, the prow of the boat tipping over the falls into a vastness that seemed to have no end.

It was only then that I noticed that there was someone else with Atropos. Right next to her – small, slight, with hair that matched the last rays of a sunset.

Red. It looks like – but it can't be, can it? It looks like her, but surely...

Arabella stood next to Atropos on the dock and watched our boat.

"Wait." I grabbed Taliesin's arm. "Stop!"

"Not now!" Jasper clutched me to his chest as the boat slipped over the edge.

We fell down and down and down, an endless fall through the sea. And behind us, I heard the sound of laughter.

AFTERWORD

The End... of the Beginning.

First and foremost, if you read and enjoyed this book please leave a review on Amazon or Goodreads! It helps other readers but also helps me know which scenes, characters, and places readers loved (or hated!). Also feel free to find me and friend me on Instagram (rhiannonh22) and Tiktok(rhiannonhargadon)

Currently Queens of Moirai is planned to be a four book series; you can pre-order Malinda's story **QUEEN OF THE BLOOD THRONE** on Amazon.

I started writing this book in 2020. At the time, it was just an idea in my head – a girl who was a bit dark, a bit sad, locked in her house. I could never have anticipated how her story would grow and take over my life, and also never expected just how many people became consumed with *wanting* to know how it would all turn out. Morena Atropos, the betrayed and lonely girl grew up, and I (somewhat surprisingly) was there to watch, jumping up in the middle of the night to record things that she said, things that she remembered.

Writing a book takes a village. I'd like to thank the following people:

My two editors. Lisa Edwards, without whom this story as its told simply wouldn't exist; and Elizabeth Bryson, who was there from the very first one thousand words, asking questions and re-reading until the final hours.

Also I owe thanks to my friend Eric Sedor-George, the person who helped me invent and refine the idea of the Cullen army; Bianca, for being my first reader of all the fragments of this series, and who cheered on Vitess and Nico from the very first day; my mother, who helped me with cover art, stickers, social media posts, and advice;

To my husband Michael, who gave me the time and space to write over these hectic years with two small children who also needed attention... the person who sacrificed the most to make this book happen was undoubtedly you. I love you.

And finally, I'd like to thank Bobby, who showed me what it was like to die with peace in your heart, unafraid.

Suggested Playlist

Fall into Me, NGHTMRE
Babydoll, Ari Abdul
Who Will Save Us, Tommee Profitt and Fleurie
War of Hearts (Acoustic Version) Ruelle
Everybody Wants to Rule the World, Lorde
Darkside, Neoni

Fight Back, Eben & Godmode
All too Well (Sad Girl Autumn Version), Taylor Swift

Made in United States
Troutdale, OR
11/07/2023

14354684R10209